be the most enduring and endearing arrival on the cop scene in the past few years."

—*Kirkus Reviews*

AVAILABLE NOW

MASUTO:
THE
HOLLYWOOD
MURDERS

HOWARD FAST

ibooks
new york
www.ibooksinc.com

DISTRIBUTED BY SIMON & SCHUSTER, INC

An Original Publication of ibooks, inc.

For
The Case of the Sliding Pool:

For Dolly, Maxie, and George,
my Three disciples at Laurel Way

For
The Case of the Kidnapped Angel:

For Paul D. Reynolds

MASUTO: THE HOLLYWOOD MURDERS
AN INTRODUCTION

L iving in Beverly Hills during the 1970s, I had the opportunity to study a rather unique habitat group. For the first year in California, I was wholly occupied with the beginning of my *Immigrants* series, California being the destination of generations of immigrants. Having struggled through 600 manuscript pages, I turned to something more relaxing.

At that time, I had completed twenty years in the practice of Zen meditation; and it occurred to me that a Zen Buddhist detective on the Beverly Hills police force would be an interesting and relaxing innovation, whereupon Masao Masuto came into being. He would be a Nisei-that is, a Japanese born in America. He would also be a Zen Buddhist, approaching the problem of murder in a Zen manner. And he would be the chief of the homicide squad in Beverly Hills: a small but remarkable city, dedicated to wealth in all of its complexities. And following the manner of Graham Greene, I would call the Masuto books "entertainments," to distinguish them from the more serious books that I had spent my life composing.

And because they would be so different from anything else I had written, I would take the pen name "E.V. Cunningham," which I had used some years before, during J. Edgar Hoover's blacklist against liberal writers.

The first Cunningham novel regarding Masuto, *Samantha*, was an immediate success, and through the years that followed, I wrote half a dozen more, continuing the adventures of my Zen Buddhist detective in Beverly Hills. In France and Italy, where the Masuto books became best-sellers, they were published under my own name, edition after edition through the years, and new editions are still being published today.

Now they are being brought back into print by ibooks, published for the first time in America under my name. As for their popularity during those long-past years, I can only say that at one bookstore book signing, I autographed over five hundred copies-which broke all records for a book signing.

So here they are again: my most remarkable Masao Masuto and Beverly Hills, that very unique city where, if murder is infrequent, it is perhaps more puzzling and more unusual than elsewhere. And I must add that I am pleased to see them under my own name.

Howard Fast
January 2001

THE CASE OF THE SLIDING POOL

CHAPTER
ONE

THE SLIDING

POOL

D etective Sergeant Masao Masuto of the Beverly Hills Police Force was a Zen Buddhist, which meant that he was willing to accept his karma and his fate perhaps with as much resignation as any man might hope for. But on this day he rebelled. His fate, he felt, had become intolerable.

He was the victim of one of the many legends that abound in southern California. This particular bit of folklore held that it did not rain after the tenth of March, whereupon Masuto had scheduled a long awaited and long overdue week of vacation time to begin on the twelfth of March. The rains began in November, as they frequently do in southern California, and for the next several months it rained intermittently and at times constantly. On the twelfth day of March it rained, and for the next six days it rained. It rained with fury and anger, as it had all winter. Hillsides turned into mud and slid down upon houses and roads; houses left their foundations and were engulfed in mud, and the dry, concrete-lined flood channel, which was euphemistically called the Los Angeles River, became a roaring torrent of white water.

Masuto's beloved rose garden, which contained forty-three varieties of rare and exotic roses, and which was enclosed by a wall of hibiscus and night-blooming jasmine, and where he had planned to spend at least one full day nurturing and pruning, became a sodden bog, and his own small and treasured meditation room, which he had built with his own hands, developed four separate leaks, so spaced as to make proper meditation impossible.

These two blows of fate were dealt to Masuto. What of his wife, Kati, and his two children—his daughter, Ana, who was nine years old, and his son, Uraga, who was eleven? Instead of the picnic at Malibu, the bicycle day on the path at Venice Beach, and the day to be spent at Disneyland, they were all cooped up, day after day, in their cottage in Culver City. Even though Masuto and his wife, Kati, were Nisei, which means that they were born in the United States of Japanese parentage, they had raised their children in the Japanese manner—whereupon neither Ana nor Uraga complained, as American children might well have done. And this only served to increase Masuto's frustration and unhappiness.

On the final day of his aborted vacation, at his wits' end for varieties of indoor amusement, Masuto produced his game of *go*. For those unfamiliar with the ancient Japanese game of *go*, it can only be said that it defies the Western mind and makes chess appear absurdly simple. According to Japanese tradition, the game of *go* was devised by the Emperor Yao in the year 2350 B.C. The true *go*—not the Western simplifications which Masuto would not tolerate in his home—is played on a board that is divided into squares by 19 vertical and 19 horizontal lines. This results in 361 intersections. Each player has 181 pieces with which to play, and the play proceeds in a manner which can conceivably be taught but hardly described.

Now, on this last day of Masao's vacation, Masuto was trying to entice Uraga into a game of *go* when the telephone rang. Perhaps providentially, for Uraga frequently won at *go*, and a defeat by his son would not at this moment have raised Masuto's spirits. Kati answered the phone and then came into the living room and informed Masuto that his boss, Captain Wainwright, chief of detectives on the Beverly Hills police force, would like to speak to him.

"Tell him I'm on vacation," Masuto said sourly.

"He knows you are on vacation. He is apologetic. But he would like to talk to you, Masao."

Masuto went to the telephone and listened as Wainwright sympathized. "I know what a pain in the ass this weather's been, Masao, and the last thing in the world I'd do would be to break in on your vacation time if it wasn't raining. But I told myself you're bored as hell, and this is your thing."

Which was Wainwright's delicate way of announcing a homicide. There was no homicide squad as such on the Beverly Hills police force. With almost two dozen plainclothes detectives in a city of not much more than thirty thousand inhabitants, there was no need for a permanent homicide detail. There were simply not enough murders, but when homicide did occur, Masuto and his partner, Sy Beckman, took over.

"If you're interested?" Wainwright added.

Masuto glanced into the living room, where his son stared bleakly at the *go* board. "I'm interested," he said, "providing I get an extra day next time."

"Good. We're up at Forty-four hundred Laurel Way. Take an umbrella. It's raining like hell."

As if Masuto didn't know.

*   *   *

Kati did not try to dissuade Masuto—at this point it was a relief to have him out of the house; but she made him wear a raincoat and take an umbrella as well, and she kissed him and clucked sympathetically over the mess his vacation had been. "Take care of yourself, please, Masao." But that was always on her lips when he left.

Driving north from Culver City across Motor Avenue to Olympic Boulevard and then to Beverly Drive, Masuto reflected on the fact that he was delighted to be back at work. He had once read somewhere that vacations are for amateurs. Could it be that he had lost the ability to enjoy anything but his work? Did he love being a policeman to that extent, or was it the puzzle, the question, the deeply mysterious and always disturbing problem of crime? Crime encapsulated the general illness of mankind, and as a Buddhist he was involved with mankind. Well, let that be as it might; it was a question he had turned over in his mind a hundred times. Answers were simple, so long as one did not dwell on the question.

Laurel Way—not to be confused with Laurel Canyon Drive, which is in Hollywood—is a Beverly Hills street that winds up into the Santa Monica foothills, a left turn off Beverly Drive just north of Lexington. The street follows the lip of a curving, ascending ridge, and the expensive houses on either side of the roadway overlook two canyons, one on either side of the ridge. Now, in the pouring rain, the road had become a shallow stream, and Masuto drove carefully, pleased that his old Datsun dealt so well with the elements; this was a day for elements. Forty-four hundred was a sprawling, stucco-covered, single-story house. There was just room in the driveway to park his car between Wainwright's Buick and a city prowl car.

As Masuto climbed out of his car and opened his umbrella, Detective Sy Beckman appeared on a path that seemed to circle the outside of the house. Beckman, a huge man, six feet three inches and built like a wrestler, grinned sympathetically. "It never rains but it pours," he said. "Me, I take my vacation in the summertime."

"Thank you. Now what have we got here?"

"Come and see. This one's a doozy."

He followed Beckman along the path, around the side of the house, through an alley of rain-soaked acacia to the terrace behind the house. It was a lovely terrace, about sixty feet long, paved in red brick, decorated with a proper assortment of palms and jasmine, with a splendid view of hills and canyons descending to the city below, and with a space in the center for a swimming pool. But the swimming pool was gone, and with it a goodly part of the terrace, leaving a gaping hole, or rather a three-sided gap in the outer rim of the terrace. Moving gingerly, Beckman led Masuto to where the outer edge of the terrace still survived, an iron railing originally placed there as a safety precaution. Where the hole was, the railing had been torn away. Now, leaning over the railing, Masuto saw the swimming pool sitting halfway down the canyon side, a wide gash in the mesquite marking its journey from its original position.

"Nothing like a little rain in Los Angeles," Beckman said. "Full of surprises."

"Masao, is that you?" Wainwright shouted.

He was in the hole left by the ambulatory swimming pool, and with him, in rain hat and raincoat, was Dr. Sam Baxter, the part-time medical examiner of Beverly Hills. There were not sufficient homicides in Beverly Hills to warrant a staff medical examiner. Baxter, chief pathologist at All Saints Hospital, doubled as medical examiner when needed.

"Get down here, but do it carefully," Wainwright told

him. "I wouldn't give you twenty cents for the rest of this terrace."

Masuto folded his umbrella and let himself down into the hole that had contained the swimming pool. Beckman followed. The rain was tapering off, and in the distance, over the Pacific, the clouds were breaking apart, revealing gashes of blue sky.

"Now that your Oriental wizard has arrived," Baxter said sourly, "I'd like to go. Never should have been here in the first place."

Masuto had resigned himself to being ankle deep in mud, but the bottom of the hole was quite firm, the water having drained down into the canyon. Actually, the excavation was in that peculiar soft rock which characterizes most of the Santa Monica hills and which is called, locally, decayed granite; and while the force of the constant winter rains had loosened the pool, over-filled it and weakened its supports to send it finally sliding down into the canyon, most of the ground it had once rested on was intact and firm, sloping from the shallow end to the deeper part. Wainwright and Baxter stood in the middle section. Masuto joined them. Wainwright pointed at the ground in front of them.

"There it is, Masao."

From the terrace a uniformed policeman called out, "The ambulance is here, captain."

"We'll be through in five minutes."

"Can I go now?" Baxter demanded.

Masuto stared silently and thoughtfully at what Wainwright had pointed to. A groove about six feet long, two feet wide and a foot deep had been gouged out of the dacayed granite upon which the pool had rested. The groove was half full of muddy water; the rest of the water apparently had been bailed out with a plastic pail that stood nearby. Lying in the water that remained, there was a human skeleton.

"Well, go ahead, ask me!" Baxter snorted. "Ask me what killed him and how long he's been dead!"

"I wouldn't dream of asking you that," Masuto said mildly. "You said 'he.' It's a man, I presume?"

"It was, and that's all I know. When we pick up the bones and get them back to the lab, I may know more and I may not. Have you seen enough, or are you going to stand there gawking at it all day?"

"I've seen enough," Masuto said.

"Then I'm going."

Wainwright thanked him.

"For what? For getting a case of pneumonia?" He stalked over to the shallow end of the pool and climbed out. "Get all the bones," he snapped at the two ambulance men, who were waiting with their basket. "And don't mess things up."

"Lovely man," Beckman said.

"Where are the owners of the house?" Masuto asked.

"Inside. Nice people. They're a bit shaken. Bad enough to lose a swimming pool—a skeleton under it doesn't add to the pleasure."

"No, I suppose not."

"You talk to them, Masao. See what you can pick up about this. The pool's been here about thirty years, so I suppose we'll come up with a dead-end John Doe. Give it a shot anyway. We can't just write the poor bastard off."

The ambulance men finished collecting the bones and departed, Wainwright following them. Masuto said to Beckman, "Let's get rid of the rest of the water in there, Sy."

"Why?"

"Did they bury him naked? I wouldn't think that shoes

are biodegradable. Where are they? Buttons, belt buckle, even pieces of cloth. There was nothing on the bones."

"Maybe it washed out. That was a damned heavy rain. It washed most of the dirt out of the hole."

"Let's look."

Beckman sighed, picked up the plastic pail, and began to bail. He got the water down to a level of about an inch, and then he and Masuto explored the grave carefully with their hands. There was nothing but bits of decayed granite and loose dirt.

Wet and dirty, the two men looked at each other and nodded.

"Buried naked," Beckman said.

"Which bespeaks a sense of thoroughness," Masuto decided. "It's a beginning."

"How's that?"

"First facts concerning the killer. He's a careful man, a thorough man. Doesn't like loose ends. A sense of neatness."

"Providing he's still alive. This was thirty years ago."

"Providing he's still alive. We also know he could operate a backhoe."

"How do we know that—you don't mind my asking?"

"He dug the grave. Conceivably, it could have been done with a pickax, but that would take hours. Anyway, here at the edge"—Masuto bent and touched two marks at the end of the grave—"that looks like the teeth of a backhoe. Most likely they had finished the excavation and the backhoe was still available. Maybe they planned to pour the concrete the following day. He could have come by at night, used the backhoe, cut out the grave, put in the body, and then packed it over with dirt."

"That's a lot of maybes."

"Just the beginning."

They were up on the terrace now. The rain had ended,

the sky in the west was laced with pink and purple clouds that formed a curtain across the setting sun. The two men stared at it in silence for a minute or so, and then Beckman said, "There's no way we're going to break this one, Masao."

"We'll see. Let's go in and talk to the people who own the place."

CHAPTER
TWO

JOHN DOE

J ohn and Mary Kelly were the fortunate "creative" pro-
prietors of a soap opera; fortunate in the fact that it
provided both of them with enough money to live in
Beverly Hills, and creative in the sense that John Kelly, a
writer, had originated the soap opera—which was called
Shadow of the Night—and Mary, an actress, was its chief
running character. John, tall, stoop-shouldered, and near-
sighted, had banged out the script, day in and day out for
five years, and Mary, blond, blue-eyed, and pretty, had
played in it day in and day out for five years. Today, being
Saturday, their single day of rest, they were at home, sitting
in the living room, comforting themselves with white wine
and trying to adjust to the loss of a swimming pool and the
ownership of a long-deceased skeleton, both in the same
day. They had already spoken to Wainwright and to their
public relations man and to the network—so that the latter
two might decide whether to make the most or the least out
of these happenings—and they were now trying to make
sense of their insurance policy when Masuto sounded their

doorbell. John went to the door and stared with dismay at the two bedraggled men. Masuto showed his badge.

"We would like to talk to you and your wife, if we might. I'm Detective Sergeant Masao Masuto. This is Detective Sy Beckman, both of us with the Beverly Hills police force. We're wet and dirty, so perhaps we should talk in the garage."

"Absolutely not," said his wife, Mary, coming up behind him. "You poor dears. Just give me your coats and come on into the living room. We have a fire going. Anyway, nothing so exciting has ever happened to us before, and here are two in-the-flesh detectives, and John, if that isn't grist for your mill, I don't know what is."

"Right on," John agreed. "Forgive my rudeness, but you're a Nisei, aren't you? I mean, on the Beverly Hills force, that's something. I mean if we can demonstrate some sanity in Beverly Hills, it can happen anywhere, wouldn't you agree?"

"Absolutely," Masuto said.

A few minutes later, sitting in the living room and drinking hot coffee, and listening to Beckman discussing a soap opera with its creator, Masuto reflected, as he had so often before, on the wedding of the tragic and the ridiculous in his work. Beckman was explaining that while his wife never missed a segment of *Shadow of the Night* if she could help it, he only caught it on his days off. "When I tell her that we were here—well, never mind that. It's off the subject."

"Yes, of course," Kelly said. "But did you ever catch a segment with the narc—Henderson, the narcotics squad."

"Afraid not."

"No? That's a pity. I would have appreciated a professional opinion."

"I think," the wife said, "that Sergeant Masuto would like to talk about the swimming pool."

"Oh? Oh, absolutely. You know, when I think of all the laps I've done in that pool with some poor devil's corpse right under me—sorry, go ahead."

"Just a few questions. First of all, when did you buy the house?"

"Just about four years ago, when the show got rolling. It was the first windfall Mary and I had since we married. We never dreamed we could afford a place like this."

"Captain Wainwright said you told him the pool had been there for thirty years. How did you know?"

"Just the word of the real estate agent when we bought the place. He said it had been built in nineteen fifty."

"Who owned it before you?"

"Carl Simmons. Very rich. He traded for a place in Bel-Air. He's in the plastics business in Irvine."

Beckman made notes.

"And how long did he live here? Do you know?"

"Six years, I believe."

"By the way," Masuto said, "how certain are you that the pool and the house were built at the same time?"

"Only what my real estate man told me. This was one of the first houses built on Laurel Way, and it set the pattern."

"And do you know the name of the pool builder? Most pools have metal plates set into them with the name of the builder."

"I suppose they do, but not ours."

"You sure about that?"

"Absolutely. I was curious about it. I asked our pool-care man about it once, and he said that back in those days, most pools were not gunnite, which is a way of spraying a metal form with concrete. Ours is—or was, I should say—

just an enormous concrete tub, with walls eight inches thick. That makes a great pool, but I guess it was just too much weight for the hillside to carry after the rains we've been having."

"That still doesn't explain the absence of the builder's nameplate."

"No, but our pool man—"

"What's his name?" Beckman asked.

"Joe Garcia. I have his address inside. He lives in Santa Monica. Do you want it?"

"Later," Masuto said. "Go on."

"Well, he said that probably the pool was built by the same contractor who built the house, and since he was not mainly in the pool business, he wouldn't have a nameplate."

"Do you know the contractor's name?"

"I'm afraid not."

"It was so long ago," Kelly's wife said. "Thirty years. Do you really think you could ever find out who put the body there—or even who the man was?"

"We have to try," Masuto told her.

"You can't write off a homicide," Beckman added.

"But how can you be sure it was a homicide?"

"It generally is when they hide the body," Masuto said. "But let's get back to the house. We've accounted for ten years. Do you know who the owner was before Simmons?"

"We think it was Jerry Bender, the comic," Mary Kelly said. "We still get some of his mail—can you imagine, after ten years."

"But I think he only lived here a year or two," Kelly told them.

"All right. You've been very helpful. Now I want you to think about this very carefully. In the time you've lived here, have you ever had a visit from a man you didn't know? Let me be more explicit. This man is between fifty-eight and sixty-five years old. He might have offered some excuse, perhaps that he was from an insurance company or from some city agency or from the water company—but in any case, he would be interested in seeing your terrace."

"Got you," Kelly said eagerly. "After all, I write these things. You're thinking that the killer might have come back, to see that his burial ground is undisturbed—am I right?"

Masuto smiled. "Quite right."

"The trouble is," Mary Kelly said, "that I can't think of anyone who fits that description. Can you, John?"

"Not offhand, no."

"But people do come around, I'm sure," Mary Kelly said. "The trouble is that John and I spend so much time at the studio. He has his office there, where he writes the show, and when you do a daily soap, it's very often eight or ten hours a day for me."

"And who takes care of the house?"

"We have a sweet Mexican lady, whose name is Gloria Mendoza. She comes in every day, cleans, and cooks if we come home for dinner. We give her weekends off, so she's not here today. But she'll be here on Monday."

"Perhaps we'll speak to her on Monday. Meanwhile, in a few hours you'll be besieged by reporters and media people. I would appreciate your not mentioning that either Detective Beckman or I are working on this case. If they ask you what the police are doing, you can refer them to Captain Wainwright."

When they left, Masuto informed Beckman that there was an old road at the bottom of the canyon from which they could reach the swimming pool.

"You got to be kidding. Aside from the mud, the brush is soaking wet."

"The way we look now, what difference will it make?"

It nevertheless made a difference, for by the time they reached the shell of the swimming pool, clawing up the brush-covered slope of the canyon, they were soaked from head to foot and their shoes and trousers had become soggy clumps of mud. Nor was anything to be found there, only the big concrete form, split along one side and perhaps destined to lie there on the hillside for years to come. There was no identifying plate or mark.

"Well, that's that," Masuto said.

"The hell with it," Beckman concluded. "He's been dead for thirty years, and another day or two won't hurt. Let's knock off and get into dry clothes."

With the end of the rain Kati removed the four pans she had set out in Masuto's meditation room to catch the leaks in the ceiling, thinking at the same time that she must have the roof repaired. She had heard that more roofs leaked in Los Angeles than in any other city because the rainy season was four months long, leaving eight dry months to lull the population into believing that it would never rain again. Well, it would, and this time she would make certain that the roof was repaired.

Tonight, the room was once again usable, but Masuto's meditation was not successful. Again and again there intruded the image of a naked man, put to death thirty years ago. The moment he arrived home, Masuto had telephoned All Saints Hospital, only to be informed by the intern on duty in the pathology lab that Dr. Baxter had left for the day. It was understandable. The bones had kept for thirty years; they would keep for another day. But Masuto found the puzzle compelling. He felt that all of life was a puzzle, and most of it beyond answer.

Later, at dinner, with Masuto and his wife eating together after the children had been put to bed, Kati asked tentatively about what horror had called him out into the rain. Her questions were always tentative, voiced with the understanding that the worst things would be concealed from her.

"We found the skeleton of a man murdered thirty years ago."

"How very awful!" But with a note of relief. If it had happened so long ago, there was surely no threat to her husband. That concerned her most.

Masuto told her the story, stressing the fact that the couple who owned the house were very nice people. It was not often that he could bring Kati a story about nice people.

"But surely there's no way you can find the killer now?"

"We'll try."

"I'm sure he's dead," Kati said firmly. "There are other punishments beside the police."

"Possibly. In any case, we'll try."

"But not tomorrow," Kati said firmly. "Tomorrow, the man on the television tells us, will be the first sunny day in a week, and we are taking the children to Disneyland."

"I was supposed to check in," Masuto told her, but without conviction. "Today is the last day of vacation. I do not work on Sunday."

"You worked today." She had changed a good deal since she joined a consciousness-raising group of Nisei women. "You can point that out to Captain Wainwright. No one else works on Sunday."

"Except policemen."

"We are all going to Disneyland."

Masuto telephoned Wainwright, who unexpectedly admitted that the bones would keep. The Masuto family spent the day at Disneyland. And on and off, when Masuto glanced at his wife, he noted a strange, slight smile of satisfaction on her lips.

*   *   *

Monday morning Masuto stopped off at All Saints Hospital and made his way to the pathology room, where Baxter's two young, bearded assistants leered at him knowingly, as if every corpse sent there by the Beverly Hills police was his own handiwork. Behind them Dr. Baxter bent over the skeleton, which he had laid out on an autopsy table.

"Well, here he is," Baxter said unpleasantly, which was his normal manner. "I suppose you want his name, sex, age, and the details of what killed him?"

"Only because of my enormous respect for your skill."

"Bunk! Anyway, his name is your business, not mine."

"Very true."

"Have you got it? No. Of course not. Do you know why some murders are solved? Because murder is an idiot game. Show me a murderer, and I'll show you an IQ of ninety-five. When an intelligent man turns his hand to murder, your numbskull police force is paralyzed."

"And is that what we have here?" Masuto asked gently. "An intelligent murderer?"

"You're damn right, which is why the body stayed in its grave for thirty years. If not for these ridiculous rains, it would have remained there forever."

"Perhaps, or perhaps nothing is forever. But acknowledging that neither of us knows the name of the victim, I'm sure you can tell me the rest."

"You're damn right I can. The deceased was a male Caucasian, about five feet eight inches tall, age between twenty-five and thirty, and killed by a knife wound, a hard, deep thrust from the rear. How do I know? Come over here." Masuto took his place on the opposite side of the autopsy table. "This," Baxter said, pointing, "counting down is the sixth of the thoracic vertebrae. Notice that scrape on the left side, actually nicked a piece of the bone. Tremendous force, drove right through the vertebral aponeurosis into the heart. A long, heavy blade, maybe something like a bowie knife, back to front, right through the body and heart and nicked this rib, right here. The son of a bitch who killed him knew what he was doing. I've seen a hundred knife wounds, but not like this. This gent had practice. Nobody drives a knife through the entire thickness of a human body unless he's been trained to do it and has done it before."

"You're sure of that?"

"Was I there? I'm sure of nothing. I'm telling you what the bones say."

"How do you know it was a white man?"

"It's my guess—shape of the skull, relationships of tibia and femur, and here in the skull, the shape of the mesethmoid, right here where it holds the cartilage. Could be a black man, but not likely. Like I said, I wasn't there."

"And the age?"

"Condition of the teeth, good teeth, two missing—knocked out, I'd guess—but not one damn cavity for you Sherlocks to fool around with dental charts."

"Why do you say knocked out?"

"Because I use my head. You can see the broken stump."

Masuto ran his finger over the stump. "Worn smooth. Not a rich man. He could have had it capped. I think your conclusions are brilliant, doc."

"You're damn right they are!"

"Well, at least you don't suffer from modesty."

"Modesty is for fools. I ought to be chief medical examiner downtown, and instead I waste my years in Beverly Hills."

"What about broken bones?" Masuto asked. "Any healed fractures?"

"Not a one." He grinned at Masuto with satisfaction. "Really handed you one, didn't I? You find the man who did in this stack of bones and I'll take back every nasty thing I ever said about you."

"If he's alive, I'll find him."

"Talking about modesty—"

"As you said, it's for fools."

Wainwright was waiting for Masuto in the police station on Rexford Drive. "I suppose you've seen the papers," he said. "This city needs flashy corpses like I need a hole in my head. Would you believe it, the city manager's blaming me for a murder took place thirty years ago."

"Who else can he blame?"

"I told him to forget about it. This is a dead end. In a few days the newspapers will get tired, and we can close the file. I'm shorthanded enough without you and Beckman wasting the city's money trying to find a murderer who's maybe dead ten years ago. Especially when our chances of finding out who was zonked are practically zilch. Beckman spent half the day Sunday down at L.A. Police trying to spot a disappearance that would fit. Nothing. We got nothing, and we're likely to get nothing."

"Where's Beckman now?"

"Over with the town records. They were closed yesterday. He's trying to find out who the contractor was and when the pool was poured. But goddamnit, I know you, Masao. I don't want any federal case made of this."

"Ah, so," Masuto said mildly. "Murder is done in Beverly Hills, and the captain of detectives is indifferent. A thousand pardons, but how does one explain that?"

"Don't give me that Charlie Chan routine, Masao. I can see you licking your lips and getting set to chase ghosts for the next two months. Meanwhile, houses are being broken into and stores are being robbed."

"Will you give Beckman and me a week?"

"Why? What have you got? Bones."

Beckman walked in. He stood watching Wainwright and Masuto with interest.

"Bones that once belonged to someone, to a white man, five feet eight inches tall, in very good health, but poor, a laborer, I suspect, and truculent—oh, about twenty-seven, twenty-eight years old."

"You got to be kidding," Wainwright said.

"Who was murdered," Masuto went on, "possibly on a Sunday by his friend, a man who had commando training in World War Two, who planned the murder very carefully, and who knew how to operate a backhoe."

"And you also have an eyewitness," Wainwright said sardonically.

"An assortment of intelligent guesses put together mostly by Dr. Sam Baxter, but it's a starting point, isn't it? I'm only asking for a week. And what a feather in the cap of my good captain if we can come up with the answer."

"I'll tell you what. Today's Monday. If you can come up with a tag for the deceased and a motive by Wednesday, you got the rest of the week. If on Wednesday you still got nothing but Sam Baxter's pipe dreams, we close the file."

"You're all heart," Masuto said.

"I'm a sucker for your Oriental flimflam, that's what I am." He turned on Beckman. "Don't stand around wearing down your heels. Get in there with Masuto and do some-thing. I got a police department to run," he said with disgust. "Crime in this city is up eight percent from a year ago, and you work on puzzles."

In Masuto's office Beckman observed that Wainwright was in a lovely mood this morning.

"Just normal good nature. What have you got, Sy?"

"I got the name of the contractor. Alex Brody on Maple Street in Inglewood. Here's the address, but whether he still lives there or is alive or dead, God knows. According to the records, the first building permit for Forty-four hundred Laurel Way was issued on May ninth, and the final inspection took place on August twelfth, both nineteen fifty. I got hold of the plans, which include the swimming pool, but there's no way of telling from the records when the pool was poured or whether it was separately contracted. If it was, it would have been a subcontract, because only one set of plans was filed."

"Was the house built on slab?"

"I thought of that," Beckman said with satisfaction. "According to the building guys they were just beginning to pour slab foundations around that time. You're thinking they would have poured the concrete for the pool at the same time."

"It makes sense. It was a slab base?"

"According to the plans."

"We'll suppose they started on May ninth, the day they got their permit. They had to put down the footings, excavate, wait for an inspection, then bring in the plumbers and lay the pipes and the ducts. It has to be three weeks to a month before they pour the concrete. Let's say the first of June—which means that our John Doe disappeared during the month of June nineteen fifty." He took a file folder from his desk and labeled it John Doe. Inside, on a sheet of paper, he wrote, "John Doe, white, age 25 to 30, height 5/8, died June 1950." He handed the file to Beckman. "There's our starting point. What did you learn yesterday?"

"From the L.A. cops—nothing. They got this new computer, and we ran through every disappearance for three years, forty-nine, fifty, and fifty-one. We turned up a lot of kids and three adult women—but nothing like an adult male. Plenty of murders, but they always managed to lay hands on a body."

"All right. I'm going to drive down to Inglewood and see if I can find the contractor. Meanwhile, check the county out with the sheriff's office, and you might as well do the adjoining counties, Ventura, Orange, and San Bernadino. Try the F.B.I. too. They keep a file on kidnapings, but I'm not sure they have one on disappearances. Anyway, check them. You might also try San Francisco and San Diego and Long Beach—"

"You don't think I'll turn up anything, do you?"

"Why do you say that?"

"If you did, you'd include every county in the state."

"And have Wainwright screaming about the phone bill?" Masuto shrugged. "Maybe you're right, but give it a try anyway. You see, I don't think this was a crime of passion, Sy. I think it was a coldblooded, planned execution. I think the killer selected John Doe because there wasn't a soul in the world who cared whether John Doe lived or died. If you want to kill someone, you kill them. It's not hard to kill a human being, and this killer was a pro. I think the killing was an adjunct to his intention and his need. His need was to make John Doe disappear—forever. That's why the body was naked."

"You'd think that with fifty thousand pounds of swimming pool on top of the body, he'd rest easy."

"No. He was or is a very thorough man. Neat, cold, calculating—and orderly. And if he's still alive, now that the body's been uncovered, he will be very unhappy, very nervous, and as sure as there's a thing in this universe called karma, our paths will cross—perhaps in the next few days."

"Come on, Masao," Beckman said, "I've seen you pull off some creepy ones, but this is way out. We may never find out who John Doe is, and now you're telling me that the killer is going to play footsie with us? How? Why?"

"All right, Sy—you tell me. Why was John Doe stripped

naked? Why was he put down under the pool? Why wasn't the killer satisfied with a plain, old-fashioned murder?"

"You'll have to ask the killer those questions."

"Or perhaps not. I've wracked my brain for reasons, and I can come up with only one. It was not John Doe who had to disappear; it was our killer. And since in our very complex society it is not enough to disappear, the killer had to become someone else. He had to have a new name, a new driver's license, a new social security card, a new birth date, a place of origin and in that place, a birth certificate. He was not content with changing his name—he was too ambitious; he planned his future. He had to have a whole new identity. Do you see it now?"

"You mean, when we find out who John Doe is—"

"Exactly. We find our killer. If John Doe was twenty-eight, somewhere there's a man of fifty-nine, living with John Doe's name and credentials."

But having recited this detailed program, Masuto felt ashamed of himself. He hated a childish display of cleverness in others, and he found it intolerable in himself. The dead man did not have to be twenty-eight at the time of his murder. He could have been two or three years younger or older. That the killer needed his identity was a guess; there could be other reasons why the body had been buried naked. And would they find the killer when they discovered who John Doe was?

"He might be dead," Beckman said, too worshiping of Masuto to list other flaws in his thinking.

"Or he might be ten thousand miles away and we might discover nothing in the end," Masuto admitted.

CHAPTER
THREE

MURDER MOST

FOUL

The City of New York includes five counties, and Chicago is synonymous with Cook County, whereby the belief is current that the City of Los Angeles and Los Angeles County are one and the same thing. But while the City of Los Angeles is enormous and sprawling, the County of Los Angeles is even more enormous—larger in fact than a number of European countries. Aside from the City of Los Angeles, there are in Los Angeles County dozens of other civic entities, small cities, villages, and unincorporated areas; and to make the situation even more confusing, many of these independent communities, such as Beverly Hills, Inglewood, Vernon, Culver City—to name only a few—are entirely surrounded by metropolitan Los Angeles. Each of these civic entities has its own police force, while the unincorporated areas are the domain of the county sheriff and his several thousand brown-clad deputies. No one planned this crazy quilt of authority; it just happened. And since it was Los Angeles, it happened uniquely. Yet one positive result of this weird complexity was an unusual amount of cooperation among the respective police forces, a fact which

Masuto was grateful for when he found two Inglewood prowl cars parked in front of the house on Maple Street, the house where the contractor Alex Brody had once lived.

On the other hand, he had a sinking feeling of unhappy anticipation, which combined with a wave of anger against his own insensitivity, the indolence and frustration which had permitted him to spend the previous day wandering with his family through Disneyland. Even as he parked his car an ambulance swung in ahead of him, and two men with a litter got out and were ushered into the small, aged, and rather shabby house by an Inglewood cop.

Masuto showed his badge to the officer, who remarked that he was a long way from home and told him to go ahead inside. The small crowd on the street watched in silence.

Whatever Alex Brody had been, he had not been rich. The living room that Masuto walked into was neat and clean, but the cheap furniture was old, the carpet worn, the walls discolored. It was crowded with another uniformed policeman, two plainclothesmen, the two ambulance men, two frightened women who sat huddled on a worn couch, and a corpse that the two attendants were lifting onto the stretcher.

Masuto identified himself and asked to look at the corpse before they took it away.

"Be our guest," said one of the plainclothesmen. "My name's Richardson. This is Macneil," he added, nodding at the other. "What I want to know is how come a Beverly Hills cop gets here a half hour after that poor lady is killed?"

Masuto was staring at the corpse. It was a very old lady, perhaps eighty years old, with thin white hair, pale, pleading blue eyes, and savage marks on her face and head.

"She was beaten to death," Macneil said. "God almighty, what the hell is this world coming to?"

"Just two blows," Masuto said. "Crushed her skull."

"We been looking for something in the room might have done it. Nothing."

"Brass knuckles," Masuto said.

"You sure or guessing?"

"That's how she's marked." He turned away and studied the room. The two ambulance men moved out with the body. "Nothing stolen," Masuto said, more as a statement of fact than as a question.

"What's to steal? That old TV wouldn't bring five bucks at a flea market. Her bag's inside on the kitchen table. Three dollars and an uncashed social security check. I still want to know what brings you here, Masuto."

"Can we please go?" one of the ladies on the couch asked. They were both in their middle thirties, frightened, tearful.

"Just a few minutes more, ladies."

"My kids will be coming home from school."

"It's only one o'clock," Richardson said. "You'll be back home long before school's out."

"What was the old lady's name?" Masuto asked softly.

"That was Mrs. Brody, God rest her soul," one of the women on the couch said. "Never harmed no one, never bothered no one. Why do these things happen? This was once a decent place to live."

"How about it, Masuto?" Richardson reminded him.

"Let's go inside," Masuto suggested.

They sat down at the kitchen table, which was covered with a hand-embroidered blue and white cloth. A delft clock on the wall matched the cloth. The linoleum was scrubbed clean and worn through. As with the living room, the kitchen was spotless.

"Cigarette?" Richardson asked.

Masuto shook his head glumly.

"You sure as hell look miserable, Masuto. Did you know the old lady?"

"No, but she would have been alive now if I had used my head."

"You'd better explain about that."

"You read about the skeleton we found under where a swimming pool had been up in Beverly Hills?"

"I read what the papers had to say."

"Well, the man who built that pool thirty years ago was Alex Brody. We got his name and address out of the town records. I imagine that he's dead and the old lady was his widow."

"And you figure Brody for the man who put the body under the pool?"

"Oh, no. No, indeed. I think the man who put the body there is still alive, and that he came here today and he killed Mrs. Brody. It was his style. He's a man who long ago was trained to kill with his hands."

"How do you know all this?"

"Some evidence, a lot of guesswork, educated guesses."

"You got a name for him?"

"No."

"You got a name for the skeleton?"

"No."

"Seems to me you don't have a hell of a lot, Masuto."

"No, not a hell of a lot. Who are the two ladies outside? Did they see anything?"

"Maybe. Let's ask them," Richardson said. "You figure maybe Mrs. Brody knew something about her husband's business which might have led you to the killer?"

"That's why she's dead."

"Still guessing. We ain't that smart down here in Inglewood. We don't make four until we got two and two."

They went back into the living room. "They live down

the street," Richardson explained. "This is Mrs. Parsons. This is Mrs. Agonian. They say they saw a man come out of the house in a hurry. They know the old lady and she don't have many visitors. So they went to the door and the door was open and they found the body."

The two women began to sniffle.

"Could you tell us something about the man?" Masuto asked kindly.

"Only from the back. We were almost a block away."

"What was your immediate reaction to him? I mean, did you feel that he was a young man or an old man or middle-aged?"

"He wasn't an old man," Mrs. Parsons said.

"He wasn't young. Maybe your age," Mrs. Agonian said, pointing to Richardson, who appeared to be in his middle fifties. "I mean that he went down the street sort of half running, you know, walking very fast."

"To his car?" Masuto asked. "Did you see a car?"

"No, he turned the corner."

"How was he dressed?"

"A business suit. He wore a gray suit."

"How tall was he?"

They both shook their heads.

"Visualize it if you can. One always has an impression of height—just your first impression. Try to remember?"

"He wasn't small."

"I think he was a big man, I mean broad, not fat, broad," Mrs. Agonian said.

"Is that all?" Richardson asked Masuto.

"I think so." He thanked the women. "You've been very helpful."

"I hope you catch him," Mrs. Parsons said. "She was a nice old lady. She never harmed a soul."

"One more thing," Masuto said. "Did she ever talk about relatives? Did she have children?"

"I don't know," Mrs. Agonian said.

"I know, I mean whatever there is to know, because she once mentioned a daughter," Mrs. Parsons told them. "But she hadn't seen her daughter for years and years. They had a terrible fight years ago when her daughter married someone she and her husband didn't want her to, and she didn't even know where her daughter was living now."

"What was the daughter's name?"

"Henrietta."

"And her married name?"

Mrs. Parsons shook her head.

"Did she have any close friends in the neighborhood?"

"Only Helen and myself. No one ever came to see her."

After the two women had left, Richardson said to Masuto, "It don't pay to grow old, it sure as hell don't. You got all you want? We got to seal up the place. We got a guy works on fingerprints, but he's off today."

"You won't find prints. I'd like to look around. Do you mind?"

"Make yourself at home. I'll tell them to hold it open until you leave."

It was a modest house, small, in the California bungalow style, with all the rooms on one floor—living room, kitchen, breakfast room, and two bedrooms. One of the bedrooms had been converted into a kind of den and TV room; the other was used as the bedroom, and on the dresser was a picture of a young man and woman. A wedding picture. The date on it was 1922. They were an attractive couple, Masuto thought. Another photo in a small silver frame revealed a teenage girl with light hair and light eyes, smiling. Masuto went through drawers reluctantly, the worn clothing of the old lady, some child's clothes, a rag doll and some other mementos, a sad, poverty-stricken past. What had happened to Brody the contractor? What misfortune? Why this awful poverty?

Masuto was looking for records, payroll lists, tax reports. He found nothing. After half an hour of searching he gave it up and called the Beverly Hills police station. "What have you got?" he asked Beckman.

"Nothing, Masao. Absolutely zilch. June, nineteen fifty, was a lousy month for disappearances in the state of California, if you don't count lost kids. And only one of those is still missing, fourteen-year-old girl."

"What about the F.B.I.?"

"Same there. Nothing that fits in. They have a millionaire who was kidnaped in Mobile, Alabama on the sixteenth of June that year, and his body never turned up, but he was only five foot six and most of his teeth were capped. What have we got here, Masao? Can a man just walk off into thin air and disappear, with nobody putting in a complaint or a missing person?"

"It's a big country. It happens."

"What do I do now?"

"I want you to find out what services trained their men in close quarter killing during World War Two. I think the O.S.S. and the Rangers did, but there might have been others. I mean the hand-to-hand commando tactics. One thing we know about our man is that he's proficient at killing, and since that was a time when killing did not go unrewarded, he may have earned himself a bronze star or an oak leaf cluster or even a medal of honor. Who knows! So see what you can dig up. It's just a hunch, but all we got to play is hunches."

"What about Brody? Did you track him down?"

"He's dead, Sy, and an hour and a half ago, his wife was murdered."

"No!"

"Two quick blows to the head and neck. Brass knuckles. Crushed her skull and broke her neck."

"He's a real pro, isn't he?"

"When it comes to old ladies, he certainly is."

"Same address, Masao?"

"The one you dug up, yes."

"Did you find anything?"

"Nothing."

"Where are you off to now?"

"Whittier. That's were Kati's Uncle Naga has a contracting business. It's time I talked to a contractor."

But before he left the Brody house to go to Whittier, Masuto telephoned the Los Angeles Police Department and asked to speak to Lieutenant Pete Bones, who was in homicide, whose path had crossed Masuto's a number of times in the past, and who had more than a little respect for Masuto's ability.

"What Chinese puzzle are you working out now?" Bones wanted to know.

"I'm interested in homicide."

"Oh? Anything special?"

"A killing without a gun. A knife or brass knuckles or even bare hands."

"What in hell are you talking about?"

"I'm asking you whether you've had that kind of a homicide today," Masuto said patiently.

"Why?"

"What do you mean, why? You're in homicide. You would know."

"So help me, Masuto, either you got a weird sense of humor or E.S.P. There was an old lady killed a couple of hours ago in Inglewood. We just got it from the Inglewood cops. Now what in hell are you up to?"

"I know about that. I'm sorry. I should have mentioned it. I'm calling from her house."

"What in hell are you doing in Inglewood?"

"It's a long story, and I'll give it to you first chance I get. I'm talking about another homicide with the same M.O."

"Tell me about it," Bones said angrily.

"There's nothing to tell. I'm asking you whether it happened."

"Oh, you're a doll, Masuto. You're cute. Now will you tell me what in hell you're talking about? Has someone been killed? Do you know about it? Or is someone going to be killed?"

"The latter is a possibility," Masuto agreed, forcing himself to be patient.

"Who?"

"I don't know."

"You call me up and tell me that someone is going to be killed and ask me whether it has happened yet, and you don't know who?"

"That's about it. I'm sorry I bothered you, Pete."

"Get your head examined," Bones snarled, slamming down the telephone. To Masuto, the click was more like a crash. He sighed and walked out of the house.

CHAPTER
FOUR

NAGA ORASHI

N aga Orashi, Kati's uncle, was among the Japanese immigrants who were rounded up and put in concentration camps during World War II. It was a shameful incident, best forgotten yet not easily forgiven, and since Naga Orashi had been brought to America at age three, he was hardly in any real sense an immigrant. By now Orashi had almost forgotten the concentration camps. Actually, though he was seventy-eight years old, he had an excellent memory, and for the most part forgot only what he chose to forget.

After the war, when he returned to Los Angeles, he built himself a cottage in Santa Monica, mostly with his own hands. By the time the house was complete his family had grown with the unexpected arrival of twins. He decided that the cottage was too small and he sold it for a substantial profit. He was then a carpenter; with the sale of the cottage he decided to become a builder and contractor, and in the years that followed he did well. His crowning achievement was to build a seventeen-story hotel in downtown Los Angeles for a group of Japanese investors. After that he turned over his building operation to his sons, content to sit on a rocking chair in the sun in the machine yard of his supply warehouse at the edge of Whittier, which is another one of the many independent towns that exist in Los Angeles County. It was there that Masuto found him, a small, wrinkled, brown-skinned man, smoking an ancient pipe and missing nothing that went on around him.

He greeted Masuto formally, if critically, explaining that "A family, Masao, is not something to be lost like rice husk in the wind. It is the fabric of mankind, even if here in this land that fact is little known and less appreciated. Where is our family? It is a year since I have seen you." He added, in Japanese, "It makes me unhappy, deeply unhappy."

"How can I apologize?" Masuto asked him. "My wife's family is more important than my own."

"Your wife's family is your family."

"Yes, and I am cursed with being a policeman, and time, which is so precious, is denied to me."

"Some of us have wondered about the life you chose."

"It is my karma."

"Don't talk to me of karma," Orashi said. "I am a Christian, as you know."

"A thousand apologies."

"I am being hard on you," Orashi said, "but I still have affection for you—even though I know that it is your work and not your own affection that brings you here."

"So, it is true. What can I say?"

"Nothing. I will tell you. You come here to talk about the skeleton found under the swimming pool in Beverly Hills."

"Yes, but how—"

"Enough, Masao! I read the papers. I exist in the world. Who else will tell you anything about a house built thirty years ago?"

"Of course."

"Have you been to see Mrs. Brody? I believe she still lives on Maple Street in Inglewood, though I have not been to see her since Alex died. So I am as culpable as you, Masao. She is very lonely, I imagine."

"No. She's dead."

"Poor woman. When did she die?"

"She was murdered this morning."

"God rest her soul. You come with bad news, my nephew."

"I live with bad news."

"Yes, I suppose you do. Do you know who killed her?"

"I think I do, but who he is, I don't know."

"Is it a game, Masao? You know who killed her, but not who he is? You have been too long with the Zen people. They teach you to talk in riddles."

"Not at all, my respected uncle. We will talk about that. Meanwhile, I am glad that you knew Alex Brody. Perhaps it will help me."

"Thirty years ago I knew all the contractors in this area. I helped Brody. He was what the young people call a loser. He was one of those who never calculate a job properly, and in their eagerness for the contract, they underbid. Up until nineteen fifty both of us built only very small houses, bungalows, such as the one he lived in in Inglewood. He wanted desperately to move into a more profitable area, and he bid on the house on Laurel Way. I told him his bid was too low, that prices were going up, and that the hillside would present difficulties. In nineteen forty-seven he had worked for me on a job, and that was how we became acquainted. He respected my ability to calculate, and he would bring me bids to look over. I did it as a favor. He was a kind man, not too intelligent, but kind, and I liked him. He knew his bid was too low, but he felt that he could cut corners. He was too honest to cut corners, and he came out of the job eight thousand dollars in debt. Real dollars, not the ones we have today. He never recovered from that loss, poor man, and ten years later he died of a heart attack."

"But he did complete the house on Laurel Way?"

"Certainly. And a very good job too."

"And he put in the swimming pool?"

"Yes, and that was a mistake. He had never built a pool before, and his calculations were way off. He had to buttress the hillside, and that was where he took his loss."

"May I explain my previous statement that you found confusing?" Masuto asked him.

With a twinkle in his eye, Naga suggested that perhaps they should speak in Japanese. "A difficult language, but not confusing. English is even more difficult and totally confusing."

"My Japanese is confusing, believe me. It confuses both myself and the listener. What I meant before, when I said that I knew who killed Mrs. Brody, was that I am quite certain I can connect him with the other murder."

"What other murder?" Naga asked innocently.

"The body placed under the swimming pool. I am quite certain, in my own mind, that the same person who put the body there murdered Mrs. Brody."

"Ah, so," Naga agreed. "And now you come to this poor old Japanese gentleman and you wish me to remember who was on Alex Brody's crew when he built the swimming pool, and when I tell you that, you will sort out the various people and you will have the murderer."

"Exactly."

"And this, Masao, is how you built your reputation for brilliance in the field of crime?"

He disliked being teased, even by Kati's uncle, whose years earned him that prerogative. "If I had such a reputation, it is undeserved. I poke around in the dark. I chase ghosts. And I hope for luck."

"Nephew, how could I possibly know who worked for Alex? It was thirty years ago. For a swimming pool, you need backhoe men, pick and shovel laborers, masons. Was the swimming pool dug in dirt or in decayed granite?"

"Decayed granite."

"And a groove was made for the body?"

"Precisely."

"Then you have two possibilities, Masao. If the killer was strong and energetic, he could have come back to the job after the crew had left for the day, and by working very hard with a pickax and crowbar, he could have dug the grave in the decayed granite. It varies, you know."

Masao shook his head. "I didn't know."

"Oh, yes. Sometimes it is so hard it must be blasted out. At other times it is as soft as gravel. How large was the hole where you found the remains?"

"About six feet long, two feet wide, a foot deep."

"Ah, so. And when he finished, I imagine he packed the soft granite back into the hole, and then when the swimming pool slid down the hillside, the rain washed out enough fill to reveal the skeleton. You think he used a backhoe?"

"Yes."

"Wrong, Masao. Shall I explain why? Over there." He pointed to where a group of caterpillar-tread machines were parked across the yard. "Those with the long necks, like geese, those are backhoes."

"I know what a backhoe is."

"But do you know how a backhoe works? You describe a grave about six feet long."

"Perhaps a few inches more," Masuto said.

"Now, the ends of the grave. They were perpendicular, like the end of a coffin?"

"More or less."

"Then we must ask, where did the scoop enter? It is not like a hand-held tool. That scoop must come down and dig its approach. It can't make the kind of a hole you describe. Now, nephew, let us have a few words on the construction of a swimming pool. The backhoe scoops it out. But if the backhoe scoops out the entire pool, how does the backhoe get out of the hole?"

"That never occurred to me," Masuto confessed. "I have never built a swimming pool."

"A humble man wins my heart. I will explain. Only a part of the hole is dug with the backhoe inside. Then the backhoe moves out of the pool and completes the excavation from above. We can do that because the scoop has a long neck which rides up and down the main hoist. In effect, the backhoe leans over the edge of the pool and scoops it out. The final shaping is done by laborers with pick and shovel, working inside the pool. Now, your murderer plans to dig a grave and bury his victim. He must wait until the backhoe is out of the pool and the laborers are finished and the concrete is ready to be poured. Otherwise how can he be sure his work will not be discovered? So we must presume that he dug the hole with a pickax shortly before the concrete was poured, that he was a laborer and not a backhoe operator. In fact, since backhoe rentals are expensive, and since Alex Brody did not own one, by the time he dug the grave, the backhoe was gone from the scene."

Fascinated by the old man's line of reasoning, Masuto listened and nodded.

"You disagree?"

"Oh, no, not at all. I am everlastingly grateful. And now,

if you will tell me where I can find this laborer, I shall be even more grateful."

"After thirty years? No, for that you must go to one of your Zen magicians."

"Zen masters are not magicians," Masuto said gently. "Just people. Surely there must be some lead, some way of discovering who worked for Alex Brody."

"Have you looked for his records? His payroll records?"

"If any survived, the murderer found them and took them."

"In any case, the killer's name would not be his real name," Naga said. "He would have been very foolish to use his real name."

"I am not looking for his name. I want the name of the man he killed."

"Oh? You puzzle me, nephew."

"Wasn't there a foreman on that job?"

"There would be, yes."

"Can you remember? Try."

The old man knit his brows. "As much as I would like to help you, my dear nephew—it was so long ago. He once used Jim Adams, who came to work for me later, but Adams died two years ago. Ah, wait—Fred—Fred Lundman. I'm pretty sure he was on that job. Fred was a good man. He went out on his own after that, and he did very well build-ing tract houses in the Valley. Yes, I do think he worked with Alex up there on Laurel Way."

"Is he still alive?" Masuto asked excitedly.

"I think so."

"Do you know where he lives?"

"Last I heard, he had built himself a fine house in Brent-wood."

"Uncle Naga, do you have a telephone? But of course you do!"

"Ah, yes. We have all the modern conveniences. Come with me."

Containing an impulse to beg the old man to hurry, Masuto followed him across the yard to the main office. "You will use my office, and I will prepare some tea. Your aunt still makes the best tea cakes I know of, and we have been entirely too unceremonious. It is not fitting."

Masuto found the number in the telephone book, Frederick Lundman, on the Bristol Circles in Brentwood, a very pleasant part of Los Angeles which lies between Westwood and Santa Monica. He dialed the number and heard it ring. It rang again and again; it rang ten times before Masuto put down the telephone and whispered, "What a fool—what an incredible fool I am!"

He dialed again, this time calling Los Angeles police headquarters, and this time the phone was answered. Masuto asked for Pete Bones. When he heard Bones's voice, Masuto said, "Here's an address. I want a prowl car there, quickly please."

"Why?"

"Damn it, Pete! Will you listen to me for once." He gave him the address. "I'm over on the east edge of Whittier. I'll go straight there, but it takes time."

"Goddamnit, Masuto, you can't push us around that way. What's going on?"

"I don't know," Masuto said tiredly, convinced suddenly that it was too late, that this part of it was over. "I just don't know." He put down the telephone and turned to face his uncle.

"I see that we will not have tea," Naga said. "I have been making light of something that is terrible."

Masuto nodded.

"We inhabit an unhappy universe, Masuto. What has happened?"

52

"I don't know. Perhaps nothing."

"You think that Fred Lundman is dead."

"I hope not. I must make one more call."

"Please."

He dialed the number of the police station in Beverly Hills and asked for Beckman.

"I got nothing," Beckman said. "This John Doe of ours stepped out of nowhere and laid down under the swimming pool and died. That's where we are and that's what it adds up to. And you want to know about bronze stars and oakleaf clusters and purple hearts, the army can lend us maybe two, three thousand names, providing you want to make a trip to the Pentagon and go through their records. So I got another notion, schools that teach kung fu and jujitsu and that stuff you specialize in—?"

"Karate."

"Right, karate. So I did a little rundown just here in L.A., and we got over four hundred places—"

"Forget it, Sy. Forget the whole thing. I want you to meet me in Brentwood. You'll get there first. It's the home of a Mr. Fred Lundman, and if everything's cool there, just hang in until I arrive. But in any case, wait there for me." He gave Beckman the address.

"You will come again on a happier occasion, with Kati and the children?" Naga asked.

"I'll come again, yes."

Driving to Brentwood from Naga's place, a disturbing thought nagged at Masuto. He had seen the toothmarks of a backhoe at the edge of the grave. Then why had Naga tried so hard to convince him that the grave had not been dug by a backhoe? Or had he been mistaken in believing that the marks had been made by a backhoe?

CHAPTER
FIVE

FRED LUNDMAN

Lieutenant Pete Bones was standing on the lawn in front of the big stucco house at the Bristol Circles, arguing loudly with Sy Beckman when Masuto drove up and parked his old Datsun behind an L.A.P.D. prowl car. On the other side of the prowl car an ambulance was backed into the driveway, and beyond that the medical examiner's car and Bones's car and then another police car. It was a quiet suburban neighborhood, very upper middle class and unused to such attention. A circle of housewives, maids, and children stood gaping and whispering.

When he saw Masuto, Bones broke off his exchange with Beckman and strode over to the Beverly Hills policeman, telling him angrily, "You got one hell of a lot of explaining to do, Masuto."

"I suppose so."

"What in hell does that mean—you suppose so? Do you know what happened in there?"

"I can guess," Masuto replied morosely.

"You can guess! You and your goddamn guesses! There are two people dead in there, and you knew damn well what was coming down. Do you know what that adds up to? It adds up to something that stinks!"

"Suppose we go inside and talk about it there."

"And more quietly," Beckman said. He was three inches taller than Bones and at least six inches wider. "Who the hell do you think you are, lacing us out like that? You got something to say, say it like a colleague, not like some crumbum hoodlum."

"Just who the hell do you think you are, Beckman? I don't take that crap from anyone!"

"Hold it, hold it," Masuto said soothingly. "Come on, let's not get all hot and angry. Pete's got a point, Sy, and it's my fault. I should have filled him in better, but I never thought it would happen like this. Not so quickly."

As they headed toward the door of the house, Bones said, "You knew this was going to happen. You knew a man and a woman were going to be killed—"

"A woman?"

"That's right. You knew it and you knew how they'd be killed and you didn't lift a finger to stop it. And if that doesn't stink, I don't know what does. I ought to read you your rights here on the spot."

"Don't be an idiot!" Beckman snapped.

"That's enough. Now you listen to me, Pete," Masuto said harshly, "this is hard enough on me without you bearing down." They were at the door now. "Hold on, before we go in there. I was afraid that something like this would happen. That's why I called you this morning. But I didn't know where or who, and the fact that I got Lundman's name and address was a streak of luck. The moment I did I called you and told you to get a radio car over here. We were too late. Yes, that stinks, but the cases where cops can prevent a crime are few and far between. You know that as well as I do. Now just let me find out what happened in here, and I'll fill you in on everything."

Bones stared at him for a moment, then swallowed and nodded. "Okay. But you fill me in—with everything."

He led them into the house. It was a well-made, well-furnished home, done in the Spanish colonial style, tile floors, good pictures on the white-painted walls. Unlike Alex Brody, Lundman had done well. In the living room there were two bodies, already on ambulance litters, two ambulance men, Lloyd Abramson, from the medical examiner's office, a uniformed cop, a fingerprint man, two other Los Angeles plainclothes investigators, and a Mexican woman in a maid's uniform who sat in a chair and sobbed.

Masuto went to the litters and stared at the two bodies. One was a woman in her middle fifties, an attractive mild-looking woman, her face tormented with a mixture of pain and surprise. "Her neck was broken," Abramson said, pointing to the livid bruise. "I can't imagine what kind of an instrument would leave a mark like that. Pete thinks he used his hand. A karate chop."

"What about that?" Bones asked Masuto. "Could he kill her like that, with a single karate chop?"

"Yes, he could."

"Could you?"

"Yes, I could."

"What the hell is this?" Beckman asked harshly. "You making jokes? Masuto was in Whittier."

"Just a joke."

"A lousy joke," Beckman said.

Masuto went to the other litter. Lundman was in his late sixties, a heavy-set man, white hair, pale blue eyes wide open. "Same thing," Abramson told him. "Neck broken. You'd think he'd put up a struggle. He's old, but he's built like a bull."

"Pull up his shirt," Masuto said to one of the ambulance men.

Bones was watching him curiously. "Go on, pull up his shirt," Bones said.

Masuto pointed to a bruise directly under the rib cage. "A hard blow to the solar plexus. If you know how to deliver it, the result is temporary paralysis. The victim doubles over. Turn the body, please," he said to the ambulance men. They turned the dead man over, and Masuto pointed to the mark on the back of his neck. "A hard vertical chop."

"You're telling me that one chop with the bare hand would kill a man of his size?"

"His size doesn't matter. The weapon is the side of the hand. A chop like that, properly delivered, would split a plank an inch thick. The first blow doubled Lundman over, paralyzed him, and put his neck in position for the second blow, which broke his neck and killed him."

"Just like that?"

"Yes, just like that." Masuto stared at Bones quizzically. "Are you going to ask me whether I could do it?"

"Could you?"

"Yes. I take it the woman was Lundman's wife?"

"Clara Lundman. Yeah. His wife."

"And the maid? Where was the maid?"

"Downstairs in the basement doing the wash. She never heard a thing. She was still down there when the cops came."

"On your call?"

"That's right."

"How long between the time she went down to the basement and the time she heard the cops?"

"About an hour and a half."

"That's a lot of wash," Beckman said.

"She says she had ironing to do."

"How long were they dead when you got here?" Masuto asked Abramson.

"Can they take the bodies away now?" he asked Bones, who nodded. "It's hard to say exactly," he told Masuto. "I got here after the cops, about a half hour later. Maybe two hours to the time I got here. A little more, a little less."

"She said she served them lunch," Beckman said. "Then she cleared up and did the dishes. It was about two o'clock, she thinks, when she went down to do the wash. I got here same time as the L.A. cops. That was just about three thirty."

"I still don't know what puts you and Masuto here at all, except for that weird tipoff. This is Los Angeles, not Beverly Hills. Sure I'm extending the courtesies—".

"You're all courtesy," Beckman remarked.

"—but there's a limit. You read me a scenario about a guy who walks in here, takes a look at the woman who opens the door for him, kills her with a karate chop, then kills her husband the same way, and then makes his exit without even touching—hey, Steve"—he called to one of the L.A. investigators—"give me those envelopes with the possessions. Yeah, without even touching this stuff. Take a look."

He emptied one envelope onto the coffee table. "Diamond ring. With the price of ice these days, it's got to be maybe sixty, seventy grand. Gold bracelet. Emerald brooch—right on the front of her dress where he couldn't miss it."

Masuto picked it up and examined it, a large emerald set in a nest of rubies. "About thirty thousand dollars," he concluded. "Wouldn't you say so, Sy?"

"Just about."

"And a Swiss watch." He emptied the other envelope. "Lundman's wallet. Four hundred and twelve dollars in cash. Another Swiss watch. Sapphire pinky ring. And six credit cards. That killer is one indifferent son of a bitch."

"Or very rich and very careful. He's not a thief, he's a murderer. He takes no chances."

"Suppose we talk about him."

"Can you give me a little more time, Pete?" He grinned at Bones. "As long as you're not reading me my rights and we're cooperating?"

"All right. I shot off my mouth too quick. It's a habit."

"I want to talk to the maid and poke around the house. And I'd like Sy to talk to some of the people outside."

"We covered that. They see no evil and hear no evil."

"Nothing?"

"Nothing to write home about. One woman saw a car pull away down the street. She thinks it was a black Mercedes. She thinks a man was driving. No plate numbers, but she *thinks* it was a California plate. Could she describe the man? No. That's it, in a town where they're maybe five thousand black Mercedes."

"Two-door or four-door?"

"She thinks four-door."

"I'd still like Sy to talk to her."

"Okay. And what do I do—sit around and wait for you?"

"It's five o'clock now," Masuto said. "If you can make it at the Beverly Hills police station at seven, I'll give you all I have. I know that takes you out of your way, but Wainwright will be sore as hell if I spell it out for you and he doesn't know what's going on. Which he doesn't. Also, I haven't eaten all day."

"You're stretching it."

"I know."

"You got any more killings lined up for me?"

"I hope not."

"Okay. Wainwright's office at seven." He turned to Beckman. "Come on, I'll introduce you to our Mercedes witness."

* * *

The Lundman maid was full of grief and fear of the cold, unpredictable Anglo world that surrounded her. She spoke English, but Masuto felt that her own language would put her more at ease, and he asked her in Spanish what her name was.

"Rosita, señor."

"Good. We will speak in your tongue. You cared deeply for the Lundmans?"

"She was like a mother to me. Who would do this?"

"An evil man. You must not think of death now, only of your own life which was spared because you were downstairs. In this house, only Mr. and Mrs. Lundman lived?"

"Yes, señor. Only the two."

"Did they have children?"

"One son in San Francisco. He is an architect. I gave the police his telephone number and they called him. He was close to them. He will feel great sorrow." She began to sob again, and Masuto waited.

"When you were downstairs, the door to the basement was closed?"

"Yes, señor."

"Were any of the machines going? I mean the washing machine."

"Yes, the dryer. I was ironing Mr. Lundman's shirts, and the towels were in the dryer."

"The man who came, he must have rung the doorbell. Did you hear it?"

"No, señor. In the basement, when the door is closed, you don't hear the doorbell. When I work down there, I leave the door open."

"Why did you close it this time?"

"Mrs. Lundman asked me to. She said she would get the door if anyone came."

"Was she expecting someone?"

"I don't know, señor."

"But when the police came, they rang the bell and you heard it. How was that? Had the clothes dryer stopped?"

She looked at him bewilderedly. "Yes, it stopped."

"But you said that even without the dryer going, when the door is closed, you don't hear the bell."

"Señor," she whispered, "the door to the basement was open."

Masuto stood up. "Come, Rosita, we're going down to the basement."

"Please, señor, not now. I am afraid."

"It will be all right, Rosita. Just stay behind me." He drew his revolver, and the remaining L.A. investigator, still in the living room, said, "What's that for?"

"I'm not sure," Masuto told him. "The killer opened the basement door. It's a million-to-one shot against him still being there, but why take chances?"

"We looked in the basement."

"We'll look again. Is there an outside door to the basement?" he asked Rosita.

"Yes, there is."

The door leading to the basement was in the kitchen, and the staircase was dark. Masuto flicked on the light. "Do you leave this light on when you work in the basement?"

"No, there is a switch at the bottom of the staircase. There are windows in the laundry room."

"He didn't leave by the basement," the L.A. investigator said. "The basement door has a dead bolt and it was locked from the inside."

They went down the stairs and searched the basement. There was a short corridor at the foot of the basement stairs. To the left was a room that contained the furnace and the hot water heater. The laundry room was to the right, and opening off the laundry room, Rosita's room. Both rooms had high, narrow windows.

"You turned off the dryer," Masuto said to Rosita. "What did you do then?"

"I was tired, señor. I went into my room and closed the door and lay down on my bed and smoked a cigarette."

Masuto noticed an ashtray with a cigarette butt in it. "Then if he had looked in the cellar, he would not have seen you—unless he went into your room?"

"Oh, my God."

"I was beginning to believe he made no mistakes."

"How's that?" the L.A. investigator asked.

"Maybe one mistake. I want to go through the house with Rosita."

"The lieutenant said to give you your head."

Masuto looked at Rosita. "How old are you, Rosita?"

"Twenty-three." She was very simply, plainly beautiful, and it occurred to Masuto that when Mexican or Japanese women are beautiful, they have a kind of beauty that no Western European woman can match, a kind of earthy openness that harks back to the beginning of things.

"You are very young, and you have a long life ahead of you. We must see that you come to no harm."

"I am so afraid."

"Now you are with me, Rosita, and there is nothing to be afraid of. I promise you that. Now we will go upstairs."

The L.A. investigator was listening to them. "She speaks English," he said with some annoyance. "You got something I shouldn't hear?"

"She's more comfortable in her language, just as I imagine you are more comfortable in yours."

"They come here and go on welfare; you'd think they'd learn to talk the damn language."

"It was their country. We came here," Masuto said gently, taking the girl's arm and leading her up the stairs.

"What the hell is that supposed to mean?"

He led her from room to room, two bedrooms, a den with a television set in it. "Look at everything, Rosita. Tell me if anything's been touched or moved."

In the bedrooms nothing had been touched. In the master bedroom, there was a jewel box on the dressing table. Evidently, the Lundmans did not believe in locking away their valuables in a safe deposit box. Masuto raised the lid and stared at the array of pearls, diamonds, and gold chains.

"She always kept them here, Rosita, like this?"

"She said they were insured, and that if she couldn't enjoy them, there was no use having them."

"She trusted you."

"Yes, señor." The tears began again.

In the den there was a large mahogany desk. It contained a file drawer. "That was opened," Rosita said.

"How do you know?"

"You see, it is not closed completely. I am careful. I keep the drawers closed."

Masuto opened the file drawer and glanced through it. "Mr. Lundman was retired?"

"Yes. Last year he retired."

Evidently, he had kept ten years of business and personal financial records. Even if his records had gone back thirty years, as the foreman on the job he would keep no records of workers. The killer must have known that. He had opened the file out of curiosity. As Masuto had already surmised, he was a curious and methodical man. He would give himself a specific length of time in the house, perhaps ten minutes, which he would consider a safe interval. He would check the house, check the basement.

Masuto shook his head in exasperation. I am working

from the wrong end, he told himself. I am following him. He's too smart for that. The only way is to begin at the beginning, but what is the beginning and why?

"Do you have a family?" he asked Rosita.

"In Mexico City, señor."

"No one here? No dear friend?"

"I am only here three years, señor, and all the time working here for the Lundmans."

"No man you love and can trust?"

"Oh, señor!"

"Then you must trust me, Rosita. I'm going to take you with me. I'm not going to arrest you, but you must not stay here. You see, the newspapers and television people, who are outside by now, well, they will report that you were here when the murders took place. You didn't see the murderer, but there is no way that he can be sure of that. And that means that he will come after you."

"Dear Mother of God, señor, what will I do?"

"You will not be afraid. You will come with me and you will do what I tell you to do. Is that clear?"

"Yes—but the house?"

"The house will be sealed and an officer will remain here until Mr. Lundman's son comes. We'll go downstairs, and you will go to your room and change into a plain dress. Pack a small bag, a change of clothes, toothbrush, things of that sort, enough for a few days. Then wait for me in your room."

They went downstairs, and as Rosita started for the basement door, the L.A. investigator demanded to know where she was going.

"To her room for the moment. I'm taking her with me."

Beckman entered as the L.A. man shouted, "What the hell do you mean, you're taking her with you! The lieutenant says she stays here."

"For Christ's sake, Billy," Beckman said, "what's with you guys? We're on your side. If Masuto says he's taking her, he's got a damn good reason."

"I'm meeting Pete Bones at seven," Masuto said soothingly. "When I see him, I'll have the girl with me. But meanwhile, I want to remind you that she's not under arrest. She can't be detained. She has the right to come and go as she pleases, and in a few minutes we're going out through the back basement door, which you can lock behind us."

"You're building one big pile of trouble for yourself, sergeant."

"We'll try to live with it."

Downstairs, Rosita was ready and waiting, and as they went out through the cellar door, Beckman said, "They are one lovely bunch, those L.A. cops. Just sweet, kind, gentle souls."

"They do their job."

"So do we. There are ways."

CHAPTER
SIX

ROSITA

They stopped to eat at a Mexican restaurant in Westwood, halfway between Brentwood and Beverly Hills. Once a small, pretty college town, Westwood was now a contiguous part of Los Angeles, although still dominated by UCLA. The little restaurant was packed with students. Rosita watched them wistfully. "They seem so alive and happy," she said in Spanish. "It's hard to understand being happy."

"Give it time," Masuto said. "We'll speak English. My friend, Detective Beckman, has trouble with Spanish."

His mouth full of tamales and beans, Beckman was having no trouble with Mexican food. He finished chewing and said, "Four years of high school Spanish—it's the way they teach, Masao, lousy. My wife says I should take a course in night school. Then I'd never see her. Maybe she's right. Anyway, we got nothing from that dame who saw the Mercedes. Now she says maybe it was a Jaguar. But I found a kid who says it was a black Mercedes, a four-fifty SL. The kid is a mavin on cars, so what he saw is dependable, but he didn't look at the plates or who was driving."

"The four-fifty is a two-door sports car. Bones said the woman saw a four-door. It's like confusing a grapefruit with a tangerine."

"That occurred to me. So maybe we got nothing."

"Which is what we had to begin with—a corpse that doesn't exist and a killer who doesn't exist."

"Except that according to you, the corpse is the killer. Bones will love that."

"I don't think Bones loves anything, not even himself. Wait for me outside the station, Sy, and then I want you to take Rosita here into our office and stay with her. Also, call Kati and tell her I'll be late."

"What do I tell my wife?"

"Tell her you've started night school in Spanish."

Rosita smiled. It was the first time Masuto had seen her smile. She was even prettier when she smiled.

When Masuto walked into Wainwright's office at the Beverly Hills police station, three men were waiting for him along with Wainwright. There was Pete Bones and with him his boss, Captain Kennedy of the L.A. police, whom Masuto had tangled with before, and a short, hard-faced man who was introduced as Chief Morrison of the Inglewood police. On Wainwright's face was a look of pained yet resigned sufferance, an expression Masuto was not unfamiliar with. "Sit down, Masao," he said bleakly.

"I'm here in Beverly Hills when I should be at home," Kennedy said, "because, goddamnit, you're pulling one of your stunts again, Masuto, and so help me God, this time you're going to give us the bottom line. The lieutenant here says he was ready to read you your rights, and maybe he went too far, but first you're down in Inglewood on a murder nobody knows about yet, and then you call Bones and tell him today is killing day and then you turn up before the bodies are cold—and just what in the hell is this all about? You people turn up a skeleton that was put under a swimming pool thirty years ago, and now we got a slaughterhouse all over L.A. County."

"It appears that way, doesn't it," Masuto agreed.

"What do you mean, appears?" Morrison snapped. "You're a Beverly Hills cop. You think something's going on in Inglewood, you call me. You don't go barging down to our turf like you got a license for the whole county. Maybe that old lady would still be alive if you had followed proper procedure."

"Would she?" Masuto asked mildly. "Or would you tell me that no crime has been committed and that there was nothing you could do? Or would you tell me that since she hadn't testified or agreed to testify at a pre-trial hearing, the rules didn't permit you to give her protection. I wasn't born yesterday, hardly, and I've been a cop for a long time. So if you're ready to listen to me and hear what I have, I'll spell it out for you. Otherwise, forget it. My boss is Captain Wainwright here. I don't owe the rest of you one damn thing."

"For Christ's sake, Masao," Wainwright exclaimed, "we're cooperating! We're not like the army and navy. We're all on the same side."

"Cool down," Kennedy said. "Maybe we're too hard on you. But if you let us in on things along the way, it would be easier."

"He don't even let me in," Wainwright said. "He's the Lone Ranger. The trouble is he's good. He's the best damn plainclothes cop this city ever had. So why don't we listen to him?"

"Go ahead," Kennedy said.

"All right," Masuto agreed. "Saturday it rained, on top of a winter of too much rain. A swimming pool on Laurel

Way slid down into the canyon, and we found this skeleton under it. We pegged it as put there thirty years ago, and my partner, Sy Beckman, put in some work yesterday and got dates and the name of the builder out of the town records. I made some guesses. One: the killer worked in the excavation. Two: the victim worked in the excavation. I have reasons for my guesses, but I won't go into them now. Anyway, thirty years go by. You don't have to be a genius to decide that the first person to see is the building contractor, providing he's still alive. Let me underline something. It was *our* killing, a Beverly Hills homicide. Alex Brody was the contractor. I had his address and I drove down to Inglewood, but I was too late. Not for Brody. He died years ago, but too late to save his wife, who may or may not have known something. The killer took no chances. He read about the pool in the newspapers or saw it on TV, and he decided to kill Mrs. Brody. If there was anything in her house to incriminate him, he took it with him. Then I called Pete here and asked about any homicide with a similar M.O. Then I drove to Whittier, where I have an uncle in the home-building business. He's an old man, and he knows everyone who operates in L.A. County. He remembered that Lundman was the foreman on that Laurel Way job, and as soon as I heard that, I called Bones and I called my partner, Sy Beckman. I was too late. Do you think I enjoy living with that? But if you can tell me where I acted improperly, I'm ready to listen."

They were silent for a while after Masuto had finished. Then Kennedy said, "You tie it all together? You're convinced that the same man who killed the body under the pool did the killings today?"

"It's too tight to be a coincidence."

"Why now?"

"Because as long as his victim was safely under the pool, he had nothing to worry about."

"Suppose Brody and Lundman were alive? What could they give us? They didn't witness the murder. Why kill them?"

"They could give us the name of the man who was killed."

"Come on, Masuto. So you got a name for the victim," Bones said. "What does that change?"

"Everything. Because my guess is that the killer took his victim's name and identity. Once you have the victim's identity, you can find the murderer in the telephone book."

"What do you base that on?" Wainwright wanted to know.

"Bits and pieces. The body was put in the grave naked. The reaction of the killer today. What Kennedy here said. Why kill people who weren't witnesses? The mind, the ego, the personality of the killer."

"What in hell do you know about his personality?" Morrison asked. He had listened scowling, looking uncomfortable at being lectured to by an Oriental.

"A good deal. He's pathological, without conscience, indifferent to any usual standards of right and wrong. He's highly intelligent in terms of being able to plan and calculate precisely. He's careful. He leaves no loose ends. He's five feet eight or nine inches in height, muscular, well built, in excellent physical condition. He exercises regularly. He's well off, possibly wealthy, compulsively neat—"

"Bullshit!" Morrison exclaimed.

"As you wish."

The others began to laugh. Still not mollified, Morrison said, "You got a murder thirty years ago, and you tell me the killer's walking around knocking off people with his bare hands. That's a hard pill to swallow. You tell our cops that he killed the old lady with brass knucks, and now it's changed to a bare hands job."

"He analyzes. When he makes a mistake, he moves immediately to correct it. The brass knucks was an error. It involves a weapon, and a weapon is incriminating. He got rid of the brass knuckles."

"And kills with his bare hands? One blow? I don't buy that crap."

"I can split a brick with one blow of my bare hand," Masuto said quietly, watching Morrison.

"Maybe we should consider that."

"Morrison," Kennedy said, "will you lay off that tack. We asked for an explanation and the sergeant's given us one." He turned to Masuto. "If all we need to turn up this bastard is the name of the man he killed, providing you're guessing right, there are ways. Someone must have put out a missing report or some kind of inquiry?"

"I don't think so. A lot of laborers are drifters, no home, no family. They pick up jobs here and there, unskilled work, pick and shovel work, fruit picking, that kind of thing. We have no fingerprints and no dental work. The man never had a cavity filled. Beckman spent most of yesterday trying to get a lead that way. Nothing."

"The F.B.I.?"

"Nothing."

"Could we go back to that Laurel Way job? Maybe someone besides the contractor and the foreman?"

Masuto shrugged. "Thirty years. We can try. But the killer's a lot more familiar with that job than we are, and if there are any leads in that direction, he'll get rid of them. Was there another murder today?"

"Not that we know of."

"Then I suspect he's closed the doors."

"What about the black Mercedes?" Bones asked.

"Beckman found a kid who says it was a two-door four-fifty SL."

"So much for that."

"Fingerprints?" Kennedy asked.

"This man wouldn't leave prints."

"Then we got nothing. Not one damn lousy thing."

"We have something," Masuto said. "The Lundmans' maid, Rosita, was in the basement of the house when it happened. The killer made a quick tour of the house, but he missed her. That's his only mistake to date."

"What kind of mistake?" Bones demanded. "She didn't see him."

"But he doesn't know that. The media's told the world that she was there."

"The media's also told the world that she didn't see him."

"He can't depend on that," Masuto said. "That could be a ploy to put him off his guard. He has to get rid of her. He's not a man who takes chances or depends on luck."

"Where is she now?" Kennedy asked.

"She's in my office with Beckman."

"I told her to stay in the house," Bones said.

"Yes. I asked her to come with me. She agreed."

"What in hell do you mean, she agreed? Where do you come off countermanding my orders in an L.A. jurisdiction? There was a cop in the house. I wanted her there."

"Just cool down," Masuto said, his annoyance beginning to show. "She wasn't under arrest. She can go where she damn pleases. I decided she wasn't safe in that house, and she agreed and went with me."

"With a cop there?"

"Yes, with a cop there."

"All right," Kennedy said. "You two can stop scrapping. She's here. What now?"

"I want you to give her key witness protection, to put her up in some hotel with guards in constant attendance."

"She's not a key witness."

"It comes to the same thing. Her life is in danger."

"So you say, Masuto. The way I look at it, you're pulling this whole scenario out of your hat. Maybe you're right and maybe you're wrong. But you know we can't treat her as a key witness. She isn't a witness. She can't testify to anything, and we can't bend the rules and spend a bundle of city money because you got intuition. She's free to go back to the house, where there'll be a cop on guard for the next twenty-four hours. That's all we can do."

"There's something else you can do."

"What's that?"

"You can pay the burial expenses when she's killed. She has no family here."

"You got a big mouth, Masuto. It's going to buy you a lot of trouble some day."

When they had gone and Masuto was alone with Wainwright, the captain said to him, "Kennedy's right, Masao. The last people in the world we need as enemies are the L.A. cops. You know that. We depend on them for a lot of things, not to mention those fancy computers they got down there. We're a small city with a small police force. All right, we got a thirty-year-old murder up there on Laurel Way. The city manager isn't breathing down my neck, and the mayor says the best thing we can do, since it's nobody anybody ever heard about, is to let the hullabaloo die down and close the file."

"You're not serious?"

"I'm serious, Masao."

"This lunatic has killed three people today, and you're telling me to close the file?"

"It's not our jurisdiction. The headache belongs to Inglewood and to Los Angeles, and we got enough headaches of our own. Anyway, this lunatic, as you call him, only connects with Laurel Way on your say-so."

"Captain, you don't believe that."

"I believe what the city manager tells me to believe. Yesterday he was on my back. Today he's off my back."

"You said you'd give me until Wednesday, and if I turned up something then, you'd give me the rest of the week. I think I've turned up a good deal."

"I said if you turned up the name of the deceased. That's what counts. Find me a movie star or a hotshot businessman under the pool, and I'll give you your head. But John Doe without even a name tag just doesn't rate it."

"But I have until Wednesday?"

"I said so, didn't I?"

"And what about the girl, Rosita?" Masuto asked gently.

"What about her?"

"She has to be put in a hotel room with protection."

"Come on, Masao, you heard what Kennedy said. Like I said, this is out of our jurisdiction. We got no obligation to this girl."

"We have an obligation to keep a human being alive. What will it cost, a few hundred dollars and a few days of time for an officer?"

"You can take her back to Brentwood. They got a cop there."

"And make her a sitting duck. No, thank you."

"Masao, I'm not made of stone, but there's no way I can justify this, no way."

Masuto went back to his office, where Rosita was carefully improving Beckman's bad Spanish. "*A qué se dedica usted?*"

"Got it. I'm a cop, right?"

"Right," Rosita said.

"How did it go?" Beckman asked Masuto.

"As it always goes, like trying to swim in a pool of molasses."

"Are they off your back?"

"For the time being."

"And what do we do with the kid?"

"What would your wife say if you pulled duty for tonight?"

"You got to ask?" He nodded at Rosita. "Is that what you have in mind? I'll tell you what she'd say. She'd say she isn't too old to divorce me."

"Then you'd better lie." He pointed to the telephone.

"Now?"

"Do it now, Sy. But let me specify that this is outside the line of duty. I can't force you."

"She's a sweet kid. If I was ten years younger—ah, what the hell!"

He called his wife, and while he made his excuses, Masuto said to Rosita, "I'm going to take you to a hotel, and Detective Beckman here will stay with you. I'm doing this because I feel you are in great danger. Hopefully, it will only be for a few days. But Mr. Beckman is a good, decent man and there's nobody in the world I trust more."

"If you say this, I believe you."

"Which is more than my wife does," Beckman said. "Where are we going, Masao?"

"To the Beverly Glen Hotel."

"You got to be kidding. That's the most expensive place in town. Wainwright would never spring for it."

"I know that. We'll give it a try anyhow. It's the last place our karate expert would look for her. Eventually he'll find her. But it gives us time. Now listen, Sy. I'll go first, with her in the car. Give me a block or so, and then follow me. If you pick up a car following us and you're sure it's a tail, cut it off and don't hesitate to use your gun. I know you can take care of yourself but this one is something else. Don't give him a chance to get close to you and don't try to put cuffs on him."

"You're thinking of the black Mercedes?"

"He could change cars—no, I'm just reacting to this insane world we inhabit. He couldn't know about Rosita until he heard the six o'clock news, and maybe they didn't have it there. It's a thousand to one shot, but I don't even want those odds."

No one followed Masuto, and Beckman pulled up at the Beverly Glen Hotel a minute or so after Masuto arrived. The Beverly Glen, a large, rambling pile of pink stucco, was almost as famous as Beverly Hills, a watering place for New York agents, actors, international jet-set characters, business tycoons, Mafia chiefs, high-priced call girls, and rich tourists who wished to rub shoulders with the general assortment of boarders. The hotel was managed by Al Gellman, a harassed, balding man in his mid-forties, who in any given month encountered everything imaginable excepting a major earthquake.

Now, in his office, he shook hands with Masuto and looked dubiously at Beckman and Rosita. "What is it, sergeant?" he asked. "We've had a quiet day so far, no drunks beating up on women, no fights at the bar, no one trying to stiff us on a room—but the day isn't over, is it?"

"I need a favor, Al," Masuto said.

"Whatever I can do. I owe you."

"I want to put this lady in a room with Beckman here to guard her, and I want it very quiet."

"You're bringing me trouble, sergeant."

"No. No one knows she's here and no one will know."

"It will cost. The best I can do with two adjoining rooms is two hundred and twenty a day."

"You said you owed me, Al. The city won't pay for this. I want three days free."

"Free!"

"With meals."

"I can't do it. It's out of the question. There's no way I can justify it."

"You find a way, Al. We've helped you out of more rough spots than you can shake a stick at. I've bent the law a dozen times. You've parked a hundred cars illegally on the streets around here, not once, but maybe two hundred times. We've never shaken you down, not for a nickel. Suppose we were to tell you the streets were off limits for parking? How many weddings would you cater then, how many balls? All I'm asking is a humanitarian gesture that won't cost you a cent. This is off season for you. You've got the space."

"If this is straight, why won't the city pay?"

"Because it's out of Beverly Hills jurisdiction. I'm not trying to con you. I'm trying to save this kid's life."

Gellman was silent for a long moment, and then he asked. "Can this be kept among us? I can't put it on the books and I can't let them register—which means I'm breaking the law."

"Let's say bending it a little. I don't want them on the register. Feed them sandwiches and coffee. They can survive on that for three days. Beckman will pick it up in the kitchen. And as far as we're concerned, no one will know."

"How about Wainwright?"

"He doesn't know and he won't know."

"Aren't you going out on a limb, sergeant?"

"I don't think so. We're breaking no law. There's no failure to register with intent to defraud or commit a crime. We're taking normal security precautions with a witness to a crime, and if the owners should come down on you, I give you my word I'll pay up myself. It won't be easy, but it won't break me."

Rosita, who had been listening intently, now said to Masuto in Spanish, "I have eleven hundred dollars in the bank I can pay."

"You'll need that money."

"My Spanish is as good as yours, sergeant," Gellman said, smiling. "I'll give you the three days. What the hell, it's a cold, hard world out there. I got a kid of my own her age."

CHAPTER SEVEN

DR. LEO HARTMAN

It was after nine o'clock when Masuto finally parked his car in front of his house in Culver City. Ever since Kati had joined a consciousness-raising group of Nisei women—with his encouragement—Masuto had been uneasy when a case kept him to late hours. There were days when he regretted his liberal stance on the question of women's rights. He had married a lovely woman who, while born in California, had been raised in the old-fashioned Japanese manner, and it was with a sense of unease that he watched the changes taking place in her character. Tonight, he expected at least some degree of annoyance from Kati. Instead, he was surprised and pleased when she greeted him with a kiss and a pleasant smile.

He undressed and lay for a few minutes in a steaming hot bath, deciding during that interval that he would make no mention of the fact that he had filled his stomach with tamales and brown beans. Even through the closed bathroom door he could hear the sizzle of tempura and faintly smell the delicate shrimp, the green beans, and the sweet potato, all of it fried to fawn-colored perfection. Kati's opinion of Mexican food would have been unprintable, had Kati been given to saying unprintable things, and Masao also knew that she had delayed her own dinner, feeding the children and putting them to bed, so that she might share her evening meal with her husband. While he could not account for this defection from the rights of modern woman, he was in no way disposed to condemn it.

Clad in a black robe, his bare feet in comfortable sandals, he sat across the table from his wife and managed to deal adequately with the tempura. But he could not refrain from asking for some explanation of her behavior.

"Oh, I did consider being very provoked at your coming home at such an hour, but then I thought of how sweet and patient you have been for the past week, locked up in the house while the rain poured down, and never complaining while your vacation was completely spoiled. So I decided that a man with your qualities deserves tender loving care—unless of course this becomes a habit with you."

"God forbid."

"Also, my Uncle Naga telephoned and told me you had been to visit him, and he was very impressed with the respect you showed him. He feels that in this barbarian society respect for an old man is most commendable."

"Your Uncle Naga never approved of our marriage. I don't think he ever forgave you for marrying a policeman."

"That's nonsense. He gave us a set of sterling silver dinnerware. I think that's very approving."

"Or a suggestion that I could never afford such a set myself."

"That is silly. Anyway, he told me that the skeleton on Laurel Way has turned into something horrible."

"Yes, it has. Your uncle talks too much."

"Uncle Naga is very clever. He said that from what you told him, you felt that the murderer had killed the man whose skeleton was found in order to steal his identity. Then the murderer could become someone else."

"Yes, more or less."

"But why should the murderer have to become someone else?"

"I don't know. I've never had a case like this, Kati. There is absolutely nothing to go on. A man was killed thirty years ago, and there appears to be no way in the world to find out who he was. I'm convinced we'll never find out who he was."

"But isn't it more important to find the man who killed him? If he took the dead man's identity, then you will know who the dead man was."

"You make it sound very simple."

"If he wanted a new identity, he must have done something terrible. He had to hide."

"No doubt," Masuto agreed.

"But what good would all this trouble and evil he went to do, if he could still be recognized?"

Masuto stopped eating and stared at her.

"Why are you looking at me that way, Masao?"

"Go on. Don't stop. What were you saying?"

"I mean that if a man does something truly terrible and he has to kill someone to find a new identity, then wouldn't the police everywhere be looking for him? Wouldn't his picture be in the papers?"

"Yes, of course," Masuto said softly. "There are really no limits to my own stupidity. Then tell me, Kati, what would he do in such circumstances?"

"He could go to Europe or Brazil. I read that such people go to Brazil."

"No, he is here."

"Why does he stay here?"

"I don't know. Apparently, that was his plan from the beginning—to remain here."

"Then, Masao, I think he would go to a plastic surgeon and have his face changed."

"Yes, he would, wouldn't he," Masuto said slowly. "I know why I continue to be a policeman. It is because I lack the intelligence to be anything else. A plastic surgeon. He could have left the country, but apparently he didn't want to."

"Could such a man be in love with a woman?"

"Yes, but how could he explain plastic surgery to a woman?"

"Tell her he was in a bad accident, an auto crash?"

"Possibly. On the other hand, he may have determined to remain here simply because this is where he wanted to be. If it was plastic surgery, then there must be some record of it. On the other hand, knowing how he works—"

"Why don't you see Dr. Leo Hartman?"

"Who is Dr. Leo Hartman?"

"The most important plastic surgeon in Beverly Hills."

Once again Masuto stopped eating to stare at Kati. "How do you know such things?"

"I read newspapers and magazines, Masao. You can go everywhere. I must stay here with the children, so I read."

As early as Masuto might arise, Kati was always awake first, and this morning, when he entered the kitchen at seven o'clock, his pot of tea and his bowl of rice was ready. Since he was already dressed in his working clothes, gray flannels and a tweed jacket, Kati expressed surprise at the fact that he apparently did not intend to meditate.

"I thought I would drive down to the Zendo," Masuto explained. "I have not been there in quite a while, and I feel a need to talk to the Roshi."

"Can he solve crimes?" Kati asked lightly.

"Only the crimes honest people commit."

"Why, whenever I ask a question that relates to Zen, must you give me an answer that makes no sense?"

"Perhaps because Zen makes no sense."

"Do you see? That is exactly what I mean."

Masuto drove downtown thinking that his wife was a remarkable woman, whom he knew very little. Well, when it is so hard to know ourselves, why should we expect to know another?

The Zendo was a cluster of old frame buildings on Normandie Avenue off Pico Boulevard. The members of the Zendo, young married people, most of them from southern California, had bought the buildings cheaply—since they were in an old, run-down neighborhood—renovated them, connected the backyards, and turned the whole thing into a sort of communal settlement. One of the houses had been made into a meditation hall with two slightly raised platforms running the length of a polished floor, and stained glass windows at one end. It was done with loving care, a cool, contemplative place. A Japanese Zen master had been sent from Kyoto to guide them, and this Roshi—as a Zen teacher is called—had been with them now for eleven years.

Masuto was a frequent visitor to the Zendo, and this morning he entered the meditation hall, removed his shoes, and composed himself to meditate. The hall was open to any who wished to come there to meditate, but by now, at a quarter to eight, the regular meditation was finished, and only the Roshi still sat, cross-legged. Masuto took his place facing the old man, and for the next forty minutes, they both sat in silence. Then the Roshi rose, and Masuto also rose and bowed to him.

"To come here with a gun in your armpit," the Roshi said, shaking his head.

"It is a part of my way of life."

"You come here only when you are troubled, as if the answers to the evils you encounter could be found here." He spoke in Japanese, and Masuto had to listen intently to follow his thought.

"And are there answers here?"

"If you are here, yes."

"I don't understand."

"Of course not. You are a fool. Can a fool understand?"

"I try."

"You know what a koan is, Masao. A koan is a question to which there is no answer. So you meditate upon it and find the answer."

"Even when there is no answer?"

"Only when there is no answer. Would it be a koan otherwise?"

Driving back to the Beverly Hills police station on Rexford Drive, Masuto reflected on his brief conversation with the Roshi and admitted to himself that he had derived little sustenance from it. Possibly, the Roshi's meaning lay in the fact that the question was also the answer. Then he would simply have to dwell upon the question.

When he reached the police station, Wainwright was waiting for him with a demand as to what in hell all this was with Beckman. "He said you assigned him to stay with the girl. Yeah, he called me. I told you we couldn't provide protection for the girl."

"It's not costing the city a cent."

"Who's paying? You? Beckman?"

"Gellman's giving us the room without charge."

"Masao, that stinks! That's taking. I run an honest force, and you're the last man in the world I'd ever accuse of taking."

"All right. If you feel that way, I'll pay for it myself."

Wainwright threw up his arms in despair. "Why? Why do you always put me on the spot?"

"I'm not trying to put you on the spot, captain. I just can't see a human being killed when I can prevent it. And as surely as the sun will come up tomorrow, I know that if he can find that girl, he'll kill her. The odds are that he will find her, but Beckman is there and I think Sy can get him first."

"Look, Masao," Wainwright said, "it's not that I don't have respect for the way you figure things. I've seen it work out too often in the past. But in this case you're guessing, and I can't go on your guesses. Morrison called me this morning. They picked up a black man who does windows down there, and they found a set of brass knucks on him and they found his fingerprints in the old lady's house. They're holding him and they're going to charge him with her murder, and that blows your theory all to hell."

"You're putting me on."

"I damn well am not! Morrison says he's going to charge him, and he feels he's got a conviction in the bag."

"I just don't believe I'm hearing this. There are possibly ten thousand sets of brass knuckles in Los Angeles, and if this black man does windows, and maybe housecleaning too, since most of them do both, his fingerprints would have to be in her house. I hate these fingerprint tricks. Has he confessed?"

"Morrison didn't mention that."

"If it were a white man, they wouldn't waste ten minutes on it. But Morrison figures he can stiff a black man and close the case and be a big hero. Well, Morrison is not only a fool, he's a malicious and meretricious fool. Any lawyer can knock that case out of court, but so help me, if it comes to a courtroom, I'll offer myself as a witness and blow Morrison's case to pieces."

"Masao, cool down! Morrison is only doing his job."

"Like hell he is! All right, I'll do something else. You gave me three days, and I'm going to hold you to your word. I'm going to hand you the killer in three days, and we'll make Los Angeles and Inglewood eat crow. Do I still have the three days? What about that?"

"You got them," Wainwright said, shaking his head hopelessly. "I said three days. You got them."

Masuto turned on his heel to leave, and Wainwright called after him, "Masao!"

"Yes?"

"Forget about paying for that room. Gellman owes us maybe a thousand parking tickets. It's time he paid off with something more than a few tickets to our annual ball."

"You're all heart," Masuto said, grinning.

"Yeah, I've been told that before."

On his way out, Masuto stopped and spoke to Polly, who ran the switchboard. She was small, very pretty, and very blond and blue-eyed, and she said plaintively, "It's nine days since you last spoke to me. What did I do wrong?"

"I've been on vacation, Polly."

"Do you know what I hate? I hate married men. I hate the institution of marriage. I hate the fact that every handsome, decent man in this town is either married or queer."

"If I believed you, I'd divorce Kati tomorrow."

"You're a liar, sergeant."

"Sometimes, yes. Look, Polly, have you ever heard of a plastic surgeon name of Leo Hartman?"

"Who hasn't?"

"Myself, for one. How old do you suppose he is?"

"Very good looking, gray hair, gray mustache. I don't know. Maybe fifty-five, maybe sixty. You can't tell with these Beverly Hills types. Maybe they do facials on each other. Professional courtesy."

"How do you know all this?"

"I read the magazines, sergeant."

"Yes, that figures. Can you get me his address?"

"Take me a moment." She riffled through the pages of a telephone book. "Here it is. Camden, between Santa Monica and Wilshire. I'll write it down for you. But don't go through with it, sergeant. You're perfect just the way you are. Don't listen to those creeps who don't like Oriental faces. I love you just the way you are."

"I'll think about it carefully," Masuto agreed.

It was only a few blocks from Rexford Drive to Camden Drive. Hartman's office was in a small, elegant medical building, and his tastefully furnished waiting room contained four ladies, none of whom, as far as Masuto could judge, was so unattractive as to require the attention of a plastic surgeon. But Masuto had discovered long ago that the only way to function as a police officer in Beverly Hills was to suspend all personal judgments and accept whatever came his way without question. He went to the little window through which Hartman's receptionist gazed out upon the waiting room, and asked to see the doctor.

"You want an appointment?"

"I want to speak to him."

"I can give you an appointment"—she consulted her day book—"oh, let us say in three weeks."

"I'm afraid I must see him immediately." Masuto showed his badge. "I'm Detective Sergeant Masuto, Beverly Hills police. It's a matter of great urgency, and I must see him now."

"But he's with a patient."

"He's not operating, is he?"

"He does not operate here," the receptionist said scornfully. "He operates in a hospital."

"Then he can leave his patient for ten minutes. Will you please tell him that I must see him now."

She stared at Masuto, who put on his sternest look, and then she rose and disappeared. A few minutes later she opened a door at one side of the waiting room. "Follow me, please."

The doctor was waiting in his office, a large comfortable room furnished with a desk, two comfortable chairs, and several expensive potted palms. Polly's description, Masuto decided, fitted him very well, except that in Masuto's judgment, Hartman was well past sixty.

The doctor sat behind his desk, and stuffed a pipe with tobacco. "Please sit down, sergeant," he said to Masuto. "Ordinarily, nothing short of an earthquake could make me break off an examination of a patient, but Miss Weller put your case strongly. What on earth can I do for you?"

"I'll only take a few minutes of your time, and I'm very grateful that you could see me now. It is a matter of utmost urgency, and you'll forgive me if I don't explain. I have a few questions that perhaps only you can answer."

"I am puzzled, but shoot."

"We'll go back to nineteen-fifty, over thirty years ago. Could you possibly tell me who was practicing plastic surgery in that year—or would it be so large a number of physicians that you couldn't possibly name them?"

"Now hold on. It depends upon what you mean by plastic surgery. Reconstructive surgery was practiced in every hospital in southern California, but if you mean elective facial surgery, a field which to a degree centers around rhinoplasty, then that narrows the field considerably."

"Yes, that's exactly what I mean."

"Then I can help you with this area. There was Amos Cohen, over in Hollywood, Ben McKeever, here in Beverly Hills, and Fritz Lennox, who worked at the medical center in Westwood. And, of course, myself. I opened my office here in forty-six, when I came out of the army. Yes, I'm older than I look, sergeant, and as yet I've had no face-lifts. I've thought of it, but I'm too old to care, and if there's one thing a surgeon dreads, it's to have some other surgeon operate on him. Now those three men I mentioned had the field practically sewn up, if you'll forgive the pun. I know. I had the devil's own time breaking in. Of course today I could give you a list of twenty, but back then cosmetic surgery was still something of a novelty, and most of those who elected it were aging actors. Today it's different. Mothers bring me children of ten or eleven years, and there's the men, more of them every year. We live in a time when beauty skin deep has become a national obsession. By the way, it's odd that you should ask me about nineteen fifty."

"Why?"

"Because that's the year Ben McKeever died."

"How did he die?"

"Terrible tragedy, terrible. His office was in a small, frame building, over on South Spalding. Lovely place. He had even fixed up his own operating room there, although for my part, I'll work only in a hospital. Well, it caught fire one night, and he and his nurse were burned to death. I don't suppose you'd be interested in the grisly details?"

"I would. Every detail you can remember."

"I really hate to go into it, hate to drag these things out of the past. It was pretty well hushed up at the time."

"It's of the utmost importance. Please. It will rest with me."

"Well, it would appear that he and his nurse were having an affair. Here's one reading of what happened. His nurse overdosed and died and either under the influence of some narcotic or in some insane fit of remorse, considering himself responsible for her death, he overdosed himself and set fire to the place. Now I'm not saying I believe this interpretation of the event. I knew Ben. He was a good man, and I never had any feeling that he was an addict, but who knows? Also, their bodies were badly burned, so I have doubts about the autopsy. When bodies are in a bad state, Beverly Hills autopsies could be slipshod. Then. Perhaps not now. We'll never really know what happened."

"What suggested suicide?"

"In a garbage container outside they found some hypodermic syringes which contained traces of heroin, and also a scrap of paper on which Ben had written something to the effect of, I know what I am going to do is wrong, but I am forced to do it—just about that, just a few words but enough to suggest suicide. But if he intended to write a suicide note, why was it found in the garbage? Why would he leave the syringes in the garbage? On the other hand, who is to say what a crazed man might do?"

"And I presume that all his records were burned, destroyed?"

"Yes. All of them. Why all the interest in Ben Mc-Keever?"

"I'm sorry, I can't reveal that now. But tell me, doctor, when exactly did this happen? Even the month of the year would help."

"I can't remember the date. But I do know it was during the summer—July or August."

"Yes, that would be right. Just a few more questions and then I'll bother you no more. First of all, how completely can facial surgery change a person's appearance?"

"Well, that depends. The nose can be changed. The appearance of the eyes—to a degree. Ears can be changed. A hairlip can be corrected, but not too much can be done with a mouth. The marks of age in the neck can be removed and certain changes can be made in the cheeks. So a person's face can be changed a great deal. Of course, the art of facial cosmetic surgery is to make changes that improve without calling attention to the operation. But the shape of the head or the jaw cannot be changed."

"And if a man came to you for extensive cosmetic changes which he obviously did not need, what would you do?"

"That depends. I would try to talk him out of it if I knew something about his background. If there were any shred of reason in his request and I considered it psychologically needful, I might go along with him. If he were an actor, I might just accept his request."

"Or if he was badly scarred?"

"That would make a difference, of course."

"Or a hairlip?"

"Of course."

"And just one more thing, the other two, Cohen and Lennox—what happened to them?"

"Cohen died of a heart attack two years ago, I believe. Lennox is retired, but still alive, as far as I know."

"I've taken enough of your time," Masuto said, rising. "You've been very helpful."

"You wouldn't care to tell me what this is all about?"

"Sometime, perhaps. Not now."

CHAPTER
EIGHT

THE MIDTOWN
MANHATTAN
NATIONAL BANK

Disconsolate, filled with a sense of defeat and frustration, Masuto returned to the police station on Rexford Drive, dropped into his chair, and put his arms on his desk, his chin on his hands, and brooded. Every trail came to a dead end; every gate was closed. A cold, calculating killer who destroyed without conscience or compunction. If he had murdered the doctor who changed his face and the nurse who assisted the doctor, he had planned it perfectly. Masuto could speculate that the killer had knocked them unconscious, shot heroin into them, planted the syringes, found the scrap of writing to plant in the garbage with the syringes, and then burned the house, destroying the doctor's photographs and records. From the little Masuto knew about cosmetic surgery, there was at least the knowledge that every surgeon had before and after photographs. The evidence was all gone, and with it the reputation of the two people he had killed.

Masuto prided himself on being beyond hate, yet he now felt hatred welling up within himself. He was locked in a shadowy struggle with a man who was an affront to human dignity, to conscience, to every concept of good and evil, indeed to the human race. According to Masuto's own knowledge, this man had murdered four people, four people who had done him no harm, for Masuto was certain that the skeleton under the pool had been a friend of the killer. Otherwise, how had the killer persuaded him to go there with him at night and alone?

The only thread was the girl, Rosita, and even there Masuto was beginning to have his doubts. The killer was careful. He might be quite certain that the maid had not seen him. This might very well be the end of the affair. Wednesday would come and go, and Wainwright would crack his whip.

Now it was twelve o'clock—noon, on Tuesday, and as if in answer to his thought, Wainwright entered Masuto's office, carrying two containers of coffee and two sandwiches.

"You look like hell, Masao. You look like you lost your best friend."

Masuto stared at him without answering.

"Here's coffee. I got corned beef and ham and cheese. Take your choice."

"I'm not hungry."

"That's a sorry note. I see you sitting in here like a whipped dog, and I buy you a sandwich, and you tell me you're not hungry."

"I'll have the ham and cheese."

"Good. I prefer corned beef."

"I know that."

"What in hell is it with you?" Wainwright demanded. "How do you get so damned involved in these things? You're a cop, not an avenging angel."

"I don't sleep well with a cold-blooded killer walking these streets or driving his Mercedes."

"How do you know he's walking these streets?"

"I know. Tell me, captain, if a question has no answer, the question should be enough—wouldn't you say?"

"I don't know what the hell you're talking about."

"Sit down and join me at lunch. Let's talk."

"Sure. I got nothing else to do. I just earn my pay by sitting around."

"You have to eat. I need someone to talk to."

"It takes me ten minutes to eat."

"Then let us talk for ten minutes," Masuto said, smiling.

"Okay. You got it. I'll take half your ham and cheese and give you half my corned beef. That way we can both be happy."

"No. I really prefer ham and cheese. How long have you been a cop, captain?"

"Too long. What is this?"

"Questions of crime. The question has to be the answer, I suppose, if I can find the right question."

"Twenty-two years, if you can get off that Zen kick of yours."

"Sixteen years for me. Thirty-eight years between us. A man sheds his identity. Why?"

"He killed someone. He jumped bail. He had to get out of the country."

"No, he has to stay here. That's the crux of it. He has to stay here. Or he wants to stay here."

"He's got family here."

"Come on, captain. This man doesn't give a damn about anyone."

"How do you know?"

"I know him. I know how he thinks. I know how he operates. Your ordinary criminal loses himself. This man didn't want to lose himself. He had other plans. And how did the cops know who he was? I mean, if they knew who he was, why didn't they grab him?"

"Like I said, he jumped bail."

"No, that's not his style."

"How in hell do you know what his style was?" Wainwright demanded. "Do you know how many people jump bail in any given month? Hundreds. A man knocks over a bank—"

"He's not a bank robber," Masuto interrupted. Then he leaped to his feet and grinned at Wainwright. "Of course, they were both in it. Together. God forgive my stupidity! That's why it made no sense—because I always thought of one, a loner, but to plan it and execute it right from the beginning, there had to be two of them."

"Will you calm down and tell me what the devil you are talking about?"

"No, sir. With all due respect, captain, I'm going to deliver this one to you signed, sealed, and rolled up."

"Like hell you are! I'm your boss, and I damn well want to know what's going on."

Masuto studied him, smiling slightly. "All right, we'll make a deal."

"No deals."

"Don't you want to hear what I've got to say?"

"No deals! What do you mean, you'll make me a deal? You got one hell of a nerve, Masuto."

"Okay, you win. No deal."

"What do you mean, no deal?"

"Just that." Masuto shrugged. "The hell with it."

Now Wainwright studied Masuto shrewdly, and then he said in a low voice, "You know what I ought to do with you?"

"Ah, so—humbly request you fire me."

Wainwright shook his head and took the last bite of his corned beef sandwich. "You are one painful, miserable son of a bitch, Masao. All right. What's your deal?"

"In one hour, give or take a few minutes, I will give you the name of the killer. Not the name of the man whose skeleton we found under the pool, but the name of the man who killed him. I want you to know in advance that this name will do us no good—now. Maybe later. But the killer has become someone else, the man he killed, and that's the name we have to find."

"So you're going to give me the name of the murderer in one hour. That's bullshit, and you know it."

"Do I make idle promises? Have you ever known me not to deliver?"

"What's this business of two of them?"

"Do you remember what I said to you before, the question is the answer? And then, a moment ago, you asked me how I knew what his style is? But I know. Why would Brody remember him? Why would Lundman remember him? Because he had a friend, a pal, a buddy, someone close to him and with him all the time. You don't remember one laborer; you remember two. 'I remember them,' people say, 'they were always together.' And then, once I realized that there were two of them, it made sense."

"What made sense?"

"Give me the hour, and I give you the name."

"All right, you give me the name of the killer. What do I give you?"

"Four more days. I want a week."

"You got it."

"A little more."

"I thought so. What else?"

"Travel time and expenses."

"What do you mean, travel time? Where do you have to travel?"

"I don't know yet, but I'm sure it's in the continental United States."

Wainwright stood up angrily. "You bug me, Masao. You come up with these wild guesses. You know what nobody else knows, and you're always pulling that Charlie Chan routine, grabbing things out of thin air. You promise to give me a name. How do I know it's the right name? Anyway, if I'm to believe you, the name is no damn good to us."

"Perhaps. Perhaps not."

"Great. Just great. And now you want a blank check to travel anywhere in the United States."

"Just plane fare. There and back. I promise not to stay overnight. No hotel bills. No perks."

"How come you don't know where?"

"I get that with the name of the killer."

"How can you be so damn sure?"

"Because the pieces have been floating around in my mind for three days, and finally they've come together."

Wainwright leaned back in his chair and stared at Masuto thoughtfully. Finally, he sighed. "I don't know. I ought to be used to the way you work. All right. We got a deal. Now get me the name of the killer. In one hour. I'll be in my office."

Wainwright left the room, closing the door behind him. Masuto took a deep breath and stretched his arms. Suddenly, he felt alive, alert, filled with energy. Grudgingly—for it went against his practice of Buddhism—he admitted to himself that this was the kind of moment he embraced, the moment when ghosts ceased to be ghosts, when the quarry was almost in sight. It was embezzlement. It had to be. An ordinary thief made no sense. An ordinary thief ends up in jail or in the county graveyard. He doesn't drive a black Mercedes thirty years later. A brutal senseless murder made less sense. This man was brutal but never senseless. The only thing that fit was an embezzlement, an embezzlement large enough to justify the planning, the killing, and the apparent power of the man who drove the black Mercedes.

He picked up the telephone and buzzed Polly.

"You want a date, Masao? Any time."

"No, dear. I want the coordinating department at the F.B.I. in Washington, the place where they have all those fascinating computers."

Masuto waited, and a minute or so later, his phone rang. A voice said, "Williams, F.B.I."

"Agent Williams," he said in his most cordial tone, "this is Sergeant Masuto, Beverly Hills police. We have a problem of the most urgent nature."

"Go ahead. I'll see what we can do for you."

"I'm talking of embezzlement. In the year nineteen fifty, between the first of April and the first of May, there was a major embezzlement in a bank. No, let me put it this way, during that time the facts of a major embezzlement came to light. We would like to have as many of those facts as you can give me."

"Can you tell me anything more, sergeant? Be more definite?"

"I'm afraid not, except that we believe the sum was over a million dollars. If you have more than one in the area of that figure, I'd like to have whatever you dig up."

"All right, sergeant. I'll have to call you back to confirm, and then I'll put it through the computer. I should have something for you this afternoon."

"This afternoon?"

"You're on California time, sergeant. It's three forty-five here. I'll get you the information within the hour."

For the next half hour Masuto paced back and forth in his office. The telephone rang once, and he grabbed it eagerly. It was Sy Beckman at the hotel, to tell him that nothing had happened and he was bored to death and his

Spanish was no better, and when could he go home. Masuto told him to calm down and that he would see him within an hour or so. "If I'm still a cop."

"And what does that mean?"

"I'll explain. I'll explain."

And then the telephone rang again, and it was Williams. "Masuto," he said, "I got it for you. Just one to fit your specifications in that time period, but it was a beauty. Two million eight hundred thousand dollars. How about that?"

"The only one?"

"The only one."

Masuto made notations on his pad. "What bank?"

"The Midtown Manhattan National Bank, upper Madison Avenue in New York. The culprit was the chief teller, name of Stanley Cutler." He spelled it out. "Twenty-five years old, Caucasian, American born, veteran with two decorations. Orphan, raised in a Buffalo orphanage, IQ of a hundred and thirty-seven, no priors. Honorable discharge, November nineteen forty-five, went to work at the Midtown Manhattan in January of forty-six, trained as a teller and rose rapidly. The embezzlement began during April, nineteen forty-nine, but wasn't discovered until an audit a year later. Classified as a brilliant piece of work, an innovation in bank embezzlement. By the way, what's your interest in this out there?"

"You'll receive a full report within the week."

"Well, the file is open, even after thirty years. No trace ever of Cutler or a nickel of the two million eight. If you've got anything, let us know."

"I certainly will. Do you have pictures and prints?"

"Both. I can wire you both and then send you a glossy through the mail."

"By the way, Williams, how tall was Cutler?"

"Five eight and a half."

"Can you send me a full description, eye color, hair, everything you have? Care of Sergeant Masao Masuto, Rexford Drive, Beverly Hills, 90210."

"Right. What are you, Masuto, Japanese?"

"That's right."

"Poetic justice if you catch up with Cutler. He fought in the Pacific."

"So it goes."

"Good luck."

Masuto put down the telephone, took a sheet from his pad, and printed in block letters STANLEY CUTLER. He then went into Wainwright's office.

"The hour's almost up," Wainwright told him.

"Not quite." He put the sheet of paper on the desk in front of Wainwright.

"What's this?"

"The name of our killer."

"Who the devil is Stanley Cutler?"

"I haven't the vaguest idea. I only know that he murdered six people."

"Six? Where do you get six?"

"The man under the pool. A doctor named Ben McKeever, his nurse, the two Lundmans and Mrs. Brody. The doctor and his nurse are pure guesswork, so we may have to scrap those two."

"Who the hell is Ben McKeever?"

"I'll tell you about it, captain. By the way, I'm flying to New York tonight on the red eye. It's the cheapest flight."

"It would be New York," Wainwright said sourly.

CHAPTER
NINE

BLIND ALLEYS

Masuto called Beckman at the Beverly Glen Hotel, and after listening to Beckman's woeful description of the state of his marriage, informed him that some respite was imminent. "You can leave her for a few hours. Have you had lunch?"

"Just finished."

"Then tell her to lock and bolt the door, and not to open it for anyone except you. Not for anyone. Make a simple code word between you, just in case she's too frightened to recognize your voice. Then get over here to the station."

"Will you talk to my wife?"

"I'll talk to her."

But talking to Sophie Beckman was not easy, and Masuto waited patiently to get a word in. "What do you mean, secrets?" she demanded. "What am I, the town crier? He can't tell me where he is or what he's doing? You're supposed to be cops, but you're beginning to sound like those creeps at the C.I.A. who won't tell Congress what they're doing, even if what they're doing is planning to blow up the world, which would be all right, but you're dealing with my husband who can't keep his eyes off any woman under ninety who comes by, and about his hands, I won't even mention—"

She paused for a breath, and Masuto said quickly, "I give you my word, Sophie, this is his assignment, and it's legitimate."

"For how long? When do I see him again?"

"Another day or two."

"Not that I'm breaking my heart to see him, Masao, but it's the way I'm treated."

"He's more miserable than you are."

"I hope so."

"Just another day or two, Sophie."

"Is he with a woman?"

"Absolutely not."

"You're lying, Masao. I could draw you a picture of the woman he's with—an oversized blonde with big boobs—"

"What did you say, Sophie?" Masuto asked with sudden excitement.

"I said I could draw you a picture—"

"Yes, of course. No, no, you're misjudging Sy. He's doing a hard and arduous job, believe me."

Finally, he managed to calm her, fortunately, since while he was talking to her, an officer entered and put a telephoto on his desk.

"For you, sergeant, with the compliments of the F.B.I."

Masuto stared at the picture, recalling with some guilt the times in the past when he had been less than generous in his opinion of the Federal Bureau of Investigation. He had to admit now that if less than long on simple intelligence, when it came to the keeping of files and the use of computers, they were without peer. Wire photos are not of the best, nevertheless it was with great excitement that he stared at the photo of the man he hunted. Thirty years had passed since this picture was taken. He saw the face of a young man, most likely blond or with light brown hair, with pale eyes, a long, thin nose, a mole prominent on one cheek, a wide jaw, fleshy cheeks, heavy brows that almost met over the nose, and thin lips. There was a scar along the left side of the jawbone.

For at least five minutes he sat immobile, staring at the photo. Then he picked it up and went into Wainwright's office, where he laid the picture on the desk in front of the captain.

"What's this?" Wainwright asked.

"Our murderer, thirty years ago. Mr. Stanley Cutler, in the flesh."

"Where did you get this?"

"Courtesy of the F.B.I."

"Masao, if this is another one of your ploys—"

"That's our man. Thirty years ago, he embezzled two million eight hundred thousand dollars from the Midtown Manhattan National Bank. That's how the F.B.I. came into it. They never found him or the money."

"Where does it connect? You're guessing again."

"Am I? Perhaps. But every instinct in my body tells me I'm right. This is the way I spell it out. The embezzlement took place over twelve months. He had a partner, whom he set up from the very beginning for the kill. That's the way his mind works."

"How the hell do you know how his mind works?"

"I told you before that I know him. Just ride with it. He needs the partner to open bank accounts, to spread the money around, maybe to buy various bearer bonds, governments, municipals. Conceivably, the partner comes to California, stashes the loot here. They take a whole year. I was going to New York to see the people at the bank and find out exactly how he did it, but that's not important now."

"You mean you're not going to New York?"

"No, something came up."

"What?"

"This picture. Anyway, it's thirty years. Who knows if there's anyone alive who can give me the information?"

"If this is our man, let's spread the picture around."

"No good, captain. It was thirty years ago. I told you he had his face done."

"What about his prints? Get them from the feds. They don't change. He worked in a bank. They got to have his prints."

"Maybe. They didn't come through." Masuto smiled. "If they do, it won't matter. He took care of things like that."

"How do you take care of prints?"

"There are ways, believe me. If a man is tough enough, he can burn them off."

"So what it amounts to is that you have nothing. You have his picture and his name, and you got nothing. Not one shred of evidence. Masao, I ought to have my head examined. I've put two men on the payroll of the City of Beverly Hills to work chasing ghosts, and I've damn near talked you into making me believe in your ghosts."

"I've called off the New York trip. That's a boost to your budget."

"All right. What do you get in exchange?"

"I want you to call Kennedy and make peace with him and borrow his police artist for tomorrow."

"Why?"

"Because we can't afford a police artist of our own," Masuto said gently.

"That's very funny. You know, Masao, there are people who tell me the Japanese don't have a sense of humor.

They're wrong. You let me talk the city manager into sending a man to New York, and now you don't have to go to New York. That's funny too. You just about tell Captain Kennedy that he's a horse's ass, and now you want me to talk him out of his police artist. That's even funnier."

"Give him a deal. Quid pro quo. He lends us the artist, we give him the murderer of the Lundmans."

"Masao," Wainwright said seriously, "I have more respect for you than you might imagine. We've worked together a good many years now, and I've seen you pull more rabbits out of the hat than you can shake a stick at. I'm even ready to believe that this is a photograph of the killer. But you still got nothing, not a shred of evidence, not one bit of anything I can bring to the D.A. That is, considering that you could find Stanley Cutler. I know you don't have a high opinion of the feds, but they got maybe the biggest facility in the world, and they've been looking for Cutler these thirty years, and they have come up with zilch. Maybe Cutler's dead, maybe in Brazil, and it's still not beyond the realm of possibility that some lunatic killed the Lundmans. God knows, there are plenty of them."

"The Lundmans and Mrs. Brody in one day—that would be stretching coincidence too far."

"It happens."

"No, I can't accept that."

"What then, Masao? You want me to promise Kennedy that we'll wrap this up and deliver him his culprit. Then we wash out. Where does that leave me?"

"You're right," Masao said after a moment. "You can't promise that. But I need that artist."

"Okay, I'll try."

He went back to his office. Beckman was waiting for him, and the telephone was ringing as Masuto entered. It was Williams, calling from Washington. "I'm sorry, Masuto," he said, "but we don't have prints."

"You'd better explain that."

"During the war Cutler pulled a man out of a burning tank. Seared his fingers. Got a citation for it."

"What about prints when he went into the army?"

"He joined up in Europe. There are no prints, Masuto, there just aren't any. Now look, if you people have a lead on Cutler, we want him."

"What about the statute of limitations?"

"There's none on retrieving the money, and we'll let the lawyers worry about the rest."

"Hold on a moment," Masuto said. "Do you have anything on that soldier he pulled out of the tank? Did he recover? His name? Anything?"

"We thought of that. No way we could trace him."

"Wouldn't his name be on the citation?"

"Not necessarily. There were witnesses to the incident. That's all you need for the citation."

Masuto put down the telephone and turned to Beckman. "We have a beauty, Sy. We have a brilliant psychopath who goes in for perfect crimes. Your average criminal has an IQ of ninety or ninety-five. Cutler's IQ is one hundred and thirty-seven. He climbed into a burning tank to save a G.I. and seared his ten fingers. At this point, I'm ready to believe he did it consciously and purposefully."

"That's crazy, Masao. No one burns himself on purpose."

"No? Perhaps not. Will the girl keep the door locked?"

"Right. She's scared enough. Did you square me with Sophie?"

"I think so. Now here's where we are, Sy. I'm going to lay out everything we have."

When Masuto had finished spelling out what he had from Williams and whatever other pieces he had put to-

gether, Beckman stared at the picture and shook his head. "What does it add up to, Masao? A picture thirty years old of a man who had facial surgery, a name that doesn't belong to him anymore, and no fingerprints. That's a stacked deck. Suppose you find him? How do you prove his identity? With Lundman dead, how do you tie him into a crime that happened thirty years ago? As far as the Lundmans are concerned, there's a perfect murder. No weapon, no witnesses."

"Except Rosita."

"Come on, Masao. She wasn't a witness. You know that. The D.A. would laugh at it."

"You're sure she's all right until five o'clock?"

"Unless he can walk through a steel door."

"That wouldn't surprise me either. Now I'll tell you what we're going to do. We're going to visit banks, not the branches, but the main offices. Here's the way I worked this out. I believe that Cutler planned this for years. He got out of the army and got himself a job in a bank. Meanwhile, he had worked out a pattern of embezzlement. That wouldn't be too hard for a man of his caliber. There are plenty of books on the great embezzlements, and in those days they were going out of their way to give jobs to vets—especially vets who had won decorations. Cutler had a partner. For some reason, I believe, Cutler selected Los Angeles for his ultimate goal, perhaps because it was the other side of the continent, more likely because most of the money in L.A. is new money. Now Cutler had a problem. Money is a problem. Two or three million dollars is a huge problem."

"I should have that kind of a problem."

"Still a problem. What do you do with it? You can't keep it under a mattress. So the way I see it, Cutler had a partner, a loyal, devoted partner who obeyed orders and who trusted Cutler with his life."

"And who ended up under the swimming pool."

"Exactly. How he got this partner we may never know. Possibly the man whose life he saved. In any case, Cutler would have chosen someone his size with the same eye and hair color, so that the driver's license and everything else would fit. Cutler funneled the money through him; it would have been too risky to try to do it himself. I imagine that for the most part they bought bonds, government bonds, company bonds, municipal bonds, all as good as cash. His partner could open accounts in half a dozen brokerage houses, and they spread their winnings over a year. But at the same time, a man like Cutler would see to it that they had some cash resources at their destination—namely L.A. At least that's my guess. I'm trying to think the way he thinks, and by now I have a pretty good notion of how he thinks. Perhaps his partner made two or three trips to Los Angeles, and each time he'd open a few bank accounts—nothing spectacular, perhaps ten thousand here, five thousand there. His partner must have been overwhelmed at the way Cutler trusted him to open the accounts in his own name, but at the same time he was signing his death warrant. Again, we'll never know how Cutler persuaded John Doe to sign on that job as a day laborer. Maybe it was simply a way to drop out of sight. You don't look for a high-class embezzler on a construction job. But persuade him he did, and there he saw the opportunity to get rid of John Doe forever, and he took it."

"And you figure we might get lucky and find two or three bank accounts for the same name?"

"It's a long shot."

"Too long, Masao. Thirty years too long."

Masuto stared at him for a moment, then he picked up the telephone and asked Polly to get him the manager at the central office of the Los Angeles branch of the Crocker Bank. The phone rang, and Masuto picked it up, introduced

himself, and stated his case. The man at the Crocker Bank, whose name was Johnson, sighed deeply and said, "I'm afraid not, sergeant."

"Why not?"

"Because thirty years is just too long. We do have a central storage depot and we do have a great deal of material on microfilm, but to be able to find and compare the names of small depositors in nineteen fifty or in nineteen forty-nine—well, I'm just afraid it's impossible."

"How impossible?"

"Impossible, sir. Well, let me be honest. I'm not absolutely sure that those records don't exist. I would have to go to our central office in San Francisco for full information. Then someone would have to spend days going through the microfilm—providing the records have been kept. We do keep records of our own accounting over that period, but names of depositors? Most unlikely. But let me say this. Give me the name of the depositor, and I'll try to track it down."

"I don't have the name of the depositor."

"What? Are you trying to make a fool of me, sir? Is this really the Beverly Hills police?"

"You can call back if you wish. This is the Beverly Hills police. We are trying to find out whether the same name appears in several banks."

"Without knowing the name?"

"The fact of the duplication would establish the name."

"Sergeant, you're wasting my time. It's impossible."

Masuto looked at Beckman and nodded.

"What did he say?"

"He says it's impossible."

"I thought so. The L.A.P.D. might cover something like that, if they could put twenty men on it and take a month.

We're too small, and who knows if the records exist? You want me to try another bank?"

"No, it wouldn't be any different."

"So what's left?"

"Rosita, the police artist, and, I think, my kinsman, Ishido."

"Who is Ishido?"

"He is Kati's father's cousin. He was an officer in the Japanese Imperial Army, and he has lived in Los Angeles these past thirty-three years. He has enormous interests in Mitsubishi and Sony, and before he retired he represented Mitsubishi on the West Coast. He is also Samurai, which may not mean much here, but still counts among the folk from the old country. Now he collects Japanese stamps and Chinese jade. He has more millions than we have fingers between us, and since he is what he is, and I am a policeman, you can imagine that he does not look too kindly upon me. I sometimes think that he has never forgiven Kati for marrying me. On the few occasions when I have seen him, he has been very courteous, but that's his manner."

"And you figure him as a connection?"

"I hope so."

"So we washed out with the banks. What do I do now?"

"Go back to the lovely Rosita."

"You know," Beckman said, "you are putting a large temptation in the face of an ordinary cop. I am human, Masao, and that kid is just too damn pretty."

"Exercise restraint."

"If Sophie ever found out, she'd cut my throat."

"We'll try to keep it a secret." And then, as Beckman was about to leave, Masuto said, "Sy, if Cutler should get on to us and somehow get into that room with you, use your gun. Don't try to take him and put cuffs on him. Use your gun, even if he's unarmed. Shoot out a kneecap or something."

"What? Are you crazy?"

"At this point, I don't know."

"He's five eight. I'm twice his size. I've never met the man I couldn't take, and I don't go for that karate crap."

"This might be the first time."

"I'll think about it."

When Beckman had left, Masuto went into Wainwright's office and stood waiting.

"Yeah," Wainwright said. "I did it."

"We get the police artist?"

"He'll be over here at ten o'clock tomorrow."

"Captain, you're wonderful."

"Yeah. Well, it's your turn to be Mr. Wonderful. Pick up a box of one dollar Flaminco cigars. Make sure they're genuine Flamincos and that they come from the Canary Islands, wherever they are. There are twenty in a box, so it will cost you twenty bucks."

"What for?"

"For Kennedy. It's part of the deal."

Masuto went back to his office and called Dr. Leo Hartman. "I would like to see you tomorrow," he said, "at about noon."

"That's impossible, sergeant."

"Yes, I've spent the day hearing that things were impossible. Let me put it this way, Dr. Hartman. You indicated that Ben McKeever was a man you admired. Perhaps I can tell you that he was murdered and his nurse was murdered. If you will give me an hour of your time tomorrow, it's possible I can bring in his killer."

"My God, sergeant, that was thirty years ago."

"His killer is still alive, free, and prosperous. Is it worth an hour of your time?"

"Are you being serious?"

"Very serious."

"All right. Come in at twelve fifteen. I can give you forty-five minutes. Will that be enough?"

"I think so."

"I'll have some sandwiches sent in. Have you any preference?"

"Whatever you choose will be fine. I'll be bringing another man with me."

"I hope you're right, sergeant. It was an ignominious way to die."

Masuto met Wainwright on his way out, and the captain asked him where he was off to.

"Home," Masuto said.

"It's only half past four. You're making an early day of it."

"I got home at nine yesterday."

"You're a cop."

"Sy's wife is talking about divorcing him. Do you want Kati to divorce me?"

"I hear your people don't go in for divorce."

"So you hear."

"I got three burglaries and a mugging. Right here in Beverly Hills. A car pulls up next to this lady's car. Two guys jump out, open the doors, grab her purse, and drive off."

"She should lock her doors."

"All right. I gave you the week. I regret it, but I gave it to you."

CHAPTER
TEN

THE POLICE

ARTIST

few minutes before the police artist arrived the following morning, the postman brought in a glossy photo of Stanley Cutler, which Williams had dispatched by express mail. The police artist arrived a few minutes before ten, a young man of about thirty, tall, redheaded, and with a Texas accent. "Well now," he said in a soft drawl, "I am mighty pleased to meet you. I'm Kenny Dawson, and you are Sergeant Masuto. I did suspect from your name that you would be some kind of Oriental. Japanese? Am I right?"

"You're right, Mr. Dawson."

"Now don't call be Mr. Dawson, sergeant. Kenny will do. I hear you got a problem that wants an artist? Of course, I would think that in a place like Beverly Hills, which I hear has more millionaires per square mile than any other spot in the U.S. of A., they would have a police artist of their own."

"We don't have call for one very often. Are you good, Kenny?"

"Good enough. Gotta admit that I put aside my dreams

of being another Frederic Remington for a steady job, but that don't mean I have sold out. Now what have you got for me?"

Masuto handed him the glossy print of Stanley Cutler. "This picture was taken about thirty years ago. As you can see, it's probably an identity photo for a job record."

"Sure enough. Same technique as passport photos."

"I want you to draw it, but to change it to conform to thirty years of aging. I can tell you that the man has not gained much weight. He stays in good physical condition. Do you think you can do that?"

"I'll give it a try. You don't have a profile, do you?"

"Just this. And we have an hour and a half. Is that enough time?"

"Plenty."

"And one thing more," Masuto added. "Can you use a medium where you can erase and make changes?"

"Sure. I'll use charcoal without fixing it, and then we can pick it up with a kneaded eraser." He looked at Masuto curiously. "By the way, you wouldn't like to explain what I'm doing?"

"Well, you're doing what few men get to do, compressing thirty years in an hour, and then we're going to consult a plastic surgeon."

"Yes, that answers my question."

The telephone rang. It was Williams, calling from Washington, and he asked about the glossy print.

"We got it. Thanks for the cooperation."

"By the way, sergeant," Williams said, "there's a ten percent finder's fee on the two million eight hundred thousand. Of course, the bank was paid off by the insurance company. That's Transwest National Insurance. They put the finder's fee on it back in nineteen fifty. I spoke to them this morning, and they say the fee is still in force, a very neat two hundred and eighty thousand dollars. Inflation puts a bite into it, but it's still a nice piece of change."

Wainwright was scowling at some papers on his desk when Masuto came into his office and sat down facing him.

"You got nothing to do," Wainwright said. "You and Beckman, you really stiffed me. He's shacked up with some cute Mexican babe, and you got nothing to do but sit here in my office with that Charlie Chan look on your face."

"So sorry, but the artist is at work, and meanwhile Agent Williams called from the Federal Bureau of Investigation, and he tells me the Transwest National Insurance Company put a ten percent finder's fee on that two million eight embezzlement, and while thirty years has passed, the finder's fee is still in force."

"You got to be kidding."

"Oh, no. No, indeed."

"Masao, bums who pull off these jobs spend it quicker than you could walk to the bank."

"Two million eight hundred thousand dollars?"

"It's thirty years."

"Let's just suppose, captain, that this particular bum has other plans. He wants to be rich and powerful. The embezzlement money is his stake. He nurtures it, invests it. Possibly he goes into some business. These last thirty years have been very rewarding here in southern California. Today he has millions."

"Still at it, Masao?"

"Suppose I'm right? All we have to do is to identify him."

"If we can't convict him for murder—and I don't see a chance of a snowball in hell that we can—then the statute of limitations has run out in the embezzlement, and he can walk around and thumb his nose at us, that is considering that you ever find him."

"Oh, I'll find him," Masuto said. "As far as criminal action is concerned, you may be right that we can't touch him. But suppose the money can be reclaimed in a civil suit? After all, there's no statute of limitations on stolen property. I read where they're still litigating World War Two disputes, and that's forty years ago."

"You may have a point there. But don't get any notions about becoming a rich cop. If it ever came to that, the money would go to the City of Beverly Hills."

"It might get us that ten percent raise we've been asking for."

"I doubt it."

"Well, one step at a time, captain. By tonight I expect to know who Stanley Cutler is."

"It's Wednesday," Wainwright said. "I expected as much."

"I'm sure," Masuto said dryly.

When Masuto returned to his office, Dawson was completing the charcoal portrait. Very skillfully, he had aged the portrait, pushing back the hairline, allowing the cheeks to expand and sag a bit, putting wrinkles around the eyes, lines on the brow and around the mouth, and loose flesh and folds of skin on the neck.

"That's very good," Masuto said.

"No, it isn't. Any art student could do as well."

"I doubt it."

"You should see my paintings. All this crap about naturalism and photorealism that's coming up now. I was doing it ten years ago, when I was just a kid. But you want to know about the art scene in Los Angeles? It stinks. A few lousy galleries on La Cienega, a couple in Beverly Hills that are even lousier. New York's the place, but they tell me you got to pay six, seven hundred a month for some small, rundown loft in Soho. I need a stake. You don't know any of the local art collectors, do you, sergeant?"

"I'm afraid not."

"Well, who does? Anyway, here it is. What do we do now?"

"We go to see Dr. Leo Hartman."

"You want me to drag all my stuff with me?"

"You might as well. You have fixative?"

"What am I—an amateur?"

"Good. I'll want to fix the drawing when we finish there."

In Masuto's car Dawson said, "The way I got it figured is this. This character ripped off something important thirty years ago and you're after him now. It had to be a homicide, otherwise the statute of limitations would have wiped it out. I would be mighty pleased to be let in on your secret, Sergeant Masuto."

"Sorry. You'll just have to be patient and read about it in the papers."

"I don't read the papers, sergeant. It's too depressing. I watch the news on TV with a pad, and I draw everything I see. That's what's responsible for the whole decay of the art scene. Nobody knows how to draw anymore. No standards. To me drawing is like playing the piano. You just have to stick with it every day of your life or you lose it."

Hartman kept them waiting for half an hour before he was ready to see them, during which time Dawson attempted to sketch one of the women sitting in the waiting room and was told in no uncertain terms that she had not come there to be an artist's model. He contented himself with sketching Masuto, and had achieved a fair likeness when the receptionist told them that the doctor could see them now.

In Hartman's office Masuto introduced Dawson while the doctor unwrapped sandwiches.

"Mighty kind of you," Dawson said. "I didn't expect lunch to come with it."

"My contribution to the good cause," Hartman said.

Masuto placed the glossy photograph of Cutler on Hartman's desk. "This is the man who may have murdered Ben McKeever. This picture of him was taken perhaps thirty-three years ago, when he went to work at the Midtown Manhattan National Bank. It's not the best picture in the world, but it's all we have. That appears to have been a rather bad scar on his jaw, possibly a war wound. Now Dawson, here, has drawn his likeness as he might appear today. Of course there's guesswork on Dawson's part, but it's a beginning. Here is what I would like you to do, doctor, if you will be so kind. The man in the photo comes into your office, as he came into McKeever's office. I don't know what went on there, and probably we never will know. But the fact is that he persuaded McKeever to change his face. Now just for the sake of our experiment, let us imagine that you are in McKeever's place. This man comes into your office and he persuades you to change his face. Now I know nothing about your practice, but I suspect that both you and McKeever would follow somewhat the same procedure. Or are there many alternatives?"

Hartman was studying the photograph. "No, not too many alternatives. Perhaps none. Is this the only picture?"

"As I said, the only one."

"If we only had a profile. But we haven't, have we."

"Here is Dawson's drawing."

Hartman put down the glossy and stared at the drawing. "It's damn good."

"Is it a reasonable reconstruction of the aging process?"

"Fairly so. I think you've made the neck too scrawny.

The photo shows a very muscular neck. I would guess that he would wear a sixteen and a half or a seventeen shirt. Age would add flesh to it, and there would be some horizontal lines under the chin."

"He is a man who stays in excellent physical condition," Masuto said.

"Oh?" Hartman looked at him thoughtfully. "May I ask how you know that if you don't know who he is?"

"In time. Could we get back to the photo? He comes into your office. You agree to change his face. What would you do?"

Hartman turned to Dawson. "How long would it take you to make a tracing of this photo—a line drawing but with all the features and marks?"

"About five minutes."

"Do it. Meanwhile we'll eat. You see," he said to Masuto, taking a bite out of his sandwich, "there is not too much you can do with the human face. We're not molding in clay. We work with flesh and bone. It's very popular in novels and movies for the criminal to go to a plastic surgeon and order a new face. It really can't be done. Now during the war I was a young surgeon in the Pacific, and since then I've done a great deal of work with people who are badly burned or injured in car crashes. In such cases, you very often do build a completely new face, but only because the old face has been destroyed, and in such cases the countenance is never quite normal."

"Why couldn't McKeever have done this with him?"

"Smash his face? Burn it? No, sergeant, we don't do such things. Cosmetic surgery is limited, thank God."

Dawson finished the tracing and handed it to the doctor. He laid it on his desk with the photograph beside it. "Suppose you change the neck on your drawing, and let me study these for a few minutes."

For the next few minutes Hartman munched his sandwich and studied the tracing and the photo. Then he said to Dawson, "Move around so you can see what I'm doing. Then you make the changes in your drawing."

"Okay, Doc. Got you."

"First thing, we get rid of the scar." He made marks on the tracing.

"Can you do that and show no new scars?" Masuto asked.

"If you're good, and Ben McKeever was good."

"Heavier neck and no scar," Dawson said.

"Get rid of the mole."

"Done."

"Now, in getting rid of the scar, we make this incision on the other side of the jaw, cut here and here, and lo and behold we've changed the shape of his mouth."

"How much?" Dawson asked.

"Just a trifle." He made the change on his tracing. "But see how it changes his appearance. A rather petulant look, but his face would light up more when he smiles. It might give him a charming smile, and I suppose that with his nature, that would be an asset. Now the nose, and there's the problem. The most prominent feature on man's face, the nose. If we only had a profile. Do you know his name?" he asked Masuto.

"Is that important?"

"It might be."

"Cutler. Stanley Cutler."

"Anglo-Saxon. Or Irish, conceivably. Irish would account for that long, pointed nose—straight, long, and pointed. We'll bob it, very simple, done it a hundred times. Here, young fellow." He made the change on his tracing, and carefully using his kneaded eraser, Dawson changed the drawing to conform.

"Ah, now we're beginning to see what the devil looks like. Now, one more simple detail, and we'll have Mr. Cutler with a face that even his own mother wouldn't recognize. Of course, that's just an expression," he explained to Masuto. "His mother might recognize him, but she'd want to know what he had done to himself. Then again, maybe she wouldn't. I think if I were doing the job, she wouldn't."

"That one more simple detail?" Dawson suggested.

"Oh, yes. Yes, indeed. You see the way his brows come together? That's perhaps the most noticeable feature on his face, that heavy line right across his brow. Well, we separate the brows. Remove a piece here, remove a piece here, and then, if we're doing a really artistic job, we lessen the thickness of what remains by about a quarter of an inch. Like this." He made the change on the tracing and pushed it over to Dawson. "See what he's become? He's no longer a sullen, miserable creature. He's quite sensitive, isn't he? The inquiring mind. Isn't it marvelous what a raised brow will do? A trick actors learned long ago. There you are. McKeever has given him a new face, a new look, a new character, and he could walk through the corridors of any police department in perfect security."

"And you could do all this?" Masuto asked. "The man's face would reveal no sign of it, no scars at all?"

"For the first few months the scars would show. After all, the trauma to the skin and flesh has been very severe."

"How long?"

"Five, six, seven months. But they are fading. By now, all trace should be gone, even to close examination."

"Is it possible for fingerprints to disappear with burns on the fingertips?"

"Yes, indeed. And even without severe burns, if one does work of a certain kind. Great mythology about fingerprints.

But you have aroused my curiosity enormously. When do you expect to arrest this man?"

"As soon as I find him," Masuto replied, knowing it was hardly that simple. "You've helped us enormously."

"It's been fascinating. Both of you very interesting." He handed a card to Dawson. "Keep in touch. I use an artist quite often, and the work pays. Give me a call next week." And to Masuto he said, "I have stifled my curiosity, but a Nisei detective on our little police force, I must say I like the notion."

"It's interesting work," Masuto said for want of anything else to say.

Outside, Dawson said, "So it goes. Art for art's sake. From police artist to the reconstruction of the faces of rich dames. I wonder what he pays?"

"Ask him."

"Right. What do you think, sergeant, am I worth twenty dollars an hour?"

"Every bit of it."

"It's not what they pay me at the L.A.P.D., but this is Beverly Hills, isn't it?"

"It certainly is."

"You got kids, sergeant?"

"Two of them."

"Well, if they want to be artists, discourage them. My uncle's a rancher, but I saw cows branded once, and that was the end of it for me. I'll ride back to your office with you and fix the drawing, and then if you're finished with me, I'll take in some of those lousy galleries on La Cienega. Might as well see what the competition is doing."

After Dawson had left, Masuto took the charcoal drawing into Wainwright and spread it out on his desk.

"What's this?"

"Stanley Cutler."

"Is this what you needed the police artist for? It doesn't even resemble the photo you showed me."

"No? Well, it's thirty years later and he's had a lot of cosmetic surgery."

Wainwright grinned and shook his head. "You are wonderful, Masao. I don't know what the hell to make of you, but you are something." He stared at the drawing again. "On the other hand, I could swear that I've seen this man somewhere."

"It's rather unique, isn't it?" Masuto said. "We discover the skeleton of a man murdered thirty years ago. The murderer has killed five other people. We know his name, and I think we know what he looks like and tonight I suspect I will know who he is, and we can't touch him."

"So you've come to that conclusion too?"

"I'm afraid so."

"Well, there it is," Wainwright said. "It happens. I think it happens a lot more than the public suspects. There's a lot of killers, a lot of criminals walking around on the streets, and the cops know it, and the cops can't touch them."

"I still have to know who he is."

"Why? What good will it do? You can't tie him into any of the murders. You can't even tie him into the embezzlement, because if he has no prints and his face is changed, there's no way ever to prove that he's Stanley Cutler."

"Don't forget," Masuto said, "that he has taken the name of the man he put under the swimming pool."

"So you say. Guesses. He could take any name. In the right places here in L.A. you can buy a social security card and a birth certificate, not to mention honorable discharge papers. So why stay with the name of the man he killed?"

"Because it gives him roots, a place of origin, a home-town. This man didn't want to lose himself. He wanted to be a man of position and power. Those are his gods, wealth and power, and to have those things, he has killed without mercy."

Wainwright looked at him long and thoughtfully. "You know, Masao," he finally said, "we've been together a lot of years. If you weren't Nisci, you'd be running this police force, although with your mind, I never understood why you wanted to be a cop. I know," he continued, waving a hand, "it's your karma. Only I don't buy that. I don't buy one little bit of it. It's something else. I've watched you through a lot of cases, and particularly through this. And most of the time, I keep my mouth shut and give you a free hand. So this time I kept my mouth shut, which maybe I shouldn't have done." He tapped the drawing on his desk. "You've gone to a lot of effort. You figured out what kind of a crime led to that murder up on Laurel Way. You tracked it down. You got yourself a suspect. You got his name and background and you got a picture of what he might look like if he were alive today—and to get this picture you had to tie in a plastic surgeon and his nurse. But I've been asking around about Dr. Ben McKeever. Masao, he was an addict, and his nurse was an addict, and he had fouled up his life from A to Z. You took what Leo Hartman told you for gospel. Well, I don't know what the relationship between Hartman and McKeever was, but either Hartman was taken in by McKeever, or he was covering. Well, that's all right. McKeever was a middle-aged man and Hartman was just starting out, so maybe McKeever threw him some bones, so to speak."

"Where did you get all this?" Masuto asked him.

"Where do you think? I called Chief Maddox, who ran the police force thirty years ago. He's almost eighty, but he has all his buttons, and he told me the circumstances. They were having an affair. The nurse's name was Mary Clancy. One of her kids smashed up a car and was killed. Mary overdosed and died. McKeever called the cops. When they got there, the house was in flames. The dirty stuff was hushed up. So this picture doesn't mean one damn thing."

"I think it does," Masuto said slowly. "It's been in back of my mind since I called the F.B.I. It's been there, and I kept chasing it away."

"What's been there?"

"Just a notion. I chase it away, and it comes back and reverses everything. Let's suppose that John Doe is Stanley Cutler, that it's Stanley Cutler's skeleton that we found under the pool, that his partner planned and executed the whole thing. Then there would be no need for concealment on the killer's part, and no way to connect him with the embezzlement. He put Cutler into the bank, showed him how to operate, and then, when the proper moment arrived, killed him."

"Then if you thought of this, why this whole business of the police artist?"

"Because I don't know. You're telling me that McKeever was in neck deep. All the more reason why he should do business with a man like Cutler. If he called the police, he could have done so at the point of a gun. But maybe that's all a surmise with no foundation. Do you want me to drop it at this point? You're the boss. You've been needling me about dropping it. Do you really want me to?"

Wainwright stared at Masuto for a long moment, and then he said, "Goddamnit, no! That murder thirty years ago was on our turf. I want you to find the bastard and bring him in."

CHAPTER ELEVEN

ISHIDO

Even Masuto, who could look at the enormous wealth and very conspicuous consumption of Beverly Hills with objectivity and without envy, related to his wife's kinsman, Ishido, with awe. It was not simply that Ishido's wealth was larger than most Beverly Hills wealth; it was the way Ishido was. Whereas visitors to Beverly Hills have often noted that it specializes in vulgarity, Ishido epitomized taste. Actually, Ishido did not live in Beverly Hills, but a few miles to the west in Bel-Air, a neighborhood with a little more posh and perhaps a good deal more money than Beverly Hills. There Ishido lived alone—his wife having died seven years before—in a large, single-story Japanese-style house, surrounded by green hedges, a brick wall, and patrolled by two armed guards and two Doberman pinschers. Ishido himself was a small, deceptively gentle and pleasant man of some sixty-five years. At the age of twenty-five he had been a colonel in the Imperial Japanese Army. When the war ended, he was the youngest general in the army. He had come to California in 1947 to represent one of the new Japanese companies that were rising out of the ruins left by the war, and now, thirty-three years later, he was retired, a multi-millionaire, and a quiet power in the Los Angeles area.

Ishido had come from a moderately important Samurai family; but moderately important or not, his was still Samurai. Masuto's father had been a gardener; and Kati remembered this as Masuto finished his dinner and headed for the door.

"Masao," she called softly.

He paused and turned to her.

"You are going to see Ishido?"

"Yes, I told you so. It's no great joy, but I have to see him. I don't know who else can help me now."

"Like that? The way you are dressed?"

He was wearing his brown tweed jacket and gray flannel trousers. The jacket was two years old and the trousers were wrinkled. He wore a white shirt without a tie and open at the neck. His brown shoes were scuffed and needed shining.

"This is the way I dress," Masuto said with annoyance. "I am a policeman, a cop. Ishido knows that. He has been kind enough to see me on very short notice—insufferably kind—and I have no intention of deluding him with the notion that a Beverly Hills cop can afford to buy his clothes at Carroll's," he said, referring to the fine men's shop at the corner of Rodeo and Santa Monica.

"But you might well convince him," Kati said, smiling, "that a Beverly Hills cop has a wife who can press trousers most excellently."

"Would it make you happy?"

"Please."

Masuto took off his trousers, and sat glumly and unhappily in his underwear in the kitchen. When his son and daughter glanced in and began to titter, he snapped at them angrily.

"What has come over you?" Kati asked.

"I have reached a point where I can conceal my ignorance from everyone but myself."

"Oh, Masao, the things you say!"

"Why didn't I trust myself? I sensed it from the beginning. There were two men. One was strong, demonic, aggressive, pathological. The other was weak and malleable. Kati, if Cutler were the strong man, there would have been no need for him to kill Lundman. Because if he were Cutler, his face would have been changed, his fingerprints absent— then how could anyone identify him or accuse him? But the other man, John Doe, he was not wanted by the F.B.I. No one was looking for him—unless Lundman or Mrs. Brody remembered. And do you know why they would remember? Because he, John Doe, and not Cutler was the strong, demonic, and aggressive one."

"I really don't know what on earth you're talking about," Kati said.

"I should have known, sensed it, but no, I spend two days looking for evidence. Well, that's over. Perhaps we'll never find him, and certainly, we can never convict him. But we shall see."

He pulled on his trousers and said to Kati, "I dislike going there. The last time I was there, I came as a kinsman and left as a policeman."

"Be natural. When you are natural, you are the most charming man in the world."

"Ah, so. Yes. I will try. Don't wait up for me. I will probably be very late."

In spite of Masuto's apprehensions, Ishido appeared delighted to see him. He did Masuto the honor of answering the door himself, a small, smiling man in a magnificent black robe. Seated in Ishido's living room, which was tastefully but sparsely furnished in the Japanese manner, Masuto accepted a paper-thin teacup from an attractive young woman in her mid-twenties. The tea was green and pungent, and after it had been poured the attractive young woman disappeared. Well, Ishido was a widower. He was entitled to live as he saw fit.

"In the past, Masao," Ishido said to him, "you attempted a discussion in Japanese. Perhaps that was unfortunate."

"We will talk in English if you prefer," Masuto said.

"It will be better. It is the tongue you were born to and the tongue I have spoken for thirty-four years. There is a legend around, Masao, that I long for the old days. Nonsense! I love Los Angeles, and I shall die here. For a Buddhist, there is no foreign land."

"I must agree with you."

"You still meditate?" Ishido asked.

"Ah, yes. Indeed."

"Good. And Kati and the children?"

"All well."

"Good. Very good. Now what may I do for you, Masao? You have come with a rolled drawing in your hand. Do you desire my opinion as an art expert?"

Masuto unrolled the sketch the police artist had made and spread it out on the low tea table.

"I will not give you my opinion as an art expert," Ishido said.

"The work of a police artist. He draws well, if mechanically."

"Of course. So very sorry for my levity. For that purpose it is excellent."

"Tell me, sir," Masuto said, "is it true what I have heard?"

"And what have you heard?" Ishido asked, smiling.

"I must go beyond common courtesy, but it is absolutely necessary if you are to help me."

"A situation not uncommon."

"I have heard that you are as wealthy as Norton Simon, with better taste and a wider circle of influence here in southern California."

"I have never counted Norton's wealth, but I have the most profound respect for his taste. Are you after him?"

"Oh, no. Certainly not." Masuto pointed to the police drawing. "Do you know this man?"

Ishido studied the picture thoughtfully. "I'm afraid not. No, I have never seen that face before. Do you know him, Masao?"

Masuto took a long, deep breath. "Yes, as a skeleton we found under a swimming pool in Laurel Way."

"Ah, so. Yes. I read about the skeleton. Who murdered the man, Masao?"

"I hope that before I leave here tonight, honored kinsman, you will tell me his name. Otherwise . . ." Masuto folded his hands and shook his head.

"Am I a suspect, nephew?" Ishido asked undisturbed.

"Heaven forbid. Our suspect is five feet eight and a half inches tall, and he weights at least fifty pounds more than you do."

"Remarkable, Masao. You know how tall he is and you know how heavy he is. Do you also know the color of his eyes?"

"Blue, I'm quite certain."

"Ah, so! We have here a game in the old sense, when they used to say that the only game worth anything was one where a human life was at stake. You have made a presumption that this man is a part of what the younger folk would call the southern California establishment."

"With all due humility, yes. And I am told that you know them all."

"Perhaps most, Masao. But satisfy my curiosity. Where did you get a picture of the man you found under the pool?"

"From the F.B.I. Except that I, being a fool, decided that this man is the murderer."

"But he is not."

"No, he is the victim."

"You pique my curiosity and my sense of the game. Let us discuss the murderer. He is five feet eight and a half, blue eyes, heavily built—and wealthy? But of course he would be wealthy if you place him in the establishment."

"In nineteen fifty," Masuto said, "he embezzled two million eight hundred thousand dollars from a bank. The embezzlement was not done by the murderer, but by his partner, whom he subsequently killed. I suspect he transferred the wealth to Los Angeles."

"Bearer bonds, some bank accounts," Ishido guessed.

"Ah, so," Masuto nodded. "But he is filled with a sense of power, aggressiveness. He must move into the community of power."

"The business world?"

"So I would guess."

Ishido poured some hot tea and sipped it. Then he closed his eyes and touched his fingers to his forehead. "Nineteen fifty-one—the latter half?"

"I can only guess, and I am reaching a point where I must doubt my guesses. The man under the pool was killed, I believe, in June or July of nineteen fifty. If it took him a year to establish himself—?"

"In what field?" Ishido asked mildly.

"I don't know. I have given no thought to that."

Smiling thinly, Ishido nodded. "Did I hear or read somewhere that these two people, the Lundmans, were killed with the bare hands of the murderer?"

"Perhaps I mentioned it. I am not sure it was in the papers."

"Karate?"

"I think so."

"So we add to our portrait, Masao. He is an enthusiast of the old art, which he perverts. To kill in karate is not only ignoble, but a perversion of all the excellence that endows the martial arts. Do you still practice, Masao?"

"Yes, when I can."

"Masao," Ishido said softly, "what hornets' nest do you stir up here? Tell me, do you have any evidence you can bring against this man?"

"No."

"So it is when you function in a democracy. Your police are very efficient, and at times, as for example with yourself, quite intelligent. But powerless. Here is a man who killed in cold blood—how many times did you say, Masao?"

"Six that I know of."

"Each killing predetermined, planned, executed with assassinlike precision, and we know of the murders and we know who he is. But we cannot touch him."

"Respected uncle!" Masuto said sharply.

"Yes?"

"You said we know who he is. True, we know who Stanley Cutler is. But I strongly suspect that Stanley Cutler is not the killer but instead is the victim."

"Ah, so. I agree."

"Then if you know who the killer is, you know who John Doe is."

"Yes. I think so. Insofar as knowledge and truth have any meaning or substance. Frequently I doubt that they do."

"Speaking philosophically, I agree with you. But in wholly mundane terms, uncle, do you know this man I seek?"

"I know one who fits your description. In nineteen fifty he bought a half interest in a small aerospace company in Orange County. I know him because we have had various business dealings and because we belong to the same country club, the West Los Angeles Club."

Amazed that his uncle, still Japanese for all his wealth and power and taste, had been admitted to the West Los Angeles Club, which had built such solid ramparts against Jews, Mexicans, and other lesser breeds, Masuto attempted to conceal his response; but Ishido simply shrugged and asked him, "Why so astonished, Masao?"

"Not at all."

"Come, come. You are absolutely amazed that they would admit me, a former officer in the imperial army, a Japanese, an Oriental, into their sacred precincts. But my dear Masao, I am inordinately wealthy—which is all that counts. Then my having been with the army of the enemy becomes romantic, being an Oriental becomes exotic, and my being rather small and withered is overlooked—and in any case, my manners are so much better than theirs. So, you see, I was invited to join. I don't play golf, but I do frequently dine there, both for lunch and for dinner. The food is excellent. Ah, now!" He clapped his hands and grinned at Masuto. "We shall all dine there together, myself, you, and the murderer."

"You can't be serious?"

"But of course I am. Not only serious but enchanted. Can you guess who this man is who fits your description? Come, Masao, I have given you one hint already—the aerospace company. Let me give you another—the gift of twelve magnificent Picassos to the Los Angeles Museum of Art."

"Incredible," Masuto whispered. "It can't be. Saunders Aerospace is the largest company of its kind in the West.

It's a prime supplier for the Pentagon. And Eric Saunders—you do mean Eric Saunders?"

"I certainly do," Ishido said cheerfully.

"You mean Eric Saunders is either Stanley Cutler or—"

Ishido poured another cup of tea and handed it to Masuto. "Come now, nephew. It is time to end this confusion. You showed me that very clever drawing of Stanley Cutler as he would be today if he were made over by a plastic surgeon. There is no Stanley Cutler. The skeleton is Stanley Cutler. Eric Saunders is Eric Saunders, very clean, as they say here, very public. No secrets in Eric Saunders's past, no need for plastic surgery or any of that nonsense. We are talking about one of a half dozen of the most distinguished citizens of southern California, an industrial tycoon of major national importance. He is the youngest son of the Earl of Newton. You know, Masao, when the old Earl died and the estate was neck deep in debt, Eric bought it and made a gift of it to the British National Trust. Didn't want it himself. He's an American citizen, member of the Republican National Committee, president of Saunders Aerospace, on a dozen boards, including several fine universities, a millionaire a hundred times over, and a member of the West Los Angeles Country Club."

"And also a murderer?"

"Who knows? But what an incredible possibility! You know, he does fit your description. Came here in nineteen fifty or so with apparently unlimited funds. People took it for granted that he had a line of credit from his British bankers. But he might well have laundered the money through Mexico and back to England and then here. He's about the height you want, blue eyes, fifty-nine or sixty, I would say, splendid physical condition."

"Is he a friend of yours?" Masuto asked.

"Ah, that would be an unhappy turn of events. No. Neither a friend nor an enemy, although I should not enjoy having him as an enemy. But if he is the man you seek, he is certainly not your common murderer."

"In some ways, yes," Masuto said. "He is as much a psychopath as any downtown hoodlum. In other ways—well, he presents problems."

"You must meet him of course?"

"Why should he care to meet me?" Masuto wondered.

"I will tell him that you are a master of the true Okinawan art."

"Karate? He practices karate?"

"Of course."

"Then he is my man," Masuto said, nodding somberly.

"No, nephew. You have no evidence. He is possibly a murderer, but not your man. No one's man."

The young woman appeared again, bearing a fresh pot of tea. She wore a black silk kimono, embroidered in gold thread. She set down the teapot and left. Ishido poured the tea, and then looked inquiringly at Masuto.

"Something troubles you?" Ishido asked, a note of mockery in his voice.

"Why do you give him to me?"

"Ah. Isn't it my duty to aid the police?"

"With all due respect, I cannot accept such an explanation."

"Then let us simply say that my karma involves Saunders. You are a Buddhist. You comprehend karma."

"How long have you known Saunders? You said he came here in nineteen fifty. Did you meet him then?"

Ishido smiled. "You are very clever, Masao, but you are also very presumptuous. I think we have talked enough. If you wish to know more about my relationship with Eric

Saunders and why I lead you to him, join us for dinner as I suggested."

A few minutes later Masuto left Ishido's house, aware that he was being used and irritated because he had no notion of why and how he was being used.

CHAPTER
TWELVE

THE BOMB

The following morning, which was Thursday, Ishido telephoned Masuto at home. Kati answered the phone, and the fact that it was Ishido placed her in a quandary. For one thing Ishido was the most romantic and unapproachable part of her life. He was wealthy beyond Kati's imagination; women had threaded in and out of his life; and he would embark for Tokyo as casually as Kati might embark for the closest supermarket. On the other hand, Masuto was meditating when Ishido called, and Kati fiercely resisted interrupting him at his meditation.

"He will return your call in a few minutes, honored uncle. A thousand apologies."

"A thousand apologies are too many, my darling," Masuto told her a while later. "Your kinsman, Ishido, is both a hunter and a game player. Like all men of great wealth, his life is a struggle against boredom, and I have displaced his boredom with a new and fascinating game. Believe me, he will find me. I cannot evade him until he sees this new game played out."

"I don't understand—"

The telephone rang.

"Ah, so! Unless I miss my guess, there is Ishido again."

Kati anwered the phone and then handed it to her husband. "It is my honorable uncle."

"I must apologize," Masuto told Ishido. "I was at my meditation."

"Of course. How insufferable of me to interrupt it. And now?"

"Now I am finished."

"Ah, so. Very good." Ishido, for all of his imperturbability, could not keep the excitement out of his voice. "I have spoken to my old acquaintance, Eric Saunders, and in spite of the fact that he has one of the most active social and business schedules of perhaps any man in southern California, he will be delighted to dine with both of us at the club tonight."

"Why?" Masuto asked coldly.

If Ishido caught the icy note in Masuto's voice, he gave no sign of it, simply repeating, "This evening at my club, Masao."

"I asked you why? Why should a man of affairs and of his importance take the time to dine with an ordinary policeman?"

"Perhaps because he understands that you are not an ordinary policeman. Perhaps because I mentioned your consuming interest in the skeleton that was discovered under the swimming pool."

"No, that's not enough. You are using me," Masuto said angrily.

"And were you not willing to use me? Of course I am using you, and you in turn are using me. This is no common homicide, Masao. You are up against a titan."

"No, sir, if you will forgive me. I am up against a sick

and vile man, a psychopath, someone who should be locked up before he does more hurt to more people."

"As you will."

"Why did he agree to dine with us?"

"Because I told him you had discovered that the skeleton under the pool was that of a man named Stanley Cutler."

"I see. And how did he react to that?"

"At first there was no reaction at all. Then he looked at me with a sort of malignant curiosity. Oh, yes, Masao, he would not hesitate to kill me should the occasion arise. Of course, I am not one of those who is easily killed, and perhaps he understands that. You see, he does respect me, or he would not have seen me so late at night and on such short notice. Yes, he agreed to dine with us."

"What is the source of your own hatred?" Masuto asked.

"My hatred?"

"Yes, your hatred."

"You press me back too many years, Masao. You are born in this country and you are not yet forty years old. Let me say only that our paths crossed in Burma many years ago, and this man, Eric Saunders, shot a Japanese prisoner in cold blood. Such things were done by both sides, but Saunders—well, I waited, and my patience was rewarded."

"There is no evidence that will convict him," Masuto said angrily. "You know that as well as I do."

"You will manage, nephew. I have faith in you."

When he put down the telephone, Kati mentioned his irritation. "What has Ishido done to annoy you so?"

"He has put me in an impossible position."

"I am sorry."

"It will be all right," Masuto assured her as he kissed her and then left the house. But would it be—and in what way? He found himself looking over his shoulder, and before he started his car, he looked underneath it and then under the hood. The threat of Eric Saunders was not simply the threat of a single man, but the threat of great amounts of money and of vast resources. Masuto knew that there was no protection against assassination, no protection against a determined killer. He might miss once, twice, three times—but in the end he would be successful. Well, perhaps Ishido was right to drive the thing to its end, whatever the end might be.

Instead of going directly to the police station, Masuto stopped off at the Beverly Hills office of Merrill Lynch, Pierce, Fenner & Smith, where his cousin, Alan Toyada, was in charge of research.

"No, don't tell me," Toyada greeted him. "They have raised your wages. You have money to invest. You're on the take now—"

"Your humor is puerile and infantile."

"It's not my humor, Masao. You're always so damn bloody serious."

"Unfortunately, I live in that world."

"Forgive the humor. What can I do for you?"

"Eric Saunders."

"Ah. And from what point of view?"

"To begin, an investment."

"For yourself? I mean—well, who knows, it is possible that Ishido passed on suddenly. Supposedly, he has no children, but from what I have heard, his heirs might well pop up all over the place. On the other hand, Kati would, I am sure, come in for a large piece of capital which should be properly invested."

"I come to you as a policeman, not as an investor," Masuto said, and possibly would have added that unless Toyada stopped babbling, nothing would be accomplished— except that Toyada was thin-skinned, as well as insensitive, a more common combination than one might suppose.

"Oh, yes, of course, Masao. But you asked me about Saunders as an investment."

"I'm curious."

"Excellent, excellent. Profits have gone up at least fifteen percent a year for five years now. Amazing record. The stock has doubled during the past twelve months."

"How do you account for that?"

"Good engineers. Space contracts. And of course their new shuttle passenger plane. They have almost a billion dollars in back orders. It's a short-haul shuttle, lands anywhere, carries two hundred and forty passengers, wide body, comfortable. Oh, yes, if I had the money, I'd buy."

"And how much of this is due to Saunders himself?"

"That's hard to say. He still plays an active role in the company, makes the hard decisions, but I hear he has his fingers in other pies as well—museums, films, politics."

"What are his politics?"

"Well, he does government work, so he's for the administration, but they say he plays both sides of the fence. I imagine he does."

"And what about his morality?" Masuto asked.

"I don't think you mean women, Masao?"

"No, I don't mean women."

"Well, you know as well as I do that you can't discuss big business in terms of morality. Rules, yes, morality, no."

"All right, Alan, rules. Does he break the rules?"

"No more than anyone else. I'm sure he pays off wherever it's necessary, but who doesn't? He doesn't raid other companies, but then he doesn't have to. He's his own steamroller and he's driving Saunders Aerospace right to the top."

"Has he ever married?"

"No, which doesn't mean he's gay. He's had a parade of women through his life."

"How does that come into your financial research?" Masuto asked curiously.

"It doesn't. I read *Los Angeles* magazine and a few of its lesser companion journals. He's mentioned frequently. Tell me, why all this interest? What do you know that I don't know, now that you've squeezed all that I do know out of me?"

"Nothing that would be helpful."

"Have you got something on Saunders? Are you going to bust him? Should we go short on the stock?"

"No way I know of that I can bust him," Masuto said.

"If you do, give me an edge."

"I promise," Masuto said.

Back at the station house, Masuto told Wainwright about his talk with Ishido and Ishido's conclusions.

"You ask me," Wainwright said, "your Uncle Ishido is leaping to some pretty dangerous and far out conclusions. Eric Saunders is not nobody. He's one of the most prominent citizens in our town, nationally known, a man of wealth and power. If one word of our discussion were to leak out of here, Masao, he could sue us right off the face of the map. And he would too. What in hell makes this Ishido so sure of himself?"

"Ishido is hard to explain. You know that he was in the old imperial army. He will never return to Japan, but he also never forgets that he is Japanese. There is some indication upon Ishido's part that he crossed paths with Saunders somewhere in the East, perhaps in Burma, and that he had a grudge against Saunders."

"Which would certainly not promote any objectivity on his part."

"Except for one thing, which worries me and complicates this even further. Last night Ishido either telephoned

Saunders or saw him in person. Ishido told him that I knew the man under the pool was Stanley Cutler and that I also knew that Saunders had killed him. You see, tonight, Saunders, Ishido, and I will dine together at Ishido's club, and I can think of no reason on earth why Saunders should have agreed to this dinner unless Ishido told him what I knew."

"What in hell does Ishido think he's up to?"

"He's playing a game."

"And where do we come in?"

"I don't know," Masuto said slowly.

"But since Saunders agreed, you feel there's no question but that he's our man?"

"None."

"So to come back to the skeleton under the pool, the reason why there was never a report of someone missing is very simple. There never was anyone missing except Cutler, and everyone concluded that he had taken off. Saunders never had to hide. He took the money, laundered it, and appeared on the scene here as a young British millionaire. And there is not a damn thing we can do about it. Then why does he want to meet you?"

"I suppose it's a conceit. He knows we can't touch him, and a dangerous game is nothing new to him. Then there's still our only ace in the hole—Rosita. I think he would like to know something about me. He is black belt karate and probably versed in all of the martial arts. Very often, Westerners who take up the martial art make a kind of pseudo-religion out of it—and I'm sure Ishido told him I have some skill in karate."

"Come off that," Wainwright said harshly. "No games!"

"The games are there."

"If you are thinking of fighting Saunders in this god-damn Chinese wrestling art of yours, forget it."

"Will he forget it?"

"You know, Masao, there's one thing you damn well better get used to. Criminals go free. Some crimes are punished; a hell of a lot of them are not. There is no way, no way in the world that you could charge Saunders and make it stick. Quite to the contrary, he may be sitting with his lawyers right this minute ready to sue the city for all we've got."

"Not really," Masuto said. "There isn't enough money on earth to make Saunders put himself on a witness stand or put me on a witness stand. We can't do anything, neither can he. It's a standoff."

"You know I got to give this to the L.A. cops and to the Inglewood cops," Wainwright said.

"Why?"

"It's procedure. You know that, Masao."

"Suppose they make waves? Suppose they decide to question Saunders?"

"That's their privilege."

"Would it hurt to hold off a day or two?"

"Would it help?"

"Maybe," Masuto said. "Nothing about this case becomes simpler, only more and more complicated. We were sure that Stanley Cutler had murdered the man under the swimming pool. Then the man under the swimming pool became Stanley Cutler, and the killer is someone called Eric Saunders whom neither of us has ever met. Let me take it one step further—"

But Matuso did not take it one step further. The telephone rang. It was Sy Beckman at the hotel, and he said quietly, "Masao, I think both doors into the corridor, Rosita's and mine, are booby-trapped. I heard some sounds, and I hiked myself up to where I could look over the transom. There's a steel box sitting in front of each door, and from the look of it, they're ratchet loaded. I alerted Gellman to keep the help away from the two doors. I thought maybe you and Wainwright should get the L.A.P.D. bomb squad over here and get here yourselves, because I'll be damned if I know what to do."

"Is there no way out except through the doors?"

"We're up three floors, Masao. If those charges are big enough, the whole wing could go. We're over the pool and the gardens, so you couldn't even get a fire truck under these windows. It's a hell of a situation, and if we ever get out of this, I'm going to get Wainwright to slap them with every violation under the sun."

"Meanwhile, I want you out of there. Make a rope of bedsheets, bedspreads, and blankets and lower Rosita to the ground, and then you slide down yourself. Now. Right now! We'll be there in ten minutes."

Then Masuto called the hotel and spoke to Gellman. "Oh, it's great," Gellman said. "You've really done it, sergeant. Just a couple of rooms for a few days, and now I got to explain to the board how come half the hotel was blown away."

"They haven't blown anything yet," Masuto said soothingly. "Just empty that wing and don't touch the booby traps. That will keep you from facing lawsuits."

"Beautiful. Now you're protecting me."

"I'm trying to."

"What's going on?" Wainwright demanded.

"Just let me call the bomb squad and I'll explain."

Driving to the Beverly Glen Hotel at top speed, Masuto said, "He uses us, manipulates us, controls us. He got her out of the room. That was all he wanted, but what could I do? What could I do? I couldn't leave them in there and let both of them die."

"For Christ's sake, Masao, nobody's died yet."

That was not so. Rosita was dead by the time Masuto or the ambulance reached the hotel. She had been shot three times while Beckman was lowering her from the window, once in the head and twice in the body.

CHAPTER
THIRTEEN

ERIC SAUNDERS

s if she were his own daughter, he hid his face to hide his tears. It was not his style to weep over the dead. He observed the routine; the routine was a necessity. Half a mile away were high rise apartments, and within half an hour, the rifle, a beautifully crafted Mauser-type five shot, was found on the rooftop of one of the apartment houses. The rifle was identified by the L.A.P.D. gun expert as a small-shop product, probably made in Italy or France about twenty years before. Masuto was uninterested. Police channels and thoroughness were not made for criminals of this type. Eventually, they would find out who made the gun, who sold it, who bought it, and it would all lead nowhere.

Beckman said, "My God, Masao, I never thought of it. It never occurred to me."

"I know."

"I figured those damn bombs were going off any moment, and then after I spoke to you, all I wanted was to get her out of there. She was a lovely kid. I was falling in love with that kid."

"I know."

"Masao, just let me get my hands on the bastard who did it—"

The bomb men didn't want anyone in the hallway where they were working, but Masuto insisted and pushed past the guards.

"Sergeant, it's off limits, even to you."

Beckman followed him, as if one could not do penance apart from the other. Stevenson, from the bomb squad, who knew Masuto, explained what they were up against. "Beckman guessed right. It's ratchet and spring. The contraption is attached with suction cups; it's wound in and then when it's flat up against the surface—in this case the door—the pawl latches on the fuse. The slightest movement blows it, and no way to get into it. It's simple, foolproof, and deadly, and so help me God, Masuto, I don't know how to handle this one."

"Unless, of course, there's no explosive in the metal box."

"I don't go in for such guesses. When I see a bomb, I function on the theory that it's loaded. This one has a clock mechanism as well as the ratchet and pawl. We'll have to empty the hotel."

"He had his marksman waiting half a mile away on a rooftop. The only function of that damn box was to get the girl out of the window."

"I can't take the chance."

"The hell with it!" Masuto said. "Come on, Sy, let's get out of here."

In the lobby downstairs Gellman stopped Masuto, pleading, "My God, sergeant, what are you doing to me? They're emptying the hotel, and half of it may be blown to kingdom come. You try to be a good guy, and this is how it ends."

"It won't be blown away," Masuto said tiredly. "I don't

know what else to tell you. I'm sorry this had to happen. The girl is dead, so she's got the real short end."

They left the hotel and Beckman said he needed a drink, and Masuto suggested a quiet place in Culver City, where they could sit and talk. Beckman had two double scotches and Masuto drank beer. "I don't know," Beckman said, "day and night together—I never met anyone like that kid, just a Mexican girl and an illegal, but the sweetest, kindest kid in the world."

"Revenge is no good," Masuto told him. "It solves nothing, satisfies nothing."

"Goddamn you, Masao, you know who did it!"

"Yes."

"I want him!"

"We all do. We're not avenging angels. We're not terrorists who make our own justice, and we're not juries. We're cops."

"What are you telling me—that we can't touch him?"

"No, we'll touch him, even without Rosita. It's not touching him—it's trying to make some sense out of this, because right now it makes no damn sense at all." He went to the telephone and called the Beverly Glen Hotel and asked for the desk. "This is Sergeant Masuto. What's the situation with the bombs?"

"Duds, sir. They went off a few minutes ago. A couple of firecrackers in each one. No damage to speak of."

Masuto walked back to the table where Beckman was working at the problem of getting drunk. "Go home, Sy," Masuto told him. "Go home and finish a bottle and sleep it off."

"What for? I got a lousy marriage. Home—home is to laugh, Masao. I'm not so old. I'm not forty yet. I could have married that Mexican kid and had everything I ever dreamed of having."

"The only world is right here," Masuto told him, putting an arm around the big man. "Come on, Sy, I'm going to drive you home."

"What about Wainwright?"

"I'll talk to him."

Masuto dropped Beckman off at his home, and then he drove back to the station and told Wainwright that Beckman was drunk and sleeping it off.

"What in hell do you mean, drunk—it's two o'clock in the afternoon!"

"I encouraged him. That Mexican kid meant a great deal to him. Stop pushing us. We're both human."

"Well, don't get your ass up. Who's pushing who?"

"Sorry, so sorry. I want this to be over."

"I told you to leave it alone and let it be over."

"Not that way."

"You think Saunders shot the kid?"

"Himself? No," Masuto said. "Did he hire the gun? A few hours ago I would have said yes, without any question. Now I don't know."

"You don't want to talk about it?"

"Tomorrow."

"You're still going to see Saunders tonight?"

"Oh, yes. That I would not miss for anything."

"Be careful, Masao."

But no, Masuto told himself as he drove away from the police station. He was not threatened, nor was he in the line of fire—unless—no, that must be expelled from his mind. He must clear his mind and know exactly what he would say to his uncle, Naga Orashi. That was Monday when he had seen Naga; what was today? Wednesday? No, Wednesday was the day with the police artist. Today is Thursday, and the whole thing began only six days ago, when the heavy rains undermined a swimming pool and sent it sliding down into a canyon. And since then four more people had died.

He drove into the yard of Naga's construction company, and there was his wife's uncle Naga, sitting in his rocking chair, as if only a few minutes had gone by since Masuto had last seen him, nibbling at cold tea rice, caked and threaded through with ginger.

"Have some," he said to Masuto.

"Thank you. I am most grateful and very hungry, since I missed my lunch somewhere during the day."

"So? Indeed? So very busy, yet you find time to come and chat with this old Japanese gentleman."

"Why didn't you tell me that Ishido operated a back-hoe?"

Naga stared at Masuto for a long moment, and then he shook his head sadly. "Granted that you were born in this country, and granted that your Japanese is abominable, and granted that you have absorbed barbarian habits—granting all this, one would imagine that you still retain some comprehension of the fitness of things."

"We are not speaking of the fitness of things. We speak about the fact that I came to you as a policeman and you saw no reason to tell me that Ishido operated a backhoe."

"Perhaps you should not have come as a policeman, Masao."

"Oh?"

"Think about it. I am Kati's mother's brother. How would you characterize us in old Japan? Shopkeepers, perhaps. Ishido is tied by a marriage to Kati's father, so she is not of his blood. Ishido is of seven generations of Samurai. His father was an advisor to the old emperor. When Ishido was twenty-five years old, he was a colonel in the imperial army. He was decorated, honored; and when finally Japan fell, he could not remain there, shamed, dishonored. You would not understand why he came here; it's an old form, the vanquished honoring the victor—a very old and honorable Japanese gesture, but one that evoked nothing from the conqueror who couldn't care less whether this young Japanese Samurai starved to death or not. Whereupon, I gave Ishido a job."

"And he learned to operate a backhoe?"

"Nephew, I did not conceal this from you. You never asked me, and it was so many years ago that the circumstances are most vague in my mind."

"But he did operate a backhoe?"

"Yes, as I recall. It was an opportunity for him to earn a bit more. Only for a while. Ishido was very clever."

"And did you perhaps rent this backhoe, driver and all, to Alex Brody when he built the house on Laurel Way?"

The old man knit his brows. "I don't know. Did I rent it or just lend it for a few days? It was so long ago."

"And Ishido with it? Come, dear uncle, try to remember."

"Possibly."

"You should have told me."

"You are chasing ghosts, Masao. The past is dead. We who are Japanese should know that better than others. How could we live if the past were not dead?"

"I am not Japanese," Masuto said unhappily. "I was born here in California. My wife was born here, and my children here."

"No, you are not Japanese," Naga agreed. "But in a manner of speaking, Ishido is your kinsman."

"I'll be back in a moment," Masuto said. He walked to his car, and from the trunk rack, he took the photocopy that the F.B.I. had sent to him. He brought it to Naga.

"You know this man?" he asked Naga.

"A thing like this," Naga said, blinking at the photo-copy, "it could be anyone. It was so long ago—"

"Or someone."

"How did you come by this picture, Masao?"

Masao shook his head. "I can't explain that now. But when I leave, honored uncle, there is no need to telephone Ishido and warn him. He knows what I know."

"I have not spoken to Ishido in more than twenty years," Naga said sadly. "I have no love or affection for him. But we are kinsmen. Of course, I am speaking out of a lack of knowledge. Mr. Lundman and his wife were killed, a terrible thing. Ishido did not do that."

"And the skeleton under the swimming pool?"

"Who knows what went on there? Who will ever know?"

"You told me the grave could not be dug with a back-hoe. It is your business to know such things. Now I must ask you again—could the grave have been dug with a back-hoe?"

Still studying the photo and without looking up, Naga said, "This is a very strange picture indeed, Masao, not of any person, but—" He switched into Japanese. "A thing lurks in shadow and asks for recognition." And then in English, "Is it not an article of your Buddhist thinking that the vibrations of the subject are in the drawing?"

"It is an article of damn nonsense!" Masuto said with irritation. "I asked you a simple question. Should I go elsewhere? There are twenty contractors in this city whom I can ask to join me on Laurel Way, and who will give me a plain answer as to whether that grave was dug with a backhoe."

"Gently, gently, Masao," the old man begged him. "Why such anger?"

"Because murder angers me."

"All right. Listen then. Your twenty contractors could not give you a firm answer. If your backhoe had a ten-inch claw spread, then it could have gouged out the grave and made the final shaping easier."

"Why didn't you tell me that the other day?"

"You know why."

"And what do you find there?" Masuto asked harshly, pointing to the photo.

"A resemblance."

"To whom?"

"To a laborer, I think. It was long ago."

"What? Or to Eric Saunders?"

"Not obviously. If I saw it somewhere, in a book or a newspaper, I would not think of Mr. Saunders."

"But you do think of him now?"

"I don't know—"

"Perhaps you have been thinking a great deal about Mr. Saunders?"

"Masao, Masao, we shelter our kinsmen when we can. I would do it for you. You would do it for me."

"Uncle," Masuto said with annoyance, "what kind of talk is that? Shelter a kinsman when he is hungry or cold, but a murderer?" He stalked over to the car, and this time he returned with the drawing the police artist had made under Dr. Hartman's direction. "And this?" he demanded, thrusting the drawing at Naga. "This is not so long ago that your memory must fail you."

"Am I a criminal that you speak to me so?" Naga asked unhappily.

"You are my revered uncle. But you must tell me the truth."

"Yes, it's Saunders. He had his face changed. I knew and Ishido knew—"

"Do you also know you are in terrible danger?"

"I am an old man. Each night I go to sleep with the

knowledge that I may not awaken. I am not afraid of danger."

For a long moment, Masuto studied his uncle. Then he asked, more gently, "What dealings did Ishido have with Eric Saunders?"

"I know very little of what went on there. I don't even know how they met. I only remember that Saunders needed someone who could speak Japanese. There was a litigation of a landholding in the San Fernando Valley, land that had belonged to Japanese nationals and was seized by the government. I think it comprised eleven hundred acres. Saunders bought the land at auction, and then Ishido joined him to fight the litigation that the Japanese nationals brought against them. Eventually, they settled, and Ishido's share was almost half a million dollars. That was the beginning of his fortune."

"And the beginning of Mr. Saunders's fortune?"

"No, he was already wealthy. The story was that he was a sort of cast-off son of an important British family." The old man blinked his eyes and then stared at Masuto unhappily. "Of course, the story is a lie."

"Yes."

"And what happened at the hotel today?"

"How do you know about that?"

"As with all things today, Masao, it was on the air immediately. Is it connected?"

"Yes."

The old man hesitated, then he said, "Be very careful, Masao."

"I always am."

"Don't think of yourself as a kinsman. I assure you, they have stopped thinking of you in that fashion."

"They? Why do you say they?"

The old man shrugged.

"Is there bad blood between Ishido and Saunders?"

"Why should there be?"

"I asked you."

"Ah, so, of course. I would think not. From what my sons tell me, Saunders made it possible for Ishido to belong to the West Los Angeles Country Club. It is not a thing that pleases me, to see a member of the old aristocracy using influence to belong to a club where the only qualification for membership is to have money and to be neither Jewish nor Oriental nor black nor Mexican. I myself would have no part of such a place, but it was something Ishido desired."

"But you say that he and Saunders have remained close all these years?"

"So I am told, so my sons tell me. In fact, I have heard that currently Ishido is engaged in negotiations with Tokyo Airlines for the purchase of some sixteen Saunders airbuses at a price of twenty-eight million dollars each—that is, acting for Saunders."

"I feel like Alice in Wonderland," Masuto said.

"Oh?"

"A children's book."

"Have I done something very wrong, Masao?"

"No—no, I think not, uncle."

CHAPTER
FOURTEEN

THE GAME

PLAYERS

Kati knew and understood Masuto better than he imagined. She understood the strange psychology operative in a man who earns twenty thousand dollars a year to protect those who make two hundred thousand and even two million. Being a policeman in Beverly Hills is certainly somewhat different from being a policeman anywhere else, and being a Nisei only complicates it further. Yet Masuto was not judgmental. He had neither contempt for wealth nor admiration for wealth. As an abstraction, he saw neither virtue nor evil in wealth; it was simply a fact of the society he worked in. Yet tonight, as he dressed himself in a clean white shirt, gray flannel trousers, and his best blue blazer—indeed his only blue blazer—Kati noticed that he appeared even more unhappy than the approaching evening should have caused him to be. She watched him toy with his gun, trying to make the shoulder holster unnoticeable under the well-fitted jacket. The jacket was too well fitted. When he stretched it to button, the gun bulged wickedly.

"Will you need the gun, Masao?" she asked gently. "Surely in the West Los Angeles Country Club an occasion to use a gun is not very likely. And anyone will know you have a gun there."

"Regulations—" Masuto sighed and put the gun aside. He selected a knitted black tie, thinking that he, like Ishido, was still a victim of the old ways. In all truth, he did not want the gun. The game precluded it.

"Masao, with a white shirt—you have nicer ties. This striped tie I gave you for your birthday and which you have never worn, well, it is much nicer than a black tie. You're not going to a funeral."

"No?"

"I haven't seen Ishido for years, but I do remember how charming and bright he is. It should be an absolutely delightful evening, if you would only relax and allow yourself to enjoy it. Who did you say the other man was?"

"Eric Saunders."

"I don't mind a bit. It's very old country, three men having dinner with no women, except geisha girls." Kati giggled. "In the West Los Angeles Country Club, geishas. Can you imagine?"

"Not very well, no."

"Oh, Masao, you are so somber." Kati was tying the striped tie now. "No one ever takes me to such a place. If they did, I would be quite happy about it." She tightened the tie fold. "There. That looks elegant. Have you ever been to the club before?"

"It's not a place I frequent."

"Then you must tell me all about it."

Not all of it, certainly, Masuto thought. Not the way the car jockey at the club looked at his old Datsun. Masuto had forgone the small conceit of using his police identification card, and in any case, it would have been out of place there and would have attracted attention to himself. He simply drove up to the door, taking his place in the line of Rolls-

Royces, Mercedes, Jaguars, Lincolns, and Cadillacs. If one can conceive of a car held at arm's length, slightly off the ground, faced with pinched nostrils, then one can understand Masuto's irritation—which he fought, telling himself, This is not the time or place for irritation. Soon, the game begins. Stay cool and steady. Which was commendable advice, since he had been fool enough to leave his gun behind—a fact which he was beginning to regret a great deal.

Ishido was waiting for him in the lobby, and he welcomed Masuto with great cordiality. "Indeed, nephew, I had thought that perhaps you might not come."

"Why? When I face a killer, I have what I might call my moment of truth. They are few and far between."

"And you are convinced that Eric Saunders is your killer?"

"You convinced me, Ishido-san."

Ishido stared at him thoughtfully. Then he bowed slightly. "Come and meet him, Masao."

Masuto followed Ishido into the dining room, a charming room done in the Spanish colonial style, the floor and walls tiled, a handsome fireplace at one end.

The headwaiter recognized Ishido, expressed pleasure at seeing him, and led him and Masuto to a table in one corner of the room. The man already seated at this table rose as they appeared and welcomed Masuto warmly. "I have heard much about you," he said.

"And I about you, Mr. Saunders."

They stood face-to-face for a moment, Masuto taller, leaner, younger—but also aware of the tremendous strength in the hand that gripped his. Saunders was built like a bull, the build of a man who is overmuscled but fights his weight successfully. For a man close to sixty, he appeared to be in marvelous physical condition, the skin tight around his face and neck, his stomach flat.

"Please, sit down," Saunders said. Masuto seated himself, Ishido on one side of him, Saunders on the other. The headwaiter was hovering over them. "I ordered champagne," Saunders said, and turned to Masuto. "You do drink champagne? Just a taste for each of us, a drink to whatever we drink to. I think we should drink lightly and eat lightly."

"For the sake of the game," Ishido said.

"Naturally," Saunders said.

When the champagne had been poured, Saunders raised his glass, but no one spoke a toast, or cheers, or anything of that kind.

"I hear from Ishido," Saunders said, "that you are a most unusual policeman. I would guess that you are studying my face with such intensity to see whether you can detect scar tissue or suture marks. But before we go any further, Masuto, I must ask whether you are wired?"

"And if I were, why should you imagine that I would tell you?"

"A sense of honor."

"Honor?" Masuto asked in amazement. "You really confront me with a thing called honor?"

"I speak of you," Saunders said. "Not of myself, not of Ishido. He tells me that you are a Zen Buddhist, that you practice meditation as well as the Okinawan art. If you tell me you are not wired, I believe you."

"I am not wired."

"I didn't think you were."

Masuto's mouth was dry. He sipped at the champagne. Actually, he did not care for champagne, and he had little desire to drink with these two men.

"I am not asking for truth," Masuto said. "To find truth between the two of you would be like seeking a lump of sugar in a pool of molasses. But you, Ishido, what advantage by lying to me?"

"Did he lie?" Saunders smiled. "Where does the truth end and a lie begin? Ishido said you very cleverly put together a picture of me, but that it did not resemble me at all."

"Then you are Stanley Cutler?"

"No, no, no, Masuto. What a dreadful mess you have made of everything. Thirty years, during which I live my life and Ishido lives his life, and then a rainstorm and a Nisei detective on a small-town police force destroy everything. I am not Stanley Cutler, Masuto, I am Eric Saunders. I was christened Eric Arthur Sutherland Saunders, and I am the youngest son of the Earl of Newton."

"Then it was Cutler's skeleton?"

Saunders laughed. "No, no, indeed."

"I think we should order dinner," Ishido said. "We will eat lightly, but we should eat and preserve the amenities. What would your pleasure be, Masao?"

"Whatever you wish."

"Surely you have a preference? Or is the company so unpleasant that you have no appetite?"

"The chicken, since you insist," Masuto said, thinking that they were both quite mad. But then, are not all murderers quite mad, and might not one say that this madness had become the condition of a great part of mankind? They chatted over the food, hardly eating, only toying with the meal. If they meant Masuto to feel the strain, they succeeded, and finally, unable to contain himself, he asked them flatly, "Which one of you killed Stanley Cutler?"

"Why? Why, Masao?" Ishido asked him. "Thirty years. What good comes of this?"

"Let me explain," Saunders said. "Since there is nothing you can ever do about it, since there is no way you can ever prosecute either of us, you should have your bone, the reward of the hunter. I would have rewarded you otherwise, but Ishido said no. Killing you would hardly be worth the price of Ishido's enmity."

"Hardly magnanimous," Masuto said. "You still plan to kill me."

"Who knows?"

"When dinner is over," Ishido said, "you may leave here, and no harm will come to you. You have my word."

"I am waiting for the explanation."

"I created Cutler," Saunders said. "He was killed in Burma. I was with him. I think I got the notion from his prints—or lack of them. Burned off in a flaming tank." He held out one hand. "Doesn't look much different, does it, but if you look closely, you'll find no recognizable prints. I turned myself into Cutler. Oh, don't think it was easy—it took months of planning, years to carry it out."

"Cutler's body?"

"I took his dog tags and blew his head off with a grenade. You have no idea how much confusion war engenders. We were of a size and he had no family, so I had the pleasant choice of being one of two persons, whichever I preferred."

"You blew his head off with a grenade," Masuto said. "Was he alive then, or was he dead?"

"Always the policeman. You want another murder to add to your list? I'm afraid I can't oblige you. He was dead when I blew his head off. I got the job at Manhattan National Bank as Stanley Cutler." He paused and smiled. Ishido took a cigar, clipped the end, and lit it. "Odd to think of it. I never fancied working at a bank, but embezzlement is so enticingly easy. Of course today with the computers everywhere, it's even easier. When I finished the job and had soaked the money away here in Los Angeles as Eric Saunders, I simply put all that was Stanley Cutler, a few cards, one or two other things, down the toilet—flushed them away."

"Then who," Masuto asked, "was the skeleton under the pool?"

"Ah, yes—the source of all our unhappiness. You see, when I was very young, I did a bit of embezzlement, but awkwardly, on a London bank. I was caught and it was hushed up because of my family, and I went into the army. Then, when I did the job at the Midtown Manhattan Bank, this Scotland Yard chap who was in on the first screw-up, drew some conclusions, got himself a a leave of absence, and turned up in Los Angeles—not to arrest me, mind you, but to threaten me into a split. Ishido happened to be with me that night. I had spotted some acreage in the San Fernando Valley and I needed a Japanese partner for the deal. The C.I.D. man was foolish enough to turn his back on me, and then there was the problem of what to do with the body. This one did have fingerprints, and I had to make sure that he vanished for good. Ishido was operating a backhoe on a job, and he suggested putting the body under the swimming pool. Well, once it turned up—there it was, with two people in L.A. who could put Ishido on that job and point a finger at both of us."

"Two people?" Masuto asked.

"The old lady and Lundman. Lundman's wife happened to be there. So it was with the Mexican girl."

"Who never saw you," Masuto said bitterly. "You damned, murderous bastard—Naga Orashi, the contractor, was the man who hired Ishido to drive the backhoe, and he's alive!"

Saunders looked coldly at Ishido, who shrugged and said, "He is my kinsman. I told you he was dead."

"You lied to me."

"I have various loyalties," Ishido said. "Don't try to understand them."

"It makes a debt you have to settle," Saunders said thinly. "You upset the apple cart."

"I changed the game slightly." Ishido shrugged.

"You know where it puts me."

"You do what you must do, Eric."

"Another kinsman?"

"Not exactly. As I said, you will do what you must do."

Listening to all this with increasing disgust, Masuto interrupted harshly. "Do you know, gentlemen, I am going to arrest both of you. I know I don't have one scrap of evidence and that not one charge will stick, but I can parade this before the media in a way that will convince the public. They will try you, even if no jury can."

"So you came here," Saunders said, "to satisfy your curiosity and to make a public spectacle of us. I would have to be childish not to have anticipated that. Look behind you, Masuto."

Masuto turned. At the table behind him, two men were sitting. They both had long, hard, sallow faces, and when he glanced at them, they nodded coldly.

"A word from me, just a movement of my hand, and you will be dead, Masuto. Don't try to arrest us. I have other plans."

"Really? What other plans?"

Masuto glanced at Ishido. He had become passive. He sat with his hands folded—as if he had placed a hood over himself and between him and the two men.

"I am a devotee of karate, of the Okinawan style."

"No, you are despoiler of a way. You desecrate and debase a noble thing. Karate is not to kill."

"No? Then what is its purpose?"

"To defend, to bring some enlightenment to those who

practice it with love and reverence. But you, Saunders, you have made it your own obscenity. You have taken something you don't understand, something beyond the understanding of men like yourself, and turned it into an obscenity, an act of murder."

"And when the old Samurai killed, Masuto, was that also an act of murder?"

Now Ishido came alive, turning to watch Masuto, who said, "If the Samurai was Samurai and he saw that the swordsman who faced him was weaker or afraid, then he did not use his sword. Do not think of yourself as Samurai, Saunders."

"I would like to," Saunders said, unperturbed. "Twelve years ago, I gave this club a karate room. I have made arrangements for its use tonight—by the two of us. I have explained to the athletic steward that we are both experts and that we intend to explore some movements. Robes and trousers have been placed there, and once we enter that room, we will not be disturbed. I am twenty years older than you, Masuto, perhaps a bit more—so I give you that sporting advantage. I may as well tell you bluntly that once we are alone in that room, I intend to kill you."

"And on my part, I am to kill you?"

"If you can."

"Whether or not I can is beside the point," Masuto said. "I am not an executioner, Saunders, I am a policeman. I do not kill people—not even people like yourself, who have surrendered all claim to being a part of the human race. Nor will I use karate to kill. That would be a betrayal of something very deep in myself."

"What is your alternative, Masuto? You're not even carrying a weapon tonight. Those two men have silencers on their pistols. They could kill you and be out of this room before your body fell to the floor. So it would appear to me that you must accept my challenge."

Masuto looked at Ishido and then at Saunders. Then he stood up. "Very well. Let's begin and get it over with."

Ishido remained at the table. He avoided Masuto's eyes. The two thin-lipped men in the dark suits also remained at their table, and moving in front of Saunders, Masuto left the dining room, passed through the lounge, and then was directed down a passageway, past a notice that said, LOCKER ROOM. It occurred to Masuto now that there were opportunities to bolt, to make a run for it. Possibly the exit points were covered by Saunders's men, possibly not; yet Masuto rejected the notion. To run now was inconceivable, and once he ran, where would the running stop? He had no intention of attempting to kill Saunders, but neither had he any intention of becoming Saunders's victim. No doubt Saunders was good, but then neither was Masuto an amateur. He was at a point where he had no plans, no scheme—and at such moments he resigned himself to the motion. Let come what would; underneath his Western exterior there was a very ancient fatalism.

They entered the karate room. It was forty feet by forty feet, and without windows. There were two large mats on the polished wooden floor, some hooks for kimonos and trousers, and a row of chairs at one end of the room. It was air-conditioned and intensely lit from above. Only a wall telephone connected it with the rest of the club.

In silence Saunders began to change. I am a middle-aged policeman, confined with a madman who believes he will kill me, Masuto said to himself, and still I do not know whether I shall kill him.

"It's not too late," he told Saunders. "You know you can't be convicted. Games like this are for witless children and madmen."

"And sportsmen." Saunders had dropped his clothes. His body was squarely built, muscular, not an ounce of fat anywhere. He slipped on the trousers and kimono, treading lightly, flexing and unflexing his fingers. "Change clothes, Masuto!"

"Sportsmen," Masuto said with contempt. "Sportsmen who kill old women and young girls."

"What the game brings. Change clothes!"

"I think not," Masuto said. "I am not a witless child. Does your white kimono give you a license to kill? You are stark, raving mad, Saunders. Do you think that the trappings of a karate match will allow you to kill me and go free? You are a pompous, bloated fool. You are sick and full of decay."

With a roar of rage, Saunders launched himself at Masuto, his arm coming around in an outside inward sword-hand strike. Masuto pivoted and let the strike pass over him. His own back-fist counterstrike missed. He sprang away, his feet, still in shoes, slipping on the floor, and Saunders was upon him with a driving upward elbow strike, which, if it had connected with the full force of Saunders's body behind it, might well have snapped Masuto's neck. It missed by a fraction of an inch, and Masuto, off balance, tried to find purchase for a shod kick to Saunders's groin. It was bad karate, but he was fighting for his life. Saunders was too quick for him, amazingly quick for a man his age, and a hard, high kick from Saunders connected with Masuto's shoulder, caught him off balance, and flung him to the mat.

For a fraction of a second Masuto was as close to death as he had ever been. He had sprawled on his back without purchase or any continuity of motion that could be turned to his defense and in that fraction of a second when he was defenseless, Saunders could have driven a kick to his throat that would have crushed his larynx and burst the blood vessels in his neck. All this Masuto knew, for in such moments the mind works with incredible speed. Then the fraction of a second passed, the lethal moment was over, and Masuto was able to whip himself off his back and into a crouch. Saunders had not moved. He stood rocklike, his motion only half begun, and then he clutched at his chest, went down on his knees, and rolled over on his back.

Masuto got to his feet and approached the recumbent figure carefully. He was ready for anything from this man, any trick, any device; but the wide open, fixed blue eyes were a valid definition. He felt for Saunders's pulse and could not find it. No question about it, the man was dead.

Breathing deeply, his whole body still trembling, Masuto went to a chair and sat down. He sat very quietly for a minute or two, composing his thoughts—bringing himself together, as he would have put it. Then he went to the telephone. As he suspected, it was an automatic switchboard. He dialed nine, and when the dial tone came on, he called Sy Beckman's number. Sophie answered. "If you want him, the bum is sleeping off a drunk, and as far as I'm concerned, I've had it."

"I want him," Masuto said.

"You can damn well have him."

"How do you feel?" he asked Beckman.

"I'm all right."

"Sy, I'm at the West Los Angeles Country Club. They have a karate room here. I need you as quick as you can make it. Now outside this karate room you may find two gentlemen in dark suits and bulging jackets. You'll know them because they're that kind. They're Saunders's hoods, and very likely one of them killed Rosita. So you can take off the kid gloves, if you feel so inclined. Be quick."

Masuto sat down again. His hands were still trembling.

He waited until his hands steadied, and then he called Wainwright at his home and told him what had taken place.

"Damn you, Masao, you killed him."

"No, sir, I did not, and he came very close to killing me."

"What about Ishido?"

"He won't run. Right now I want you over here with the ambulance from All Saints Hospital. I want to get his body out of here and have Sam Baxter do an autopsy before anyone knows he's dead."

"You mean no one knows he's dead?"

"I know it. I presume he knows it."

"Damn it, Masao, you know what I mean. You can't sit on a corpse like that. He's not just anybody. He's Eric Saunders."

"I'm not sitting on it, captain. We—myself and what was Saunders—are in the karate room at the club. I imagine Saunders's two baboons are outside the door, and they're both armed and nasty, and I see no reason to open the door and invite their reaction—since I am not armed. And Eric Saunders, I remind you, was a murderous pig."

"Why didn't you say that in the first place? I'll have a squad car over there in a few minutes—"

"No."

"What do you mean, no?"

"Sy Beckman's on his way. Please, captain, let him take care of it."

"You said there were two of them."

"Let Sy take care of it, please."

"No, sir. I am sick and tired of you two running around like this was your own private vendetta."

"Well, as you wish—"

"Masuto, why do you pull these things on me? I've given you clowns more leeway than any sane chief would give a couple of cops, and now suppose the D.A. comes up with a vendetta killing—suppose he says you went overboard and took the law into your own hands? You know what I mean. How do I answer that?"

"I didn't touch Saunders. He died of a heart attack."

"Then why do you need an autopsy? The bastard is dead. It's over."

"I think he was murdered."

"Oh, no, not again."

"Yes, I'm afraid so," Masuto assured him. Now sounds were coming from outside the heavy door to the karate room, and Masuto said, "I must hang up now. Please hurry."

He went to the door and opened it. Beckman filled the doorway, a man in a dark suit hanging limply from each of his huge hands. He flung them into the karate room, where they lay on the floor, bleeding and moaning. Then, panting, he said, "What do you want me to do with these two loathsome bastards?"

"Cuff them and read them their rights, Sy. Concealed weapons, resisting arrest, and with a little luck, maybe murder one."

"And who's that?" Beckman asked, pointing to Saunders.

"Eric Saunders, alias Stanley Cutler. Very dead—very dead indeed, Sy. My God, what is today?"

"Thursday, all day."

"And it was only last Saturday that we found the skeleton."

"That's right. Is it over, Masao?"

"Almost."

"What's left?"

"A few loose pieces. Odds and ends."

"How come the cops aren't here?" Beckman asked suddenly. "I don't mean us. I mean the real cops, the guys in the blue uniforms?"

"Any moment now. I gave you a head start. I thought you'd want to deal with these two."

"I dealt with them," Beckman said.

CHAPTER
FIFTEEN

SAMURAI

I t was almost midnight, and the pathology room in the
basement of All Saints Hospital was deserted except for
Masuto, Dr. Sam Baxter, and Dr. Alvin Levine, the resident pathologist whom Masuto had dragged out of bed and
pressed into service. Naked and white and sliced open,
Saunders's corpse lay on the table. Baxter, washing his
hands, said to Levine, "You don't have to close. Just put
him on ice. He'll hold."

"You'll be back tomorrow to close him?"

"Why? He's dead, isn't he? Any damn fool can sew him
up. Even a witless ghoul like Masuto here can sew him up.
Well?" he demanded of Masuto. "Are you satisfied?"

"With what?"

"With what I told you. Cardiac arrest."

"So you told me. What caused it?"

Levine, bending over a microscope, straightened up,
took a test tube from over a flame, and shook it slightly. "I
think I have it," he told Masuto. "You noted the high thyroid
level?" he said to Baxter.

"So what?"

"It's triiodothyronine."

"He might have been taking it on prescription."

"Why?" Levine wondered. "He's not the type. Anyway, he took enough to kill him."

"How would it work?" Masuto asked him.

"The amount he had in him might result in a brief illusion of energy, then a very rapid heartbeat—so rapid that the heart muscle forces itself into cardiac arrest."

Baxter nodded. "That's possible."

Masuto went out into the street, and for a few minutes he stood in front of the hospital, breathing the cool, sweet night air. Then, with a deep sigh, he climbed into his car and drove to Bel-Air, to the home of his kinsman, Ishido. The electric gate that guarded Ishido's driveway opened up for Masuto, and the servant who opened the door of the house for him said, in Japanese, "Come in. My master is expecting you."

"It is very late—"

"No, he is expecting you."

In the living room Ishido was pouring tea that had already been prepared. He wore a white gown and black slippers and sat cross-legged by the table.

"Join me, please," he said to Masuto.

Masuto sat by the table and accepted a cup of tea.

"No doubt you come from the hospital, where an autopsy was done on that sick and worthless flesh."

"You condemn a friend."

"We were never friends," Ishido said. "Circumstances drew us together."

"You saved my life," Masuto said. "It incurs an obligation."

"Which you cannot repay."

"Not in this life. Perhaps in another."

"Ah, so—and you, the cold and enlightened policeman, you believe the old way, that we live and live again?"

"Who knows? I believe many things."

"You are a strange policeman, Masao. Yes, I gave the thyronine to Saunders in his food, in his tea, so it is quite true that I have murdered him. But I also saved your life. Or did I? Could you have defeated him?"

"I don't know."

"And now you have come to arrest me?"

"If I had not come," Masuto said, "others would come."

"I understand."

"Do you? I take no pleasure from this. I know of the Samurai only what I have read and what the old folks tell me and what I see in silly films."

"You are telling me, nephew, that I have dishonored my lineage?"

"Worse. You have dishonored yourself. And why did you lie to me about Eric Saunders and Burma?"

"That was not a lie. The man he killed was my friend."

"And so you committed murder for the benefit of Eric Saunders. Come on, uncle, that is too much. This is a moment for the truth."

"And what do you know of the truth? You are an American, Masao. I am something else, beyond your understanding. I could have killed Saunders thirty years ago. The punishment would hardly have befitted his crime. To me, death is not what it is to you. It is easy to die. So I did what I had to do, and it gave me a weapon to hold over Saunders. The whole story is in my vault at the bank. He knew that, so he could not kill me with impunity—and I waited. I let him build his empire, and I waited for the moment to bring him and his empire down in ruins."

"And the moment was tonight?" Masuto asked sardonically.

Ishido smiled. "No, nephew, the moment was not to-night. Tonight I changed my plans. I had no desire to see you die. I seek no sympathy. There is simply a matter of the fitness of things." He stood up now, and he made a slight formal bow to Masuto. "I shall not run away, nephew, but I need a few minutes to prepare for my absence and to change my clothes. If you will wait here?"

Masuto nodded. Ishido went into the next room. Masuto sat cross-legged by the table, staring at the tiny cup of green tea that Ishido had prepared for him.

And then he heard the woman scream, a piteous wail of grief.

Masuto rose and went into the next room. A woman was huddled in a heap on the floor, sobbing. Ishido knelt on a velvet cushion, a bit of incense burning before him and both hands clasping the knife that was buried in his breast.

Masuto helped the woman to her feet and led her out of the room. "He is gone," Masuto told her, speaking Japanese slowly and carefully, "but he departed honorably. Now there are things we must do."

THE CASE OF
THE KIDNAPPED
ANGEL

CHAPTER
ONE

THE KIDNAPPED
ANGEL

As a Buddhist policeman on the Beverly Hills police force, Detective Sergeant Masao Masuto abhorred superstition. For one thing, it went against his Zen training, for another, it defied common sense; so when a day began not only badly but improbably and continued in such manner, he refused to blame anything other than coincidence. The day was early in November, close to his birthday, which marked him as a Scorpio; but his distaste for the nonsense called astrology—which pervaded Los Angeles—was as great as his distaste for any other superstition.

For all that, he found it quite extraordinary that he should be interrupted by a thief during his morning meditation. He had begun his meditation at six A.M., in the first faint gray light of dawn. His meditation room was a tiny sun porch at the rear of his Culver City cottage, where he lived with his wife, Kati, and his two children. Since the two children were of different sexes, there was no bedroom to spare. Masuto did not complain. Indeed, he was grateful for the nine-by-twelve sun porch, which was large enough, since it contained no furniture other than a meditation mat and pillow; and there he was, sitting on the pillow cross-legged in what is known as the lotus position, wrapped in his saffron-colored robe, when a sixteen-year-old Chicano boy forced open one of the windows, climbed through, and stood facing him.

For a long moment the Mexican boy stood motionless, staring at the nisei detective, who sat motionless, returning the stare. For Masuto, it was a double effrontery—first that a thief should invade a policeman's house, and second that he should be interrupted in his meditation. Then the boy, digesting the fact that Masuto was alive, turned to flee, and Masuto thrust out a leg and tripped him. Then, with the boy's arm in a hammerlock, Masuto said, "Get up and don't struggle, because if you do, your arm will be broken."

Kati, alarmed by the commotion, arrived at the meditation room in time to hear this, and her comment was, "I don't believe this. A little boy, and you threaten to break his arm?"

She was right. The Chicano boy was quite small. Masuto let go of his arm and led him from the room by the collar of his shirt. Masuto was slightly over six feet tall and, at this moment, somewhat ashamed of himself. The boy was skinny and shivering.

"I didn't do nothing. Let me go," the boy said.

"He's a thief," Masuto explained to Kati. Now Masuto's two children, Ana, age eight, Uraga, age ten, were also watching, standing in their nightclothes and regarding Masuto with what he could only interpret as accusatory stares.

"Why don't you let him go?" Kati asked.

"He's a thief. I'm a policeman."

"You're a cop?" the boy said. "My God, I got as much brains as a cockroach, breaking into a cop's house."

"What's your name?" Kati asked him.

"Pedro."

"And you're hungry. Did you have any breakfast?"
He shook his head.

"And that did it," Masuto explained to his partner an hour later in the homicide office of the Beverly Hills police force. "This kid breaks into my house, and Kati feeds him."

"You know what it is, Masuto. It's those consciousness-raising sessions she's been going to. Did you call the Culver City cops?"

"No."

"You let him go?"

"I have to live with my wife. Anyway, he swore up and down he'd never done it before and wouldn't do it again, and the only weapon he had on him was a screwdriver. If I turn him over to the cops, it's either a suspended sentence or juvenile. Either way, he gets a record and maybe worse."

Masuto's partner, Detective Sy Beckman, nodded. "Maybe you're right. But I hate these stupid kids. Amateurs. We can deal with the professionals, but the amateurs screw things up. I don't know—no more lines of professional pride. These days everything is amateur. Maybe this kidnapping too. It has the earmarks."

"What kidnapping?"

"Angel Barton was kidnapped, and the captain's car was stolen. The two ain't connected, except that Wainwright's sore as hell. That's a coincidence—your house broken into and Wainwright's car stolen. Do you suppose they're after the Beverly Hills cops?"

"When did that happen?"

"The car?"

"No, the kidnapping."

"Sometime last night. I just got here ten minutes ago, so I'm not filled in on the details. Wainwright threw these files at me to play shuffleboard with—they're all on people associated with Mike Barton, but from here what we got is strictly nothing."

"Where's the captain now?"

"In his office with a roomful of civilian brass. He called twice to ask where the hell you were."

At that moment the telephone on Masuto's desk rang. He picked it up and Wainwright's voice asked him where the hell he was.

"I'll be right in."

In the dozen steps between his office and Captain Wainwright's—he was chief of detectives in the Beverly Hills police force—Masuto tried to remember and piece together what he knew about the Bartons. He knew at least a little and sometimes a great deal about most of the celebrities who lived in Beverly Hills, which is not to say that he knew many of them personally. What he knew of the Bartons had been gleaned from newspapers and from his wife, Kati, who was a much more enthusiastic movie fan than Masuto. Mike Barton was one of a half-dozen or so bankable stars, which meant that his name alone, associated with a film project, was enough to bring in the financing necessary to make the film. It was said that he had been paid a million and a half to star in his last film and that he was asking two million for his next. He was a tall, well-built man, with a craggy face, russet hair, and blue eyes, and given the right director, he could perform as an actor. Masuto tried to recall him on the screen, and while he felt he must have seen one of his films, he was not absolutely certain.

Concerning Barton's wife, Angel, his information had come totally from Kati, who read the gossip columns and pored over the picture magazines and was absolutely enchanted by both the name and the public image of Angel Barton.

The most intriguing thing about Angel Barton was that

she had no traceable past, not even a real name available to the columnists on *The Hollywood Reporter* and *Daily Variety*. When questioned on this subject, she simply smiled her wonderful smile, and her husband, in reply to the same question, told reporters that since her name was Angel, she had obviously dropped from heaven. He himself had christened her Angel, and neither of them would discuss any prior existence. This was taken by the media as a publicity stunt, and while several enterprising reporters set out to discover who Angel actually was, none of them were successful. The secret was well kept.

And as Kati had put it to her husband, "She does look like an angel." More precisely, she looked like the romantically remembered Marilyn Monroe, with the same golden curls and wide blue eyes. She had a very faint, almost undiscernable foreign accent which no one could place and a way of making any man she spoke to feel that he was the most important member of the male world. She and Mike Barton had been married two years ago, but whether it was her first marriage or not Kati had never mentioned. The rest of what Kati had told him about Angel Barton was of no great consequence, nor could Masuto recall much of it as he entered Captain Wainwright's office.

The small office was crowded. Joe Smith, the city manager, was there, along with Al Freeman, who was the mayor—an honorary, unpaid job—and three other men, introduced in turn as Frank Keller of the FBI, very young, very pompous; Jack McCarthy, Barton's lawyer; and Bill Ranier, Barton's business manager. McCarthy was in his late fifties, overweight, sure of himself, with a wide local reputation among film people; Ranier was middle forties, thin, nervous, impatient.

Wainwright wasted no time. "This is Masuto," he told Ranier and McCarthy. "I'll settle for him and his partner, but

I can't have hands off. Once Barton informs the police, it's a police matter."

"I know, I know," said McCarthy. "I advised him. But you know damn well, Captain, that a smart kidnapper will not pick up the ransom if he suspects a trap."

"Jack," the mayor said soothingly, "if there's one thing we're all together on, it's that nothing must happen to Angel. But Barton can't handle this alone."

"He's not alone. He has Bill and me."

"Not enough," Wainwright said. "You know that as well as I do, Mr. McCarthy. I'll tell you what I'll do. I know Barton's convinced that his house is being watched and that maybe there's even an inside connection, and we got to respect the threat that his wife will be killed if he even speaks to the cops. There'll be no phone taps, and the feds will use our place here as their command post. Now Sergeant Masuto here is the best man we got. A hell of a lot of gardeners are Japanese or nisei. We'll fit Masuto up with a gardener's pickup and he'll change his clothes and drive out to Barton's place and go in through the back door the way a gardener would. Barton's an actor, so he can raise hell with Masuto for interrupting him today if anyone's listening and then he can find a way to talk to Masuto alone."

"I don't know whether Barton will buy that."

"He'll buy it," Freeman said. "I'll drive out first and talk him into it. But when it comes to the drop he wants to be alone, absolutely alone."

"Let him work that out with Masuto," the city manager said. "Barton has the last word, but when there's a crime in our city limits and we're informed, we have an obligation to pursue it."

"I'll arrange for the car," Wainwright told them. "Nothing's going to happen until the banks open. I'd appreciate it if one of you filled Sergeant Masuto in. Then he can go home and change clothes, and still get to Barton's soon after nine."

"I'll go there now," Freeman said, and then asked McCarthy, "are you worried about carrying the money, Jack? I can meet you at the bank."

"No sweat. You stay with Mike. He's alone, and he'll need all the support he can get."

Freeman left with Wainwright. The mayor put his arm around McCarthy and assured him of the city's support. "Everyone loves Angel. I wouldn't want to be in the kidnapper's shoes if anything happens to her. You tell Mike that we're at his disposal. The whole damn city's at his disposal."

"That'll help."

They left McCarthy with Masuto, who said, "You'll forgive me if my questions are blunt. I have to get home and change clothes, and I want to get to Barton's as early as possible. First—how much is the ransom?"

"A million dollars."

"Has Barton got it?"

"He'll get it. Yes, he's got it."

"When did the kidnapping take place?"

McCarthy stared at Masuto thoughtfully for a long moment before answering. "They say you're good. Are you that good?"

"I'm a cop," Masuto said. "I do my job."

"That's fair enough. The Bartons have a place out at Malibu. Last night there was a party at the Malibu Colony. Mike felt rotten, headache, maybe a touch of the flu. He talked Angel into going without him, and he told her that if it got to be past midnight and she was enjoying herself, she shouldn't try to drive home but stay over at their Malibu place and come in today."

"That sounds like an understanding husband."

"They have a good relationship. Mike went to sleep. At

three in the morning he was awakened by the kidnapper's
call. The man told Mike he had Angel and that the ransom
was a million."

"Who gave the party?"

"Netty Cooper. She was married to Sam Cooper, the producer. They're divorced. She got the house at Malibu."

"What did Barton do then?"

"He drove out to Malibu. His house had been broken
into. There were signs of a struggle—broken lamps, over-
turned chairs."

"Did he then go over to Cooper's place?"

"No. The kidnapper had warned him to keep it quiet. For
all Mike knew, the party might still be going on."

"Is his house in the Colony?"

"No, about a mile away."

"He's a cool-headed man."

"Yes, he is."

"And what was his next move?" Masuto asked.

"He telephoned me from the beach house and I met him
here at his home in Beverly Hills. It was about six o'clock
in the morning then. I persuaded him to call Al Freeman.
The kidnapper had been very emphatic about what would
happen to Angel if he communicated with the police, but
Al felt he must call in the feds. Then I talked to Bill Ranier.
A million dollars in cash is a very large order, Sergeant. No
one bank carries that kind of cash. Fortunately, both Bill
and I have good connections with a number of banks."

"But you found the cash?"

"It's promised. It's being put together and it will be delivered to the Central Bank of Los Angeles by nine-thirty.
I'll pick it up there. The kidnapper said he'll call in his in-
structions for the drop at noon."

"Did Barton talk to his wife when the kidnapper called?"

"Oh, yes."

"What did she say?"

"She was frightened. Mike says she could hardly talk. What does a woman say in a situation like that?"

"If he repeated her exact words and if you can remember them, I'd like to hear them."

"What difference does it make? Time is running out."

"It might be important."

McCarthy shook his head and knit his brow. "I don't know. 'Help me.' I think. 'Get me out of this, please, Mike.' Something like that. I didn't press him."

"Do they have a security system in their house at Malibu?"

"I think so, yes."

"It connects with the Malibu police?"

"I really don't know." He looked at his watch. "Suppose you hold the rest of your questions for Mike when you get out there. I have to get over to the bank."

Masuto nodded, and as McCarthy left, Wainwright entered the room. "The gardener's rig will be downstairs in a few minutes, Masao. I swear I don't like this. It's lousy police method, and the feds are leaning on us and screaming special privilege. What in hell do they expect? It's Beverly Hills not Hell's Kitchen. There's more weight in this town than at a fat farm, and it all leans on us."

"When he goes to make the drop," Masuto said, "should I try to follow him?"

"No. We have to leave him clear."

"I don't like it. It's wrong."

"I know. It's lousy police work."

"I don't mean that," Masuto said. "It's wrong on his end."

"What does that mean?"

"I don't know. It just doesn't wash."

"Sure. And when you get something more than one of

your goddamn Oriental hunches, I'll talk about it. Meanwhile, keep an eye out for my car."

"What do you mean, keep an eye out for your car?"

"My car was stolen. Didn't Beckman tell you? My car—right here in Beverly Hills, standing in the driveway of my house."

"That is adding insult to injury. Still, Captain, if you insist on driving a Mercedes, you take the risk that goes with it."

"What do you mean, Mercedes? The car's twelve years old. I bought it for nine hundred dollars and put three thousand into it. Sure it's a Mercedes—ah, the hell with it! We'll find it. Meanwhile, get into some old clothes and look like a gardener."

"I am a gardener," Masuto replied as he opened the door to leave. "I grow the best roses, the best tomatoes, and the best cucumbers in Los Angeles. It's a relief to pretend to be something I understand."

Masuto stopped to look into his office, where Beckman still labored over the files. "I hear you've turned gardener," Beckman said.

"I wish it were permanent. What have you got?"

"Not much, but Mike Barton is an interesting guy. Angel isn't her name and Barton isn't his."

"What is his name?"

"I'm not absolutely certain, but maybe it's Brannigan. Also, he gambles."

"Everyone gambles."

"Big. Also, which I'm not sure about either, cocaine, and maybe the Angel sniffs a bit as well."

"Can you find anything on her?"

"I'm looking."

"Keep looking. From what I'm told, the drop will take place at twelve noon. This has to be kept very quiet, but the

big brass convinced Wainwright to leave him uncovered when he makes the drop."

"That's crazy!" Beckman exclaimed.

"Maybe yes, maybe no. I don't think it makes much difference. I'll see you later."

The gardener's truck was downstairs, an old Ford pickup with two lawnmowers sitting in the loading area. There were also picks, shovels, two bags of lime and a rolled-up hose. It had a cranky clutch and it bucked as Masuto backed out of the parking area.

It was just nine o'clock when he parked the pickup in front of his house in Culver City. Unlike New York City, there was no regulation requiring Beverly Hills policemen to live in Beverly Hills. If there had been, they would have to have been very wealthy policemen indeed. The small cottage in Culver City, only a few miles from Beverly Hills, was Masuto's base, his retreat, his argument that the world he lived in was not entirely insane and bloodthirsty. There was his home, his wife, his children, his tiny meditation room and his rose garden. Now his children were at school, the teen-age burglar had departed and evidently his wife, Kati, was out shopping, for the house was empty. He changed into old shoes, work pants, and a blue shirt, and as he was ready to leave, Kati entered, her arms full. Masuto took the bags of groceries from her and carried them into the kitchen, while Kati told him how delighted she was that he had been given the day off and was prepared to work in his garden.

"I am not going to work in the garden. In two minutes, I shall drive off in that truck parked in front of the house."

"The gardener's truck?"

"Yes."

Kati shook her head bewilderedly.

"I have not become a gardener. It's a costume for my

assignment. I'll tell you about it tonight. Until then—" He spread his hands.

"Ah, so. We are man and wife, but still I'm not to be trusted. Very old Japanese, Masao," she said, shaking her head. Kati was the gentlest of souls, but since she had joined a group of nisei women in the process of consciousness raising, she had developed a vocabulary of protest and disapproval. "Old Japanese" was a part of it. Masuto kissed her, refused to argue the point, and left the house, reflecting that as a Zen Buddhist he was poorly developed indeed. He should have been able to see her point of view. Well, one day he would change all that—one day when he had completed his twenty-two years on the force and was in a position to receive his pension. When that time came, he would spend at least six hours a day in meditation in the Zendo in downtown Los Angeles. Until then, unfortunately, he was a policeman.

Or was he just that, a policeman and no more? What was the point, the focus of his existence? With all his years of meditation, he had not experienced enlightenment, or satori, as the Japanese called it. He was more romantically inclined than people suspected. His wife, Kati, knew that her husband was a most unusual man, but even she did not suspect that there were times when he saw himself as a member of the ancient samurai. That was sheer fantasy. His family was not of the samurai, but out of plain peasant people, for all their success here in this new country; but at a moment in history Zen Buddhism had been the religion of the samurai, and for all of his failings, Masuto was a Zen Buddhist—and how so different from the samurai? The film the Japanese had made, which was titled *The Seven Samurai*, fascinated Masuto. He had seen it three times, brooding over the mentality of these seven men who must save a village, even at the cost of their lives, a village where they had no connection—except perhaps the human connection. That was very Zen.

And was that why he lived out the role of a policeman?

Or did he live simply for the occasional puzzle that broke up the dull routine of robberies? In all truth, he loved his work. That was his burden, his karma, to make his life out of the bleakest, the most horrifying aspects of what is euphemistically called civilization. Be that as it may, his problem now was to go disguised as a Japanese gardener, to the home of a film star, and to try to find out why said film star was unwilling to involve the police in the kidnapping of his wife. Wainwright would have seen it differently; he would have insisted that Masuto's responsibility was to find the kidnapper and to protect Angel Barton—if, conceivably, she could be protected. Why, Masuto wondered, did a part of his own mind reject that notion?

Then he put his thoughts aside. It was best not to think, not to speculate. More must happen.

Mike Barton's home was on Whittier Drive, north of Sunset Boulevard, at the extreme western edge of Beverly Hills. In a wealthy and elegant city, this was one of the wealthier and more elegant neighborhoods, enormous houses of twenty and thirty rooms sitting in manicured jungles of exotic tropical plantings. Barton's house suited the neighborhood, a strange combination of oversized Irish cottage and French chateau, painted white, surrounded by a whitewashed stone wall. A high iron gate opened to the driveway, and as Masuto turned into the entrance, the gate opened, indicating that someone was expecting him and had noted his approach. He drove around to the back of the house, as a gardener would, and as he got out of the car, Bill Ranier, Barton's business manager, came out of the back door to meet him.

"All right, Sergeant, you're here," Ranier said. "I don't

know how good this idea is, but since your people insist, Mike agreed to go along with it. Just remember that he's pretty damn disturbed, so don't try to break him down. He's going to do this his own way, and any pressure or strongarm tactics can only hurt Angel—maybe kill her."

"I don't use strongarm tactics," Masuto said softly, "but it might be worth noting that in Italy, where the payment of ransom is forbidden by law, people have tried to operate this way, without the police. It doesn't help. The same number of kidnap victims are killed. If Barton would cooperate, we might get both the kidnappers and his wife and a million dollars to boot."

"Well, he won't. He's going to do it his way."

"Is the money here?"

"Inside. McCarthy got here a few minutes ago."

"In what form? What kind of bills?"

"Fifties and hundreds. We have the numbers, but hell, there's no problem with laundering it. Billions of petrodollars floating around the world, so I guess we can kiss it good-bye."

"Possibly. I think now I'd like to talk to Barton. By the way, how many servants are in the house?"

"He keeps three in help, Joe Kelly chauffeurs and doubles as a butler when he has to, Freda Holtz—she's the cook—and Lena Jones, the maid."

"Does Kelly do the gardening?"

"No, Mexican gardener comes in twice a week, not today. Now look, here's the scenario we worked out. I tell Mike you're here. He yells and puts up a fuss. I calm him and tell him he might as well talk to you. That's for any big ears. I tell him it will help to pass the time and ease the waiting. Then he comes outside and walks with you through the plantings. He's got a small greenhouse at the other end of the property, so you can go in there and talk. It should make some sense to anyone who might be listening."

"You only mentioned the three in help. Are there any others?"

"Just his secretary, Elaine Newman."

"Is she here today?"

"Not yet. She comes in around ten, but she could be early or late. Mike doesn't hold her to strict hours."

"Does she know about the kidnapping?"

"No, and we decided not to tell her. When she comes in, I'll send her over to my office to get some papers and my secretary will keep her waiting there and then she has to pick up a manuscript for Mike. That will keep her out of it until noon. This is still off the record, and according to the kidnapper, we have to keep it that way."

"All right." Masuto nodded. "I'll wait right here for Barton."

CHAPTER
TWO

MIKE BARTON

Masuto had occasionally speculated on what makes a "bankable" star, a term very expressive in Hollywood if nowhere else in America. Certainly it was not theatrical talent, not appearance—though appearance was important—not beauty, not brains, but rather an indefinable thing which some called charisma for want of a better name. It was not connected with the way an actor lived his life, treated the other sex, was or was not a doper, a drunk, a liar, or a thief. It was something that cut through all that, recognizable yet undefinable—and whatever it was, Mike Barton possessed it. He was onstage as he stepped out of his house, and he strode over to Masuto with a kind of assurance reserved for his narrow clan, yet lacking, Masuto felt, any of that tired inelasticity that comes from fear and sorrow. He was a star, but not a very good actor.

He shook hands and said, "Let's walk, Sergeant. My house has big ears."

"Whose ears?"

"Damned if I know."

"Kidnapping for ransom is planned. It's not decided on

the spur of the moment. Someone must have known that your wife would spend the night at the beach house."

"Who? I didn't know it myself. Angel didn't know. We decided that she should show up at the party because Netty's a dear old friend. I had a splitting headache and I felt too rotten to trek over to Malibu. I told Angel that if the party was a drag, she should cut out of there at ten o'clock or so, but if she was having fun and decided to stay on, she shouldn't try to drive back here. Hell, that's what the beach house is for."

"But the people at the party would know that she planned to stay overnight."

"Some of them, maybe. I suppose Netty would know. Where the hell is all this leading, Sergeant?"

"The woman who gave the party, Netty Cooper—did you talk to her?"

"Come on, come on. My wife was in trouble."

"Still," Masuto persisted, "someone must have known that she would be at the party—"

"Sure. People knew that."

They were at the greenhouse now. "I guess we ought to step inside," Barton said, "just in case someone's watching. It'll make some sense for me to be walking in the garden with you."

Inside the greenhouse Masuto asked him, "Who might be watching?"

"Goddamnit, Sergeant, you get me at the worst moment of my life and ask me questions that make no damn sense."

"I'm sorry."

"All I want is to get back into the house and wait for the phone to ring."

"I can understand that."

"Then it makes no sense for me to be out here talking to a gardener. You keep asking me who is watching. How the hell do I know? But someone knows every move I make and every move Angel makes, and they're going to think it's funny as hell for me to be out here with you. Furthermore, let me tell you this: If anyone follows me when I make the drop and Angel is hurt, I swear to God I'll sue Beverly Hills for every dollar they got in their treasury."

"No one will follow you."

"Then I suggest you get your truck out of here."

Masuto nodded, reflecting that to be a policeman in Beverly Hills was quite different from being a policeman anywhere else in the world. He watched Mike Barton stride across the garden to the house, the stride and bearing of a thoroughbred horse, and then Masuto walked to his truck, got in, and drove out of the place. A few minutes later he parked the pickup at the police station on Rexford Drive, ignored a uniformed cop who wanted to know whether he had changed his profession, and then climbed the stairs to Wainwright's office.

"Back already?" Wainwright asked sourly.

"He didn't want me there. He raised hell and told me to get out."

"Great. We pay a hundred dollars to rent the truck for a day and we get ten minutes out of it."

"Beverly Hills can afford it."

"They don't pay for it. It comes out of our budget. Did you get anything?"

"Not really. Some impressions."

"Well, just sit on them. The city manager was in here and he wants us to keep hands off. Ranier and McCarthy are out there with Barton, and they'll be in touch with us once Barton pays the ransom. When Angel is returned, we can move in and investigate."

"And if Angel isn't returned?"

"Let's take it one thing at a time."

"I'd like to go out to Malibu now," Masuto said.

"What for?"

"I want to see his beach house and I want to talk to Netty Cooper, the lady who gave the party where Angel spent last night."

"The Malibu cops are handling that."

"I know, Captain. Nevertheless, she resides here. The Malibu cops would expect us to stick our noses into it."

"I don't want trouble with the brass, Masao. They want us to keep hands off."

"Absolutely. I'm not tailing Barton or interfering with him. I'm looking at a place where a crime was committed, a break-in and a kidnapping. It would be derelict on our part not to look into it, and it would undoubtedly open us to various charges that—"

"All right. Do it. I'm sick of being told when to be a cop and when not to."

"I'd like to take Beckman with me."

"What for? You need the company?"

"For protection. He's bigger than I am."

"Take him and get the hell out of here!"

His desk still covered with files, Beckman was talking into the telephone when Masuto entered. He put down the phone, and Masuto told him, "Come take a ride. We'll drive over to my house, I'll change clothes, and then we'll head out to Malibu. Unless you got something out of this morning?"

"We'll talk in the car," Beckman said. He was a big man, three inches taller than Masuto's six feet, heavy-set and slope-shouldered. He sat in Masuto's old Datsun scrunched over and observed that when you scratched the surface of anyone, what came up was pretty damn strange.

"How's that?"

"You want to know about Angel. Well, I put out every

line we have. I called Gloria Adams at the *L.A. Times* and I called Freda Mons at the *Examiner*. Between them they know about every celebrity in the country, when they pee and when they cut their fingernails and who they're in bed with, and I even called Elsie Binns at S.A.G., who knows practically every actor in the world, and do you know that none of them could come up with even a license tag for Angel Barton. That is, before two and a half years ago, which was when she moved in with Mike Barton. So who is she and where was she and where does she come from?"

"How about her maiden name?"

"That, Masao, is a lulu. Nobody, but nobody, has the vaguest notion what her maiden name was, or whatever her last name was, maiden or not."

"What did they call her? They must have called her something."

"They called her Angel."

"What about the Motor Vehicles Bureau?" Masuto demanded. "Did you try them? If she drove a car before she was married, she had a license."

"I'm slow but not stupid, Masao. Sure I tried them. They're a pretty lousy organization to begin with and they don't break their backs doing things for the Beverly Hills cops, and when I told them that all I had was a first name and an address, they didn't exactly applaud me. Nothing. So I called the L.A. cops who got some good computers. Zilch. Zilch wherever I turned. Two and a half years ago, that lady just didn't exist."

"She existed. Now what about Barton?"

They were at Masuto's cottage now, and Beckman suggested that they save Barton for the ride out to Malibu. "Otherwise, we got to talk about the weather, which doesn't change, and football, which ain't your game anyway."

It was after eleven now, and Kati, delighted to see her

husband at midday, immediately began to prepare food.
"I'm not hungry," Masuto said. "I'll change and then we'll
have to go." Beckman was hungry, and Kati fried a large
hamburger, which he wolfed down with a glass of milk. "I
expected tempura," he explained to Masuto when they were
back in the car. "You didn't expect me to pass up an offer
of Kati's tempura."

"You ate hamburger."

"That's what I got. I'd have to be a pig to turn it down
and ask for tempura."

"I guess you would."

It was about twenty-five miles from Masuto's home in
Culver City to the old Malibu Road, the location of the Bar-
tons' beach house. When they were on the Pacific Coast
Highway heading north, Masuto reminded Beckman about
Barton. "You said his real name might just be Brannigan.
Why 'might just be'? A good many film actors change their
names. It's no great secret."

"It is and it isn't, Masao. In the old days Jewish and
Italian and Polish actors used to sit on their real names, and
sometimes their real names were absolutely secret, actors
like Leslie Howard and Kirk Douglas and Tony Curtis to
name only a few. But after the war things changed and you
got people like George Segal and Sylvester Stallone who
don't give a damn and lots of others too. But with Barton,
it's different."

"How's that?"

"Well, think about the way he looks, a kind of a cross
between Robert Redford and Ronald Reagan. He's got to be
Irish or Wasp, so you don't think of him changing his name.
But his past is as blurred as the Angel's. He turned up here
in Hollywood in 1964 and it seems that for two years he
did everything except act—washed dishes, waited on tables,
pumped gas. Then he got some bit parts in TV, and then he

pulled off a major role in a series—and from there, zoom. He's one of the top ten. But who is he? Nobody seems to know."

"A hundred million people have seen his face. How does he hide?"

"Maybe he don't have to hide. You hide if you're on the run, if there's a want out for you. If it's just a background you're maybe ashamed of, or some kind of nastiness that won't help the image, or maybe even something you want to forget, you change your name."

"Then where did the Brannigan notion come from?" Masuto reminded him.

"I talked to Gloria Adams at the *L.A. Times*. She says that in the interviews with fan magazines and such, Barton just blurs his past—admits to being an Easterner from upstate New York, but she mentioned that two years ago she got a letter from back East. She tells me her column is syndicated all over the country, and this letter says that Barton's real name is Brannigan and that he comes from Schenectady in New York. So she asked Barton, and he says it's a lot of hogwash, so she just forgot about it, because crazy mail is a part of her job. She wanted to know how come the Beverly Hills cops were suddenly interested in Mike Barton, but I put her off and told her that if something broke, she'd be the first to know."

"Did you call the Schenectady cops?"

"I did that, but they don't have fancy computers, and they said that for anything seventeen or eighteen years ago it would take a couple of days to get into their old files."

Masuto nodded. "That's good work, Sy. From here on we'll just take it as it comes."

"You think he'll ever see Angel again?"

"Somehow, I do."

"It's almost noon. By now Barton's made the drop."

"I would presume so."

It was just past twelve when they turned left off the Pacific Coast Highway at old Malibu Road and pulled up in front of the Malibu police station. Joe Cominsky, the Malibu chief of police, had started out as a uniformed cop with Sy Beckman when they were both members of the Los Angeles police, and now he shook his hand warmly. "It's been a long time, Sy, many moons."

"I envy you. If you've got to be a cop, I suppose Malibu's got everything else beat."

"It has its points. Glad to meet you, Sergeant," he said to Masuto. "Maybe you're just what we need on this, because this Barton thing is sure as hell a Chinese puzzle."

"The sergeant's not Chinese. He's nisei."

"I know, I know. Just an expression. No offense."

"Forget it," Masuto said. "I know what you mean. I'd like to look at their beach house, and then I'd like to talk to Netty Cooper. I'm sure you've been talking to her."

"Just got back from there."

"Then you have a list of the guests last night?"

"It's a Who's Who of the film business. You know the kind of people we got out here in the Malibu Colony. Top directors, top stars, top producers. The thought of a couple of them sneaking down the road after the party to kidnap Angel Barton is just bananas."

"Were there no people from outside the Colony?"

"Fred Simmons, the producer, and his wife. Simmons is sixty-seven with a bad ticker. They left about eleven. Fred Simmons has more millions than you could shake a stick at. He's no candidate."

"How many people were there?"

"About twenty altogether."

"I'd like to talk to Mrs. Cooper."

"Absolutely," Cominsky said.

"And to have a look at the Bartons' beach house."

"Sure. Suppose we go along there now. I'd like another opinion. When I said Chinese puzzle before, I wasn't making an ethnic crack. I meant the puzzle part of it. It's just a mile down old Malibu Road. I'll drive you there."

"Then Angel never had to touch the highway. She just drove down Malibu Road. I suppose someone could have been waiting, watching for her car."

When they reached the Barton beach house, Cominsky pointed to the slope on the inland side facing the house. "Nothing there but mustard grass. No place to hide."

"On top?"

"Maybe. There's a road up there, between here and the Pacific Coast Highway, so I guess they could have parked there and watched. But let's look at the house."

The house was one-story and brown-shingled, presenting a blank wall to the road. The entrance was on the beach side, and alongside the house, nestled between the Barton house and the adjoining house, an alley led through to the beach. Cominsky opened the door to the alley, explaining, "Most of the people here leave passkeys with us."

"No garage?" Masuto asked.

"Not here. Very few of them. People park in the space in front of their houses."

"I don't see her car?"

"They took it—a yellow two-seat Mercedes. Worth over forty grand. We put out an APB on it, but no word yet."

"And when they left, was the gate open?"

"Right. Hold that thought, Sergeant. The gate wasn't jimmied. Either they opened it with a passkey, or they came around from the beach. And the nearest public pass-through to the beach is a quarter of a mile away. Just follow me through here."

The passageway was no more than three feet wide, the

house directly on the left making a windowless wall. In the Bartons' house there were several side windows, all of them covered with fretted iron grillwork.

"What about these people next door?" Masuto asked.

"Divorced actor. He does westerns in Spain. Been there three months and not expected back until next month."

They emerged into the blazing sunlight of Malibu Beach, the white sand stretching in front of them, a man walking a dog, a youngster in a wet suit trying to surf, and four pretty girls playing volleyball. The Barton house had a broad shaded porch facing the ocean, and in front of it and three steps down, a wooden terrace enclosed by a picket fence. On the terrace were tables under striped beach umbrellas—folded now—lounge chairs, and dining chairs. Cominsky opened the gate at the side of the picket fence and led them across the terrace.

"Barred on the road side, but not the beach side."

"The water kills thoughts of evil," Masuto said, and Cominsky glanced at him strangely.

"Yet the evil persists," Masuto added, smiling. "Only the sand is washed clean. Forgive me, Chief. I'm also puzzled."

"Oh? Yeah," Cominsky agreed. "Just take a look at this front door." He unlocked a police padlock that had been bolted to the door and stood aside. Masuto and Beckman stared at the door, which had been attacked in two places by a jimmy and forced open. In the lower corner of the window, next to the door, was a stick-on label with the legend HELMS SECURITY.

"Helms ties into police stations," Masuto said. "Was this tied into yours?"

"You're damn right, Sergeant."

"You tested it? It was working?"

"Absolutely."

"And you had someone on duty?" Masuto persisted.

"Even if we didn't, there's an alarm bell attached that can be heard a mile away on this beach."

"In other words," said Beckman, "she never turned on the alarm."

"Come inside."

They stood in the living room of the attractively furnished cottage—grass rug, wicker furniture with bright blue upholstery, good prints on the walls. Masuto stood staring, captivated. Two of the prints were askew, a lamp was knocked over and smashed, a chair was turned over, and the grass rug was pulled out of place.

"I want you to see the bedroom," Cominsky said.

"In a moment." He was trying to recreate a struggle in his mind and to fit it into what had happened in the room. Beckman, who knew him well, watched with interest. "All right," Masuto said.

"There are three bedrooms." Cominsky led the way. "This is the master."

The bedclothes were rumpled, a nightgown on the floor. As Masuto studied the scene, Cominsky walked over and touched a switch next to the bed. Above the switch, a red light glowed.

"This is the alarm switch. The light's on when the switch is off."

"I should think it would be the other way," Beckman said.

"No, this makes sense. You put out the lights, and then the red light reminds you about the alarm."

"What time did she leave the party?" Masuto asked.

"About one P.M. When they all live in the Colony, the parties tend to run late."

"But it was a weekday. Most of them would have to be in the studios very early."

"Yeah. She was one of the last to leave."

"And Barton got the call at three A.M. That leaves two hours. Unless they were stupid enough to make the call from here, they had to break in and take her somewhere. If they were watching her, why didn't they intercept her? Why break in at all? And if she went straight to bed, why didn't she reach out and turn on the alarm?"

"You tell me," Cominsky said.

"And if she wasn't asleep, why didn't she reach out and turn on the alarm when she heard the door go?"

"Was the bedside lamp on?" Masuto asked.

"It was."

"You had the place dusted?"

"Early this morning. We don't look for anything there."

"Can I use the phone?"

"Be my guest."

He called Beverly Hills and got through to Wainwright. "It's one o'clock," Masuto said. "What do you hear from Barton?"

"Nothing."

"Did he pay the ransom?"

"According to Ranier he got the call from the kidnappers over an hour ago and left just before noon, taking the million dollars with him."

"Never said where he was going?"

"Not a word."

"Did Ranier listen in on an extension?" Masuto asked.

"He says he didn't. He's there with McCarthy, waiting for Barton to show. Where are you?"

"At Barton's beach house."

"Did you find anything?"

"Confusion. I'd like to talk to Netty Cooper while I'm out here."

"Why not? Aside from the confusion, you got any ideas, Masuto?"

"Too many. If you want me, you can call the Malibu station. They're right outside the Colony."

He put down the phone and turned to Cominsky, who asked him if he had seen enough.

"I think so." He picked up the nightgown and looked at it—white silk, white lace. He put it to his face to smell it. Cominsky grinned. Beckman said, "I never knew you went in for that, Masao."

"Only lately."

Cominsky padlocked the cottage door again.

"If the system is turned on with the bedside switch," Masuto said, "then what happens when you open the door from the outside?"

"There's a switch in the lock that turns it off. It's not foolproof, but it's a damn hard lock to pick."

"Does your screen at the police station tell you when the alarm systems are on or off?"

"Yes. The officer on duty says it was off."

"Here on this part of the old road," Masuto said, "what kind of people live here?"

"Mostly the same kind you find in the Colony down the road, only with less money for the most part. Of course, some of them, like Barton, use their houses only on week-ends, and some of the houses, like this one, are as classy as the houses in the Colony. Some people don't want to live in the Colony, and then the houses at the Colony aren't for sale very often. You get writers, actors, directors, lawyers— you name it."

Masuto turned toward the ocean, staring at the incoming waves, apparently lost in thought. "I'd like to live here," Beckman said. "I guess I'd rather live here than anywhere else."

"Time was, and not so long ago," Cominsky told them, "that you could buy one of these houses for forty, fifty thousand dollars. Now there isn't one you can touch for less than half a million."

Masuto smiled thinly and shrugged. "Let's go back to the station house." He had been thinking that Malibu Beach was very beautiful. But most of the world was very beautiful until men touched it.

CHAPTER
THREE

MALIBU BEACH

B ack at the Malibu police station, Masuto found a message to call Wainwright at the Beverly Hills station.
He made the call and was put through to Wainwright,
who said, "What was taken has been returned."

"Very cryptic and interesting."

"I got a room full of reporters. I'll call you back in five
minutes."

Masuto put down the telephone and asked Cominsky,
"How much has this leaked?"

"Who knows, Masuto? I did my best. The local news
people were here. They always are when there's a break-in
on the beach, but I didn't say word one about the kidnapping. They wanted to know were any of the Bartons in the
house. I had no comment for that."

"What about Netty Cooper?"

"She had to know something was going on when I got
the list of her guests. But I didn't mention the kidnapping.
That won't help. It'll come out before the day's over."

"Angel's back."

"How do you know?" Beckman asked him.

"I spoke to Wainwright. He had a room full of reporters. I guess that means it'll be out. The chief's right. You can't sit on something like that."

"Well, thank God," Cominsky said. "She's a nice lady. I'd hate to think that anything happened to her. Is she all right? Did they rough her up?"

"I don't know. Wainwright didn't fill me in on any details."

"I'm starved," Beckman said.

"You can grab a bite at the drugstore in the shopping center across the road. It's not great, but it's all right. Or you can drive down to the pier and eat fancy."

"We have to wait for Wainwright to call back."

A few minutes later the call from Wainwright came through. "Masao," he said, "I'll be leaving for Mike Barton's place in about an hour, and I want you to meet me there."

"You said his wife is back?"

"Right. No harm done except some tape marks on her mouth and wrists. She says she was snatched out of her Malibu house by two men who wore stocking masks, taken somewhere, and finally dumped on Mulholland Drive, just to the west of Coldwater Canyon. She walked to the firehouse and they drove her home. McCarthy's with her, and that's the story he tells me. I got to meet with the mayor and city manager again, because they think they can sit on this and I got to tell them they're crazy."

"What about Mike Barton?"

"No sign of him yet."

"Did you put out anything on him? He should be back by now."

"Not yet, Masao. You know, he could have made the drop fifty miles from here. The kidnappers could have split up. One takes Angel, one goes to pick up the money. What are you thinking?"

"I don't know exactly what I'm thinking," Masuto said. "It's nothing I can put my finger on. It's just a smell. It doesn't smell right."

"No, it stinks, and I don't know why either, except when there's a crime and people tell the cops to keep hands off, well, that stinks for me."

"Who else is at his house?"

"Ranier's still there, and there's a uniformed cop I just sent over and told to sit in his car on the street, and if they don't like that, they can stuff it. What did you find in their beach house?"

"Puzzles. Questions."

"You might go straight to Barton's place."

"Well, we're here, so we might as well talk to Netty Cooper who had the party here last night. It's one-thirty now. I should be able to get to Barton's place by three or a little later."

"Okay. I'll meet you there."

"Try to hold McCarthy and Ranier there. Also the three servants and a woman called Elaine Newman. She's his secretary."

"Hold on, Masao. We can't detain anyone. You know that."

"Just ask them, politely."

"I'll try. But we got nothing to detain anyone on."

"We're not arresting them. All I want to do is talk to them."

"I'll try."

They stopped at the drugstore where Masuto ordered a bacon and tomato sandwich and Beckman ordered ham and cheese on rye. "Didn't you just eat lunch at my house?" Masuto asked him.

"Sure, but that was a long time ago."

"Yes, I suppose it was."

*　　*　　*

It was only a couple of hundred yards from the police station to the gate to Malibu Colony. At that point, where one turns off the Pacific Coast Highway to the old Malibu Road, the Colony is directly to one's left, a manned gate, and then beyond it a row of some of the most expensive houses in southern California. Masuto had frequently reflected on the lot of a detective trying to juggle the payment of bills, mortgage, doctor, dentist, grocery, insurance, etc., on a policeman's salary while protecting people who earned more in one year than a policeman could earn in a lifetime.

At the Colony gate, the guard looked at Masuto's identification and shook his head. "Heavy today—heaviest day we had in a long time. First the local fuzz and now fancy Beverly Hills cops. What goes on?"

Masuto shrugged.

"Come on, I'm on your side."

"The creature came out of the sea," Beckman said.

"Funny, funny."

"Which is Mrs. Cooper's house?"

"Down there. You can't miss it, painted bright yellow."

They drove through and parked in front of the yellow house. A Chicano maid opened the door and asked them to wait. In a few minutes she returned and asked them to follow her. Unlike the Barton house, this one had a proper entrance facing the road. It was two stories, had striped awnings, an entrance way, a huge living room-dining room with baroque furniture painted white, and, facing the sea, tall glass sliding doors. Netty Cooper was sitting on the deck-terrace with a man—a tall, elegant, good-looking man of about fifty. He was dressed in gray flannels, sported a carefully combed and barbered head of iron gray hair with pale gray eyes to match—and a face that was vaguely familiar.

"Two Beverly Hills detectives," Netty Cooper said with obvious relish. "I never knew they had any detectives on the Beverly Hills police force, only those handsome men in uniform with the pale blue eyes, and so polite, so very polite. But you do have to be polite to be a policeman in Beverly Hills, don't you?" Her own eyes were very pale blue. She was a slender, attenuated woman in her middle forties, with a long face, long neck, long trunk, and long legs. Her dyed yellow hair was piled on her head, and her nail polish was so dark it was almost black. She wore a beach dress of pale green, and her sandals revealed toenails painted the same color as her fingernails.

"Yes, ma'am—very polite," Beckman said. Those who didn't know Beckman and took him at his appearance, that of an oversized running back, were often surprised by his irony. Masuto was watching the man. He recognized him now, Congressman Roy Hennesy.

"And of course you've come about poor Angel's kidnapping."

"How do you know that Angel Barton was kidnapped?"

"Oh, one knows. This is a very small place. What has happened to our Angel?"

"She has been returned unharmed."

There was a pause, and then Hennesy said, "Thank God. Kidnapping is a horrible thing."

"I am Detective Sergeant Masuto. This is Detective Beckman."

"How nice! How very nice! And this is Congressman Hennesy, a dear friend. Masuto. How nice to think that we have a Japanese detective on the Beverly Hills police force. I spent three months in Japan, and I would love to chat about it. So many things I didn't understand. You could be so helpful."

"I'm afraid not. I've never been to Japan."

"Really? Then you must go."

"Yes. Thank you for the suggestion. Meanwhile, I'm much more interested in the Barton kidnapping."

"Oh? Are we on the list of suspects?"

"So sorry," Masuto said, "we have no suspects but would appreciate information."

Beckman watched him narrowly. Masuto rarely displayed anger, but when he fell into what Wainwright called his Charlie Chan routine, he was provoked and dangerous.

"How disappointing! I always wanted to be a suspect."

"Were you at the party last night?" he asked Hennesy.

"I was. But I assure you, I did not kidnap the Angel. If I had, I would never return her. I would give up my seat in Congress and find a desert island somewhere—a place where she and I could live out our lives in idyllic ecstasy."

"Ah, so. And does she feel that way about you?"

"Sergeant, must you be so literal? Half the men in Los Angeles are in love with the Angel," Mrs. Cooper said, and then to Hennesy, "but you are a very heartless man to sit there and tell me you dream of running off with the Angel."

"My apologies, and the disclaimer must include the fact that I am here with you, while the Angel snuggles in the arms of her devoted husband. How devoted, I wonder? How much was the ransom, Sergeant?"

"I have no idea," Masuto said.

"Close-mouthed—ah, well, an officer in pursuit of his duty."

"Did you leave the party before or after Mrs. Barton?"

"I really don't know."

"You mean with all your talk about a desert island, you didn't notice whether she was gone or not?"

"She left before Mr. Hennesy did," Mrs. Cooper told him. "I don't think any of my guests were candidates for a kidnapping—Jack Fellows and his wife, more millions than they know what to do with, the Tudors—well, a star does not dash around kidnapping people—Kennedy, only the most successful director in town, the Butterworths and the Goldbergs and the Lees. Not a very large party, Mr. Detective, and no one who is a potential for your kidnapper. If you think that any of my guests walked out of here and went over to the Barton place and kidnapped Angel Barton, you are absolutely out of your mind."

Masuto stared at her for a long moment; then he nodded. "We'll be going now—oh, one thing. Which of your guests live here in the Colony?"

"The Lees and the Goldbergs. Are you going to grill them as well?"

"I haven't grilled you, Mrs. Cooper."

"The Goldbergs are four houses down, the Lees are the sixth house."

"And, Congressman, when did you first learn about the kidnapping?"

"About two minutes before you arrived, Sergeant. I've been here about an hour, but Mrs. Cooper was upstairs doing her bath and things. I walked around to the beach side and made myself comfortable on the terrace. We're old pals. And, by the way, I didn't think you were serious about who left first, and I was rather put off by your questioning me. I did leave before Angel, if that matters."

"Thank you," Masuto said coldly.

Outside, Beckman let out his breath and shook his head. "They are a pair. She's a normal Beverly Hills type phony. The congressman's a fuckin' pain in the ass. They almost had an indictment out on him once, and then it was squashed, and they go on reelecting him. You want to keep your hands in your pockets if you get too close to him."

"What now?" Masuto asked him. "The Lees or the Goldbergs?"

"Let's give the Goldbergs a shot."

The Goldberg house was painted pink. Mrs. Goldberg was small, with dark hair, dark eyes, fiftyish, and had a schoolgirl figure and a good coat of tan. Her house was furnished in beach baroque, apparently de rigueur in the Colony, but with accents of pink. She asked them to sit down on the pink chairs on the terrace and poured Cokes for each of them.

"How exciting to have two real live detectives here. Wait until Joe gets home and I give him a blow by blow. Only poor Angel—"

"She's safe, Mrs. Goldberg. She's home, unharmed."

"Oh? Then I'll be bitchy and rescind my sympathy."

"I take it you don't like her?"

"Ugh! You see, I don't hide my feelings."

"That sounds like very strong feeling."

"It is. You see, Detective Masuto—that is it, Masuto?"

"Yes, indeed. And this is Detective Beckman."

"You see, I wasn't born to this sun-drenched, orange-ridden, never-never land. Joe and I made it the hard way, and he's just about the best producer in the business, so I don't have to be a diplomat, or an ass-licker, whichever you prefer. Now this is not a place without its gonifs and stinkers, as I'm sure you know, but this Angel is a beauty. Yes, indeed—even for the film business." She stopped and shook her head. "But I'm sure you're not interested in Angel."

"But we are. Please go on."

"Where do I start and where do I stop? Don't ask me to go into Angel Barton on my own. Ask me questions."

"All right. We've just come from Netty Cooper's house. She told us that you and your husband were at the party last night."

"We were. Netty's all right. She just keeps hurting all over with rejected-woman syndromes, three divorces—but since we're a community-property state, she's done brilliantly financially. Joe says she's worth at least five million."

She has fangs and she's no one's fool, Masuto reflected, asking her, "How did you find out about the kidnapping?"

"Sergeant, Joe, my husband, is producing Mikey's new film. In this kind of trouble, he would tell Joe before he told his own mother. Mikey isn't poor, but to put together a million dollars in a few hours is not easy. Joe always maintains a large liquid position, just in case he wants to tie up some literary property or a director. Joe was able to put his hands on two hundred thousand or so, and with Bill Ranier and Jack McCarthy pitching in, they were able to supply what Mikey needed for the ransom. But a million dollars for the Angel—ah well—"

"You keep saying Mikey," Beckman put in. "You must be very close to Mike Barton."

"He's like a son to us. Joe ran into him over in West Hollywood one day, pumping gas. You see—" She paused. "You see, I want to tell you this because I just don't like the smell of what's happening here, and both of you look like decent men. But please don't blow it all over town. Joe went to great effort to give Mikey a certain aura. So if this can be just among us?"

"I'll try," Masuto agreed. "We're involved with a crime, so I can't promise anything. But we'll try."

"Good enough. Mikey's father had a grocery store in Flatbush. That's in Brooklyn. We knew his father and we knew Mikey as a kid. His name then was Bernstein."

"You're kidding," Beckman said. "You mean he's Jewish?"

"What's so strange? You're Jewish, aren't you?"

"I look it."

"No law says you have to."

"And what about this rumor that his real name was Brannigan and that he came from upstate New York?"

"If you read Gloria Adams, you'll find a lot of rumors. When Joe and I were living in Flatbush and trying to make it the hard way, I saw Mikey every day, the sweetest, most willing, most decent kid I ever knew. The only kinkiness in him was that he wanted to be an actor. Then we came out to the Coast and lost touch with him, and then one day, about sixteen years ago, Joe met him at a gas pump. He brought the kid home, and we fed him and made him stay with us. Joe got him a part in a TV film, and he liked what he saw and got him an acting coach. From there on it was step by step, until he became the Mike Barton of today. We love Mikey, so I don't want to put Joe on a pedestal as Mr. Good Guy, but without Joe he would be another of the ten thousand unemployed actors around town. I don't say Joe didn't profit. He made eight films with Mikey, and six were enormous money-makers. But that's not why he did it."

"He had already changed his name to Barton when your husband met him?"

"Yes. He wanted it that way, and Joe let it stay. They decided on a mysterious past, and it worked, for what it's worth."

"And how did he meet Angel?"

"That's another well-kept secret—" She hesitated, studying Masuto and Beckman thoughtfully.

"But you're going to tell me," Masuto said deliberately. "You're not a chatterer, but you've decided to tell me a number of things. May I ask why?"

"Is why important?"

"I think so."

"I'm afraid. There's something happening here ever since Mikey married her, and it frightens me. He's changed. A lot of stars and semi-stars in this town cat around like they're in competition. Mikey wasn't that way. There were a few girls in his life whom he really cared for, but he didn't marry until he met Angel. He lived with one lady for five years, and while they were together he never looked at another woman. He has one real weakness—one, maybe a dozen. Who hasn't? Mikey wouldn't win any prizes for smarts. He's sweet and kind, but not too bright. But the one real weakness I'm talking about is gambling. It's a sickness, and he's a big loser. He met Angel in Vegas, where she was dealing blackjack, and he fell for her like a ton of bricks. She had been on the job only a few days, and already she had the reputation of wanting nothing to do with any of the studs around the place. She walked off the job with him the next day and they came back to L.A. together and she moved in—and it didn't work, not one little bit. It was a rotten, screwed-up marriage from the word go."

"Not according to the media," Beckman said.

"You can talk to the media or you can talk to me. The Angel that the fan magazines write about—the sweet, gentle, compassionate creature—doesn't exist. The real Angel is by no means a sweet, warm woman. She's a controlled cake of ice."

"They say she has a slight foreign accent."

"She's French. She claims to have learned her English dealing at Collingwood's in London."

"Which you don't believe?"

"Joe's been to Collingwood's. He says they don't have lady dealers."

"If the marriage is so bad," Masuto asked her, "why do they stay together?"

"You never met Mikey?"

"This morning. I talked with him at his house."

"All right. He paid a million dollars for her. He adores her, pays his price, and gets nothing, absolutely nothing, in return. If you want reasons, talk to a psychiatrist. It's nothing I understand, nothing Joe understands. If she told Mikey to lay down at the front door so she could use him as a doormat, he'd do it. The one real fight Joe ever had with Mikey was when Mikey wanted him to put Angel into a picture."

"Why?" Beckman asked. "She's beautiful."

"Beautiful, Mr. Beckman," she said patiently, "is a salable commodity in Grand Rapids or St. Louis. In Hollywood you can't give it away. On any street in West Hollywood, you'll see ten girls as beautiful as Angel, and if you walk through one of the studios, you'll see a hundred. Of course, they don't have her press, which comes from being married to Mikey."

"Still, if Mike Barton wanted it—"

"When you have ten million dollars riding on a picture, you don't make gifts of starring roles. Anyway, Joe agrees with me. She can work her charm in a living room, but she's not enough of a woman to make it on the screen."

"What exactly do you mean?"

"I don't really know what I mean. I'm Jewish. I look at Detective Beckman here and decide that he's Jewish. Maybe if I wasn't Jewish I wouldn't know. I'm a woman, and when I look at Angel and talk to her—well, something's missing. It's just a feeling. I can be very nasty when I put my mind to it."

"One more thing, if you can still put up with our questions. At the party last night, who left first, Angel or Congressman Hennesy?"

"They left together."

"You're sure?"

"Quite sure. But if you think Hennesy's involved in the kidnapping—no. It's not his style. He's a white-collar crook—payoffs, bribes, influence peddling."

"You seem to know him."

"Ah, Detective Masuto, you live here in the Colony, and you know a great many people, some nice, some not nice at all."

"Where does Hennesy live?"

"A few miles from here."

"Is he wealthy?"

"That's hard to say. You see, a public servant is always so ready to sell at almost any price that it's difficult to say whether poverty or larceny is the motivating factor."

Masuto nodded, repressing a smile. "Thank you. You've been very helpful and informative."

"How often do we get two good-looking city detectives out here in Malibu?"

"Even if you do look Jewish," Masuto said to Beckman when they were outside in the car.

"She's a tough little lady. I wouldn't want to get on the wrong side of her."

"Still, it's puzzling," Masuto said. "One loves Angel, one hates Angel. Nobody gives any reason why."

"You're going to look for reasons why a dumbbell falls in love, you got to be crazy."

"You think he's a dumbbell?"

"She does. She may love him like a son, but she don't give him even passing marks. Anyway, Masao, I think that as far as we're concerned, the case is closed. The feds will step in, and they want all the cards where a kidnapping is involved. Anyway, the break-in part of it and the snatch itself was in Malibu, so it drops into the lap of the Malibu cops. We might as well head back to Beverly Hills to Barton's place, and then I can tell my wife I actually saw Mike Barton in the flesh. That'll give her meat for the coffee klatch for the next two weeks. Unless you want to talk to Lee?"

"He's a screenwriter, isn't he?"

Beckman consulted his notes. "That's right. Cominsky says he's the hottest writer in the business."

"We'll skip him. I don't want any more imagination. I already have too many notions of what happened here last night."

They were on Sunset Boulevard, heading east toward Beverly Hills, when Masuto's radio lit up. It was Polly at the switchboard at the station house.

"Where are you?" she asked him.

"Just east of Sepulveda."

"Let me try to patch you through to the captain. He's been trying to get you."

"Masao?" Wainwright's voice was flat and bleak. "Where the hell are you?"

"Just passing the university."

"Well, get your ass over here to San Yisidro, just up from Tower."

"Why?"

"Because Mike Barton is sitting here in his car with a bullet through his head."

CHAPTER FOUR

SAN YISIDRO

S an Yisidro is a road that winds up into the Santa Monica Hills, branching off from Tower Road a short distance from Benedict Canyon. For about a mile and a quarter San Yisidro is within the city limits of Beverly Hills, and then the road goes on into Los Angeles. It must be noted that Beverly Hills itself is an island, entirely surrounded, not by water but by the City of Los Angeles. San Yisidro is a very elegant neighborhood, but there are spots where the cactus and the mesquite still grow untouched as they have for the past hundreds of years.

It was at one such spot that Mike Barton's black Mercedes was parked, drawn up on the shoulder of the road, the central attraction for two Beverly Hills police cars, Wainwright's car and Dr. Sam Baxter's car. A uniformed policeman stood in the road, waving the curious by. Masuto and Beckman parked behind a prowl car and then joined Wainwright at the Mercedes. The door was open, and Baxter was examining the body of what had been Mike Barton. On the other side of the seat Sweeney, the Beverly Hills fingerprint man, was dusting the car and the dashboard.

"When did you find it?" Masuto asked Wainwright.

"Half hour. Officer Comdon was patrolling the road, and he saw the car. Barton looked alive just sitting there, which is why, I guess, other cars passed it by, but Comdon figured he might be lost or something."

"When was he killed?"

Wainwright nodded at Sam Baxter, and Masuto went over to the doctor and asked him.

"How the hell do I know?" Baxter snapped. "Was I here? All right, we'll play the guessing game." He looked at his watch. "It's four-thirty now. I'd say he's been dead four hours, and that's just a guess, and if you put me on a witness stand, I'll say it's a guess."

"Thank you, Doc. Next to your skill I admire your sweet nature most. What killed him?"

"A gun. What in hell do you think killed him?"

"Yes, of course," Masuto said humbly. "I thought perhaps you could tell us what kind of a gun."

"The bullet's still in his skull. When I open him up and take it out, I'll give you all the details. Meanwhile, from the entry hole, I'd guess it was a twenty-two, and since the bullet didn't go through, I'd say it was a twenty-two short. A guess, you understand? But what the hell, if I did my work the way you people do yours, my whole life would be guesses."

"Yes, our work is hardly as precise. How far away was the gun when the bullet was fired?"

"You're sure you don't want the name of the killer?"

"Only if you have it."

"The gun was no more than twelve inches away. Powder burns. If you want me to do all your work for you, I'd say that his killer was sitting in the car with him. Barton turned away, and the killer put the gun to the back of his head and fired."

"And then wiped every print from the inside of the car," Sweeney said. "Took his time and polished the inside and the door handles like he was working in a car wash."

An ambulance drew up now, and two attendants pulled a stretcher out. Beverly Hills was not large or violent enough to require its own morgue and pathology room, and they had a long-standing arrangement with All Saints Hospital for the use of both facilities. Sam Baxter, chief pathologist at All Saints, doubled as medical examiner when his services were required.

The ambulance pulled away, Baxter following it, and Wainwright, studying the car thoughtfully, asked Masuto whether he had any ideas.

"Too many." He had squatted down by the rear wheel, feeling the dirt. "It rained day before yesterday. If the killer was parked here waiting for him, there should be tracks on the shoulder in front."

Beckman anticipated him. "Right here, Masao." Wainwright and Masuto joined him. "Do you know," Masuto said wryly, "television has become an enemy. It gives the criminal the benefit of a writer's imagination." The tracks had been there, but they were deliberately scuffed out.

"Still," Beckman said, "he was parked here, which means that two cars were sitting here, and maybe people don't remember one car, but somebody's got to remember two of them."

"You know it makes no sense," Wainwright said. "It's happened enough times that kidnappers kill the kidnapped person, but why kill the man who's making the drop?"

"Yeah, why?" Beckman added.

"It makes no sense only if there *was* a kidnapping," Masuto said.

"Then what in hell was it?"

"Barton parks here to meet someone. He has a million

dollars with him. The person he meets is parked in front of him. Is it a kidnapper? He doesn't tell Barton to drop the money and drive on. Instead, he leaves his car, gets into Barton's car, talks to him, and then kills him. No evidence of any struggle in the car, just a simple, friendly murder by your friendly kidnapper."

"Just hold on," Wainwright said. "If you're talking about a faked kidnapping, tell me how it makes sense. Sure Barton had to have some help to raise the million on short notice, but it's covered. He has over a million dollars in property and securities, so it's his money. Now what in hell does he gain by faking a kidnapping and paying out a million dollars of his own money?"

"I have a notion," Masuto said, "but I don't know whether I'm right."

"Suppose you let us in on your notion."

"Let me find out whether it makes any sense, Captain. Then I'd like to talk to the lot of them at the Barton place, Ranier and McCarthy and the Angel and a lady by the name of Elaine Newman, and also the three servants. If any of them left the Barton house, I'd like you to get them back in there and have Sy sit on the place until I get there."

"And that's going to help you find out who killed Barton?"

"I know who killed Barton."

"What!"

Masuto spread his hands and shook his head. "Not your way. I have no evidence. I see some kind of a crazy jigsaw puzzle, and I don't know what it is or why it is. So don't ask me to name any names."

"Why the hell not?" Wainwright demanded angrily.

"Because I can't do it that way. You know me a long time. This is like a dark tunnel and I'm feeling my way through."

Wainwright stared at him for a long moment; then he nodded. "All right, Masao, I'll play it your way for the next twenty-four hours. Then I want the name."

"Fair enough."

"Now what time at Barton's?"

"It's five now. Suppose we say between seven and seven-thirty."

Masuto left Beckman with Wainwright, and from San Yisidro he drove to Woodruff Avenue in Westwood, where his cousin, Alan Toyada, lived with his wife and three children. Toyada, who had been chief research analyst at Merrill Lynch for a number of years, had resigned to teach economics at U.C.L.A. and to conduct his own investment business. Masuto hoped to find him at home, and his hope was rewarded. After a series of polite greetings to the wife and the three children, he sat down in Toyada's study and explained that he had a problem.

"Which is why you're here, of course. What has happened to us since we nisei have become Americans? We abandon all the old ways. Family counts for so little. Do you know how many months it is since we have seen Kati and your children?"

"Too many. One lives with so much nonsense that the important things go by the board."

"How is Kati?"

"Very well. She has joined a consciousness-raising group, all nisei women. I think I approve."

"Do you? You might remember that one of the great advantages of being nisei is that one usually has a nisei wife. When you salt the kettle too much, it's very easy to spoil the stew."

"Perhaps. But I think we should talk about women's rights another time. Right now I have a problem that I present to your superior knowledge."

"Oh? Possibly the Barton kidnapping?"

"How do you know about the kidnapping?"

"Caught it on the radio driving home. The Angel was returned and the Bartons are happily reunited."

"Not quite. Mike Barton is dead—murdered."

"My God! When did that happen?"

"A few hours ago."

"Do you know how, why?"

"How—yes. Shot in the head. But why—" Masuto shook his head. "That's why I come to you."

"To tell you why Mike Barton was shot? I am overwhelmed, Masao. A simple investment counselor called upon to explain the evil that men do. Actually, I am very flattered."

"You are by no means a simple investment counselor. You know more about the curious mythology of money than anyone else I might go to. So please try to help me."

"How can I refuse?"

"Very well. I'll be as brief as possible. Angel Barton was kidnapped. The ransom was a million dollars. The ransom was paid and Angel was released unharmed. My guess is that whoever received the ransom payment murdered Mike Barton. But it is the kidnapping itself that puzzles me."

"More than the fact of a crime?"

"Much more. In the first place, I don't believe that there ever was a kidnapping. I am convinced that Barton and his wife arranged a false kidnapping. But why?"

"Did he borrow the money?"

"No. But even if he had, his price is a million and a half dollars a film. But he didn't borrow the money. Of course, since he had only a few hours this morning to put together the million dollars, he had to go to the banks for cash, and he was helped by his producer, his lawyer, and his business manager. But every dollar was backed by securities Barton owned. Which means that he arranged a kidnapping and paid a million dollars of his own money to himself—or at least so he planned."

"You're sure the kidnapping was fraudulent?" Toyada asked him.

"If not, I should put away my police credentials and spend my declining years pumping gasoline. It was not only faked but stupidly faked."

"And your problem is to understand why it should have taken place at all?"

"Exactly. You see, early this morning, when Barton rejected any intervention on the part of the police or the FBI, I began to suspect the validity of the kidnapping. Then, as events unfolded, my suspicions were confirmed. The only thing that makes no sense whatsoever is the reason for the charade."

"But, Masao, when you found Barton's body, did you also find the million dollars?"

"No."

"Ah, so!"

"Yes, very Japanese. Do you do it purposely?"

"A habit of my father's."

"You would have made a good policeman, but my disgraceful profession is enough for the family to endure. Of course the person who killed Barton had motives easily understood. He wanted a million dollars. And this person also knew about the kidnap plot, whether or not he was directly involved in it. But Barton—?"

"Masao, you are a victim of the fact that policemen are grossly underpaid. The explanation is really very simple."

"It is? I feel like a fool already."

"Nonsense. It is simply outside your province. Mike Barton earned well over a million dollars a year. This money is paid as wages, and it is taxed by the government at a rate of fifty percent. But he also had very substantial additional income, which is categorized by the government as un-earned income, and which in Mike Barton's case would have been taxed at a rate of seventy percent. Now what this in-come is, I have no way of knowing, but it's a safe guess that it was substantial."

"What kind of income?"

"Dividends on security holdings. Rents from real estate. Possibly shares in profits of films, depending on how they might have been structured. Any number of sources for what the government calls unearned income. Now when an actor works in a film, regardless of how much he is paid, a substantial part of his wages is withheld, just as a part of your own wages is withheld for tax purposes. But to some extent he decides how much should be withheld, and if there is a difference in the government's favor, he makes it up on April fifteenth, the date for filing. If there is a difference in his favor, the government sends him a check. Of course, you are aware of this. But with unearned income and with the income of self-employed professionals who are paid by fee as independent contractors, there is no withholding. The re-sponsibility for the payment of taxes rests with the individ-ual, and he must anticipate his tax and pay it to the government in four installments. Now keeping that in mind, let's return to Mike Barton. We'll propose that he needed a large amount of money desperately and quickly. Why? Was he being blackmailed? I leave that to you. You say that the million dollars was collateralized by securities? Are you sure? Have you checked? The money was put up by his friends—have they seen the securities? And how much of the million was an overdraft granted by the bank? If he has one of those enormous Beverly Hills houses, that would be security enough for an overdraft. But what have you checked?"

"At this point, nothing," Masuto said unhappily. "I saw no reason to question his friends concerning the securities."

"So we don't know how much of that million was his, but we can accept the fact that a substantial part was. He would have to clean out his bank accounts. Anyway, he needs money quickly and desperately. What to do? He and whoever was in it with him concoct a plan. Fake a kidnapping. Pay out a million dollars in ransom, which he can claim was his own money, and then take a million-dollar deduction on his income tax. If the entire million is in the seventy percent bracket, he nets a cool seven hundred thousand dollars of clear profit—plus his original million. But even if it's all in the fifty percent bracket, he has a very neat half a million dollars in profit. Of course, since the bills would be recorded, he'd have to launder the money. But no difficulty there. He pays the ten percent fee. It's regular big business south of the border and in the Bahamas."

"And the treasury allows it?"

"Masao, when a child is kidnapped, people bankrupt themselves to pay the ransom, and most kidnappings are not faked. Internal Revenue is pretty damned heartless, but this is America, and you know how people's hearts go out to a kidnap victim."

"And it's more or less foolproof, isn't it?"

"Except for stupidity, which you tell me this is laced with. However, considering that he would have paid ten percent to the launderers, Mike Barton would be holding nine hundred thousand dollars in cash. That's a lot of cash. What would he have done with it?"

"That's the question, isn't it? When I know that, I'll have all the other answers."

"How's that?"

"Just a guess that whoever killed Mike Barton did it for the money. I find the money, I find a killer—or killers."

CHAPTER
FIVE

THE HOUSE ON

THE HILL

N orth of Sunset Boulevard, in Beverly Hills, the land rolls up to the Santa Monica Mountains. The gentle slopes and hillocks are cut by several canyons, and the real estate in this area constitutes one of the most expensive residential neighborhoods in the entire country. The Barton home was on a hilltop just high enough to look out over the Beverly Hills Hotel, a Spanish colonial house on an acre of ground.

It was dark when Masuto pulled into the driveway, and four cars were already standing in the parking area. Beckman was waiting outside the front door, talking to a uniformed Beverly Hills cop, and he greeted Masuto with relief. "You got a houseful of angry citizens," he told Masuto, "especially McCarthy and Ranier, who insist that we got no right whatsoever to keep them here."

"We haven't. Why do they stay?"

"They tell it that the only reason they're here is to protect the rights of the Angel and to keep her from being bullied by the cops."

"Why do they think we'd bully her?" Masuto wondered.

"Because when they asked Wainwright whether they were suspects, he said that he had to take the position that everyone who knew about the kidnapping was to some degree suspect. He said it more diplomatically, but McCarthy blew his top anyway. Barton's secretary—her name's Elaine Newman—went to pieces when she heard about the murder."

"Oh? And how did Mrs. Barton take it?"

"I don't know. She's been in her room since she got back. The doctor's been here to see her."

"What doctor?"

"Their family doctor, name of Haddam. He's gone now."

"And what about the FBI?"

"That kid, Frank Keller, was here. He nosed around and asked a few questions. Didn't seem to know what the hell he was doing."

"And the captain?"

"The captain went home to have dinner. McCarthy told him that any harassment of Angel Barton would result in an action, and that he'd sue the hell out of the city, and you know how the captain reacts when one of the wealthy citizens threatens to sue the city. He says that you can handle it, because since you know all about who murdered Barton, you can go easy on everyone else. What about it, Masao? Do you know?"

"Sort of."

"What the devil does 'sort of' mean?"

"I know and I don't know."

"Sure. That clears it all up."

Beckman led the way into the house. "What about the press?" Masuto asked him.

"They were here, also the TV guys. Wainwright and McCarthy spoke to them. I told Frank, the officer at the door, not to let anyone in, except first he talks to you."

Masuto was studying the house thoughtfully. Earlier in

272

the day he had seen it only from the outside. Inside, it displayed the slightly insane baronial overbuilding of a film star's house of the nineteen thirties—tile floor, huge center staircase, stained glass windows, light fixtures like chateau lanterns, mahogany doors and trim and white plaster between heavy wooden beams.

"They're in the living room—or were—over there." He nodded at an archway.

Masuto went down two steps, through the archway, and opened a heavy door. The living room was at least forty feet long, with a high, beamed ceiling, an overstuffed couch, some easy chairs, and an enormous fireplace with a box large enough to take five-foot logs. No fire burned there now. The three people in the room were almost lost in its immensity—McCarthy talking on the telephone, Ranier at a long deal table with papers spread in front of him, and in one of the big, overstuffed chairs, her legs drawn up under her, her eyes staring sightlessly into space, a very pretty, slender young woman who, Masuto surmised, was Elaine Newman. She had dark hair and dark eyes and wore almost no makeup, and her face had a chiseled quality that Masuto responded to immediately. After he and Beckman had entered the room and stood just inside the door for a long moment, the girl turned to look at him, but without curiosity. Ranier glanced up from his papers and McCarthy finished his phone conversation.

"We met this morning," Masuto said. "I'm Detective Sergeant Masuto."

"Yes." McCarthy nodded. "I suggest you get on with your inquisition and let us get out of here. I already informed Wainwright that you have no damned right even to suggest that we stay and be questioned."

"Only for you to help us," Masuto replied gently, "as citizens and as friends of the murdered man."

"They weren't his friends," Elaine Newman said unexpectedly and tiredly. "Don't call them his friends."

"Shut up, Elaine!" Ranier snapped.

"Why? Are you going to kill me too, you blood-sucking son of a bitch?"

Ranier leaped to his feet and came around the table. "I won't stand for that! I don't have to stand for that! I don't have to listen to that foul-mouthed cunt!"

Beckman interposed himself, blocking Ranier's advance. "Let's all of us just take it easy," he said. "Why don't you sit down, Mr. Ranier?"

For a moment or two Ranier faced up to Beckman's enormous bulk; then he retreated and dropped into a chair. Beckman turned to Elaine Newman and said, "Why don't we go inside for a little while, Miss Newman. Suppose we find the kitchen and make us some coffee. I can use some, and I guess you can too." He glanced at Masuto, who nodded, and then he helped the girl out of her chair and led her to the door. "Can I go home?" she asked Masuto plaintively.

"In a little while. After we've talked. Go along with Detective Beckman and try to relax."

After Beckman and the girl had left the room, Ranier turned to Masuto and told him angrily, "I resent this. I resent having to stand here and be accused of murder by that little bitch."

"Bill, Bill," McCarthy said, "no one is accusing you of murder. Elaine is just shooting off her grief, and it's a relief to have some grief around here. Anyway"—he turned to Masuto—"Bill doesn't have enough guts to kill anyone."

"Thank you," Ranier said sourly.

"And Mike was his meal ticket. Who kills the goose that lays the five percent?"

"He was your meal ticket too!" Ranier shouted. "Talk

about bloodsuckers—you soaked him with fees that were unreal."

"Which eliminates both of us as murder suspects. That ought to please you."

"That's enough of that," Masuto said sharply. "The fact of the matter is that Mike Barton is dead and someone killed him, and I have to make some sense out of this. All this talk of suspects is meaningless. We have no suspects. We have every reason to believe that Mr. Barton was killed for the million dollars of ransom money. Why whoever received the ransom found it necessary to kill him, we don't know. I'm hoping that one of you gentlemen can enlighten me."

"Have you spoken to Angel?" McCarthy asked. "She saw the kidnappers."

"You spoke to her?"

"We both spoke to her," Ranier said, "but she wouldn't talk about it—"

"She couldn't," McCarthy interposed.

"Then she couldn't. The doctor said she was in shock. Then when she heard about Mike's death, she went to pieces completely."

"Where is she now?"

"In her room."

"We have reason to believe," Masuto said, "that the person who killed Mr. Barton was known to him, perhaps a good friend."

"Mike had lots of friends."

"And no friends," McCarthy put in. "You have friends when you earn less than two hundred thousand a year. Above that, you have appendages. When you're a star, you have the star-fuckers, and the woods are full of them."

"Were you his friend?" Masuto asked gently.

"I'm going to ignore the insinuation. I was his lawyer. Bill here was his business agent."

"Yes, of course." Masuto studied them thoughtfully. "Mr. Barton, it appears, was killed some time between twelve-thirty and one o'clock. Without any insinuations, believe me, I must ask you gentlemen where each of you were at that time?"

"Right here," Ranier replied.

"Well," McCarthy said, "you did run back to your office."

"Later. Much later."

"Come on, Bill, it was not much later."

"What in hell are you trying to do?" Ranier demanded angrily. "Set me up?"

"I'm not setting you up. For Christ's sake, what are you so jumpy about? No one's accusing you of killing Mike. You're the last person in the world who had any reason to kill him. But the plain truth of the matter is that Mike got the ransom call at twelve noon on the button, and he bombed out of here with the money two minutes later. You left about ten minutes after that, and it was half-past one when you came back."

"I drove straight to my office."

"And where is your office?" Masuto asked.

"On Camden. My secretary keeps a log. She logs me in and she logs me out. She can bear witness to that. I had some work that had to be attended to. I didn't stay to finish it. I brought it back here with me."

"And when did you get back here?"

"It was about one-forty-five, I think. "Lena Jones—she's the maid—she let me in."

"And while he was gone, for an hour and forty-five minutes, where were you, Mr. McCarthy?"

"You know you have no damned right to ask me any questions."

"I know that. You don't have to answer."

276

"I was right here, in this room. I made some phone calls, but I was right here."

"Alone?"

"Yes, alone. But Mrs. Holtz brought me a sandwich and coffee."

"When was that?"

McCarthy shrugged.

"You know damn well when it was," Ranier said. "You were eating the sandwich when I got back. You offered me the other one. I didn't even take time for lunch," he told Masuto.

"So what? I never left this room. Right now I would like to leave it. I've been cooped up here all day."

"You are both free to leave whenever you wish," Masuto said.

"If you're going to subject the Angel to questioning, I think I'll stay," McCarthy told him. "I'm her attorney."

"As you wish. And if you think of anything more you would like to tell me, I'll be in the kitchen."

"I'll take you there," Ranier said.

"I'm sure I can find the kitchen, and I would like to talk with Miss Newman privately."

"Can he do that?" Ranier demanded of McCarthy.

"Why not? I'm not her attorney and you're not her business manager."

"You know what she's going to say."

"I have no idea," Masuto said. He walked out of the room and through the hallway into what was apparently a butler's pantry. A sallow-faced man in his sixties sat there, reading a copy of *Sports Illustrated*, and he looked at Masuto inquiringly but without speaking.

"Sergeant Masuto, Beverly Hills police."

"I'm Kelly, the chauffeur."

"You live here?"

"Over the garage."

"I'd like you to stay in the house tonight. I want to talk to you later."

"Where would I go?"

Masuto went past him and opened a swinging door into the kitchen. It was an old-fashioned kitchen in size, better than twenty feet square, and recently modernized into the glittering perfection that most Beverly Hills homes required of their kitchens—but with the color scheme, perfection fled. The floors were yellow tile. The refrigerator, stove, and sink were finished in pink, and the walls in tile of mauve and tan. In the center of the room, at a large butcher-block worktable, Beckman sat with three women: the secretary, Elaine Newman; a stout, middle-aged woman whom he introduced as Mrs. Holtz, the cook; and a thin black girl who dabbed at her swollen eyes and who was introduced as Lena Jones, the parlormaid. Beckman himself was finishing a plate of stew and the last of a large mug of beer, and imagining she saw a look of disapproval on Masuto's face, Mrs. Holtz said, "Let him eat. Better the food shouldn't go to waste. Nobody has any appetite today."

"You hungry, Masao?" Beckman asked him.

He shook his head, thinking nevertheless that it was past his dinnertime and that he'd hardly get home much before midnight.

Mrs. Holtz pressed him, and Masuto relented to the extent of a cup of coffee and a slice of pie. Then he asked the maid and the cook to wait in the dining room, telling them that he would like to talk to them later. When they had gone, he said to Beckman, "Get the chauffeur's full name and phone into L.A.P.D. See if they have any priors on him."

"His name is Joseph. Joseph Kelly," Elaine said. "He has a record, if that's what you're looking for. But he wouldn't kill Mike. Mike's the only one who's ever been decent to him. He was just a drifter without a hope in the world when Mike picked him up and gave him a job."

Masuto nodded at Beckman, who left the room. Sitting opposite the girl, he studied her thoughtfully.

"You're a nisei?"

"Yes."

"And you're the cop assigned to this case?"

"Yes."

"That means you have to find out who killed Mike."

"I hope to."

"Well, it's no big deal. I know who killed Mike."

"Oh? Who?"

"The Angel." She said it with loathing.

"Inside, you suggested that Ranier killed Mr. Barton."

"Maybe he did."

"Both of them?"

"They're both worthless bloodsuckers."

"You hate people."

"Some people. But I loved Mike. I was the only one around him who did, aside from Mrs. Holtz and Lena and Joe Kelly. All the rest"—her voice sank to a whimper—"oh, my God, it's like killing a kid, like killing a little boy. Why? Why did they do it?"

Masuto waited until she had regained control of herself, and then he asked her, "What about Joe and Della Goldberg? Did they love Mike?"

"I guess so. But after he married Angel—"

"The relationship cooled?"

"Yes."

"How long have you worked for Mike Barton?"

"Two years. Since right after he married Angel."

"What did your work consist of?"

"His correspondence. Also, he always wanted to write a book. All the stars do. They have this guilt thing about being where they are, and mostly they can't justify to themselves why they are where they are, and they feel that writing a book about themselves will be a way out. Poor Mike. He tried, but it was all too complicated."

"He dictated to you?"

"Yes. But we didn't get very far on the book. Twenty or thirty pages."

"I would like to read it, if you would allow me."

"Sure. Sure, why not?"

"Why do you hate Mrs. Barton?"

"The Angel? Because she's a phony. Because she's a mean, heartless bitch and because she gave Mike nothing but misery."

"Why didn't he divorce her?"

She thought about this for a while, and then she shook her head. "I don't know."

"Perhaps he loved her, the kind of love that demands nothing in return."

"Bullshit!" she said angrily. "My heart isn't broken because I lost a job. Mike has been my lover since almost the first day I was here. Are you going to tell me he loved that cold bitch?"

"I'm telling you nothing, only asking."

"I don't know why I'm talking to you at all."

"Because we both want to find out who killed Mike Barton, and I must ask questions which will disturb you. I ask you again, why didn't he divorce her?"

"He would never tell me. She had something on him."

"What?"

"I just don't know."

"Guess. You must have turned this over in your mind a thousand times."

"Ten thousand times."

"You say he didn't love her, yet he was willing to pay a million dollars ransom."

"Come on, Sergeant."

"What does that mean?"

"That whole kidnapping was a fraud. That little louse Ranier designed the whole thing."

"Why?"

"I don't know why. But I do know this, that if it were a real kidnapping, Mike wouldn't have given twenty cents to get her back. Oh, he might have had to make a public display of some kind, but keep the cops out, keep the FBI out? No way. I can see how Mike might have paid the kidnappers a million dollars to keep her—but to get her back? You've got to be kidding."

At this point Beckman came into the kitchen and said, "Masao, we got company. Della Goldberg is here with her husband, Joe, and Netty Cooper, and Roy Hennesy, the congressman from out in Malibu. They all claim to be dear friends of the deceased, so I put them in the living room."

"Dear friends," Elaine said bitterly.

"There are also a lot of media characters and Gloria Adams from the *Times*, and I guess I owe her."

"Keep them out—no reporters. You don't owe her that much. Let them go over to the station house and get it from our P.R."

"What P.R.? We don't have any P.R."

"Mac Bendix—he always knows what's going on, and he'll pump the captain and keep them up-to-date. But no reporters in the house. Also, if you can, keep the maid and chauffeur apart from the guests."

"Mrs. Holtz wants to make coffee. She says if you have guests, you got to feed them. The black kid is serving drinks. I don't know how I can chase her out."

"All right, let it go. What about McCarthy and Ranier?"

"They're still here, hanging in."

"I got a feeling they're all going to hang in. Do me a favor, Sy. Call Kati and tell her I'm here open end. I don't know when we'll get home."

Elaine Newman was staring at Masuto with interest. It was the first moment that some of the pain had left her face. As Beckman left, she said softly, "You know what you're doing, don't you?"

"I like to think so. I'm not sure."

"How come a man like you is a small-town cop?"

"We can talk about that some other time, and Beverly Hills is not any small town. Right now we come back to Ranier. Why are you so sure he engineered the kidnapping?"

"Because poor Mike didn't have enough brains to work it out, and the Angel has plenty of viciousness but not too many smarts."

"Why do you think Ranier planned it? Mind you, I neither agree nor disagree. I just want to know why you think so."

"Yes, I've been thinking. I got here about ten. I was here when you pulled that silly gardener charade—saw you through the window. Mike was in a black mood, not worried, not grief-stricken over the Angel, just mean and angry because he had been talked into doing something he didn't want to do. Usually he's gentle as a lamb. Or was. My God."

"Easy," Masuto said. "Try to relax. This has been very hard, but you're young and your whole life is ahead of you."

"You ever been in love, Sergeant?"

"Yes."

"Then don't tell me my whole life is ahead of me. I'm all right now. I was telling you about Mike's mood. I tried to talk to him, but that was no good. He wouldn't talk. I think I lost my temper and said something about if the kidnapping was real, why didn't he bring in the cops and the

FBI? Then he told me to get out of the room. Ranier was there, and the way he looked at me, he could have killed me right then and there."

"You still haven't told me why you think Ranier planned it?"

"He was Mike's business agent. You work in Beverly Hills, so you know what a business agent is. He takes five percent of everything Mike earned, and do you know what Mike earned? It's only November now, and already Mike earned over three million dollars. It sounds like a lot, doesn't it? It sounds like enough to run a small country. But look what happens to it. First of all, Ranier takes his five percent off the top. Then McCarthy takes another ten percent off the top as Mike's agent—my God, what's wrong with me? I keep talking about him as if he were alive."

"I thought McCarthy was Mike's lawyer."

"He is. But he also acts as his agent. That's common enough. A lot of lawyers do it. He draws up the contracts with Joe Goldberg and takes his ten percent for that. Then again, as when Mike was sued by Bert Bailey, his stunt man, McCarthy defended the suit. His fee for that was seventy thousand dollars. Then the feds step in with their income tax, and every bum in town with his hand stretched out, and Mike's family back East, and Mike never said no to anyone. I'm not saying that Mike doesn't need a business agent. He could no more handle that kind of money than a five-year-old. But Ranier is a crook, and I bet that when it comes to probating Mike's will, you'll find that he doesn't have twenty cents. Ranier's taken care of that. That's why Ranier rigged the kidnapping and he and Angel murdered Mike."

"Tell me about Angel."

"You don't believe me."

"I believe that you have passionate feelings," Masuto

said. "I can't afford to have passionate feelings. I'm a policeman. I need proof, evidence."

"Haven't I given you enough evidence?"

"Not evidence, Miss Newman. Opinions. And I respect your opinions. I need your opinions."

"You're the strangest cop I ever met."

"Perhaps you've met very few. You said Mr. Barton didn't love Angel. Was there ever a time when he did love her?"

"I suppose when he married her."

"You suppose? Didn't he ever talk about it?"

"No! You keep asking me these questions. I'm sick. My whole world has gone down the drain, and you keep asking me about that bitch who killed him."

"Because I must. How did she feel about him?"

"Indifferent. What shall I say? They had separate rooms. Sure they appeared together at parties now and then. That was P.R. Otherwise she went her own way and Mike couldn't have cared less."

"What was her own way?"

"I don't know. No one knows. She has that little voice and that phony beatific smile, and it takes the whole world in."

"Was she having an affair with Ranier?"

"I don't know."

"Do you know where she came from?"

"France. Mike told me that once. It's all he ever told me about her. He wouldn't talk about her."

"But you say Mr. Barton loved you."

"Yes, yes, yes, damn you!"

"Then you must have discussed a future. That's the way people are, people like yourself, people with strong feelings."

"Yes, we discussed it. It was someday, always someday.

When he no longer had to be a star," she added. Her eyes were filmed with tears. "Being a star. What a beautiful fate! Take a sweet, decent dumb kid from Brooklyn and turn him into a symbol for a nation of lunatics. I'll tell you what he said to me, Mr. Detective, and then you can make something out of it with your smart-ass, slant-eyed know-how!" Her anger poured out at the whole world and at Masuto, because he sat facing her. "He said he'd divorce that bitch just as soon as he could afford to face the world as a clown, as a ridiculous joke."

"A clown?"

"Yes. You heard me. A clown!"

"Miss Newman," Masuto said gently, "I can understand your feelings, but nothing is helped by venting your anger at me. We both want the same thing—to find out who killed Mike Barton."

"I told you who killed Mike."

"Then let's say we want to prove it, and to do that, you have to help me. Will you?"

For a long moment she hesitated; then she nodded. "I'll try."

"Good. Now a moment ago you said that Mike Barton felt he would have to face the world as a clown. You're sure that's the word he used?"

"Yes, clown."

"And a ridiculous joke?"

"That's what he said. A clown. A ridiculous joke."

"But why?" Masuto insisted. "Why those words? He could have said a fool, a turkey, a sucker, a shmuck—those are words used by a man out here who feels he has been taken to the cleaners by a woman. They're like code words. But a clown?"

"What difference does that make?"

"I think it makes a difference. Perhaps we'll talk about

it again. You're upset, Miss Newman. Let me help you a little."

"How can you help me?" she demanded.

"Let me try. Empty your mind. Try to think of nothing at all. Just be here. We'll go on with this discussion, but if you can, simply hear my questions and give me answers, but don't evoke any images beyond that. Will you try?"

"It sounds crazy, but I'll try. I'll try anything. Otherwise I'll just go out of my mind."

CHAPTER SIX

THE RETURNED ANGEL

I f you don't mind," Masuto said to Elaine Newman, "I'd like you to remain in the house for a while. That's not a police order or even a demand. It's just that you know a great deal about what went on here, and I'd feel comfortable if you were here."

"I can stay,' she agreed listlessly. "There's a room upstairs that I use when I work late—or when Mike wanted me to stay over. Angel didn't object. I'd like to lie down for a while and see whether I can think my life into some kind of order."

"Does the door lock?"

"Yes." She looked at him curiously.

"Lock it." And as she got up, "One more thing, Miss Newman, tell me about the house."

"This house?"

"Yes. How many rooms, where they are—that sort of thing."

"Sure. There are six bedrooms upstairs, the master bedroom, which is Angel's, another bedroom which was Mike's—they've been in separate rooms since I came here to work—the room I use when I stay over, and two guest rooms. Behind the kitchen, through that door"—she pointed—"two servants' rooms. That's where Mrs. Holtz and Jonesey stay."

"Jonesey?"

"The black kid, Lena Jones. Joe Kelly sleeps in a little apartment over the garage. Through that door"—she pointed again—"the butler's pantry. No butler, just the pantry, and that door at the other end of the kitchen leads to the break-fast room. From the pantry one swinging door leads into the dining room, and the other opens into the hallway. You remember the way you came in with the big staircase facing you and the living room on your right. On the left there's the dining room, and at the front of the house, in front of the dining room, there's a library or den or whatever, and that's where I worked and took care of Mike's correspon-dence."

Beckman and Mrs. Holtz came into the kitchen while Elaine was speaking. "She insists," Beckman said.

"Because," Mrs. Holtz said, "it's after eight o'clock al-ready, and some of these people eat no dinner. I don't have people in my house, I should let them starve."

"One more thing," Elaine said. "There's a game room with a pool table in the basement."

"You tell them," Mrs. Holtz said to Elaine. "Did Mr. Bar-ton ever let anybody go hungry?"

"No, he fed the hungry."

"Where's Mrs. Barton?" Masuto asked Beckman.

"In her room. The doctor gave her a sedative and said she was to be left alone until he returned tomorrow."

"Crap! That's a load of crap!" Elaine exclaimed. "That lousy quack can't tell the living from the dead. I say she's up there in her room drinking champagne and eating caviar and celebrating."

"We'll see," Masuto said quietly, watching Mrs. Holtz, who had listened in silence to Elaine's outburst. "Right now, Sy, take Miss Newman here up to her room." When they had left the kitchen, he asked Mrs. Holtz, "Do you like Mrs. Barton?"

Her face stiffened. "I don't talk about the dead."

"Mr. Barton's dead, not his wife."

"To me, she's dead."

He went into the living room then. It was occupied by Netty Cooper, Congressman Hennesy, Della Goldberg, and her husband, Joe.

"Did Mr. McCarthy and Mr. Ranier leave?" Masuto asked them.

"Downstairs playing pool," Netty Cooper informed him.

"Yeah," Joe Goldberg said, "such is respect for the dead. Who are you?"

"The policeman I told you about," his wife said. "He is Detective Sergeant Masuto." Her eyes were red from weeping, and her voice trembled as she spoke. She fought inwardly to remain calm. "Where is Elaine? I want to see Elaine."

"I sent her up to her room," Masuto said. He went to the archway that led to the foyer and called Beckman. When Beckman appeared, he said to him out of the hearing of the others, "Take Mrs. Goldberg upstairs to Miss Newman's room. Make sure she locks the door again." And to Mrs. Goldberg, "If you go with Detective Beckman, he'll take you to Miss Newman."

After Della Goldberg left the room with Beckman, Hennesy asked Masuto whether he was new in the Beverly Hills police force.

"No, Mr. Hennesy, I'm not new to the force."

"Then you know that we don't browbeat people in Beverly Hills. We don't push them around."

"Yes, thank you for reminding me of that."

"Now, if you don't mind, we'll leave."

"Oh?"

"We're not leaving the house. Not yet. With cops all over the place, Angel needs someone to protect her. When you go, we'll go."

"Yes, of course. But before you go, might I ask you where you were at twelve-thirty today?"

"You know where I was, Sergeant. I was sitting on Mrs. Cooper's terrace out at Malibu, where you met me."

"That was considerably past twelve-thirty."

"That was considerably past the time I got there."

"How long was he there?" Masuto asked Mrs. Cooper.

"This is insufferable!" Hennesy said. "What in hell right do you have to stand there and question us?"

"The same right you have to refuse to answer," Masuto said, smiling.

"You're goddamn pleased with yourself, aren't you, taking over this house and pushing heartbroken people around."

"Oh, don't make such a fuss, Roy," Mrs. Cooper said. "I'm delighted to answer this Oriental gentleman's question. Do you know, Mr.—"

"Sergeant Masuto," he said politely.

"Do you know, Sergeant Masuto, one of the most unpleasant things a hostess can do is to look at her watch while guests are present. It's a crude signal that she wants them to leave. I wouldn't dream of doing it. So if the congressman says he was on my terrace at twelve-thirty, why he was. That's all there is to it." With that she took Hennesy's arm and they walked out of the living room.

"They're a cute pair, Officer," Joe Goldberg said. "They are that, a very cute pair." He was a short, fat man, bald, with a pair of sharp eyes hidden under shaggy brows. He took out a cigar now, offering another to Masuto, who shook his head. He clipped the end of the cigar and lit it, took a sip of the drink on the table next to his chair, and then puffed deeply and with satisfaction. "Lousy ticker," he said, "overweight, smoke too much, and here I am and poor Mike's dead. It's a stinking, fucked-up world, Officer, but I'm sure you know that."

"It has occurred to me. Tell me, was Mr. Barton on a picture when this happened today?"

"My latest. Half filmed, and it goes into the cutting room trash can. Five million dollars down the drain."

"But surely you were insured?"

"Yeah, insured. But that's not the game, is it? It takes a year to set up a film before the cameras begin to grind, and that year isn't insured. I lost my star and, like Della says, we lost a son too. Poor Mike—poor dumb bastard."

"Who do you think killed him?" Masuto asked casually, dropping into a chair facing the producer.

"Come on, come on, since when does a cop ask you that? This is my first murder, Sergeant—Masuto, isn't it? You're a nisei, if I'm not mistaken?"

Masuto nodded.

"I think I've seen your name in the papers. You're a pretty smart cop. The Japanese are damn smart, too smart for the rest of us, I'm afraid."

"I'm just a policeman, and you produce motion pictures," Masuto reminded him.

"I'm not sure that my job takes more brains than yours, and certainly a lot less guts. No, I have no idea who killed Mike, but I could name a lot of people who have a damn good reason for killing him, and they're all in this house— his friends, horseshit, pure, unadulterated horseshit."

"Please go on, Mr. Goldberg. You intrigue me."

"Start with McCarthy. He and Mike got into an argument at the Bistro two weeks ago, and Mike hit him across the face with his open hand. I don't know what the fight was about, but they tell me Jack just took it and stalked away. I don't know whether that's a reason for murder, but I suspect that McCarthy hates his guts."

"Still he rallied around this morning when the kidnapping took place."

"Ah, money talks. Mike is his best client. As for Bill Ranier, I've been pressing Mike to dump him. Ranier's a crook, and a business agent who's a crook is something no one needs. Ranier knows Mike was about ready to part company with him. As for that little tart they call Angel, she's not shedding any tears over Mike's death. I imagine it was the answer to her prayers."

"And the congressman and Mrs. Cooper?"

"She's a silly woman, and you can drop her off the list. Hennesy is another matter. Shady, and once very close to being indicted for bribe-taking. They say he's mad about the Angel, but that's a thin rumor. The Angel is shacked up with someone, but who it is I don't know. But then a million dollars talks pretty damn loud, doesn't it?"

"So they say. And yourself, Mr. Goldberg?"

"Sure." Goldberg nodded, staring at his cigar ash. "Don't leave me out. I could have killed Mike ten times over—for being a horse's ass, for marrying that bitch, for not divorcing her, for letting Ranier rob him blind—ah, what the hell difference does it make now?"

"Why didn't he divorce her?"

"You know, there was a time when Della and me, we were like a mother and father to Mike. He would invite himself to dinner two, three times a week. He would bring his dates for our approval. He would beg Della to read his lines with him. Oh, I don't claim it was all disinterested affection for the kid. I made him a star and he was worth his weight in gold to me. But beyond that, we were both crazy about him—until—" He stared at Masuto. "You want to listen to all this garbage?"

"Yes, I do."

"Okay. Until he met the Angel. She was dealing twenty-one in Vegas. That was two—two and a half years ago. Mike was a hot gambler, but the stories about him losing two or three hundred thousand in a session are pure bullshit. When Mike went to Vegas, he'd take a couple of thousand with him and when it was gone, he was finished. Well, as I said, he meets this Angel, it's love at first sight, and she quits her job which she had only a few days. They're married right there in Vegas and she comes back with him, and for a week or so Mike is happy as a clam, and then it's over."

"Same question, Mr. Goldberg. Why didn't he divorce her?"

"Did you ask Ellie Newman? She's a nice kid. She and Mike were in love with each other."

"I asked her. She claimed she didn't know, and the closest she ever came to an answer from Mr. Barton was his belief that it would make him a clown, a joke in the eyes of the world. I guess he intimated that it would end his film career."

"Poor dumb kid. Well, that's more of a reason than I ever got. She had something on him. I don't know what it could be—" He shook his head hopelessly.

"And the kidnapping this morning. Did you buy it, Mr. Goldberg?"

"What do you mean, did I buy it?"

"I mean," Masuto said slowly, choosing his words carefully, "did you feel that it was a real kidnapping or a faked kidnapping?"

"How the hell should I know? Sure I knew that Mike wouldn't have given twenty cents to get her back, but the public wouldn't buy that, and if Mike had refused to pay the ransom for his wife's life, that would wash him out as a working star. We talked about that, and I agreed that he should pay it."

"Did you also agree that he should keep the police and the FBI out of it?"

"Did he? I didn't know that." He shook his head worriedly. "Why would he do that? He had to pay the ransom, but I'd think he'd have the cops in there every step of the way." He stared at the curl of smoke rising from his cigar. "Sergeant?"

"Yes?"

"How long do we have to stay here?"

"You don't have to stay here at all. You can leave whenever you wish."

"Well, I'll wait until my wife finishes talking to Ellie."

Masuto nodded and left the room. Beckman was in the hall outside talking into a telephone. Masuto waited. Beckman put down the telephone.

"Where are they?"

"Downstairs in the game room."

"Any of them leave?"

Beckman shook his head. "It's like they're all watching each other. Mrs. Goldberg is still upstairs with Newman. Angel's still in her room."

"And Kelly?"

"He's in the kitchen with Mrs. Holtz. The black kid is downstairs. They keep her running for drinks. By the way, Doc Baxter called. It was a twenty-two short, just as we thought, and he still fixes the time of death between twelve-thirty and one. One more thing—" Beckman paused, relishing the moment. "Wainwright had a couple of cops canvassing the houses on San Yisidro. They found a kid who saw a yellow two-seat Mercedes drive by at about twelve-thirty or so. He remembered it because it's his dream car, and he never saw it before."

"Did he notice who was driving, a man or a woman?"

"No. He was at an upstairs window, being sick with the flu, so he never saw who was driving."

Masuto thought about it for a while, and then he said to Beckman, "Sy, I want to talk to Angel Barton, and I don't want anyone else talking to her first. So go upstairs and wait for me outside her room. No one goes in—but no one. And if she wants to leave, just delay her. I won't be more than ten minutes."

"This Dr. Haddam said—"

"I don't give a damn what Dr. Haddam said."

"Okay, Okay, Masao. What's eating you?"

Masuto laughed and shook his head. "I'm sorry, Sy. We live in an insane world."

"What else is new?"

"I try to suspend judgment. Sometimes that's almost impossible. What did you find out downtown about Joe Kelly?"

"He has a record, like Miss Newman said. Seven priors. In and out, he spent maybe twenty years in jail, all of it theft, grand larceny, petty larceny. He's a thief, that's all. He got out on parole eight years ago, and Mike Barton hired him. He's been clean ever since."

"All right. Go upstairs now. I'll join you in a few minutes."

Masuto went into the kitchen. Kelly and Mrs. Holtz sat at the kitchen table, each with a cup of tea. Mrs. Holtz was a woman of at least fifty, possibly even sixty years. She was crying, yet seemingly unaware of the tears rolling down her cheeks. Kelly sat watching her, his long, lined and battered face impassive. But that, Masuto realized, could be misleading. A man who had lived Kelly's life would be beyond the point of revealing emotions facially. Masuto felt the tragedy of his own aloofness, but it was a tragedy mankind shared, the tragedy of being fragmented, of each person being walled away from the suffering of others. There was little left for those two people. In all likelihood Kelly could never find another job.

Masuto pulled a chair up to the table, waving Mrs. Holtz back to her seat as she started to rise. "Don't get up, please."

"I'll get you a cup of tea, Sergeant. A piece of cake."

"No. No, thank you. Just a few questions."

"You might as well know about me," Kelly said. "I got a record."

"I know."

"I never slugged anyone and I never shot anyone. I was never busted for carrying a gun."

"I know that."

Mrs. Holtz evidently did not know it. She stared at Kelly in astonishment.

"And I never left this place today."

"Yes. Then you saw Mr. Barton leave with the ransom money?"

"I was washing a car in front of the garage when he pulled out. He had a big brown suitcase, and he put it on the front seat of the car next to him."

"What time was that?"

"Maybe ten, fifteen minutes past twelve, because after he pulled away I turned off the water and came into the kitchen here for my lunch."

"That was twenty minutes after twelve," Mrs. Holtz said. "I remember."

"Why do you remember the exact time?" Masuto asked her.

"Because inside, in the living room, Mr. McCarthy and Mr. Ranier was having terrible argument. Joe heard it too.

He said, 'What do you think? Maybe they're hungry.' It was joke. I said, 'No, it's only twenty minutes after twelve.' "

"Did you hear what they were saying?"

"I don't listen. Maybe Joe?"

He shook his head.

"Mrs. Barton was kidnapped," Masuto said, "and in great danger. Yet you were able to joke about things."

Mrs. Holtz shrugged. "Is terrible not to care about someone, but she was never nice to us."

The telephone rang, and Masuto picked up the extension on the kitchen wall. It was Klappham, on night duty at the station house. "The captain left me this number, Masao," he said. "Bones down at L.A.P.D. called and left this message for you. They picked up the yellow Mercedes. It was parked on Fourth Street downtown. No damage. Mint condition and the key in the lock."

"Did they dust it?"

"I was just going to tell you, wiped clean."

Masuto hung up the telephone and turned back to Kelly. "Did you ever drive for Mrs. Barton?"

"Sometimes."

"Did you ever take her to meet anyone?"

"Maybe, but I don't know who she met."

"What does that mean?"

"Well, a lot of times, I drive her down to the Music Center. I drop her off and she'd tell me when to pick her up. Same thing out to Malibu, if she didn't want to bother to drive. We got that big Lincoln Continental chauffeur car, with a bar in it and a telephone and all that garbage, and I guess it made her feel pretty classy riding around in it. She didn't like my driving, but when you been busted as many times as I have, you drive careful, and when she was alone with me she could really let go. She could talk pretty damn dirty. Sometimes she'd cuss me out in French. I don't know the words, but from the way she spit it out I knew she was cussing me. She was always after Mr. Barton to dump me and hire someone else."

"Did you ever take her to meet a man—I mean did you ever actually see her with a man?"

"Once, when I had to pick her up at the County Museum, she was kissing someone."

"Who?"

"That's it. I was coming down Wilshire, maybe two, three blocks away. When I got to her, he was gone."

"Yes. Do you know whether either of the Bartons owned a gun?"

"Yes," Mrs. Holtz said. "Yes. She left it one day on her dressing table. No, not on it—inside. You know how the top comes up with a mirror. It was there, and Jonesey saw it. It scared her to death. Jonesey was cleaning the room, and she came running to me."

"Did you see the gun?"

Mrs. Holtz nodded.

"Can you describe it for me?"

"It was small, silver, very small. Like a toy gun. Like guns you see, but they're really cigarette lighters."

"Thank you. I'll talk to Miss Jones later. You've been very helpful."

Masuto went upstairs then and joined Beckman, who was waiting for him outside the door of Angel Barton's room. "Anything?" he asked Beckman.

"Quiet as a grave. Nobody in, nobody out. There's still reporters and TV characters outside, but Dempsy's held the line against them. You'd think the telephone would be ringing constantly, but the black kid they call Jonesey tells me that they have an unlisted number and they keep changing it. Still, you'd think a star would have loads of friends."

"You'd think so," Masuto said. He tapped at the door of Angel's room. "Where's Miss Newman and Mrs. Goldberg?"

"That room, down the hall," Beckman said, pointing.

Masuto knocked at the door again, waited a few seconds, and then turned the handle and opened the door. The room was pink and white—white carpet on the floor, pink walls, white bed, pink coverlet, two pink and white angels suspended by wire from the ceiling fleeting over the bed, mirrors on one whole wall, white baroque furniture, a pink and white chaise longue, and lying on it, half-reclining, Angel Barton in a pink robe over a white silk and lace nightgown. Her hair was a hairdresser's triumph—long, spun gold, and two wide, innocent blue eyes stared at them out of a Marilyn Monroe face.

The two men halted just inside the door, staring at Angel, who returned their stare unblinking.

"Sy, close the door," Masuto whispered.

He closed the door and said, "Masao, what the hell goes on here?"

Masuto walked over to Angel Barton and picked up her arm. There was no pulse and the hand was cold.

"Is she dead, Masao?"

He pushed the lids down over the staring blue eyes. "Very dead, I think." On the floor next to the chaise longue there was an empty hypodermic needle. Beckman picked it up with his handkerchief.

"How long?" he asked Masuto.

Staring at Angel thoughtfully, Masuto said, "The hands are cold. Twenty minutes, half an hour." He was examining her arm. There was a single puncture mark. "What's the smell?" he asked Beckman, who was sniffing the air.

"Ether."

"I thought so. Go downstairs, Sy, and tell Dempsy that no one leaves the house. I've been stupid, and I don't want to go on being stupid. Then call the station and tell them to get another cop over here and to inform the captain. Then call Baxter and tell him we want him and an ambulance."

"He'll love that."

"We'll try to live with his displeasure."

Beckman was studying the hypodermic. "No prints."

"No, he wanted to get rid of it, so he wiped it and dropped it."

Beckman left the room. Masuto walked over to the dressing table and raised the lid. There was the gun Mrs. Holtz had spoken about. It was a small, expensive purse gun, twenty-two caliber and probably, Masuto guessed, of Swiss make. He took it out, hooking his pinky through the trigger guard and then brought it into the light of a lamp, studying it carefully. It bore a clear set of prints which, he was convinced, would match those of the dead Angel. He then wrapped it in his handkerchief and dropped it into his pocket.

He then walked over to the dead Angel and stared at her thoughtfully. She was indeed a very beautiful woman, even in death. He tried to analyze his own feelings. Had he been the cause of her death? Was his own failure to anticipate it to be condemned? Should he have known? There was something missing. He was not attempting to exonerate himself. There was simply something missing.

He bent over the dead woman now and raised one of the eyelids he had closed before, peering at the cold blue eye it revealed. Then he lowered the lid again. There were two doors at one side of the bedroom. Masuto went to them now. One led to a bathroom, where tile and sink and tub were in varying shades of pink. The other door opened on an enormous walk-in closet.

Masuto flicked on the closet light, staring at the racks of dresses, slacks, and evening gowns. One entire wall of the closet was devoted to a shoe rack, holding at least a hundred pairs of shoes and, at the bottom, four pairs of riding boots. He then went through the racks and finally found, not on the racks, but carefully folded on a shelf behind the dresses, six pairs of whipcord breeches. What this added up to, Masuto could not for the life of him imagine. Possibly nothing. Possibly she liked to ride. In the detective stories he read occasionally, everything pointed in a specific direction. But here were things most curious that pointed nowhere.

CHAPTER
SEVEN

THE DEPARTED

ANGEL

You don't need me," Dr. Baxter said sourly. "I don't have to dance attendance on every corpse you clowns turn up. I was in the middle of my dinner—"

"It's ten o'clock," Wainwright said apologetically.

"Civilized people eat late, and if you think I'm going to spend all night doing an autopsy, you're crazy. I'll get at it in the morning."

"All we want to know," Wainwright begged him, "is why she died."

"Because her heart stopped. It causes death."

"Come on, Doc, be reasonable."

"Are you reasonable? What do you think they pay me to be medical examiner for this silly town of demented millionaires. All right, you want to know what she died of? I'll tell you what she didn't die of. She didn't die of an overdose of heroin, if that's what you're thinking. She's not a user."

"Was she murdered?"

"How the hell do I know whether she was murdered? I'm not a cop, and I can't read the minds of the dead. When I cut her up, I'll tell you what I find."

"You can take her away," Wainwright told the stretcher bearers. They left the bedroom with the body, Baxter stalking after them.

"He's a doll," Beckman observed. "He's just a sweet, good-natured doll."

Sweeney, glancing up from his search for fingerprints, blamed it on Baxter's profession. "You do that kind of work, it's got to show."

The photographer was still working his flashbulbs. "The body's gone," Wainwright said tiredly. "That's enough. Take what you got back to the station and develop it."

"I don't know how the word gets around. Maybe it's ESP," Beckman said. "But there's two TV crews outside and four or five reporters. Someone's got to talk to them."

"I'll talk to them. Just tell them to wait and be patient." Beckman left the bedroom. Wainwright slumped down on the chaise and said to Masuto, "What makes you so damn sure she was murdered?"

"It had to be. Only I didn't have enough sense to realize it."

"I don't know what in hell you're talking about, Masao, but I know one thing. This afternoon you told me you knew who killed Mike Barton. No more games. I want the name."

"All right. But it doesn't finish anything. Angel Barton killed her husband—but only in a legal sense. She was with a man, and the man pulled the trigger. Of course, she was part of it. They planned the thing together. And the stakes were high—one million dollars in cold cash, and if it worked, anything she was entitled to in his will." Masuto reached into his pocket and took out the gun he had wrapped in his handkerchief. "Here's the gun that killed Mike Barton."

Wainwright stared at it speechless. Sweeney came over, lifted the little pistol carefully by its trigger guard, and examined it in the light of a lamp.

"As lovely a set of prints as I've ever seen."

"Where did you get it?" Wainwright demanded.

"Over there—in her dressing table. Where the killer had placed it after he finished with Angel. The prints are excellent. He put them on the gun after Angel was dead, pressing her fingers to it."

"And how did he kill her?"

"I don't think we'll ever know that. My guess is that he knocked her out with something, perhaps ether, and then he injected her vein with air. I don't know whether that can be proven in an autopsy. They may find traces of something in the syringe. He was desperate and in a hurry, and I guess he decided to make it look like suicide. It was a stupid, witless crime from the moment it started this morning."

"Yeah, when it's not stupid, we don't even know that a crime took place. I guess you're right about the gun, but we'll let Ballistics decide. You said this morning, you think the whole kidnap caper was a rigged job?"

"A kid's job. I think the husband, Mike Barton, was in on it, and then his Angel double-crossed him and brought someone else into it. Or maybe the whole thing started with the killer. I couldn't make any sense out of the kidnap thing until I spoke to a cousin of mine who's an expert on legal ways to cheat Internal Revenue, and he said that there would have been a big tax break for Barton."

"Except that from what I hear, neither Barton nor the Angel were smart enough to figure it out."

"Exactly. There's another small matter," Masuto said. "The killer is right here in this house."

"You're sure?"

"Very sure. No one came in when it was done, no one left."

"That's beautiful." Wainwright rose and began to pace the room. "Pink and white, pink and white, she must have really seen herself as some goddamn kind of angel. They don't want a cop for my job, they want a diplomat. Downstairs, we only got one of the most prominent lawyers in town, a top film producer, a hotshot business manager, and a congressman. Plus a chauffeur with a record long as my arm."

"Not to mention a number of women who are probably a lot smarter than the men."

"And a fed. That kid from the FBI pushed his way in and started bugging me about what was his role in all this. I told him how the hell did I know what his role was? He's a goddamn idiot. He's got a notion that the Mafia is mixed up in it because he heard we found a syringe in here."

"Is he still here?"

"Prowling around downstairs. I can't throw him out. We've had too many run-ins with the feds."

"We'll both be very kind to him."

They had their opportunity almost immediately. As they went downstairs from the second floor of the Barton house, they saw Frank Keller waiting for them at the foot of the staircase, his pink-cheeked, snub-nosed face set in a grimace of determination. He was wearing a carefully pressed gray flannel suit, a white shirt, and a tie with brown and maroon stripes. Masuto, who wore an old brown tweed jacket over rumpled trousers and a tieless shirt, had once been asked by another FBI man whether he always dressed that way or only when in disguise.

"I've been trying to work out my role here," Keller said. "I don't want to push in like a bull in a china shop."

"That's very considerate of you," Masuto agreed.

"On the other hand, there's been a kidnapping, even though both the victim and the ransom payer are dead. You know, it's a national tragedy. I don't think anything quite like this ever happened before. You think of Mike Barton and you think of Robert Redford, Al Pacino, John Wayne—although I don't think it would have happened to John Wayne in just this manner."

"I guess not," Masuto agreed.

"Of course, the murders are a local matter, if murder is the correct term?"

"We think Angel Barton was murdered," Wainwright told him. "We won't know for certain until after the autopsy. We found a syringe and a puncture mark—which is all we know for sure."

"You could do one thing that would be very helpful," Masuto said.

"Be glad to."

"We can be pretty certain that if Mrs. Barton was murdered, someone here in the house at this moment killed her. And we can work up a background on every one of them except Mr. Hennesy."

"Congressman Hennesy?"

"That's right."

"But surely," Keller protested, "you can't suspect Congressman Hennesy of an act of murder."

"I have to. I have to suspect every one of them."

"We're not accusing him or anyone else," Wainwright explained, talking softly, since from their position at the foot of the stairs they could hear the chatter of voices from the living room. "Believe me, here in Beverly Hills, a thing like this is no picnic. One wrong move on our part and we could face a million-dollar lawsuit—and that fellow McCarthy in there is one of the sharpest lawyers in town. That's why we'd like you to get us a rundown on Hennesy. Your office must have everything there is to have on him."

"I'll try. I don't know what they'll say in Washington. Is he involved in the kidnapping?"

"I don't know," Masuto said.

"Does anything point in that direction?"

"If you wanted to point it, you could. He was at the same party Angel attended the night she was kidnapped, but when we talked to him about it this afternoon, he seemed to have forgotten that he left the party with her. He offered a lie as an alibi without being accused of anything. I don't know what it adds up to, but if you want to make a connection with the kidnapping for the people in Washington, there's enough there."

"All right. I'll do my best. But it won't be sooner than noon tomorrow."

"We understand."

"You don't mind if I stick around for a while?"

"Be our guest," Wainwright said generously, and then he led the way into the living room.

They were all there—McCarthy and Ranier and Joe Goldberg and his wife, and Congressman Hennesy and Mrs. Cooper and Elaine Newman—with Beckman leaning his huge figure against a grand piano and watching them with calculated indifference.

"You have no right to hold us here," McCarthy said immediately. "You know that, Captain Wainwright. From what I gather, you don't know what caused Angel Barton's death. This is Beverly Hills, and I find it outrageous that this over-sized officer of yours"—he indicated Beckman—"should tell us that we are not to leave."

"If he told you that, he was mistaken," Wainwright said placatingly. "Of course you are free to leave whenever you wish. I only suggested that we would like to have a few words with you, that is with any of you who don't have to leave immediately. You were friends of the Bartons, and in that capacity you could be very helpful. But if you wish to leave, Mr. McCarthy, there's no reason why you shouldn't."

"For how long?"

Wainwright turned to Masuto. "Ten, fifteen minutes," Masuto told them. "Your assistance would be invaluable. But as the captain said, any of you who wish to leave now are free to do so."

No one moved. Hennesy said, "Since as a concerned citizen I am to be part of this charade, I'd like a drink."

Wainwright nodded at Lena Jones, who was hovering in the doorway. She came forward slowly.

"Take orders from all of them," Masuto told her. "Is Kelly still around?"

"He's in the pantry. He'll make the drinks."

"All right. Bring back the drinks, and then we're not to be disturbed."

While the people gathered in the living room were giving their orders for drinks, Beckman walked over to Masuto and whispered, "Any way to smell their hands, Masao?"

Masuto chuckled. "Want to try? Ether leaves an odor, but there's soap and perfume."

"Just a notion."

To Wainwright, Masuto said softly, "I want to tell them that Angel was murdered."

"Will it help?"

"I think so."

"Is it one of them?"

"Or Beckman or myself or one of the three servants. No one else was in the house."

"Go ahead and do what you got to do."

"I'll step on toes."

"There's no other way. The city manager will be in my office tomorrow morning yelling his head off. But he'll yell at me, not at you. So just take it with a grain of salt if I put you down and save face."

"I'm all understanding."

Jones returned now with the drinks, and when she had

left the room, Masuto said to the assembled company, "I must begin by telling you that Angel Barton was murdered, and we have every reason to believe that she was murdered by the same person who killed her husband. I must add that the murderer is still in the house, since no one entered or left this house since at least an hour before the murder took place. That doesn't mean the murderer is in this room, not necessarily, since there are also three servants in the house. This information does not change what Captain Wainwright said before. There are no charges against any of you, and any one of you is free to leave when he or she pleases."

"And to be tagged as your mysterious killer!" Mrs. Cooper snorted.

"This whole procedure is outrageous," McCarthy said. "I challenge your statement that no one entered or left this house this evening. There are French doors, a kitchen door, a basement door—there are windows. How dare you come in here with your asinine conclusions and browbeat a group of people whose only sin is that they were the close friends of Mike and Angel Barton!"

"There'll be no browbeating, Sergeant!" Wainwright snapped.

"Terribly, terribly sorry," Masuto said. "Please forgive me if I gave any impression of browbeating. You may leave now, if you wish, Mr. McCarthy."

"I have clients here. I will not leave them without legal protection."

"Would anyone else like to leave?"

No one moved.

"Then I must tell you, as Mr. McCarthy certainly would have, that you have the right to ignore any questions I may ask you. I shall question each person in turn, and I would appreciate it if the others did not interfere. Except, of course,

Mr. McCarthy, who will be duty-bound to advise his clients not to answer when he feels they should not answer."

"I'm not sure I want to answer any of your damned questions," Hennesy said.

"As you please, Congressman. I'll start with Mrs. Goldberg."

Beckman had moved behind them. He sat on the piano bench, his notebook out.

"Do you ride, Mrs. Goldberg? I mean horseback."

Della Goldberg observed him with interest, smiling slightly. "As a matter of fact, I do. I mean, I try. It's silly at my age, but most of the things one does out here are silly."

"Where do you ride?"

"In Malibu. My husband and I keep horses at the Grandview Corral.

"And you both ride?"

"We both try."

"Thank you. And you, Mr. McCarthy, do you ride?"

McCarthy stared at him, his face set.

"Of course he does," Mrs. Cooper said, "and I don't blame him for refusing to answer a stupid question like that. And I ride, if you intend to ask me that dumb question. At the same Grandview Corral."

"I ride occasionally," Ranier volunteered. "I don't know why you want to know and I couldn't care less. At Crushanks, in the Valley."

"And you, Mr. Hennesy?"

"I think I've had enough of your nonsense, Masuto. I didn't like you when I met you this afternoon, and I like you less now. The abuse of police power is one of the things I like least in this democracy of ours. To have a very mournful occasion like this turned into a circus is more than I can endure. I think I'll leave." He stood up. "Will you join me?" he asked Mrs. Cooper.

"As a matter of fact, I was thinking the same thing." She rose too.

"I'll go with you," McCarthy said, and to Ranier, "I'd advise you to do the same thing, Bill."

"I'll stay," Ranier decided.

McCarthy, Hennesy, and Mrs. Cooper left the room. Masuto heard the door slam as they departed from the house, and Wainwright took the moment to whisper to Masuto that he was going home. "It's your ballgame, Masao," he said. "I'm going to get to the city manager tonight, before McCarthy shits all over us. And be careful," he added, dropping his voice still further. "We got McCarthy and we got the congressman, and those are two mean bastards. So for God's sake, keep it cool and don't involve us in any lawsuits. And don't make any arrests. These people aren't going anywhere."

The Goldbergs, Miss Newman, and Ranier sat quietly, waiting. When Wainwright had left, Joe Goldberg said, "What now, Sergeant? I'll admit I am an appropriate candidate for murdering the Angel, if I had enough guts to murder anyone, which I haven't, but poor Mikey I would kill only for his stupidity, and no one kills because someone they love is stupid."

"Mikey wasn't so stupid," Della Goldberg protested. "He was trusting."

"Which, carried to the extremes he carried it to, was simply another form of stupidity."

"Will you two stop!" Miss Newman cried. "You just can't stand the fact that Mike decided he didn't need another mother and father. Calling him stupid because he loved people and trusted them!"

"I think you'd better go home, Miss Newman," Masuto said gently. "You've had a long, terrible day." And to Beckman, "Take her outside, Sy, and have a squad car drive her home."

"I have my car here," she muttered, the tears beginning.

"All right, if you wish. And please give Detective Beckman your address and phone number."

"Anything more?" Goldberg asked after the girl and Beckman had gone.

"Yes. Do you know whether Hennesy rides?"

"He rides," Ranier put in.

"What is this riding business?" Goldberg asked. "How does it fit in?"

"I'm not sure I know."

Beckman came in then and told Masuto that Kelly had asked whether he could go to his room. "He sleeps over the garage."

"Yes, he can go." And then to Ranier, "How do you know Hennesy rides?"

"I was once a guest out at Albermarle, near San Fernando. They told me he keeps a horse there."

"That would cost a bundle," Goldberg remarked. "Hennesy doesn't have a pot to pee in."

"Hennesy's on the take. When he needs money, he gets money. All right, I don't smell of roses. It takes one to know one."

"What kind of take?" Masuto asked.

"I can give you a list of what a congressman can do for you as long as your arm. He does it."

Keller, the FBI man, spoke up for the first time since he had entered the room and said, "That's a serious accusation, Mr. Ranier."

Ranier looked at Masuto hopelessly. "Is he kidding?"

"I think not. He's a federal officer."

"And you work in this town," Ranier said to Keller, "and you never heard that Roy Hennesy is a crook?"

"Come on, Bill," Goldberg said, "you don't call a man a crook until you can quote chapter and verse. Anyway, I've had enough of this whole thing. My wife and I would like to leave, Sergeant."

"If you wish, of course."

As he rose, he asked, "Are we still suspects?"

"Did you or your wife kill the Bartons?"

"You know damn well we didn't!"

Masuto shrugged. "At this point, I know so little."

The Goldbergs departed, leaving Masuto with Ranier and Keller. Ranier rose, took a few paces, leaned over the piano with his back to the two men, and then turned to Masuto and said, "I want to talk to you."

"Very well."

"Alone."

"All right." And to Keller, he said, "You might as well tie it up for the night, Mr. Keller. We've lost everyone except Mr. Ranier, and he wants privacy."

Keller was not to be dismissed so easily. "Those are very serious charges, Mr. Ranier, and directed against a congressman, they become even more serious. Unless you can back them up with hard evidence, they are certainly actionable."

"Screw him!" Ranier said angrily. "If Hennesy wants to sue me, let him sue me. I don't give a damn. If your goddamn Justice Department knew its ass from its elbow, you wouldn't have people like Hennesy making a career out of the take!"

"I don't think this ought to go any further tonight," Masuto told them. "We're all tired and upset. If you want to go into this with Mr. Ranier, I suggest you do it tomorrow."

Keller seemed ready to stand his ground. Then he nodded. "All right, I'll take it downtown, and then we'll see.

Good night, Sergeant." He showed his displeasure by not even glancing at Ranier as he left.

"Stupid son of a bitch," Ranier said.

"You wanted to talk, Mr. Ranier."

Ranier dropped into a chair and put his face in his hands. Tired, Masuto sat facing him. Masuto waited. He rarely urged anyone to speak; it was better to wait.

When Ranier looked up, his face was drained. It was the thin, parched face of a man who had run all his life without ever catching up with himself. "You got me pegged for Angel's murder," he said finally. "You got me pegged for Mike's murder."

"What makes you think so?" Masuto asked.

"Don't give me that soft Oriental shit, Masuto. I know who you are and how you work. I haven't lived in this town for twenty years without knowing which side is up. I know about you and how you work, and goddamnit, I won't go down for two killings."

"If you didn't do them . . ." Masuto shrugged.

"Look, I'm going to come clean with you. I don't know whether what I did was legal or illegal, but it wasn't murder. Whatever you may think, the truth is that I was trying to help Mike. I liked Mike."

Beckman came in now. "What about it, Masao? Should I take off?"

Masuto nodded, and Beckman left. Ranier was staring at his hands. "I liked Mike," he said softly, "but he was a damn idiot. Who else but an idiot would marry Angel? And I didn't steal from him. I made good investments, but it was real estate and the money was tied up. He owed half a million dollars in taxes, and he didn't have it. The money should have been paid in September, and here it is November. And why? Because he'd sneak off to Vegas and drop a hundred grand in one night. So I cooked up the kidnapping.

That's right, it was my idea, a stupid idea, but I'm not the first one to go stupid. We had to borrow most of the money, but we could pay it back after we laundered it, and we'd make half a million and better out of the tax deduction. Mike and Angel agreed to go along with me, and now they're dead."

"Was any of the money yours?"

"About a hundred thousand dollars."

"Suppose you tell me exactly how you laid it out."

"Some of it you know. Angel made the fake entry out at Malibu, and then she drove her car to my place. She had the key, and she was there until twelve o'clock. Then she made the call to Mike, and after that she was supposed to drive downtown to Fourth Street, where Mike would pick her up. They'd leave the car there, and the story would be that after Mike had made the drop on San Yisidro, or claimed that he made the drop, he was instructed by the phony kidnappers to pick her up in Benedict Canyon, and then he was to bring her back here."

"Why drive to San Yisidro at all? Why didn't he go straight downtown and pick up his wife?"

"In case he was followed. He had two suitcases with him in the car. He was to park around a curve on San Yisidro, and wait to see whether he was followed."

"And what was intended to be done with the money?"

"He would leave it in the trunk of his car until we turned it over to be laundered."

"And who was going to launder it?"

Ranier hesitated now. Masuto waited. Then Ranier shrugged and said, "Hennesy."

"Ah, so!" It slipped out. He disliked the expression. "Then Hennesy was in on the kidnapping?"

"No. I mean, not to my knowledge. Mike hated him. The Angel could have told him, but I don't know. We were going to wait a few days until things quieted down, and then we'd make our deal with Hennesy."

"And how do you know Hennesy wouldn't blow the whole thing?"

"Hennesy? Come on, Sergeant. Mr. Hennesy has a reputation to uphold."

"What did Angel do when her husband didn't appear?"

"She waited for an hour, and then she took a cab. She dropped it a few blocks away and walked here to the house."

"You met her when she returned?"

"That's right. I opened the door for her, and as soon as I saw her without Mike, I knew that we'd screwed up. My first thought was that Mike had taken off with the money, but that made no sense. I told Angel to go up to her room and go into shock or something, and I'd call Dr. Haddam, and she wasn't to talk to anyone until we found out what had happened to Mike and the money."

"Where were McCarthy and Miss Newman when you spoke to Mrs. Barton?"

"He was in the living room. She was in the library. They came out while I was talking to Angel, and she threw a hysterical fit and rushed up to her room."

"You spoke to Mrs. Barton in the hallway at the door?"

"Yes."

"I presume they did not overhear you?"

"No. We were whispering."

"And why are you telling me all this, Mr. Ranier?"

"I told you before. I'm not going to take a murder rap. I know I'm the prime suspect. Sooner or later you'd find the key to my apartment in Angel's purse or somewhere. I said my secretary was in my office and saw me when I went back there. I lied. She wasn't there, so I have no alibi for the time I was away. And then that bitch Newman accused me of murdering Mike. You put it all together, and you got enough to bring it to the D.A. That's why I'm leveling with you."

Masuto regarded him thoughtfully for a few moments, and then he said, "I don't think you killed Mike Barton, Mr. Ranier, and I don't think you killed his wife."

"Well, thank God for that."

"I might still bring it to the D.A."

"Why? You just said you didn't think I killed either of them! You going to frame me?"

"Not for murder. There are other matters."

"What other matters? I've been stupid, but I committed no crime. There was no kidnapping as such. You can't indict me for a dumb trick."

"How about the million dollars?"

"I'll pay it back if I have to ruin myself. I'll be ruined anyway when this gets out."

"And conspiracy to defraud the government?"

"Come on, Masuto, you know you could never prove such a conspiracy. If you testified, I'd deny it. I made no confession."

"Well, that would depend on what the FBI decides. It's a federal matter. On the other hand, they might be willing to make a deal with you."

"What kind of a deal?"

"If you were willing to testify against Congressman Hennesy."

"My life wouldn't be worth a cent if I did. You know that."

"Well, it's up to you."

"Why don't you get Hennesy on this? He's always been crazy about Angel. She could have tipped him off, and then with Mike dead, they split a million between them."

"So you think Hennesy killed Barton?"

"Why not? It's a good guess."

"I think you should go home, Mr. Ranier. It's almost eleven o'clock."

CHAPTER
EIGHT

MRS. HOLTZ

They had all departed, the living and the dead, leaving Masuto alone in the house with the servants. He was tired and he was depressed. In its outer countenance, Beverly Hills was the most beautiful of cities—lovely palm-lined streets, immaculate lawns, splendid examples of every tropical plant that money could provide; and behind the façades of the million-dollar houses, a bitter commentary on the happiness that money buys. He thought about it for a while, and then he thought, as so often before, about giving it all up—and then wondered, as so often before, what else he could do. He had a profession, and he was very good at it, but it was too much like the pathology of Dr. Baxter; he cut and dissected and put the bits and pieces under his own peculiar microscope, and then he had to live with what he discovered.

He called his wife. She never asked when he would come home. The tone of his voice told her things. "You are unhappy and depressed," she said to him. "Has it been bad?"

His thought was that he struggled to retain some faith

in the human race, and when that slipped away, it was very bad indeed. But he said, "Not too bad, Kati."

"I'll wait for you. You haven't eaten."

"How do you know that?"

"I know you."

He put down the telephone. A sliver of light gleamed from under the kitchen door, and Masuto went through the pantry and into the kitchen. Lena Jones sat at the kitchen table with Mrs. Holtz. Their teacups were empty. They just sat there.

"I wait until you leave," Mrs. Holtz said to Masuto, "then I lock up. Go to bed," she said to the black girl.

"I'm afraid."

"Nothing will harm you, so go to bed."

"I won't be able to sleep. I'm too scared."

"It's all right," Masuto told her gently. "No one will harm you now. Tell me, Lena, where were you when Mrs. Barton returned this afternoon?"

"Upstairs, cleaning Mr. Barton's room."

"Did you happen to look out of the window? The room is at the front of the house, isn't it?"

"I did look, yes."

"Why? Was there some special reason?"

"The window was open. I heard Mr. Kelly call out."

"From where? I mean, where was Kelly?"

"I guess in his room over the garage."

"And you heard his voice. What did he say?"

"I think, hey, Angel."

"Angel? Not Mrs. Barton?"

"Once I heard him call her Angel," Mrs. Holtz said. "Like he was making fun of her."

"And from the window, you saw Mrs. Barton?"

Lena nodded. "Coming up the driveway. Walking slow, like she didn't hear Mr. Kelly at all."

"She didn't respond to his shout?"

"No."

"How did she look?"

"Terrible. She was dragging herself."

"Did you see a taxi pulling out of the driveway?"

Lena shook her head and began to sob.

"You go to bed," Mrs. Holtz said. "Right now, you go to bed."

Still sobbing, Lena Jones stood up and walked out of the kitchen.

"Sit down," Mrs. Holtz said to Masuto. "I make you a nice cup of tea. Or maybe coffee?"

"Tea will be fine."

She put a kettle of water on the stove and started the light under it. "A few minutes," she said. "Tell me, you like your tea strong like the British drink it or weak like the Americans drink it?"

"Weak."

"I'm sorry I don't have Japanese tea. It's green, yes?"

"Sometimes."

"And you're Japanese? I mean I know you was born here, the way you talk, and on the police."

"Yes, I'm Japanese. When we're born in America of Japanese parents, we're called nisei."

"I'm asking too many questions? I'm nosy?"

"Please feel free to ask me anything."

"Myself, I'm Polish. I was in a concentration camp." She pulled up her sleeve to show the tattoo mark. "I was a young girl. I don't like to talk about how I survived." As she spoke, she cut several slices of sponge cake and set the plate in front of Masuto. "Mike's favorite cake. Poor boy."

"It looks delicious," Masuto acknowledged. "But I'd rather not."

"Japanese don't eat cake?"

"Of course they do. But my wife is waiting up for me with dinner, and if I don't finish every bit of it, she'll be hurt."

"You're married! So if your wife is waiting, why don't you go home already?"

"Because I wanted to talk to you again, Mrs. Holtz."

"You give me credit for more brains than I have. Tell me something, I know you're not Jewish, so what are you, a Christian?"

"I'm a Buddhist."

She shook her head. "I think I heard about it, but I don't know what it is."

"It's a way of living, acting, being, of knowing who you are."

She poured the tea and placed it in front of him. "Sugar?"

Masuto shook his head.

"So tell me, please, how do Buddhists feel about Jews?"

"The same way they would feel about any other people."

"And none of them hate Jews?"

"Buddhists try not to hate."

"That's nice." She sat at the table, facing him, a shapeless woman whose lined face was etched with suffering. "That's very nice, Mr. Masuto. Hate is so crazy, so unreasonable. Someone like Kelly, he has to hate Jews, he has to hate colored people, he has to make life miserable for poor Lena."

"I thought he was very fond of Mr. Barton."

Mrs. Holtz shrugged. "Not so fond. Sure, Mike was good to him. Maybe nobody was ever so good to Kelly as Mike. And Kelly liked his job. But he'd get mad at Lena and yell, 'Get that lousy Jew nigger out of here.' Then he'd complain about the Jew food I cooked. Not with Mike where Mike could hear him. And I'll tell you something else. He has a gun."

"How do you know?"

"Because Lena was cleaning his room and she saw it."

"Perhaps Mr. Barton wanted him to have a gun."

"Maybe. I don't know."

"We think," Masuto said, "that Mrs. Barton was blackmailing her husband. Miss Newman seems to feel that strongly. Do you have any notion of what she might have held over him?"

Mrs. Holtz shook her head. "They had terrible fights at first, and then, about a year ago, they stopped fighting."

"Do you know what the fights were about?"

"I wouldn't listen. I liked Mr. Barton too much. I couldn't bear to listen."

"Did Lena listen?"

"Lena's a good girl. She wouldn't listen."

"No, of course not," Masuto said, his tone easy and without threat. "But you yourself, Mrs. Holtz, you live here, you must have known what went on in this house."

"I'm not a spy," she said with annoyance.

"No, of course not. And I'm not talking about ordinary blackmail on Mrs. Barton's part. It was something she knew about him, or something about herself. Miss Newman indicated that it would wreck Mr. Barton's film career if it came out—and that this was the reason he stayed married to Angel."

"He must have had a reason. They weren't like a man and a wife. They had separate rooms. Sometimes for days they didn't even talk to each other."

"Was he in love with Elaine Newman?"

"You think Elaine killed Angel? You're crazy, Mr. Policeman."

"No, I don't think she killed Angel."

"She loved him, he loved her, that's a sin?"

"Did Angel know?"

"What do you think? She knew and she didn't care. She had Mike's money. She lived like a queen."

"Who do you think killed Mike Barton?"

Mrs. Holtz answered without hesitation. "Kelly. He killed both of them, and now Lena and me, we're here alone with him. Why don't you do something about that, Mr. Police-man?"

"I don't think you're in any danger, Mrs. Holtz. We'll have a policeman in the front hall all night, and tomorrow we'll go into the question of whether Kelly has a permit for the gun. Only one more question. Who were Angel Barton's friends?"

"Who could want to be her friend?"

"I'm sure she had friends. She was a beautiful woman. Who did she go out of her way to see?"

Mrs. Holtz thought about it for a while, her face set. Then she shrugged. "Maybe they were her friends."

"Who?"

"That congressman, Hennesy, and Netty Cooper."

Masuto had finished his tea. "Thank you," he said to her. "You've been helpful. Try to get a good night's sleep."

In the hallway, Officer Voorhis was dozing over a copy of *Sports Illustrated*. He blinked sleepily at Masuto. "I wasn't really asleep," he explained.

"Try being really awake."

It was a cold night for southern California, the temperature down to forty-five degrees. Masuto drove through a Beverly Hills as dark and empty as a city long forgotten and de-serted, as dark and empty as a graveyard. Too much had happened in a single day; he couldn't cope with it or digest it properly, and he did what Zen had trained him to do. He emptied his mind of all thought and conjecture and let himself become one with his car, the dark streets and the night, along Olympic Boulevard and south on Motor Avenue to Culver City. It was a half hour past midnight when he pulled into the little driveway alongside his cottage, entered his house, and embraced Kati.

"It's so late. Why did you wait up for me?"

"Because my day doesn't finish until I see you. I have good things for tempura. It will only take a few minutes."

"I couldn't face real food now," Masuto said. "A boiled egg and some toast and tea."

"Then have your bath and it will be ready. The tub is full, and there are hot towels."

"The children are all right?"

"The children are fine. Ana won a prize for her ecology poster. She drew a beautiful picture of a deer. Do you think she will grow up to be an artist?"

Masuto laughed. It was good to be back in this world. "She is an artist," he said to Kati. "Perhaps we all begin as artists. Then it leaves us."

"Must it?"

"Perhaps not with Ana, if we are wise."

"It's very hard to be wise," Kati said.

"The hardest thing of all, yes."

"But much easier to be helpful. Have your bath and I'll prepare some food."

"In a moment. I want to step outside and look at the roses."

"In the dark?"

"There's a moon, and the smell is best at night. It's some small consolation, Kati. November is the best month for roses, and I've hardly looked at mine."

Of course they showed no color, even in the moonlight, but the air was full of the odor, subtly threading its way through the stronger scent of night-blooming jasmine. The rose garden was Masuto's hobby, his delight, his own proof that even as a policeman he retained some small trace of the artist. His backyard was small, thirty feet wide and forty feet deep, but he needed no more space than that. Except for the explosive climbers that made a fence around the yard, the roses were spare, skeletonlike stems that burst into a variety of glory. That appealed to Masuto—the thorny stems and the marvelous blooms of color and scent.

He stayed with the rosebushes a few minutes, but it was enough. Then he went into the house and had his bath.

CHAPTER
NINE

THE ZENDO

When Masuto's universe was too greatly askew, when the face of reality dissolved into too many grotesques, he would rise early in the morning and drive to the Zendo for meditation. Ordinarily, he did his meditation each morning in his tiny room in the house; but to meditate with others in a place given to meditation was more gratifying. Now, dressed, he kissed Kati gently. She opened her eyes and complained that it was still dark.

"It's half past six. I go to the Zendo first."

"The children won't see you," she said plaintively.

"Perhaps I can get home early this evening. I promise to try."

The Zendo was in downtown Los Angeles, a cluster of half a dozen once-dilapidated California bungalows that the students and monks who lived there had restored. All around it was the decay and disintegration of the inner city. The dawn light was just beginning when Masuto parked his car in front of the Zendo, and then as he stepped out, he felt himself grabbed in a tight embrace from behind. A second young man appeared in front of him, put a knife to his stomach, and said, "Just take it easy, turkey." Then, still holding the knife to Masuto's stomach, he pulled aside his jacket and saw Masuto's gun. "Son of a bitch, the chink's a cop! We got us a fuzz!"

Masuto felt the grip around his arms slacken for just an instant, enough for him to drive his elbow into the ribcage of the man behind him, at the same time, pivoting, so that the knife thrust intended for him took the man who was holding him in the side. The wounded man screamed and let go of him, and Masuto leaped away with his gun out.

Fifteen minutes later, a squad car drove away with one of the muggers, while an ambulance carried off the second one, and Masuto found himself abashedly and uncomfortably facing a group of monks in their brown robes. They made no comment, and Masuto, who was trying to frame an explanation or apology in his own mind, found none that would do. Whereupon, he bent his head and walked into the meditation hall. Half a dozen people were still there, sitting cross-legged on cushions on the two slightly raised platforms that ran the length of the room. At one end of the room, the old rashi, the Japanese Zen master, sat in meditation. The half dozen included two monks, a young, pretty woman, and three middle-aged men who looked like business executives. Masuto took off his shoes and joined them, his folded hands still shaking from his experience. He tried to fall into the meditation, but after what had happened outside, it was very difficult.

One by one, the other meditators finished, made their bow to the rashi, and left, until only Masuto and the old man remained. Masuto's half-closed eyes were fixed on the floor in front of him. He heard the rashi move, and then the old man's feet, encased in straw slippers, appeared in front of him. Masuto looked up.

"You bring violence with you," the rashi said, speaking Japanese.

"It met me on the street outside."

"Ask yourself where it came from."

"I am deeply sorry. I disturbed the peace of this place."

"Are you all right?"

"I am not hurt, if that's what you mean."

"I can see that you're not hurt."

"Then I must answer no."

"Then look into yourself. Even a policeman can know why he is a policeman."

"I will try, honorable rashi."

Leaving the Zendo, Masuto realized that he was ravenously hungry, and he pulled into a short order place on Olympic. Bacon and eggs and fried potatoes and four slices of bread and two cups of coffee helped to restore his equanimity. It was ten minutes to nine when he arrived at the station house. Beckman was waiting for him, along with Frank Keller, the FBI man.

"Your hunch was pretty good," Keller said to Masuto. "And this is confidential as hell, but we've been running an investigation on Hennesy for the past seven months. The Coast Guard grabbed a boat off San Diego and picked up a kilo of cocaine. Hennesy's name was in the boat's log. It could be another Roy Hennesy, because the name's not that uncommon, but when you put it together with the other tidbits about Hennesy's moral stance, it could mean something. The department's cooking up a move against a number of public officials who are a little less than kosher, and they don't want anything to upset the apple cart. So unless you tie him in directly to kidnap or murder, they'd just as soon let him be."

"Have you ever known the goddamn feds not to tell you to keep hands off?" Beckman said with annoyance.

"Forget it," Masuto said.

"I'll be at my office downtown," Keller said, his feelings bruised. He stalked out.

"You don't have to lean on him," Masuto told Beckman. "He's a decent kid, for a fed."

"What have you been drinking, the milk of human kindness? Anyway, the captain wants to see you right off. He's in his office with Dr. Haddam—the one who came to see the Angel."

"Out at Malibu," Masuto asked him, "what kind of a dress was Netty Cooper wearing?"

"What?"

"Come on, think."

"It was sort of like a kimono, pale green."

"Yes. Long sleeves? Enough to hide needle marks?"

"I think so."

"Good. Wait for me. This can't take too long."

In Wainwright's office Dr. Haddam was protesting. He was a neat, stout little man, with steel-rimmed glasses, bald, and a high-pitched voice that proclaimed his irritation. "I find this whole thing highly annoying, if not unethical. Why didn't you call me when Mrs. Barton died? I'm the family physician. The family—"

"I told you before, Doctor, there is no family. They are both dead. We have no indication of family beyond that. This is Detective Sergeant Masuto."

"Then I wash my hands of the whole matter."

"Yes, if you wish. But we'd like to ask you a few questions."

"I don't have to answer any questions. Indeed, I don't intend to. I'm a busy man. Call my nurse, make an appointment, and if I can find the time, I will talk to you."

He started to leave, and Wainwright said evenly, "A hypodermic syringe which contained something that was apparently the cause of Mrs. Barton's death was found beside her. Since you were the doctor in attendance, this puts you in an awkward position. Surely you realize that."

The doctor stopped short, turned slowly to face Wainwright, and growled—a valid growl for so short a man. "How dare you! That, sir, is actionable! I'm a practicing physician and a resident of Beverly Hills for twenty-five years, and you dare—"

"Please, sir," Masuto said, spreading his hands, "you read an implication that was not there. We found the hypodermic and Mrs. Barton is dead. We simply must ask you the circumstances of your visit to her."

"You found a hypodermic!" he snorted. "What was in it? What caused her death? Why didn't you call me then?"

"We don't know what caused her death," Wainwright said. "The autopsy is being performed right now at All Saints Hospital."

"You don't know! And you call yourselves police!"

"What did you do for Mrs. Barton?" Masuto asked. "What condition was she in? What did you prescribe?"

"I prescribed nothing."

"Oh?"

"Nothing."

"Did you examine her?"

"No. She wouldn't let me near her. In fact, that ill-natured woman drove me out of the room."

"But you were her physician."

"I was Mr. Barton's physician. Now I shall tell you what happened, and that's the end of it. Mr. McCarthy asked me to see her. I went into her bedroom, and she snarled at me to get out—and used very abusive language, I may add. There are sides to that Angel the public never saw. Then Mr. McCarthy went into the room, and I heard her snapping at him. She threw a shoe at him as he left. She slammed the door after him. Then the maid appeared with a tall glass of ice and apparently Scotch whisky. I would presume at least four ounces of whisky over the ice. She said that their butler or chauffeur, what is his name?"

"Kelly."

"Kelly. Yes, he had sent it up. Then Angel opened the door, took the glass, and so help me God, drained down most of it."

"You were standing in the hall?" Masuto asked.

"Yes, with McCarthy. The maid was at the door. Mrs. Barton handed her the glass and slammed the door in our faces. Then I left. She did not strike me as a woman who required either a sedative or an examination. A psychiatrist, perhaps. Now you have my story, and I would like to leave."

"Of course," Masuto said. "You've been very helpful. We are most grateful."

"Well, there you are," Wainwright said, after the doctor had departed. "Unless he's lying."

"No, he's telling the truth. He knows we can check it out with McCarthy. He's a doctor, not an actor, and that beautiful indignation could not be manufactured."

"Do you suppose Kelly killed her?"

"I don't know."

"You don't know. When this thing was ten minutes old, you told me you knew who killed Barton. Has your Chinese crystal ball collapsed?"

"Even Sweeney no longer classes all Orientals as Chinese—"

"Get off your high horse, Masao. They're all leaning on me, like we were Scotland Yard instead of a two-bit small-town police force."

"It was only yesterday. We're making progress."

"Tell me about it."

"What the good doctor told us helps."

"That's bullshit, Masao, and you know it, and I know how you work. You got something, and you're not opening your mouth about it. Now, I'll tell you what I'm going to do. I'm going to search that Barton house from cellar to attic, and I'm going to find that million dollars."

"It's not there."

"How the hell do you know?"

"Because I think I know where it is. Now, wait a moment," he said as Wainwright began to explode. "Just hold on. That doesn't mean I know where it is."

"Then what in hell does it mean?"

"It means that I could make a guess, and then if we act on my guess and go ahead and get a search warrant and search the place and find nothing, we'd be in for a lawsuit that would make your year's budget look like peanuts."

"All right, tell me—no, the hell with you. Get out of here and make this thing make sense."

"When will Baxter finish the autopsy?"

"He says by noon." Masuto started for the door. "One thing," Wainwright added, "how does Kelly figure?"

"I don't know."

"He's a part of it?"

"I think so."

As if he had heard the question, Beckman entered the office as Wainwright was saying, "Maybe I'm a cynical old cop, but I never trusted a reformed ex-con."

"You mean Kelly?" Beckman asked.

"That's right. I mean Kelly."

"Well, Dempsy just called. He took over at the Barton place from Voorhis, and he says that the ladies are worried because Kelly didn't show this morning and Kelly's place over the garage is locked, and what should he do?"

"Tell him to do nothing," Wainwright said. "You two get over there, and let me know what you find. If Kelly skipped with that million, you will have a hell of a lot of explaining to do."

"What did he mean by that?" Beckman asked Masuto as they left the building.

"He wants to search the Barton place. If Kelly skipped with the money, he'll blame us for not searching the place yesterday."

"Do you think he did?"

"No."

"Then where is he?"

"I imagine he's right there in his room."

"Come on, you know Dempsy. He'd pound on the door and yell loud enough to wake the dead."

"Nobody yells loud enough to wake the dead. Take your car, Sy. I'll follow you to the house."

"Wait a minute, Masao—what are you trying to tell me? That Kelly is dead?"

"Perhaps. Civilization, or what we have of it, stops short at a million dollars. It's a strong inducement."

CHAPTER
TEN

THE LOSER

Officer Dempsy was waiting in the driveway when Masuto and Beckman pulled their cars up in front of the garage. A TV unit was there, photographing the house, and one of the men in the unit recognized Masuto and came over to ask whether there were any new developments.

"Not that I know of," Masuto said. "Anyway, I don't do the P.R. You know that. They'll give you the story over at headquarters."

"You know they give me nothing. Anyway, we want pictures. If I could talk to the servants?"

"Absolutely not."

"I don't have to talk to them. Let us photograph them."

"No."

He went back to his unit, and Dempsy said, "They've been driving me crazy, Sergeant. Anyway, the two ladies are too scared to come out of the house, and I wouldn't let them in."

"Good. Now where's Voorhis?"

"Home, sleeping."

"Wake him up and get him over here. Now, as I understand it, Kelly's place is over the garage."

"That's right."

"Two entrances," Beckman said. "I checked it out yesterday. There's one door at the top of that staircase outside"—he pointed to the farther wall of the garage—"and another at the end of a passageway on the top floor of the house. Same passageway leads to Mrs. Holtz's room and the maid's room. Both doors have those locks with the little thing in the handle. You turn it, and then you can close the door from the outside and it's locked. No keys. I asked Kelly about that. He said there never were any keys while he worked here."

"You tried both doors?" Masuto asked Dempsy.

"Sure. The doors are the kind you can kick in, but I didn't want to try that until you gave the word."

"What do you think, Masao?" Beckman asked. "Can we force entrance, or will we be asking for trouble?"

"Who from? Both owners are dead, and if Kelly's alive, why would he lock the doors?"

"Do you have sufficient cause?"

"A man could be half dead in there. That's sufficient cause."

Before they went into the house, Masuto said to Dempsy, "No media inside the house. If Ranier or McCarthy or any other friends of the Bartons show up, tell them to wait and get me. And when Voorhis arrives, I want to see him. Now get him over here."

Masuto and Beckman went into the house and through to the kitchen. The two women turned from their work to stare woefully at the detectives.

"What happens now, Mr. Masuto?" Mrs. Holtz wanted to know.

"We'll see. I want to get into Kelly's room. I'm told there are no keys."

"That's right. Kelly never asked for them. He said he didn't need them, so Mr. Barton never had them made."

"Is it a single room?"

"No, two rooms, a bedroom and a little sitting room. The outside door is into the sitting room. Kelly always kept that locked, but he never locked the door into the hall upstairs."

"But we hardly ever went into his rooms," Lena said. "When we had to go in there and clean, it made him mad. He tell us to stay out, with a lot of badmouth talk."

"Mrs. Holtz," Masuto said, "I have to address you as the caretaker of the house, simply because there's no one else responsible. I'm informing you that I have good reason to believe that Kelly is injured and requires help. I want you to understand that considering these circumstances, I shall break down the door."

Mrs. Holtz sighed and shrugged. "If you must, you must."

"Servants' quarters," Beckman said as he led Masuto up the kitchen stairs and into a shabby hallway. "Four rooms here, and Kelly's place. I guess they don't build them like this anymore. That's it," he said, pointing to the door at the end of the hall."

"Kick it in, Sy."

Beckman raised his size fourteen shoe and let go at the door. It flew open, the bolt tearing out of the jamb, and they walked into Kelly's bedroom. There was a single bed, neatly made up, and pasted on the wall, several tear sheets from skin magazines.

"Super neat, some of these ex-cons," Beckman said.

Masuto opened the door to the sitting room. Kelly sat in an ancient armchair, a crooked smile on his face, his eyes wide open. There was a bullet hole in the center of his forehead.

"Poor bastard," Beckman said. "Poor dumb loser."

"It was his karma."

"Spends the best years of his life in jail and ends up like this, hates the whole world, hates Jews, hates blacks, and the poor dumb bastard never knew what he was doing."

"That's it. He never knew what he was doing."

"Why?" Beckman wondered. "Why did they kill him?"

"He wanted some of the million dollars. Probably, he didn't want too much. He was always a petty thief. But whatever he wanted, it was more than his life was worth."

"The same killer?"

"No, I don't think so," Masuto said slowly. "We have three murders, and we have three murderers."

"Come on, Masao, why? Why three?"

"Because I think I know who two of them are, and neither of them could have killed Kelly."

"I'll call the captain. What about Doc Baxter? He's doing the Angel's autopsy."

"I want him here. I want to know when Kelly died. Tell the captain that, and let him fight it out with Baxter."

For a while after Beckman had left, Masuto stood staring at the dead man. It would be comfortable, he felt, to believe, as his ancestors had, that people lived many lives, and that perhaps in one of them Kelly would have found some peace. Now three people were dead, a simple, bloody case of greed—vulgar and grotesque.

Masuto went back into the bedroom and opened the top drawer of the old chest that served as Kelly's wardrobe. He pushed aside underwear and a rumpled shirt, and there was Kelly's gun, an ancient automatic pistol, rusted and clogged in the barrel. When he had worked out the clip, he saw that it was empty. If anyone had tried to fire the gun, it would have blown up in his face, a gun that Kelly had picked up somewhere, perhaps in a garbage dump. Aside from the gun, the two small rooms revealed nothing that could relate in any way to his death. No writing, no pens, no pencils. Perhaps Kelly had been illiterate. There were half a dozen magazines, *Playboy, Penthouse*, two suits in the closet, a pair of sneakers, an extra pair of shoes, a razor and shaving cream on the sink in the tiny bathroom and only aspirin and a laxative in the medicine chest. A plant with several red geranium blossoms served as the only touch of color or decoration.

Masuto closed his eyes and stood silently until he heard steps in the passageway. It was Beckman returning, and with him, Officer Voorhis.

"Oh, Jesus," Voorhis said. "When did that happen?"

"While you were on duty last night. What happened, Voorhis, did you fall asleep?"

"Sergeant, I swear to God—"

"I don't want that!" Masuto snapped at him. "I want to know whether you fell asleep, and I want the truth!"

"Jesus, Sarge, this place was quiet as a tomb. Maybe I dozed a little, but I didn't sleep."

"You can explain the difference another time. Where were you?"

"In the front hall."

"Did you go out and patrol the grounds?"

"Yes."

"How many times?"

Voorhis hesitated.

"The truth," Masuto said.

"Once."

"Great. Just great. And when was that?"

"About an hour after you left."

"So from one o'clock until Dempsy relieved you, you

just sat in the hall and dozed, as you put it. You didn't sleep, you dozed. That's a damn easy way to earn your pay."

"I told you it was quiet as a tomb. Nothing moved."

"When you were awake or when you were sleeping? Never mind. Did you hear anything, the shot, the sound of a car?"

"Nothing, Sarge. I never heard a sound."

"Beautiful!" Beckman exploded. "You're one smart cop, Voorhis. You're put on duty to guard a house and a murder takes place right under your nose."

"For Christ's sake, what am I, a platoon? I was in the front hall. There's an outside entrance to this place, and whoever killed him must have used a silencer. The ladies didn't hear anything, so why are you leaning on me?"

"All right, Voorhis," Masuto said. "Go back to the station and write out your report." And to Beckman, "The ladies heard nothing?"

"Nothing. And the walls and doors in this servants' wing are paper thin. So he must have used a silencer."

"I suppose so."

"That's a steady hand. A gun with a silencer and pop—right between the eyes. That's very professional shooting, Masao, and cool too. It wouldn't be a contract, would it?"

"Not likely. There just hasn't been time enough to set something up. This is the result of what happened yesterday." Masuto peered closely at Kelly. "No powder burns. He probably stood across the room. Sy," he said, turning to Beckman, "I want you to go out to Malibu and search the Barton place. You'll have to sweet-talk Cominsky to get in there, but I don't think he'll mind."

"He searched it, you know."

"But he wasn't looking for something."

"What am I looking for? The million dollars?"

"No, it's not there."

"Then what?"

"I don't know," Masuto said.

"But not like Cominsky, I'm looking for something. Only I don't know what."

"That's right."

"If you say so."

"And one more thing. After that, Sy, I want the war records, if any, of McCarthy, Goldberg, Ranier, and Hennesy. I want to know what they were in the service—rank, division, job, whatever you can come up with."

"And who took commendations for pistol marksmanship?"

"That would help."

"And where will you be?"

"Here, I suppose. Or at the station."

Only a few moments after Beckman left, Captain Wainwright stalked in, followed by Sweeney with his fingerprint kit, Amos Silver, the police photographer, and Dr. Baxter, who said cheerfully, "Live in Beverly Hills. A short life but a merry one. What goodie do you have for me now?"

Masuto pointed to Kelly's corpse, visible through the door to the next room.

"Went out with a smile," Baxter said. "Few of them do."

"You're a damned ghoul," Wainwright muttered.

"Pathology, dear Captain, is a ghoulish business. Let's have a look at him. Would it surprise you if I said he died of severe trauma of the brain? No, it would not. No powder marks. I'd say the shot was fired from at least ten feet. Took the back off the skull, perhaps a thirty-eight. And of course you whiz kids are waiting for me to tell you when he died. Not easy. Not easy at all," Baxter complained, flexing Kelly's fingers and feeling his cheeks. "At least six hours. That's the best I can do."

"Which would put it back to four o'clock in the morning."

"Give or take an hour."

"And when you autopsy," Masuto asked, "you can certainly pin it down more closely?"

"Ah, the autopsy. Just happen to be in the midst of an utterly fascinating autopsy—one Angel Barton."

"What have you got?" Wainwright demanded. "What killed her?"

"Ah, there's a question," Baxter said, smiling impishly. "But, you see, I am not quite through, and not one word until I finish. I'll have some surprises, depend on it. Tell you what, send our Oriental wizard over to the hospital in an hour or so, and I'll give him chapter and verse. Now I'm on my way—unless there are any other questions about the deceased?"

When Baxter had departed, Wainwright asked, "Why do I hate that man?"

"He's a good pathologist," Masuto said. "I suppose it's just his nature to be nasty."

"Have you searched the place?"

"Nothing that means anything. As Beckman said, the poor devil's a loser—all his life. This gun was in a drawer of the chest."

"This gun can't be fired. Why do you suppose he hung on to an old piece of junk?"

"It probably gave him a sense of security."

The photographer finished his work, telling them, "I'll have prints in an hour or two." The ambulance men arrived as the photographer left, straightened Kelly's body with difficulty, and carried him out.

"I hate this," Wainwright muttered. "I hate this whole case. Is there any hope of winding it up, Masao?"

"Tonight perhaps."

"You got to be kidding."

"No. I know who killed Barton—"

"His wife? How the hell do you ever prove that? She's dead."

"You're right. I don't think we'll ever prove it, and if she weren't dead, I don't think we could ever convict her. I'm not sure we could convict the other two—"

"Two of them?"

"I think so. One killed Angel, and someone else killed Kelly. We have three murders, three murderers."

"Beautiful—that's just beautiful." He stared at Masuto. "I never know when you're telling me something you know or handing me a line of crap. You think you can clean this up tonight?"

"I think so, yes."

"All right, who killed Angel and who killed Kelly?"

"I think I know who killed Angel. Kelly . . ." He shook his head. "But if you can get them here tonight, I think I can give it to you. Kelly and Angel both."

"Who? Get who here? How do you get people here? Are you indulging in some goddamn literary detective fantasy?"

"McCarthy, Ranier, the Goldbergs, Mrs. Cooper, Miss Newman, and Hennesy."

"Masao, have you lost your bearings. You don't do such things."

"It can be done."

"How? Do I arrest them? Do I kidnap them?"

"Have someone reach each one of them and tell them that tonight we are going to expose the killers. You can't force them to come, but they'll come."

"You read that in a book."

"I don't read murder mysteries," Masuto said with some annoyance. "It's bad enough that I live with it. Do you want me to read about it as well?"

"I read them," Sweeney said. "You put them in one room and you get the killer. It's pure bullshit. Every time I read one of them, I ask myself why those clowns don't take a look at the way ordinary cops work. Like crawling around this place looking for fingerprints. From what I see, this Kelly never had a visitor. All the prints match up."

"With what?" Wainwright demanded. "How the hell do you know that they match up?"

"Because," Sweeney replied, smiling thinly, "when you tell me this joker has a record, which was yesterday, I pull a set of prints from the Los Angeles cops and I got it right here with me."

"Yeah, you're a real smartass cop," Wainwright said and, turning to Masuto, "I don't like it. Anyway, how can you be sure they'll come?"

"I'm not sure. But look at it this way, Captain. There are two draws—curiosity and guilt. These people like to talk, and this is something to talk about, something to make them shine at a dinner party or whatever. On the other hand, the guilty ones will feel they're pointing to themselves if they don't show."

"And how about this Angel business, Masao? Do you really think you know who killed her?"

"I'm guessing. I could be wrong."

"And when you get them here, what then?"

"I think I know a way."

"You're sure it's one of them?"

"Two of them," Masuto said. "Will you give it a try?"

"All right. But I'll be going way out on a limb, and so help me God, Masao, if you leave me hanging there, I'll take it out of your hide. What time?"

"Let's say nine o'clock. And I'll need some money."

"What do you mean, you'll need some money?"

"You'll get it back."

"When?"

"Tonight."

"All of it?" Wainwright asked suspiciously. "What the hell is it for if I get all of it back?"

"Trust me, please."

"How much?"

"A thousand dollars."

Wainwright regarded Masuto sourly. "All right. But I want it back, every cent of it. I'm going to the station house now, and I'll pull a draft for you and you can cash it at the bank. Are you going to call these characters?"

"If you could do it," Masuto said gently, "it would be much more meaningful. You've got the rank and they'll be impressed with a call from you."

Wainwright stared at him, shook his head, turned on his heel, and walked out. Sweeney, putting his equipment together, looked at Masuto with respect. "That was beautiful," he said. "That was like Moses getting water from a rock. The captain will never be the same again."

"I think he took it very well."

"Look, Sarge, do you expect any significant prints from this place?"

"No."

"Then why the hell do you let me work my ass off?"

"You're fingerprints. If you don't look for fingerprints, the captain would be very upset. You know that."

"The hell with you!" Sweeney said, and stalked out. A minute or so later, Masuto followed him.

Downstairs in the kitchen Mrs. Holtz and Lena Jones sat at the kitchen table, depleted, their faces full of hopeless fear. Elaine Newman stood at a window, staring at the gardens behind the house. She had come there while Masuto was upstairs in Kelly's quarters, and now as he entered the kitchen, she turned slowly to face him.

"Will it stop? Will you ever stop it?"

"It's over now."

"I didn't know a thing like this could happen here—in America—in Beverly Hills. How can such a thing happen here?" Mrs. Holtz said.

"I just don't know what to do," Elaine said to Masuto. "What do you do? Do we keep the house going? Do we close it up? Who pays the wages of Mrs. Holtz and Lena—yes, and myself. I know it's selfish and unfeeling to talk about such things, but what am I supposed to do?"

"Did you call McCarthy? Wasn't he Barton's lawyer?"

"I called him. He doesn't return my calls. He isn't very fond of me."

Masuto went to her and put his arm around her shoulders. "We'll finish it soon," he said softly. "You've been through your own hell, but that will end." Suddenly, her face was pressed into his jacket and she was sobbing uncontrollably. He held her like that for a moment or two, and then he said, "Will you help me? I need your help."

"Yes."

He took out his handkerchief and handed it to her, and she dried her eyes.

"Where do you work, Elaine? I mean in what room?" He quite deliberately called her by her first name. Masuto was not unaware of the fact that he was a very good-looking man, that women liked him and trusted him.

"Suppose we go there now. We'll talk." He turned to Mrs. Holtz and Lena Jones. "Don't be afraid. We have a policeman in the front hall. Let him answer the door."

"Will you be here?" Lena Jones asked desperately.

"For a little while. But the policeman will be here all day."

"You can't blame them," Elaine said as they walked to

the library. "They're frightened. So am I. They live here. Where can they go?"

Dempsy was in the front hall. "Listen," Masuto said to him. "There are two women in the house, in the kitchen. I want you to look in there every half hour or so, make them feel comfortable. They're afraid."

"Sure."

"And no one else comes into the house—no one. Except Miss Newman here. If she leaves, she can return. But no one else. And if anyone gets nasty about it, call the captain."

She led Masuto into the library. It was more or less a standard Beverly Hills library or den, with wood-paneled walls, shelves of leather-bound books, tufted leather furniture, and bad pictures. There was a large desk and a typewriter.

"Sit down, please," Masuto said to her.

She curled up in one corner of the couch. Masuto sat facing her. "I'm all right now," she said.

"I know. You're a survivor."

"A woman alone in this town who isn't a survivor—well, I don't have to tell you."

"No, you don't. Now, you were here when Mike Barton left with the ransom money?"

"Yes. I told you that."

"How big was the suitcase?"

"Oh, about this size." She motioned with her hands. "You know the size you can bring on the plane with you? Well, I'd say it was a size larger."

"Is it one of a matched set?"

"Yes, it is."

"Could I see the set? Where would it be?"

"In the closet in Mike's room. I'll take you there." She led the way upstairs. Unlike Angel's room, this was plain, almost drab. The closet was a large, walk-in affair with,

Masuto reflected, enough suits, jackets, and slacks to outfit the entire Beverly Hills police force. The luggage was lined up on a shelf, a space showing where one of the suitcases had been removed. Masuto pulled out the one next to it and studied it. "Just one of each size?"

"Yes, in that design, just one of each size. There are other suitcases in the storeroom."

"The same design?"

"Oh, no, quite different."

"Do you know where they came from?"

"They're from Gucci."

"The place on Rodeo Drive?"

"Exactly."

"Do you suppose they'd have another just like it?"

"I'm sure they would. It's a standard item."

"Well, that helps. Would you mind coming with me to Gucci to make sure I get the right thing?"

"Sure, if it's going to end this business."

"I think it will."

At Gucci's, fifteen minutes later, Elaine selected the suitcase.

"How much is it?" Masuto asked.

The clerk, who had been observing Masuto's creaseless gray flannels, his old tweed jacket, and his tieless shirt, said coldly, "Four hundred and twenty dollars."

Masuto responded with stunned silence, and Elaine stepped into the gap and said, "This is Sergeant Masuto of the Beverly Hills police force. We need the suitcase only for a single day, not for travel purposes, but simply as an exhibit."

Masuto took out his badge. "It will be returned, undamaged, tomorrow."

"I'll have to speak to the manager," the clerk said, and when the manager was apprised of the situation, he told them that he was delighted to be of some service to the Beverly Hills police. "You might mention the name Gucci," he said, "but only if it's convenient."

Outside, Masuto said to Elaine, "You, my dear, are a remarkable young woman."

"I think you're a remarkable cop," she returned.

CHAPTER ELEVEN

THE AUTOPSY

Masuto deposited the Gucci suitcase in the trunk of his car and drove Elaine back to the Barton house, explaining on the way about the proceedings scheduled for that evening. "I want things to be as loose and easy as possible. Mrs. Holtz can have cake and coffee for those who want it. Can Miss Jones mix drinks?"

"I'll help her. But what makes you so sure they'll come?"

"They'll come. This is not simply Beverly Hills, it's the American dream factory. Each one of them has either a starring or a supporting role, and they wouldn't miss it."

"And that's what the suitcase is for?"

"Perhaps. You know, Miss Newman, there is a Zen belief that what one sees is illusion. The reality is what one refuses to see."

"Yes, and now it's Miss Newman again."

"I'm a policeman."

"And married?"

"And married."

"They always are."

Leaving her at the house, Masuto drove to All Saints

Hospital and made his way down a flight of steps to the basement and the pathology rooms. Dr. Baxter was waiting to welcome him with a malicious smile.

"Finished, Doctor?" Masuto asked pleasantly.

"I, my Oriental wizard, am finished. You have just begun."

"I am sure you will make it less difficult for me."

"Oh, no. No, indeed. I intend to make it damned confusing for you. Not with Mike Barton. A simple case of a bullet in the head, twenty-two caliber. Not with Mr. Kelly, whose skull was blown open with a thirty-eight. But with the Angel—ah, there we have a nest of worms."

"You know what killed her?"

"You're damn right I do. I'm a pathologist, not a cop. Would you like to hear what killed her?"

"Very much."

"Good. Then come over here and have a look at the body of the deceased. Having seen only one puncture hole on the arm of the deceased, you Sherlocks concluded that the Angel was not a user. Nothing of the kind. In her circle it is not fashionable to mark the arm. She used her thighs."

Masuto turned away, and Baxter covered the body. "Squeamish, huh? Now let me tell you what killed her. It was a combination of three things—Scotch whisky, chloral hydrate, and a large dose of heroin."

"Chloral hydrate?"

"The venerable Mickey Finn. My guess is that it was mixed into the whisky, which would put her to sleep, and while she was in slumberland, someone not concerned about marking the beautiful arm slipped in and shot her full of heroin."

Masuto made no response to this, his carefully constructed puzzle tilting and crumbling, and Baxter watched him with satisfaction. Then his usually impassive face creased in unhappiness, and he whispered, "Oh, my God, what a fool I was."

"Not alone, young fellow," Baxter said cheerfully, "not alone by any means. One among many, because now comes the whammy. Brace yourself." Silent, Masuto stared at him. "You can't guess? Come on, throw a wild one at me."

"I don't know what the devil you're talking about," Masuto said tiredly.

"Kind of upset you with that three-way knockout. By the way, any one of those three, the Mickey, the whisky, or the heroin would probably not be lethal. Put them together, and you have a one-way ticket into the great beyond. Still waiting for the whammy?"

"Yes, my good doctor," Masuto said coldly.

"Okay, here it is. Your Angel is not a woman. She's a man." Pleased with himself, he waited for Masuto's reaction.

"Is this another manifestation of what passes for your sense of humor?"

"Really getting to you today," Baxter said, rubbing his hands together. "As a matter of fact, it's pretty damn funny, isn't it?"

"You are the coldest, most inhuman imitation of a healer I have ever encountered!" Masuto said angrily.

"Healer? Hell, no. I am a pathologist, sonny, and don't you ever forget that—and a damn good one. And what I said before goes. Your Angel is a man."

"All right, I'm listening." His anger passed. Now the last few pieces were falling into place. "Please explain it."

"Have you ever heard of sexual reassignment?"

"You mean the medical change of a man into a woman?"

"Exactly. There have been half a dozen notorious cases and several thousand that the public never hears about. Now you take our Angel here. A rather small, delicately built man, not a homosexual, decides that he's a woman in a man's body. Some authorities feel it's a fixation. Others that it's a genetic error at birth. He goes to Denmark or France—or even up her to Stanford—where they've been doing it lately."

"Just what do they do?" Masuto asked.

"You want the whole thing?"

"Yes."

"All right. It begins with chemotherapy procedure. There are two families of hormones that play a major role in determining who is a man and who is a woman, the androgens and the estrogens. Both are present in both sexes, but in a man the androgens predominate and in a woman the estrogens predominate. The first step in sexual reassignment is to reverse the role and put the man on massive doses of estrogens. That starts a biochemical process of change. The male functions cease. The growth of the beard slows, the hips become rounded, then the entire musculature takes on a feminine aspect. Even the breasts begin to increase."

"Just from the hormones?"

"You're damn right, just from the hormones. But that's just the beginning. Electrolysis takes care of the beard. That's permanent. Then we go into the operating room. Silicone discs are implanted in the breasts. And then they do something called a bilateral orchiectomy, which, without going into details, mean, the changing of a man into a woman through operative procedure, removal of the testes and the conversion of the penis into an artificial vagina—and that's what you have lying there on my table, a woman who was once a man. Would you like to have another look?"

Masuto nodded, and once again Baxter removed the rubber sheet that covered Angel Barton's body. Even after having listened to Baxter's detailed lecture, Masuto found it hard to believe that he was not looking at the body of a beautiful woman. Watching him, Baxter said, "You start with a very handsome young man, you get a beautiful woman."

"Could she have intercourse?"

"After a fashion."

"What does that mean?"

"She's altered. That doesn't make her a whole woman. We're not God."

"Then eventually Mike Barton would have known."

"Unless he was a total idiot."

"Poor fool in a kingdom of fools," Masuto muttered. "The idol of millions married to a man who became a woman—his terrible secret. What clowns we are. That was his word. The only word. The proper word. How could he let the world know?"

Baxter covered the body. "Not a bad day's work. As for our movie star. He danced—and he paid the piper."

"I would appreciate it if you could sit on this for twenty-four hours."

"I'll be delighted to cooperate," Baxter said. His victory had almost mellowed him, but he could not resist adding, "I regret that I haven't handed you the killers on the same silver platter, but the city does pay you gentlemen for service."

Masuto departed without replying. His car was parked behind the hospital in the lot, but he felt a need to walk, and as he walked, circling away from the hospital and toward Sunset Boulevard, he once again contemplated the ridiculous anomaly of a Zen Buddhist policeman in Beverly Hills. Why did he go on with it? Why did he continue? What kind of karma brought him to this ultimate barbarism which was also the glittering crown of a monied civilization. These were questions he had proposed a hundred times before. They always remained unanswered.

He walked back to his car and drove to his home in Culver City. It was only one o'clock, and Kati was both alarmed and delighted.

"This is my spiritual and physical nourishment for today. I have eaten wretched food, and tonight I shall not be home before midnight. I have a half hour, dear Kati. Can you prepare something?"

It was a sudden descent and an imposition. She had just fed her two children and sent them back to school, and now she was in the midst of her ironing. The nisei women in her consciousness-raising class, which she had begun to attend a full year ago, would have voted to send Masuto out to a lunch stand. But since none of them were witness, Kati embraced her husband, and after she had assured herself that no injury or other tragedy had sent him home, prepared the tempura from the night before with amazing speed.

She sat opposite him, watching him eat. In spite of her consciousness-raising class, it was her pleasure to watch him eat.

"We live in a wilderness," he said.

"It's those terrible murders. I was listening to the news this morning, after the children left for school."

"Death is always terrible. But this is a sickness."

"Why do they do it, Masao?"

"Money, hatred, revenge."

"It frightens me so," Kati said. "Not because I expect anything to happen to me. I'm not afraid of such things. I wasn't afraid of that skinny Chicano boy who was such a foolish burglar. But because I lose my faith in the whole world."

"One should neither have faith nor lose faith. What is faith? This is the way things are."

"But why? Why are things this way?"

"Because we lose touch with what is real and then we invent what is not real."

"That's Zen talk," Kati said with irritation. "I don't understand it."

"Perhaps I don't understand it myself," Masuto said gently. "I need a few minutes to myself, a few minutes to sit and meditate."

But Kati's food helped more than the meditation, and driving back to Beverly Hills, he felt better, reflecting on what a primitive thing a man is, that a bellyful of good food could color the whole world differently. When he entered the police station, Beckman was waiting for him.

"Bingo," Beckman said to him. "Do you want to hear about it?"

"In a few minutes. First, where's Wainwright?"

"In his office. I got something for both of you to hear."

In Wainwright's office Masuto closed the door and faced Beckman and Wainwright.

"You're getting them tonight—all of them," Wainwright growled. "And so help me, Masao, you'd better come through!"

"Ah, so," Masuto said. "Would the honorable captain listen and stop shouting at me?"

"Not if you give me that shogun crap."

"I am trying to inject a note of lightness into a very miserable affair. I have been to All Saints Hospital, and I have been lectured to by our Dr. Baxter. It would appear that the Angel was a heroin addict. The glass of whisky that was handed to her when she returned was laced with chloral hydrate—"

"A Mickey," Beckman said.

"Exactly. And when she passed out, someone came into her room and shot her full of heroin."

"That would do it," Beckman agreed.

"More to come. The Angel was a man."

When Masuto had finished giving them every detail of Baxter's story, they still were unwilling to accept the facts.

"I just don't buy it," Wainwright said. "You can't turn a man into a woman—yeah, maybe into some kind of freak, but the Angel was no freak. She was one of the most beautiful dames I ever saw. She's been photographed and interviewed."

"She was stacked," Beckman said. "Those weren't falsies. Hell, that dressing gown didn't half cover her. She was all woman and built like something out of a *Playboy* centerfold."

"And she started out as a man. We may hate Baxter, but he's no fool. I saw the autopsy. So let's not waste time arguing about it. Now we know what she held over Mike Barton and what she blackmailed him with. As he saw it, if word got out that he had married a man, and that's the way they would have put it, he was done, finished as a star."

"No question about that," Beckman said.

"Perhaps, perhaps not. But that's the way he saw it."

"Didn't he know? I mean, when he married her?"

"Would you know?"

"You mean they could have slept together?" Wainwright asked.

"So Baxter tells me."

"I'll be damned."

"Do you think they knew?" Beckman asked. "I mean, the others."

"Maybe. If they did, they all lied. But maybe they didn't know—except—"

"Except who?"

"Kelly," Masuto said. "Well, we'll see. You said they're all coming?"

"That's right."

"Sy and I will get there by eight-thirty. We still have a few things to do."

Back in his own office Masuto said to Beckman, "All right, Sy, let's have it."

Beckman was still bemused. "What was she, a man or a woman?"

"Baxter calls it sexual reassignment. It's a long, complicated operative and hormonal procedure, and he says it's been done thousands of times."

"But how could Barton—"

"Come on, Sy. How could you? How could everyone else?"

"You tell me. It gives me the creeps. Was she an addict?"

"Yes."

"Heroin?"

"Yes."

"You know, Masao," Beckman said, "if anyone else was working with you, and you say to him, go out and search, he might just ask you what he was searching for."

"All right, you found it," Masuto said, looking at his watch.

"Well, why the hell didn't you tell me what I was looking for?"

"Because I didn't know what you were looking for."

"And now you know?"

"That's right."

"You are one weird son of a bitch, Masao. All right. I turned that place upside down. I found these in a jar of cold cream." He took three small ampules, each covered with a stretched rubber top, out of his pocket and placed them on Masuto's desk. "You know what they are?"

"Heroin?"

"Prepared stuff. I had Sweeney run a test. High grade,

pure heroin, medicinally prepared, according to Sweeney, and legally imported from England."

"Illegal. I don't think a doctor can prescribe it in California, but I suppose that if you pay enough, you can get it. Well, that's what killed her, that and the whisky and the chloral hydrate."

"Where's the fourth ampule?"

"In the garbage at the Barton place, I imagine, or in a garbage dump somewhere. It wouldn't help us. Everyone's too smart about fingerprints these days. That was good work, Sy, damn good. Now what about the war records?"

"I unloaded that one on Keller. You were very nice to him, so he was very glad that we don't hate the FBI the way the L.A. cops and the New York cops do. I explained that we were a very small outfit and that we appreciated what the FBI could do for us. He said he'd call in the information as soon as Washington worked it up."

"Today?"

"That's what he said, this afternoon."

Masuto looked at his watch again. It was twenty minutes to three. "How long to get to the bank from here?"

"Our bank? Five minutes."

Masuto dialed the number of the Barton house. Elaine Newman answered, and Masuto said to her, "About that suitcase of money—did you see it open? Did you see the money?"

"Yes."

"Can you remember the bills on top? Tens, twenties, fifties?"

"They were twenties. I think—no, I'm pretty sure. I heard them talk about it after Mike left. Twenties."

Masuto did some quick calculations, and then he said to Beckman, "Sy, Polly has a draft for a thousand dollars waiting for us at the desk. Take it to the bank and get fifty twenty-dollar bills. Then stop at a stationery supply place and get ten reams of twenty-pound bond paper."

"How do I pay for the paper?"

"Tell them to bill us. Better hurry."

After Beckman left, Masuto sat at his desk, his eyes half-closed, his hands folded in his lap, and began to put the pieces together. He assembled them in his mind and let them fall into place, like the bits and pieces of a jigsaw puzzle. He was sitting like that when a cop opened his door and told him that Wainwright wanted to see him.

The city manager was in Wainwright's office, and he offered Masuto a bleak nod. "The captain's been telling me about tonight, Sergeant, and I don't like it. I think you ought to call it off."

"Why, if I may ask?"

"Because you're playing with fire. Jack McCarthy is one of the most important lawyers in Los Angeles, and a resident of this town to boot. Joe Goldberg is one of the biggest producers in town, and Ranier is a damned important businessman. And Hennesy—Sergeant, he's a member of the House of Representatives. You have money there and you have power, and sure as hell they'll slap us with a lawsuit that'll curl our hair."

"On what grounds? No one's being forced. No one's being charged. They're coming because they wouldn't miss tonight for the world. They're coming to see a killer exposed. I promise you that they will not be badgered or provoked. In fact, I won't even question them."

"Then what the devil do you want them for?"

"Because one of them murdered Joe Kelly, and because that man is an accessory to the murder of Mike Barton."

"Sergeant, I have a lot of respect for you, and I know what your record is. But how do you know that?"

"What I know is meaningless and unimportant until I

can prove it, and unless you let this take place tonight, I doubt that I'll ever be able to prove it."

"Captain Wainwright tells me you're convinced that Angel killed Mike Barton."

"I am, yes."

"Can you prove it?"

"Possibly. Tonight."

"And who killed Angel?"

"I think I know, but I have no evidence, none whatsoever."

"I'd still like to know."

Masuto shook his head. "Then it would be an empty accusation. I don't do that. But about tonight, I can assure you that there'll be no heavy-handed police methods. I think you should allow it to proceed."

The city manager looked at Wainwright. "Captain?"

"I'll be there," Wainwright said, "so you can have my word that whatever is done will be done with a light touch."

"All right. But I'm holding you responsible. This kind of thing, three murders in one household, does the city no good. The sooner it's cleaned up and forgotten, the better off we'll all be."

Masuto's phone was ringing as he entered his office. It was Frank Keller, the very young FBI man, obviously pleased with himself. "I got it all, Sergeant," he told Masuto. "Shall I send the records over?"

"Can you give me the salient points over the phone?"

"Can do. Start with Joseph Goldberg. World War Two. Enlisted in 1942. Field artillery. Do you want the unit and battle record?"

"No. What about marksmanship citations?"

"Goldberg ended up a lieutenant, field commission. Small arms—that's common in the field artillery. McCarthy was World War Two as well, tank driver—can you imagine, with that paunch of his? Also small arms. Ranier was in the Korean War, quartermaster corps, no citations, and also in the Korean War, Hennesy served with the Coast Guard, rank of midshipman. That's it, very briefly. Should I send the records over?"

"I would appreciate that," Masuto said. "And thank you for your efforts."

Beckman came in while Masuto was speaking. "Anything?" he asked.

"Not much. They all know how to use a pistol."

"The paper's in my car. Ten reams—do you know what that weighs?"

"About the same as a million dollars in twenty-dollar bills, more or less."

"And the money's here," patting his bulging pockets. "It's a nice feeling to walk around with a thousand dollars in your pockets."

"Do you know where there's a paper cutter—one of those power jobs?"

"We could try City Hall. They should have one. I get the drift of what you're going to try, but what about the suitcase?"

"Courtesy of Gucci."

"Same one?"

"So Miss Newman says. I promised to return it, so we'll handle it carefully. Now let's try for the paper cutter."

Beckman took a packet of currency wrappers out of his pocket. "You forgot about these."

"So I did. I wonder what else I've forgotten."

CHAPTER
TWELVE

THE SUITCASE

It was well after six o'clock before Masuto and Beckman finished cutting the paper and arranging the piles, topped by twenty-dollar bills, in the suitcase. While they were at work, Wainwright stopped by and watched them for a moment or two, and then said, "It's an old trick. What makes you think it will work?"

Masuto shrugged. "It's a shortcut. Maybe it won't work."

"You got anything else?"

"Something, not much."

"Whoever it is, he was in it with Angel."

"Yes."

"Then he could have killed Mike Barton."

"He could have, but I don't think he did," Masuto said.

"He could have killed Angel. One less to split."

Masuto shrugged.

"What does that mean?"

"I don't think he killed Angel. I think he killed Kelly."

"And what do we do about Angel?"

Masuto shook his head.

"You know," Wainwright said, "you are one secretive

bastard, Masao. You're supposed to be part of this police force, not a goddamn supercop."

"I never think of myself as a supercop," Masuto replied, smiling. "I crawl through mazes and I try to guess what goes on in the minds of poor tortured madmen. Do you want me to drag you in with me every time I get some crazy notion."

"All I want you to do is to level with me."

"I try."

"And just keep an eye on that suitcase. I want that thousand dollars back."

"Not to mention the suitcase," Beckman said, "which cost four hundred and twenty dollars at Gucci."

"Goddamnit!" Wainwright snarled. "Who paid for it? Did you charge it to us?"

"Gucci lent it to us, as a gesture of goodwill toward the Beverly Hills cops."

"Clowns," Wainwright muttered as he stalked out.

They ate at Cantor's on Fairfax Avenue. Beckman wanted tempura, but Masuto had eaten tempura for lunch and he had no great love for Los Angeles Japanese restaurants. He told Beckman that he had a craving for chicken and matzo-ball soup so they went to Cantor's. Masuto would not talk about the case. He dodged Beckman's question and talked about the TV version of *Shōgun*, the matzo balls at Cantor's, and the problem of inflation on a cop's salary. Then, as they were leaving, he said to Beckman, "Do you know where to break the connection so that a car can't start?"

"Nothing to it."

"All right. Tonight, after they arrive, if there's a key in the car, put it into your pocket, and if there's no key, break the connection. But I don't want the cars damaged, I just want none of them able to start."

"No sweat."

"And if anything happens, just let it play out. No rough stuff, no daring moves, no jumping anyone. Just watch me and play my game."

"What are you looking for?"

"Just being careful."

It was eight o'clock when they got to Mike Barton's house, and the only car in the parking space was Elaine Newman's Mustang. Dempsy, still on duty, came out to meet them.

"No one here yet?"

"Only Miss Newman. She's been here all afternoon. The cook and the maid—that's all."

"Good. Now, listen, Dempsy, if something happens to-night, no guns or rough stuff. If someone has a gun, no shooting if you can help it. Play it very cool."

"What do you expect, Sergeant?"

"I don't know. Maybe nothing."

Beckman carried the suitcase into the house. "You know, Masao," he said, "I never thought of money being heavy. This is heavy."

Elaine Newman had opened the door for them, saying, "Thank God you're here, Sergeant. This place is spooky. What have you got in there?"

"About nine and a half reams of bond paper and some twenty-dollar bills. Do you have a closet in the library where you can stow it until we need it?"

"Absolutely." She was alive this evening. She had broken out of the torpor of her grief. "Get him," she said eagerly. "Get him, please. Not only for Kelly, but for Mike too."

"What do you mean by that?"

"Angel killed Mike, didn't she? That's what you think?"

"How do you know I think that?"

"You sit in this library, and you can listen to half the house. It's these old-fashioned hot-air vents. I overheard you talking to the captain. You know she killed Mike, but if she was in it with someone else, then that makes him guilty too, doesn't it?"

"Perhaps. I don't decide matters of guilt or innocence." He looked at her thoughtfully, reflecting that she was not beautiful, not even very pretty, but there was intelligence in the face and the wide-set, dark blue eyes were unusually striking. You saw the eyes before you saw anything else, and a head of rich thick brown hair framed them very well. She was an odd contrast to the woman Mike Barton had married and, very likely, Masuto decided, a complete reaction.

"Then get the evidence," she said evenly.

"I'll do my best." He turned to Beckman. "Cover the door, Sy, and steer each one into the living room. I don't want them wandering around the house. Be gentle but firm."

"It's like a goddamn convocation of nobility."

"Our nobility, for what it's worth. Lend a hand, please," he said to Elaine.

"Most of them I can't stand to look at."

Masuto smiled. "Rise above it. Serve coffee. Ask for drink orders. Be a sort of hostess."

"Must I?"

"You're all we have. Where are the ladies?"

"In the kitchen."

Going to the kitchen, Masuto tried to remember when he had spoken to the captain about Angel being the killer. Had it been here in the house? Too much had happened in the past thirty hours. Things ran together. In the kitchen was the warm, homey smell of baking. Lena Jones was filling a tray with cups, saucers, and cake plates. Mrs. Holtz was slicing a loaf cake.

"It smells wonderful," Masuto said.

"Have a piece."

"I just finished dinner."

"Have a piece. It won't hurt you. I'll pour a cup of coffee."

He sat at the table and munched the cake. "You're right. It's absolutely delicious. Lena," he said to the black girl, "yesterday, when Mrs. Barton died, Dr. Haddam tells us that you brought a glass of ice and whisky upstairs and that Mrs. Barton drank it. Can you tell me exactly how that came about?"

She was frightened. She stared at Masuto without answering.

"She's just a child," Mrs. Holtz put in. "You know what it's been like in this house yesterday and today? I'll tell you what happened. Kelly came into the kitchen. Lena and me were here. He says to Lena, 'There's a glass of whisky on the bar. Bring it up to Mrs. Barton.' I tell him, 'Why don't you bring it up yourself?' Then he curses. I don't want to speak bad of the dead, but he had a foul mouth. Then he stamps out of the back door."

Masuto nodded.

"You like sugar in the coffee?"

"No, just black. Lena," he said to the maid, "don't be afraid. Just tell me what you did then."

She took a deep breath. "I go out then and get the glass."

"What kind of glass?"

She went to the closet and took out a tall highball glass. "Same as this."

"Can you remember how many ice cubes were in it?"

"Three, I guess."

"You're a very observant young woman. And how high was the glass filled?"

She touched the glass about three quarters of an inch from the top.

"The doctor," Masuto said, "guessed that it was Scotch whisky."

"That's what she drank."

"Scotch is not quite as dark as bourbon or rye. Would you guess that it was all whisky, no water."

"Yes, sir, that's what I thought."

"And what did you do then?"

"I brought it upstairs. Mr. McCarthy and the doctor was just outside the door, and I hear it slam as I come upstairs. Then she opens the door, sees me, and grabs the drink out of my hand. She was shaking. She just drains it down and then pushes the glass back at me and slams the door again."

After that Masuto sat in silence for a few minutes, finishing the cake and the coffee. Then he said to Lena, "Do you think you can serve our guests tonight?"

"Yes, sir."

"They'll be here soon. Miss Newman will help you. Most, I imagine, will want drinks. Some will have cake and coffee. Then, at about a quarter after nine, I'll get up and speak to them. When that happens, I'd like you to leave and stay here in the kitchen with Mrs. Holtz."

The Goldbergs were the first to arrive. They came at ten minutes to nine, and looking at the fat little man with a fringe of white hair around his bald skull, and thinking of the field artillery officer who got a field commission, Masuto reflected on the callousness of time. Captain Wainwright arrived a few minutes later, and then after him, Congressman Hennesy, Mrs. Cooper, and then Bill Ranier. It was ten minutes after nine before Jack McCarthy got there, completing the group, and he said to Wainwright, "I'm here only because Joe Smith asked me to come. Otherwise, I'd have no part of this nonsense."

Wainwright thanked him for coming. Elaine Newman took orders for drinks. Lena Jones poured coffee, her hands shaking just a bit. Della Goldberg and Bill Ranier had coffee. The others had drinks. Beckman stood unobtrusively at the entrance to the room. Elaine Newman took a seat apart from the others, who had seated themselves on three large couches that made a conversation area in front of the grand piano.

At half past nine Wainwright rose and spread his hands for silence. "I don't want you to think of this as an inquisition," he said. "Nothing of the sort. We asked you to come here tonight to help us inject some clarity into our thinking about this case. It's a shocking case, and it does the city no good, and until it's cleared up, it will engender fear where there's no reason for fear. Our procedure tonight will be very simple. Detective Sergeant Masuto will outline some of the salient points of the case, and when he finishes, anyone who wishes to can comment. That's about it."

Masuto stood up, and out of the corner of his eye he saw Lena Jones slip out of the room. There were no doors to the living room, but Beckman was planted solidly in the archway that led to the hall. The four men and the two women seated in the horseshoe of couches watched Masuto expectantly. Wainwright and Miss Newman were behind him.

Netty Cooper was finishing her second drink. "I think this is very thrilling," she said. "Our brilliant Fu Manchu is going to expose a murderer."

"Netty, don't be an ass," Hennesy said.

"Since you're an asshole, what difference does it make?" she replied.

"Lovely, lovely," Della Goldberg said.

"Oh, shut up and fry your own fish. Or make her the killer. Do make her the killer."

Masuto waited.

"I think we all ought to shut up and get this over with," McCarthy said.

"Can we begin?" Masuto asked. Silence. "Very well. Yesterday, Mr. Ranier informed me that the kidnapping of Angel Barton was not a kidnapping but rather a scam to defraud the government of income taxes."

"That was confidential!" Ranier cried. "You have no right—"

"I have every right," Masuto said coldly. "You did not put it to me as confidential. You laid it out in an attempt to save your own hide."

Ranier's face tightened, but he said nothing.

"The plan, in brief, according to Mr. Ranier, included himself and Mr. and Mrs. Barton. According to Mr. Ranier, Mike Barton was in default to the government for half a million dollars in back taxes, to which extent he would benefit from the swindle."

"Not true!" Goldberg snapped. "We had the same accountant. Mike was in default only fifty thousand dollars, and he had bonds to back that up."

"I told Masuto what Mike told me," Ranier protested lamely.

"Then, gentlemen and ladies, if Mr. Barton was not in default, we must look for another reason for his participation in so stupid and unworkable a scheme. Perhaps I can enlighten you—I mean those of you who are not already aware of what I am going to say. The woman, Angel Barton, had undergone a process of what is called sexual reassignment, a process which through hormonal treatment and surgery turns a man into a woman. This was the secret with which she blackmailed and controlled Mike Barton for two years."

Masuto watched the faces. McCarthy's face was full of disbelief. Goldberg was untouched. He knew. Della Goldberg burst into tears. Netty Cooper shook her head in disbelief, and Hennesy sat with his mouth open. Ranier's face was unchanged, set tight. Masuto turned to look at Elaine Newman. She was staring at the floor.

"So the kidnapping now stands in a somewhat different light," Masuto said. "Mike Barton was blackmailed into it, as he was blackmailed into remaining with Angel Barton, as he was controlled and manipulated—"

"I pleaded with him," Della Goldberg burst out. "I begged him to let the world know and be damned. Joe offered him an unbreakable five-picture contract if he would divorce that devil, but he wouldn't. He said it would be the end of his life, the end of his career."

"The plan," Masuto said, "as Mr. Ranier laid it out to Mike Barton, was for Angel Barton to meet him at San Yisidro, take the money, drive to downtown Los Angeles, park her car, and take a taxi back here. Instead, she altered the plan—with or without Mr. Ranier's approval, we have yet to discover—and when she met her husband, she sat down next to him in his car, diverted him somehow, took her gun from her purse, and shot him."

"Without my knowledge or approval, if there's a shred of truth in what you're saying, which I doubt!" Ranier shouted, and then turning to McCarthy, "Jack, can he do this? Stand there and slander me?"

"If he's slandering you," McCarthy said coldly, "it's actionable. You're not required to say anything or even to remain here."

"I damn well intend to remain here while he's spouting this garbage!"

Without appearing to respond to the interruption, Masuto continued. "Then, her husband dead, Angel put the suitcase in her car, drove downtown, and then took a cab back here. When she arrived here, she told Mr. Ranier what had happened, and he asked her what she had done with the gun. To his horror, she had forgotten to dispose of it. She gave it to him and he probably hid it for the moment behind some books in the library."

"I won't even dignify this fantasy with a denial," Ranier said.

McCarthy rose, one finger hooked on his belt. "You, sir," he said to Masuto, "have concocted a story which points directly to a man who is a client of mine. You have offered not one shred of evidence. Indeed, if you had any such evidence, you would not have provoked this charade, and since you cannot arrest Mr. Ranier, you have chosen to slander him. Let me be precise. You accuse him of conniving with Angel Barton to steal a million dollars, a hundred thousand of which was his own money—"

"Or his clients' money," Goldberg snapped. "The man's a business manager."

"I'll thank you not to interrupt me, Joe. But to get back to Sergeant Masuto's actionable accusations. You charge that the money was placed in Angel's car. You say she drove downtown, left the car, and returned here by cab. But when she returned, she had no money, no suitcase—"

As McCarthy spoke, Masuto nodded slightly at Beckman, who left the room.

"—which makes the first hole in your incredible concoction. And if Mike was being blackmailed so readily—" He stopped in mid-sentence as Beckman entered the room carrying what was unquestionably a very heavy suitcase. He placed the Gucci bag on the floor in sight of the group and opened it. The sight of the open bag, filled with what were apparently neatly stacked bundles of twenty-dollar bills, drew a collective gasp from the audience, the response of people to a magician who takes a very large rabbit out of an empty hat. Masuto watched Ranier, whose tight, controlled face revealed nothing. The silence was drawn like a stretched rubber band, until Netty Cooper said shrilly, "Is that the ransom? Good heavens, did you have it all this time?"

"I didn't have it," Masuto said.

Coldly and angrily, Ranier said to McCarthy, "I want you to witness the fact, Jack, that my home was entered and searched illegally. I had no knowledge of the fact that Angel had put the ransom money in my house. I only discovered it an hour before coming here, and I intended to take up the matter with Captain Wainwright."

"Did you have a warrant to search his house?" McCarthy asked Masuto.

"No."

"Then I'm afraid you're in for trouble, Sergeant."

"Possibly." He nodded slightly at Beckman, who closed the suitcase and latched it.

"No, sir. Not possibly, but indubitably. Your conduct of this charade has been both disgraceful and actionable. You have read too many mysteries, sir. What fiction allows, the law prohibits—"

Still, Masuto watched Ranier.

"—and I am absolutely amazed, Captain Wainwright, that you could lend yourself to this. However, this is not the end of the matter, only the beginning."

"May I finish?" Masuto asked sharply.

"I see no reason why this slander should be continued," McCarthy said.

"Your client is free to leave," Wainwright said with annoyance. "He was not forced to come here."

McCarthy looked at Ranier, who rose but made no move to leave. "Let's hear the rest of what this turkey has to say," Ranier said bitterly. "We might as well get all of it."

"Joseph Kelly," Masuto said, "was, as you all know, Mr.

Barton's chauffeur. He was a man with a long prison record. Barton gave him a chance and employed him. Last night he was murdered. He was murdered because, standing in the butler's pantry, he overheard the conversation between Angel Barton and Mr. Ranier when she returned here after the kidnapping."

"Just hold on!" McCarthy interrupted. "You're digging your own grave, sir! You're accusing my client—"

"Let me finish!" Masuto said harshly. McCarthy paused. "I'm not making any accusations that can't be backed up. There were two women in this house last night, Lena Jones, the maid, and Mrs. Holtz, the housekeeper, and both of them were awakened by a loud gunshot. Miss Jones looked out of her window and saw Mr. Ranier leaving Kelly's quarters."

It came like a bombshell. Even Wainwright and Beckman had not been ready for this. Only Elaine Newman appeared not to be surprised, sitting relaxed, a tight smile on her lips. The others were staring at Ranier, who shouted, "That's a damned lie, Masuto! That's a concoction out of the whole cloth! You set out to frame me here tonight! Loud gunshot! You son of a bitch, you said yourself that the gun had a silencer and that no one heard anything!"

"Wrong, Mr. Ranier," Masuto said. "No one except Captain Wainwright here and Detective Beckman knew about the silencer. How did you know, sir? How did you know that Kelly was killed with a gun that had a silencer?"

"You told me."

"I did not."

Ranier looked about him, stared at the three policemen who were standing calmly, then reached into his jacket, drew a gun, and stepped clear of the couches, covering the three policemen, who did not move.

"Nobody moves," Ranier snapped. "Just put your hands up and keep them there."

Just the slightest nod on Masuto's part to Beckman and Wainwright. They put up their hands, as Masuto did.

"Bill, you're crazy!" McCarthy cried. "What in hell are you doing? Can't you see that this is a frame? You're playing into their hands."

"You—Newman!" Ranier said. "Pick up that suitcase and set it down by my side."

"Of course," Elaine replied. "I'm delighted to be of assistance, Mr. Ranier." And with a show of strength amazing in a woman so slight, she lifted the suitcase, carried it over toward Ranier, and then deliberately stumbled so that the whole weight of the suitcase caught him in the side. As he doubled over, Masuto sprang, grasped the wrist that held the gun, pointing the gun down as it went off. An instant later Ranier was lifted off the ground in Beckman's bearhug while Masuto forced the gun from his grasp. Then Beckman cuffed him.

"You bitch!" he snarled at Elaine Newman. "You filthy, lousy bitch!"

The room was in chaos, the others crowding around, Dempsy running in with his gun drawn, Elaine Newman smiling calmly, and Wainwright telling Masuto, "Read him his rights—slowly, carefully, every word of it. His lawyer's listening, so I don't want any mistakes from here on in."

"I arrest you for the murder of Joseph Kelly," Masuto said. "This is an admonition of rights. You have the right to remain silent—"

The voices were stilled. They stood in silence, listening to Masuto recite the formula as if it were some kind of prayer. When he had finished, Wainwright said to Dempsy, "Take him down to the station and book him for murder one and put him in the cage."

"I'd like to talk to him," McCarthy said.

"Downtown. Not here."

"I'll see Judge Lacey tonight," McCarthy said to Ranier. "We'll get bail."

"I doubt it," Wainwright said.

"We'll see," McCarthy said, and started to leave.

"One moment," Masuto told him. "Detective Beckman here fixed all your cars so they wouldn't start—just in case Mr. Ranier made it to his car. Give him five minutes."

By ten-thirty the last of them had gone, leaving only the three policemen and Elaine Newman, who was in the library. She said she had bills to pay, odds and ends to clear up, and she wanted it all done with so that she could get away to San Francisco for a few days, see her mother, and begin to forget what had happened here.

Wainwright was staring unhappily at the Gucci bag. "What did you say was the price of this suitcase?" he asked Masuto.

"Four hundred and twenty dollars."

"Well, it has a bullet hole in it, so unless you can work it out with the Gucci people, that's four hundred and twenty dollars out of your pay, Masao."

"What? You wouldn't do that."

"Wouldn't I? After your performance here tonight? You miserable son of a bitch, with your wild-eyed guesses and Chinese insights. You had nothing when you came in here tonight, nothing, and you hornswoggled me into backing you up and putting my job on the line. If Ranier wasn't such a stupid slob, he would have laughed you right out of the force."

"Wise men don't murder."

"Bullshit on your goddamn philosophy." He held up the gun. "This is all we got. And if this isn't the gun that killed Kelly, we got nothing."

"I think it's the gun."

"You think so. God save me from what you think."

"Even if he should beat the murder charge, it's a good arrest. We have him for armed robbery, for using the gun to get the suitcase out of here, and the feds can bring a conspiracy to defraud Internal Revenue against him. Also, I suspect that when they go through his books, they'll find enough illegal use of funds to send him away for a while."

"Maybe."

"Why don't you wait until Ballistics tests the gun and matches it. Then you can let go at me."

"Resisting arrest," Beckman put in.

"I'm going home," Wainwright said. He gave the gun to Beckman. "Drop it off at the station." But at the door, he turned back and said to Masuto, "Who killed Angel?"

Masuto shrugged.

"Don't give me that goddamn inscrutable crap of yours. I asked you a question."

"I can't answer it."

"You mean you don't know? Was it Kelly?"

"No."

"You're lying to me, Masuto. What is it? You got something you're going to dazzle us with?"

"No."

"Every damn reporter and wire service and TV camera in southern California is going to be at the station tomorrow. What do we tell them?"

"Tell them we have promising leads."

"Do we?"

"No."

"You think Ranier killed her and you got nothing to back it up."

"I think the person who killed Angel Barton was sitting in this room tonight, and we haven't one shred of evidence to back up a charge, and I don't think we'll ever have any."

"I've never known a lack of hard evidence to stop you before."

"It stops me."

"You can tell the media that a finger of suspicion points to Kelly," Beckman said. "The poor bastard's dead and that takes us off the hook."

"I hate that kind of thing."

"Then keep the file open," Masuto said. "Something may turn up."

Wainwright left. Beckman put the gun in his pocket, stretched, and yawned. "What about this Gucci suitcase?" he asked Masuto.

"Bring it down to the station, Sy, and separate the real bills and put them in the safe. I'll go over and plead my case with Gucci tomorrow."

"Okay. You coming?"

"I'll have a word with the two women in the kitchen. They must be pretty frightened. You go ahead."

"See you tomorrow," Beckman said as he went out.

CHAPTER
THIRTEEN

EVIDENCE

Masuto went into the kitchen, where the two women were sitting at the kitchen table. They had not left the kitchen since Lena returned there and they sat at the table in a kind of rigid expectation.

"What was the shot we heard?" Mrs. Holtz asked Masuto. "We were afraid to go in there."

"Nothing. Mr. Ranier's gun went off, but no one was hurt." Except myself, he thought ruefully, to the tune of four hundred and twenty dollars.

"Mr. Ranier?"

"Yes. He was the one who killed Kelly. We arrested him."

"A man like that! In his position!" Mrs. Holtz shook her head.

"Did he kill Mr. Barton?" Lena asked tremulously.

"No. Mr. Barton's wife killed him."

"How terrible!"

"Yes."

"And what happened to her?" Mrs. Holtz asked.

"Someone killed her."

"Death, death—it's so terrible."

"It's over now," Masuto told them. "It's all over. You're absolutely safe here."

"Should we just stay here?"

"I think so. As I said, it's absolutely safe. You can go on charging whatever food and supplies you need, and according to what Mr. Goldberg told me, payment will come out of the estate—as will your wages. Mr. Goldberg thinks that the house and most of Mr. Barton's estate was left to Miss Newman, but there's a bequest of ten thousand dollars to each of you—again according to Mr. Goldberg, so that should be helpful."

"Ten thousand dollars?" Both women looked at him in amazement and disbelief. "I can't believe it," Mrs. Holtz said, and Lena said, "I never in all my life—I'm just a black woman. Why he leave me that money?"

"He was a generous man. He knew how it felt to be poor," Mrs. Holtz said.

"Miss Newman is still here," Masuto told them. "She's in the library. So don't be alarmed if you hear someone walking around. I'll be going now. As I said, there's no danger, nothing for you to worry about."

He left the kitchen then and went to the library. The only light there was a green-shaded desk lamp. Elaine Newman sat at the desk, writing. She glanced up as Masuto entered, her face quite lovely in the dimmed light.

"May I come in?" he asked.

"Please. I'm just trying to tie up some loose ends. Mike's mother and father are dead, but there are a few relatives in the East who must be notified. The funeral's tomorrow, and while Mr. Goldberg's taking care of that, he wants me to write something for him to read at a memorial meeting which will be held a week later. It's not easy."

"No, I suppose not—to write about someone you love. No, it wouldn't be easy."

"You're a very sympathetic man, Sergeant Masuto."

"For a cop."

"I didn't mean that."

"No, I'm sure you didn't. You're leaving tomorrow?"

"After the funeral. I must get away for a while, and my mother will fuss over me, and I guess I need that right now. I feel very bereft and alone in the world."

"That's understandable."

"Won't you sit down, please?"

Masuto dropped into a chair, facing her.

"How did you know it was Ranier?" she asked him.

"I knew it, but I had to confirm it. That silly trick with the bag did it."

"But how did you know it?"

"There was a hundred thousand dollars of his own money in the bag—or his clients' money. That would make no difference. It was money he had in his hands. He was taking no chances. He would kill before he ever let that money out of his hands."

"And the money's at his house?"

"We'll have a search warrant in the morning, and we'll pick it up."

"I still don't understand how you knew," she said.

"The first thing he asked Angel when she entered the house was whether she had dropped the money at his house."

"But you weren't here when she came back."

"But you were, Miss Newman, here in this library. So you heard Angel—you yourself mentioned how the air vents carry sound—and I imagine Kelly, who was in the pantry, heard it as well."

"Really?" She put down her pen and looked at Masuto with new interest. "But there's no way you could have known whether or not I was here in the library, since you were not in the house."

"Perhaps."

"And I suppose you're also guessing that Kelly was in the pantry and that he overheard from there. Do you think that is why he was shot?"

"Yes. Probably he tried to shake down Ranier for part of the million dollars."

"And Ranier killed him."

"Yes."

"You still haven't explained how you knew about Ranier."

"Ah, so." Masuto stared at her thoughtfully. "You told me," he said.

"What?"

"Yes, Miss Newman, yesterday in the living room, after Mike Barton was killed, you lashed out at Ranier. You said something to the effect of, 'Are you going to kill me too?' "

"Did I? Truly?" She appeared not at all disturbed.

"Yes, you did."

"Well—" Elaine sighed. "I was upset, distraught, and I had to lash out at someone. Bill was there. I never liked him, and I begged Mike to get rid of him. He was stealing Mike blind. But come now, Sergeant, you didn't build your whole case on what I blurted out in a fit of grief and anger?"

"No, I didn't. You're absolutely right. And I wasn't wholly certain until our little ploy with the suitcase worked. But on the other hand, Miss Newman, I never for a moment believed that you would have indulged in that outburst unless you knew something. You're not the type. You are very cool, very collected, very much in control of yourself. There was also no doubt in my mind that Angel Barton had killed her husband. Of course, I could have been wrong."

"I don't think you were wrong."

"I know you don't," Masuto said, "because you were here in the library, and you heard Ranier ask Angel whether she had taken care of Mike, and you heard Angel tell him that she had. Then, I suppose, Ranier asked her what she had done with the gun, and she said she had forgotten to get rid of it. Ranier must have been very angry, and he took the gun from her and dropped it behind a row of books in here—"

"And never noticed I was here?" Elaine smiled.

Masuto pointed to the door. "You see how it opens inward. You simply stepped behind the door. Very cool and quick-thinking. If Ranier had seen you, he would have killed you."

"How amazing!" Elaine looked at him and nodded. "What a remarkable man you are, Detective Masuto! I had always thought that policemen had no imagination, but you have a marvelous gift of fancy. Please go on. I can't wait until I hear what happened next."

"You must have brooded about it for a while. I'm sure you loved Mike Barton a great deal. You would have made him a good wife."

"You're damn right I would!" she said, almost harshly, and then she began to cry. "Forgive me, please." She wiped her eyes with a tissue. "I'm all right."

"Can I get you anything? A drink?"

"No, I'm all right."

Masuto watched her and nodded. "You, you would have made him a good wife. You would have mothered him, and you have the wit and intelligence he lacked."

"Stop it! I don't want to hear about that! If you wish to continue your fairy tale, then do so. Otherwise, please go."

"I'll continue, Miss Newman. I don't know where you got the chloral hydrate, but I can guess. I would say that Angel had it and you found it in her medicine cabinet when she was out, and deciding that she intended to use it against Mike, you appropriated it. How you must have hated her! Of course, you knew her secret. Well, you waited for the proper moment, and it came when you heard Kelly shouting for Lena to get the drink and take it up to Angel. You had the chloral hydrate. You stepped into the hall and dropped it into the glass of whisky. Kelly had meanwhile gone into the kitchen. Then you waited until the coast was clear, took the gun from its hiding place, slipped up to Angel's bedroom, and found her unconscious, the chloral hydrate having done its work. Apparently, you knew where she hid her syringe and heroin—I don't think anyone else could have known that—and you gave her a large dose of heroin. I don't know why you took the ampule with you, possibly you were startled by some sound. You would have used the gun if you had to, but there was no need. You put the gun in her dressing-table drawer and you left. I suppose you flushed the ampule down a toilet. Yes, you must have hated her a great deal."

Elaine was herself again, and she smiled with approval. "What a stunning pattern of events you've invented. And you make it all fit together as neatly as a jigsaw puzzle. You're right about one thing, Sergeant. I hated Angel. Of course I knew about the sex change, but since it was Mike's secret in life, I was determined that it should be his secret in death. His Angel was a devil in human form, and I shed no tears for her. I'm glad she's dead. But tell me, do you actually believe this fairy tale you've put together?"

"I'm afraid I do."

"Are you going to arrest me for the murder of Angel Barton?"

"Only if you are willing to make a confession and sign it."

"And wouldn't I be a fool to do that, Sergeant Masuto?

You haven't one tiny shred of proof or evidence to back up this complex story of yours. Not even enough to arrest me."

"I know that."

"And if you did, Mr. McCarthy, who was Mike's lawyer too, would be so happy to slap the City of Beverly Hills with an enormous false-arrest suit, not to mention defamation of character and mental stress."

"I know that too."

"I worshipped Mike. I adored him. He was my lover and my child at one and the same time. Bill Ranier was as guilty as Angel of Mike's murder. She pulled the trigger, but he was an accessory before the fact and after the fact. And I'll tell you something, Mr. Detective, in three years he'll be out of jail. You lied about Lena Jones. She's no witness. So what will they get Ranier for? Conspiracy to defraud the government? Resisting arrest? You said it yourself. He'll be out in three years or less."

"Possibly," Masuto agreed. "Unless you testified against him."

"You do so want life to fit your fantasies. But, you see, I wasn't in the library and I did not kill Angel, and I'm afraid we must leave it there."

Masuto stood up. "I don't believe in revenge, Miss Newman. The person who takes the revenge pays too great a price."

"But justice? Do you believe in justice, Detective Masuto?"

"I'm not sure that any of us are wise enough for justice. I'm not sure I know what justice is."

Elaine walked with him to the door. "I wish I could know you better, Mr. Detective. You're a very strange and interesting man."

"We never truly know another person," Masuto said. "Even Angel Barton had a spark of something human and wonderful buried inside her. Perhaps no one ever tried to find it."

"Whatever you think I've done," Elaine Newman said, "you're not making it any harder for me to live with it. I knew Angel Barton. You did not."

She stood at the door, watching him as he walked out and over to where his car was parked.